BEAST CHILD

D1045578

VOYAGES OF THE FLYING DRAGON

BEAST CHILD

BEN CHANDLER

RANDOM HOUSE AUSTRALIA

The creation and development of this book was assisted by the South Australian Government through the Carclew Youth Arts Board.

A Random House book
Published by Random House Australia Pty Ltd
Level 3, 100 Pacific Highway, North Sydney NSW 2060
www.randomhouse.com.au

First published by Random House Australia in 2011

Copyright © Ben Chandler 2011

The moral right of the author has been asserted.

All rights reserved. No part of this book may be reproduced or transmitted by any person or entity, including internet search engines or retailers, in any form or by any means, electronic or mechanical, including photocopying (except under the statutory exceptions provisions of the Australian *Copyright Act 1968*), recording, scanning or by any information storage and retrieval system without the prior written permission of Random House Australia.

Addresses for companies within the Random House Group can be found at www.randomhouse.com.au/offices.

National Library of Australia
Cataloguing-in-Publication Entry

Author: Chandler, Ben
Title: Beast child / Ben Chandler
ISBN: 978 1 86471 979 6 (pbk)
Series: Chandler, Ben. Voyages of the flying dragon; 2
Target audience: For secondary school age
Dewey Number: A823.4

Cover illustration and design by Sammy Yuen
Internal design and map by Sammy Yuen
Typeset by Midland Typesetters, Australia
Printed in Australia by Griffin Press, an accredited ISO AS/NZS 14001:2004 Environmental Management System printer

10 9 8 7 6 5 4 3 2 1

FSC
www.fsc.org

MIX
Paper from
responsible sources
FSC® C009448

The paper this book is printed on is certified against the Forest Stewardship Council' Standards. Griffin Press holds FSC chain of custody certification SGS-COC-005088. FSC promotes environmentally responsible, socially beneficial and economically viable management of the world's forests.

THIS BOOK IS DEDICATED TO MY PARENTS,
MUM AND DAD,
FOR TEACHING ME TO BE PRACTICAL IN
ALL THINGS — THEN TURNING AROUND AND
ENCOURAGING ME TO DO THE OPPOSITE
BY FOLLOWING MY DREAMS.

'These are natural enemies. But what creature could be so low and treacherous as to murder the people of its blood?'

He thought: it is a pity that there are no big creatures to prey on humanity. If there were enough dragons and rocs, perhaps mankind would turn its might against them.

T.H. White
The Book of Merlyn

◉ THE CREW OF THE HIRYŪ ◉

Mayonaka Shishi	Captain
Arthur Knyght	First Officer
Anastasis Greygori	Ostian Diplomat
Kami Tenjin	Records Keeper
Gekkō no Niji Shin	Helmswoman
Long Liu	Doctor
Kenji Jackson	Navigator
Yūrei no Gōshi Yami	Swordsman
Lenis Clemens	Engineer
Misericordia 'Missy' Clemens	Communications Officer
Andrea Florona	Lookout
Chō no Jinsei Hiroshi	Cook
Kami no Suzume Shujinko	Cabin Boy
Aeris	Bestia of Air
Aqua	Bestia of Water
Atrum	Bestia of Darkness
Ignis	Bestia of Fire
Lucis	Bestia of Light
Terra	Bestia of Earth

⊙ CONTENTS ⊙

◉ TRAINING ◉

Lenis saw the fist coming. *Sweep right arm up to block. Something about a crane, or a seagull . . .* Yami's instructions churned through his mind, but it was too late. The blow caught Lenis just beneath his ribs. The air rushed out of him. He doubled over and another strike connected with his chin, snapping his head up. Something smashed into his chest and sent him flying backwards. His head bounced against the *Hiryū*'s deck as he fell. False lights flared across his vision.

Again.

'You are not a fighter.'

'Enough, Shujinko.'

The voices sounded very far away.

Lenis's frustration roiled inside him. He took it and twined it through his anger. His focus turned inwards as he sought to harness his emotions. He grabbed hold of them, crammed them together. They writhed against one another, against his control of them, but slowly he constricted them, tightening them into a ball of rage. In a moment he would unleash it on his opponent, sending him out over the airship's railing and down to his –

No! Lenis felt his sister flinch at his mental scream. *Not like that!* He drew in a long, shaky breath, just like Yami had taught him, but pain erupted in his side, turning it into a wheeze. Even so, his vision began to clear. The outline of his assailant came into focus above him. Lenis could feel the contempt his attacker had for the boy he'd just beaten, but underlying it was a deep current of fear. A fear of heights, of flying. Lenis knew that he could use that against him, to overwhelm his opponent with his own emotions, but he didn't want to do that to anyone, not since he'd reduced the Warlord of Shinzō to a quivering mess a couple of months before.

Lenis's assailant showed no signs of granting him mercy. 'You are far too slow.'

'Lenis is slow because his body is not accustomed to combat, Shujinko,' Yami said. 'His mind works quickly, but his body must be trained to obey without thought.' This last statement, Lenis guessed, was directed as much at him as his sparring partner. 'It will come in time, as no doubt it came to you.'

Shujinko said nothing for three heartbeats, and then, 'Sir!'

Yami came over and helped Lenis to his feet. Dull aches from older bruises clashed with Lenis's fresh injuries, but if he wanted to learn how to fight then he couldn't afford to rest. These training sessions were not what he had expected. True, he had been the one to ask Captain Shishi if he could learn Shinzōn martial arts, and he had been excited when Yami volunteered to be his teacher, but Lenis hadn't counted on the new cabin boy's involvement.

Lenis squared his shoulders. 'I'm ready to go again.'

Yami was still gripping his shoulder. 'Perhaps we should ask the doctor to look at you first, Lenis.'

The Shinzōn swordsman ran his free hand down Lenis's side. The pain in his chest sharpened at the pressure, causing Lenis to gasp as he collapsed against his teacher. Perhaps a little bit of rest wouldn't be a bad thing after all.

Yami helped Lenis cross the deck. As they passed Shujinko, the cabin boy said, 'Nice match.'

Lenis stiffened in Yami's arms. He could feel the older boy's satisfaction. These training sessions would have gone a lot smoother if Shujinko didn't enjoy beating him so much. He never gloated over his victories, but he didn't have to. Lenis knew exactly how he felt about them. One of the problems with being empathic was that you couldn't escape the true emotions of others, and Kami no Suzume Shujinko *really* didn't like Lenis.

At the forward hatch Lenis let go of Yami's arm and used the railing to support himself down the stairs. His mentor followed along behind; his silent shadow. Yami's emotions were always harder to sense than those of other people. He was a reserved man by nature, but he had also erected strong barriers within himself, holding things back he didn't want to feel. Even if Lenis wished to break through those barriers, he knew that Gawayn was trapped somewhere behind them. The Kystian soul's chaotic emotions were constantly at war within Yami, striving to take control of his body. Ostensibly, this had been done to the Shinzōn man to prevent him from ending his own life, but Lenis had seen other things that could arouse the dormant Kystian, such as the presence of Demons.

It took Lenis a long time to reach the galley. Each step brought a fresh stab of agony to his side. He kept his breathing shallow to minimise the expansion of his chest, but that didn't do much to ease his pain. As he reached the bottom step he was immediately overwhelmed by love and contentment. For a moment, Lenis forgot his pain as Suiteki's sheer joy enveloped him. The baby dragon left her bed by Hiroshi's stove and ran over to him, her nails digging first into the wooden floor of the galley and then into Lenis's leg as she climbed up his trousers. Lenis grimaced, picking Suiteki off before she could snuggle inside his robe. The last thing he needed was an enthusiastic baby dragon clawing at his damaged ribs.

He held her to his face, looking deep into her silver eyes, wrapping her in his own love and delight in seeing her. Suiteki shivered in pleasure, her miniature claws digging into his skin, raising fresh welts on his wrists and hands.

He was already covered in white scratches that had not yet had a chance to heal. He was going to have to trim her nails.

Yami cleared his throat from behind them. Lenis carefully cradled Suiteki in the crook of his arm as he continued on to the doctor's cabin. The baby dragon made short, high-pitched caws and scrabbled against his grip, wanting nothing more than to curl up inside Lenis's robe, next to his heart. Her craving for heat was as large as her appetite. When she wasn't curled up next to Hiroshi's stove or snuggled in with the Bestia, she was pressed up against Lenis, wrapping herself in his body heat. Even though it was early spring, the air was still bitterly cold. Lenis suspected the skies above Heimat Isle were constantly frigid. The mountain ranges that covered the island looked as though they hadn't been free of snow for a very long time. Nothing grew near the summits and there was no sign of life, either animal, human, Bestia, or Demon. For the last, at least, Lenis was thankful.

The *Hiryū* and its crew had been forced to winter in Nochi, the capital of Shinzō, despite their desire to pursue Shōgo no Akushin Karasu. They had last seen the mercenary in Asheim, the capital of Ost, where he had claimed to be in possession of the stones of ebb and flow necessary for unlocking Suiteki's power. That was before the crew of the *Hiryū* had even found the dragon egg, and long before Suiteki's birth. Their delayed departure had given the mercenary's trail time to grow even colder, but the unseasonable weather that had sped their return flight to Shinzō had finally broken the very afternoon they were scheduled to depart. They were only now on their way back north, hoping to make up for lost time by flying over Heimat Isle, rather than taking the longer, safer route from the southern tip of Heiligland.

As Lenis raised his free hand to knock on the doctor's door, Long Liu opened it and clucked his tongue.

'Again?' The doctor shook his head, sending debris flying out of his wild mane of hair.

'Just my ribs.' Lenis hissed as he tried to take a breath and then stumbled inside as the doctor motioned him in.

'So, I shouldn't bother with the blood pouring out of your head?'

Lenis's hand went to the back of his skull, which caused his ribs to shift again. His fingers felt something sticky, and when he brought his hand back around to his face he saw that they were covered in blood.

'How . . . ?' He felt light-headed. Yami took him by the shoulders and lowered him onto the bunk in the middle of the doctor's cabin.

'You hit your head on the deck,' Yami told him.

'I didn't even feel . . .' Lenis trailed off. Somehow the damage to his ribs had overridden the aching of his other injuries, but now that he knew he was bleeding the ribs didn't seem so important. He swallowed past the lump that constricted his throat. 'How bad is it?'

Yami's voice was as calm as ever. 'Head wounds always bleed excessively. As long as you haven't cracked the bone, there will be nothing to worry about.'

'Great,' Lenis mumbled.

The doctor handed him a small vial. Lenis drank its contents in one swig, throwing his head back and wincing as his vision clouded. He had learned early on that however effective the doctor's tonics were it was usually better not to ask what was in them. This particular concoction was bitter and made his tongue tingle, but a moment later his pain dimmed. First the older bruises he'd earned during earlier training sessions faded, and then the more immediate throbbing of his ribs, chin, and finally his head quieted. Lenis felt his lips twitch up into a smile.

Long Liu made him lie on his stomach. As the doctor began prodding the back of his head, Lenis felt himself falling towards sleep. He barely noticed Suiteki wriggling her way under his chin and was only vaguely aware of Yami talking to him. 'It is good that you have begun training, Lenis. I have been anxious. I do not know how I will protect both you and your sister if one of you . . .'

Whatever else Yami had to say was lost in Lenis's dreams.

○

Missy watched Lenis's training session through the crystal dome of the bridge. She was hardly surprised her twin brother needed Yami's help to get below decks. Barely a day went by when Lenis didn't end up visiting the doctor. He'd spent most of the time they were marooned in Nochi fiddling around with the *Hiryū*'s engines, but the moment Shujinko had boarded the airship, Lenis had begun acting strangely. He'd asked Captain Shishi if he could learn to fight, which was not at all like Lenis, and he'd also begun to consume vast amounts of food. Missy had no idea how her brother fitted it all in his stomach, but Chō no Jinsei Hiroshi, the old cook, seemed delighted by Lenis's newfound appetite and was constantly offering him things to eat. Missy assumed it was a boy thing, but she was beginning to worry about their supply levels.

All that food probably accounted for Lenis's recent growth spurt. The twins had always been of a height in the past, but now her brother was taller than Missy by at least six inches. He was almost the same height as the cabin boy, who was two years older. Those two did not get on. Things had been a lot more fun when Namei was on board. Then, the *Hiryū*'s voyage had seemed like some grand adventure. That all changed in the skies above Asheim when Lord Butin had ordered Namei's throat cut.

Missy shivered and recalled why they were flying above Heimat Isle. They were returning to Asheim to try and pick up Karasu's trail, which meant there was a good chance they'd have to face Lord Butin again. Missy glanced at Princess Anastasis. The princess of Ost was staring vacantly out of the crystal dome. Lenis described her as 'empty' because he couldn't sense anything from her. This was because she had given most of herself, including her emotions, to her Lilim Disma. In exchange, Disma had given most of her power to Anastasis so that she would be strong enough to kill Butin.

Missy had no such desire for revenge. She had loved Namei – everyone on the crew had – but killing Lord Butin wouldn't bring the cabin girl back to life. Assuming he could be killed. Butin posed as a man, but he was actually a Lilim with enough power to control a Demon, and that made him very dangerous.

Between Karasu, Ishullanu the Demon King, and Lord Butin, the crew of the *Hiryū* had plenty of enemies but only one weapon. Suiteki was their last hope of stopping the spread of the Wastelands and the Demons that infested them, but without the stones Karasu had in his possession she would never grow into a fully-fledged Totem with enough power to stop the Demon King's army. Ishullanu's generals were corrupted Totem and Jinn, the powerful ancestors of the Bestia and the Lilim, and there was no telling how many lesser Demons they commanded between them.

Missy looked around the bridge at her crewmates. Captain Shishi and Arthur Knyght were great warriors, and Gekkō no Niji Shin and Kenji Jackson were strong fighters too, but even if the entire crew worked together, they were still only a few people against an entire army. She caught herself staring at the princess. The girl had given up almost everything to gain the power to fight her enemy. Would it be enough to destroy Lord Butin? Missy didn't know, but the crew would need powerful allies if they were going to have any hope against their adversaries. Missy wondered what sort of power a Lilim had. She knew there weren't many of them left since the Great War, but if the crew could somehow find those who had survived, could they convince them to help fight Ishullanu? Lilim shared their power by forming pacts with humans. Could a pact be forged that would grant someone enough power to stand against a Caelestia, the race of gods more powerful than any other creature, who had given birth to the Jinn and the Totem? There was only one way for Missy to know.

She turned to the princess. 'Excuse me, your highness?' Anastasis regarded her blankly and made no reply. Missy cleared her throat and tried again. 'May I ask you something?'

'Is it about Butin?' The princess delivered the words in her usual monotone.

'Indirectly,' Missy hedged. 'I was wondering how much power a Lilim can bestow on a human.' Anastasis said nothing. 'I mean, would they be able to give you enough to defeat Lord Butin?'

'Yes.'

Missy waited, but the girl provided no further information. 'What about a Totem, or a Jinn, who had been turned into a Demon? Could a Lilim make you strong enough to defeat a Demon Lord?'

Anastasis didn't even shrug. It seemed she wouldn't answer any of Missy's questions unless they were directly related to her desire to kill Lord Butin. Missy tried to frame her next question in such a way that Anastasis would answer it, but before she could, Disma spoke.

'No, Missy.' The princess's Lilim was sitting on Anastasis's shoulder. Her wings were folded against her back and her tail was wrapped around the girl's waist. 'A Lilim's power is not equal to a Jinn's or a Totem's. We are the children of the Jinn, just as the Bestia are the children of the Totem, and both are descended from the Caelestia.'

Missy looked from the princess to her Lilim. 'So how much power do you have?'

'More than you.' Disma smiled widely, revealing her fangs, and then winked. 'You humans are physical beings. You are bound by the limitations of the physical world. This makes you weak. We belong to the spirit realm, which has no limits, but we cannot affect your world unless we form a pact with one of you. By forming a pact, something is given and something taken by both parties. Through us, you gain access to the realm of the spirits, the place of primordial and elemental powers. We, in turn, can enter the physical world. The more you give, the more we give. The more you lose, the more we lose.'

'So, the more Anastasis gives to you of herself, the more power she can draw from the spiritual realm and the more ...' Missy searched for the right word, '*physical* you become?'

'Yes.'

'What happens when a person gives everything?'

Disma looked quickly at the princess, and Missy was sure something passed between them but couldn't tell what. It wasn't any sort of communication she could fathom, but there had been *something*. 'For a time,' the Lilim said, 'that person is very powerful. Then they die.'

'Die?'

The Lilim smiled her wicked smile again. 'How could they live without the desire to eat, to drink, to draw breath?'

Missy mulled this over. 'Then what happens to the Lilim? Do they go back to the spiritual realm?'

Disma shook her head, sending a ripple through her blue hair. 'No. When a person gives us everything, and I mean *everything*, we enter fully into this place. We become physical creatures.'

'So, you die too?'

'Sometimes.'

'Sometimes?'

'You cannot live without dying. That is the way of the world. But not everything that has a physical form is alive.'

Missy glanced around at the others on the bridge. They had been following the conversation closely. 'What does that mean?'

Disma looked her in the eye. Missy felt pierced by her red gaze. There was something disturbingly human in that stare, but also something so totally foreign that Missy knew she would never be able to fathom this creature. Not completely. 'What I mean, Missy, is that not all Lilim choose to manifest as living creatures when they enter the physical realm, and of those of us that do, not all of them choose death. When a pact is done, there are ways . . . well, you have seen what remains of the Lilim who were bonded to the Greygori line.'

Missy shuddered, remembering all of the statues in the King's audience hall in Asheim, the place where she had first met Lord Butin. When she had been standing in that hall amongst the statues, she had thought they were so perfectly carved that they could almost have been real Lilim turned somehow to stone. She'd never imagined she'd been right about that.

'So,' Missy said, 'when a pact is done, you can choose to die, or to live forever as a statue?'

Disma flicked her hair in such an offhand way that Missy wondered if the trait were something she had taken from Anastasis. 'Oh, it needn't be as a statue. That was the Greygori way, but really any physical object will do.'

'Isn't that *worse* than death?'

'I have no idea,' Disma countered, 'as neither fate has yet befallen me.' She paused. 'It is a cruel trick, don't you think? We yearn so for the world of physical things, yet the cost . . . the Bestia have it easier, I think.'

Lenis woke slowly, drawn to consciousness by the dull throbbing of his body. He was in his bunk in the engine room.

Yami had probably carried him there after he had succumbed to the soporific effect of Long Liu's medicine. Lenis was getting used to the aches and pains that accompanied his training. The fact that he could feel himself getting stronger made them bearable. He might not yet be a match for Shujinko, but he was confident that, in time, he could beat the older boy on his terms, without falling back on his empathic abilities. Ever since he had used his powers to subdue Warlord Shōgo Ikaru, Lenis had been aware of them growing in ways he had not expected. He had always been able to feel what others felt, to form bonds with Bestia and sense what they most needed or wanted, but he had never suspected that he would be able to affect the emotions of others, or to use his own feelings to exert influence over them.

His altercation with the Warlord had been an awakening. Ever since, his powers had grown stronger, his sense of others more pronounced. In quiet moments when he lay alone on his bunk, he had even begun experimenting with his own emotions, taking hold of them and manipulating them intentionally instead of by instinct, which was what he had done when in the Warlord's grasp. It was not that he wanted to control anyone – since Nochi he had never attempted to overpower someone with the force of his empathy – but he was intrigued by what he could do simply because he could do it. Lenis wanted to test the limits of his developing powers. He would never actually use them against someone, he told himself, unless they were trying to do him harm, but if he did ever have to use them again, he wanted to know what he was doing.

Sometimes, when his training had left him tired and battered, he entertained fantasies of throwing Shujinko over the railing, propelled by the power of the boy's own fear, but Lenis knew he would never exact such revenge. Not really. He didn't have it in him to intentionally hurt someone and, he had to admit to himself, Shujinko *was* helping him learn to fight. Maybe he didn't want to help Lenis. Maybe he took a little too much pleasure in pummelling Lenis senseless. Maybe he didn't like Lenis at all, but whatever he felt, however much he punished Lenis during their training bouts, Lenis was still getting stronger. He grinned as he imagined the day when it was Shujinko who had to limp to the doctor's cabin.

Lenis suddenly cried out as a sharp pain erupted in his earlobe. Suiteki had soon learned the most effective way to get Lenis's attention.

'Come here, you.' Lenis reached up and grabbed the baby dragon around the midriff. She allowed him to pick her up, hanging limply from his hand as he held her above his face, her tail wrapped around his forearm. She didn't seem to be growing at all, though at the rate she was eating Lenis had expected her to be as big as her mother by now. Suiteki scrabbled against his hand, and Lenis brought her down to his chest. Her tiny claws dug through his robes and into his skin. 'You can't be hungry again.'

But she was. He could feel her hunger as an ache deep in his own belly. He'd never known a Bestia to be so hungry so often, but Suiteki wasn't a Bestia. She was a Totem. The rules Bestia Keepers usually followed in the care of their charges were, he suspected, largely irrelevant when it came to caring for an infant Totem.

With a sigh, Lenis hauled himself off his bunk and headed towards the galley. The Bestia radiated what Lenis could only describe as a parental tolerance and affection for the baby dragon. They barely stirred in their hutch as he passed them by. Ignis raised his head and flicked one of his ears before settling back down amongst the pile of furry bodies. Suiteki gave a high-pitched squawk in response to the flame Bestia's attention. Briefly, she struggled against Lenis's grip, suddenly overcome by the desire to bury herself amongst the Bestia and their warmth, but then Lenis's stomach growled, reawakening her own hunger. Caring for her, Lenis decided, wasn't all that difficult. How hard could it be to keep her warm and fed?

○ FLIGHT TO FRONGE ○

Missy startled as Andrea Florona, the *Hiryū*'s lookout, called down through the airship's speech tube. 'There's smoke to the west, Captain Shishi, over the shoulder of that peak, three points from the northwest.'

Kenji Jackson looked up from his map table. 'That'd be Fronge, down on the coast. Nothing to –'

The lookout cut the navigator off. 'There's a lot of it, Captain. Too much for household fires, and it's black.'

Arthur Knyght, the *Hiryū*'s first officer, frowned and crossed his arms over his massive chest. 'Could it be factory smoke?'

There came a rustling of papers from the navigator's desk. 'There's no record of any factories in Fronge. It's a mining town, but they ship all of their ore to the mainland for processing.'

Missy's curiosity got the better of her. While the others discussed what the smoke could mean, she threw her spirit-self out of her body and went to take a look. Her awareness sped west, up to and over the snow-topped shoulder of the mountain Andrea had pointed out. She saw the smoke immediately. It was everywhere. Great billowing black masses of it obscured an otherwise white and blue world. Soon everyone on the *Hiryū* would be able to see it, even if they kept their northern heading. Even this far away Missy could feel the acrid tang of it stealing into the back of her throat aboard the bridge.

If Missy had been relying on her eyes she would have been blinded by the smoke and soon lost her way, but her spirit-self didn't *see* with physical eyes, so she was soon able to pass through the blackness to the source of the smoke. Unsurprisingly, it was a fire. A big one. Missy was reluctant to get any closer, not because of the heat – her spirit-self was immune to physical harm – but because a fire this large could only mean one thing. The entire town of Fronge was burning.

Missy built up her courage and entered the inferno. She could sense the flames devouring the buildings of Fronge around her, eating into any wood it could find, lapping at anything made of stone, but she couldn't sense any life. She lacked her brother's ability to sense spiritual energy, so she had to scan the burning town methodically, searching for stray thoughts just as Raikō had taught her when he had forced her to search for a cure for the Wasteland sickness. Now, as then, the search proved futile. She couldn't sense any minds. The people of Fronge must have fled when the blaze started, or else – Missy heard something then that would have sent shivers down her spine and the hair to stand up all over her body, if it wasn't safely back aboard the *Hiryū*. It was a psychic scream, and it was coming from the far side of town.

Missy raced through the blazing streets, searching for the source of that terrible cry so full of pain and panic. Two more joined it, then even more until there were too many to count. Missy drew closer, dreading what she would find. The cacophony of mental anguish suddenly began to diminish. One by one the mental cries cut off. One by one the people of Fronge died.

The *Hiryū* was too far away to save them, and there was nothing Missy could do in her spirit form, but she felt compelled to be there, to witness the deaths of the people of Fronge. They were on the next street over. Missy went flying straight through a still-blazing, half-collapsed building. She emerged into a giant square. The townspeople huddled in the centre of it, away from their burning homes. They were mostly dressed in trousers and linen shirts, including the women, and were covered in soot and ash, but the warriors encircling them wore drab-coloured Shinzōn robes. Missy drew a little closer, trying to work out what was going on. Were they making sure no one got close to the blaze? But surely the people wouldn't be *trying* to get any closer. Then two of the Shinzōn guards grabbed a young man with blond hair from within the pack of townspeople. They carried him, screaming, over to the building Missy had just passed through and threw him into the blazing house.

Missy reeled, unconsciously drawing her spirit-self back even though she couldn't be seen. The blond man screamed as his skin blistered, but the guards ignored him. Another pair grabbed a girl, no more than six years old, and dragged her across the square.

Missy fled, tearing through the air in her attempts to get back to the *Hiryū*. She could feel her body screaming, was vaguely aware of the others asking her what was wrong. She slammed herself back into her body and wrenched her cries under control.

'We have to get to Fronge!' she shouted.

Arthur placed a hand on her shoulder, trying to steady her. 'Miss Clemens –'

'*Now!*' she shouted him down. 'They're killing the towns-people! They're throwing them into the fire!'

'They're what?' Shin demanded.

'Who?' the captain asked.

Missy glared at him. 'Does it matter? We have to go! There isn't time!'

Captain Shishi nodded. 'Miss Shin, please correct our course. Mister Jackson, how long until we reach Fronge?'

The navigator scribbled something on a scrap of paper. 'At our current speed, Captain? A little over an hour.'

'No!' Missy cried. Great sobs burst out of her. 'They'll all be dead by then!'

She reached inside her jacket and felt the Quillblade, the *shintai* of Lord Raikō the Thunder Bird. It was throbbing slightly as if in anticipation, as though it could sense her fear and anger. She hadn't used the Quillblade since she and Lenis had summoned Lord Raikō to defeat Ishullanu, the Demon King. She didn't even know if she could use it on her own. The first time she had tried, Raikō had plucked her soul out of her body and tethered it to himself. It had taken the Clemens's combined will to take control of the Demon Lord that had once been Raikō and turn him against Ishullanu. She drew the blade out of her jacket and felt it stiffen in her hand, turning into a sword as it absorbed her fear and fed off her anger. All her doubts disappeared. To save the people of Fronge, she would once again attempt to summon the Lord of Storms.

◉

Lenis startled. Something was wrong with his sister. He launched himself off his chair and out of the galley. Suiteki squawked in annoyance, and Yami called after him, but Lenis ignored them both. The ache in his ribs exploded, sending waves of blood to his head and making him dizzy. He pushed through them. Missy was in trouble.

He ducked under the mast-shaft, wincing again at the pinch in his side. As he reached the foot of the stairs leading up to the bridge, a wave of nausea hit him. Missy's fear, the thing that had woken him, had suddenly vanished, and he knew what that meant. His sister was holding the Quillblade.

Lenis didn't like the way the *shintai* fed off Missy's emotions. It reminded him of a leech, sucking something out of his sister she would have been better off keeping.

'Lenis!' Yami had recovered from his shock quickly and was right behind him as Lenis climbed the stairs, two at a time. The swordsman reached up and grabbed Lenis's hand.

'It's Missy,' Lenis panted as he spun on the swordsman. Yami nodded and dropped his hand. Together, they continued up.

When they reached the deck they had to push past Shujinko, who was headed below deck. The cabin boy scowled but didn't complain. He never did. Instead he maintained a stiffly formal façade that Lenis was starting to understand was the Shinzōn manner for expressing dislike. He preferred the open hostility he used to get in Pure Land, back when he was a slave.

Two more steps and Lenis was on the bridge, just in time to see Missy raising the Quillblade above her head.

'Missy, stop!' Lenis reached to grab her hand.

'Lenis, I have to! You don't know –'

But in the instant they touched, he did know. He saw what she had witnessed in the burning town of Fronge. He saw the Shinzōn guards drag the young man to the inferno, saw them throw him in, saw them snatch a young girl from her mother's arms . . . but he saw something else, too, or rather *someone* else. Someone his sister hadn't recognised because she'd never seen him before. Lenis had, though, months before in the Wastelands to the west of Gesshoku, outside the ruins of the temple of Seisui.

'Karasu.' Lenis let his hand drop. 'It's Karasu.'

Missy brought the Quillblade down to rest in her lap. 'Karasu's there?'

Lenis nodded. 'The one with the giant sword strapped to his back.'

'Mister Clemens,' the captain interjected, 'is there any way to increase our speed?'

Lenis kept his eyes locked with his twin's, but he nodded again. 'I've made some modifications to the engines. I think I can almost double our current top speed.'

'Very well, please do so. We must reach the city of Fronge as soon as possible.'

'Yes, sir.' Lenis was still looking at Missy. He nudged his chin towards the Quillblade. It was lying in her lap but was still in its sword form.

Missy lowered her gaze and took her hand from the hilt. Slowly, almost reluctantly, the Quillblade turned back into a golden feather. 'Please hurry, little brother.'

Lenis turned to go. 'Just make sure everyone holds onto something.'

He ran down to the engine room, satisfied his sister would not attempt to summon Raikō again. He understood her desire to do so, to turn the Thunder Bird on Karasu and his men, but unleashing a Demon Lord on Fronge wouldn't help the people there, even if the Clemens twins were able to harness his power as they had done in their battle with the Demon King. They could end up causing more damage than they prevented.

Fortunately, the *Hiryū* had other weapons at its disposal. Most of the crewmembers were warriors, and the airship had its cannon, but none of them would do any good if they didn't reach Fronge soon. The alterations Lenis had made to the engines were designed to increase its speed exponentially. Ever since he had discovered he could successfully channel the energy of two Bestia through the machinery almost simultaneously, an idea had been maturing at the back of his mind. The months spent in Nochi had given him the opportunity to put that idea into practice.

As he moved into the engine room, Lenis scooped up Ignis. The flame Bestia licked Lenis's chin as he carried him over to the remodelled engine block. Originally there had only been one hatch and one engine block. Now there were two. Aeris was already in the left compartment, channelling pressurised air through the airship and its wing balloons. The pressurised air system was a relatively new design that had many advantages over the old combustion engines, as they required less power from the Bestia running them and could maintain flight for far longer periods. For raw power, though, the combustion system was far superior, but so much of its energy was needed to maintain air density in the wing balloons that it was simply too inefficient to be practical.

Lenis had worked out a way to combine the two systems. By carefully controlling the flow of energies through the engines, he could use pressurised air to maintain their altitude and combustion to propel them forwards. At least, that was the theory. There were risks involved. It wouldn't take long for Ignis's power to heat the machines to a point where Aeris's energy would combust. Mixing pressurised air with extreme heat could easily blow the engines apart, along with the rest of the airship, but for a short period Lenis could increase the engines' output, essentially doubling the *Hiryū*'s speed without seriously endangering his Bestia.

Lenis pulled open the right hatch and placed a squirming Ignis inside. The Bestia immediately started preparing itself for the process of channelling its power into the machines. Lenis worked quickly, making several minuscule adjustments to the dozens of new levers he'd had to install to maintain precise control of the twin channels of Bestia power. If he were off by even a fraction, the whole thing would literally blow up in his face, and the survivors of Fronge would be fed to the fires of their town.

Taking a deep breath, Lenis closed the hatch and took a hold of the second ignition lever. He grabbed the speech tube with his other hand and shouted into it, 'Hold on!'

He pulled the lever. For two heartbeats, nothing happened. Lenis was just about to recheck the engines' settings when they roared into overdrive. Heat flared up from the machinery, but Lenis had anticipated that and had reinforced the insulation of the whole engine block during the overhaul. He was just about to congratulate himself when the *Hiryū* surged forwards, throwing him against the back wall of the engine room.

◉

Missy was pushed back into her chair as the airship leapt forwards. She heard Shin swear from her post at the tiller. The *Hiryū* veered wildly out of control as the helmswoman lost her grip. For a moment Missy was convinced they were going to crash into the mountainside, but then Shin got the tiller under control and they swept smoothly by it, their port wing balloon sending up a great spray of snow as it brushed the shoulder of the mountain.

Missy heard a scream and looked down on the deck. Everyone had secured themselves at Lenis's warning, even Andrea up in her crow's nest, but Shujinko either hadn't heard or hadn't taken her brother seriously. The cabin boy was sprawled out on the deck, crying for help as the force of their flight dragged him aft. She saw he was in no immediate danger. As long as Shin held them steady, the worst that could happen to him would be falling down the stairs leading below decks. Shujinko obviously didn't realise that, though. He kept screaming and scrabbling for a handhold. Missy had to remind herself that this was the first time the *Hiryū*'s new cabin boy had ever flown on an airship.

She was considering getting up and giving him a hand when they suddenly plunged into the smoke coming from Fronge.

'I can't see anything,' Shin croaked from the tiller.

The smoke quickly filled the bridge. Missy started coughing along with everyone else, but she was the only one who could guide them now. She pulled her scarf up over her mouth and detached her spirit-self from her body. Its wracking cough soon faded into the background as she rushed on through the smoke, once more into the smouldering town of Fronge.

They had come farther and faster than she had thought possible. Whatever Lenis had done to the engines had *more* than doubled their speed. Missy made her way quickly to the square. The number of townsfolk had diminished greatly, she noticed with a pang of guilt. However fast they were going, it wasn't fast enough. She brought herself back to her body. The old records keeper, Kami Tenjin, was kneeling next to her, shaking her shoulder.

'What is it?' Missy asked through a hoarse throat.

Tenjin was visibly relieved. 'I thought you had lost consciousness.'

He pulled her down to the floor, where the smoke wasn't quite so thick. She tried to get her breath back. Missy couldn't see anything beyond a couple of feet, much less out of the crystal dome. The smoke was too thick.

'We're almost through,' Arthur called from the direction of the bridge's entryway.

'Mister Clemens,' Missy heard the captain call from somewhere on the hazy bridge, 'please reduce our speed.'

A moment later the engines groaned and the *Hiryū* slowed. Missy and Tenjin were thrown forwards, their momentum sending them crashing into the back of Arthur's legs. All three fell down the stairs to the deck, landing in a pile on top of Shujinko as Tenjin cried out.

'Lord Tenjin!' Arthur called.

Missy righted herself. Tenjin remained sprawled on the deck, clutching his leg. Missy crawled over to him and touched his shoulder. 'Are you all right, Lord Tenjin?'

He looked up at her, soot turning the creases in his face into dark lines. 'I believe I have hurt my ankle, Miss Clemens.'

'Come on,' she said, pulling one of his arms around her neck, 'I'll help you to the doctor.'

Shujinko took the old man's other arm. 'I will take him.'

The cabin boy looked pale but composed. His thoughts were awhirl. Missy didn't have the patience to sort through them. She left Tenjin in his care and ran over to the railing. It was easier to see out here on the deck now that they had passed through the smoke. The sky behind them was black with it still, but they were now upwind of it. Missy took a moment to orient herself.

'We've overshot the town,' she said to Arthur and then followed him back to the bridge. 'We have to come about. The square is near this end of Fronge.'

Arthur nodded. The bridge was still filled with smoke. The first officer relayed the order and the *Hiryū* came about.

A moment later they began to descend. Missy's throat felt raw, and tears were pushing against her resolve to hold them back. How many people had died while they raced to Fronge? Was there even anyone left to save? And what would have happened if they hadn't been passing at this exact moment?

The *Hiryū* landed with a familiar thud that shook the entire vessel. Missy followed the others out to the deck. Looking over the fore railing she could just make out the top of the wall surrounding Fronge and the black smoke rising from behind it.

'Missy!' Lenis had come up on deck. He had two of his Bestia with him – Aqua, who had an affinity for water, and Atrum, the Bestia of darkness.

'Lenis!'

Missy grabbed her brother's hand just as the captain started giving orders. 'Our first concern must be the safety of the people of Fronge.' As Missy looked around at her fellow crewmembers, she saw each of them nod, their faces grim in their determination. All of them had gathered to hear the captain's orders. With the exception of Tenjin, they would all be going into Fronge. 'Princess Anastasis, would you mind opening the gate?'

The Ostian princess remained unmoved by what was happening in the town. Missy knew she didn't care about the people dying behind the walls because she couldn't. She had given too much of herself to Disma, the Lilim she was bonded to. Disma was sitting on Anastasis's shoulder, whispering into her ear, flapping her wings and twitching her tail.

Without warning the princess leapt over the railing, apparently spurred into action by whatever Disma had been saying to her. Anastasis held her giant hammer above her head and swung it down as she landed in front of the walls. Her weapon hit the wooden portion of the metal-bound gates and a dull boom echoed along the length of the wall, sending the *Hiryū*'s deck shaking.

Missy held her breath and squeezed Lenis's hand tighter. Every moment they delayed, another person was consigned to the flames. She looked up into her brother's face. He was pale; no doubt his empathic abilities were being overwhelmed by the terror and grief of the townspeople behind the wall. Aqua was pressed up against his leg, and Atrum was nestled in the crook of his arm. The blind, black-furred Bestia had wrapped his tail around her brother's neck, but Lenis gave no sign that he even noticed. Missy shook his hand and he shivered, coming back to himself.

'The princess got their attention,' he said to her and smiled, a bare lifting of the corners of his mouth. 'They've stopped.'

Missy didn't need to ask what they had stopped doing. She knew all too well.

Anastasis lifted her hammer and brought it down again, fracturing the wood within the metal bindings of the gate. Still, it held. She struck again and again, showing no signs of restraint or tiring. Missy could see the muscles in the princess's neck and arms straining every time she lifted her mallet, but her face remained immobile, as though it cost her no effort at all. Each time her hammer connected with the gate, the wood and bindings gave a little more. Missy had seen the devastation Anastasis could inflict with her mallet before, back in the prison of Asheim. Then she had used her barrel-sized hammer to smash through the doors of the crewmembers' cells in a single blow, and later she had helped fight off Lord Butin's Demon, Nue. The gates of Fronge were proving resilient, but finally, with a sharp snap that tore through the crackling of the fires and the rushing of the wind, the gates split open.

Lenis held Missy back as the others poured through the gate. He was looking at her oddly, and it took her a moment to realise he was trying to tell her something.

Wait, she sent the thought into his mind. *What was that?*

Let the others handle Karasu, he replied.

But –

We need to get the stones.

What?

Her brother went on, perfectly calm, *You and I are going to find Karasu's airship. It must be somewhere in the square. We've got to sneak on board and find the stones of ebb and flow. This might be the only chance we get.*

Missy felt her knees suddenly weaken. Her hand moved involuntarily towards the Quillblade inside her robe.

If she could only touch it, the *shintai* would absorb her fear and allow her to think clearly. Lenis squeezed her other hand hard. She let her free hand drop.

Don't, Lenis's thought cracked through her mind. *We have to be quiet if we're going to sneak on board their airship.*

Missy didn't know what to do. She felt paralysed. She'd been so desperate to get to Fronge so she could help the townspeople, but Lenis's plan made sense. He hadn't lost sight of their true mission. They had thought it would take months to track down Karasu, and now here he was. He had the stones they needed to unlock Suiteki's power so she would be a match for Ishullanu the Demon King. They had to take this chance, but where would that leave the people of Fronge? Missy firmed her resolve and put her trust in her crewmates. They could take care of Karasu. It seemed impossible that they had just stumbled upon him like this. What were the chances it would happen again? She and Lenis had to try and steal the stones of ebb and flow from him.

How are we going to sneak on board? she asked.

In answer, Lenis dropped her hand and reached up to stroke Atrum's fur. The colour returned to his cheeks. A genuine smile appeared on his face. It was a familiar look, and it told Missy that her little brother was planning some crazy stunt. She found herself mirroring his grin.

⊙ STEALING THE STONES OF EBB AND FLOW ⊙

Lenis pulled his sister behind him and edged up to the shattered remains of Fronge's gates, doing his best to ignore the townspeople's fear. An undercurrent of tension thrummed through him. He could imagine the crew of the *Hiryū* facing Karasu's warriors in the square, each eyeing the other, seeking an advantage. He just hoped the others could distract the Shinzōn mercenary long enough for him and his sister to reach Karasu's airship, sneak aboard, and steal the stones of ebb and flow. This could well be their last chance to get them.

He risked a peek around the splintered wood of the gates. As he had imagined, the crew were facing off against Karasu's warriors. The two groups were almost evenly matched, but behind them about fifty townspeople huddled together, surrounded by even more of Karasu's men. The flames of the town had died down, the glowing embers of a deeper heat barely masked by the blackened timbers and stone of Fronge. Lenis could feel it, even from all the way across the square. If the captors left their charges, Karasu would have the advantage, but then the townspeople would be free. They had no weapons, but perhaps given the opportunity they would help the *Hiryū*'s crew fight off their tormentors.

Lenis poked his sister in the ribs. *Missy, I want you to hang onto my hand,* he thought, and she nodded. *No matter what happens. Atrum is going to cloak us, just like he did the* Hiryū *back in Itsū when we escaped the Warlord's forces. It should work, but we have to maintain physical contact . . . I think.* He felt her uncertainty and was grateful she trusted him enough not to raise any objections. *But I also need you to listen to what is going on with the others.* Lenis felt his own excitement building as he outlined his plan. Somehow communicating it to his sister made it seem like more of an adventure, a stunt like the ones they used to pull back when they were slaves in Pure Land, and less of a reckless and desperate plan upon which so much depended. *If Karasu tries to return to his airship, we need to know about it.*

Missy nodded again and squeezed his hand. He could sense her nervousness and also her desire to draw the Quillblade. For a moment he considered suggesting she do just that. He needed her clear-headed, but he pushed the notion out of his head before it formed into a thought she would notice. Instead, he wrapped her in a portion of his own exhilaration and anticipation, and saw her square her shoulders in response.

He took a deep breath and bent his head down to speak softly into Atrum's ear. It came out just above a whisper, though there was no way any of those gathered in the square could have heard him, 'Now, Atrum.'

The Bestia's tail tightened around Lenis's shoulders and his blind eyes closed. Nothing happened. At least, not that Lenis could see. He could feel Atrum's power at work, though, and knew he was doing whatever he did to make them invisible. Lenis looked at Missy, who dropped his hand for a moment, gasped, and then groped around as though she couldn't see it.

He grabbed her hand instead. *Looks like it worked.*

I couldn't see you at all! Not even your shadow!

But you can see me when we're touching?

Missy nodded.

Lenis took a deep breath and let it out slowly. *Let's hope that means we're invisible to everyone who isn't touching us.*

He took another breath and held it before stepping into the gap in the gates. No one seemed to notice them. He pulled his sister after him and hurried across the square, angling away from the others. Still nothing. It worked! Atrum had made them invisible.

He turned his attention to other matters. *What's going on, Missy?*

Sorry. There was a pause. *Captain Shishi is talking with Karasu.*

Missy stumbled and Lenis instinctively tightened his grip on her fingers. *Are you all right?*

Missy nodded. *It's hard to listen in and walk at the same time. I'll be all right. Can you see Karasu's airship?*

This way. Just take one step at a time.

Now that they were behind the walls, Lenis could see Karasu's airship to the north of the square, well away from the crouching villagers and the fires that had all but destroyed Fronge. There were two guards standing by the ropes leading up to the airship's deck, but their attention was fixed firmly on what was happening in the southern end of the square, their hands wrapped around their swords' hilts. Lenis glanced towards the gathering. His crewmates were arrayed against Karasu's men, but he couldn't hear anything that was being said above the wind and the noises coming from the dying town.

Lenis shook Missy's hand. *What are they saying?*

Karasu is talking . . .

As Missy communicated the conversation in the square, Lenis led them towards the mercenary's airship, slowly, so his sister wouldn't trip again. She staggered along behind him as though she were half asleep.

'How is it you have come to be here, Captain Shishi?' Karasu asked.

'We were searching for you, Sir Karasu.'

There was a pause. 'Indeed? What an extraordinary coincidence that you have found me here, of all places.'

'The gods do not deal in coincidence.'

Lenis almost snorted. The captain was an advocate of what he called the Way. He didn't believe in fate, or in letting gods or anyone else direct his destiny. *Is he joking?*

It's a ploy, Missy replied. *He's trying to throw Karasu off guard.*

Is it working?

Shh! I'm trying to listen.

Lenis stifled a retort. The ropes leading up to Karasu's airship were twenty paces away, behind the two guards. Although Lenis was confident they could sneak around them, he was worried about the ropes. He couldn't hold Missy's hand and climb at the same time. They would need a diversion. He had wanted to save that for later, in case Karasu returned to his airship, but he didn't see any way around it now.

He edged them around the two oblivious guards until they were almost touching the airship's hull. Then he stopped and squeezed Missy's hand again.

Missy, I need you to send a message to Aqua.

Aqua? Missy asked, still half-listening in on the confrontation brewing at the southern end of the square.

I sent her around the wall, Lenis told her. *She should be close to the burning ruins now.*

What do I tell her?

Just tell her it's time. She knows what to do.

Lenis felt his sister depart. The part of her that could communicate with Bestia was gone, flying out along the western edge of the square in search of Aqua. Lenis tried to maintain his calm while he waited for her to return. She wasn't gone that long, but every second felt impossibly drawn out. From one heartbeat to the next Lenis expected battle to break out in the square, or for Karasu to withdraw to his airship. The crew would try to stop him from leaving, but their focus would be on protecting the remaining townsfolk.

Suddenly Missy was back. *Okay, she got the message, but what is she going to . . .* Missy's mental voice trailed off as a high-pitched squeal came from the west. *Oh.*

Billows of steam rose up from behind the encircled townspeople. Aqua's affinity for water meant that she could draw moisture out of the air and condense it. The colder the air the better, and though the heat of the fires was intense, the mountains of Heimat Isle were very cold. Aqua had no trouble generating enough water to douse the coals of a burnt building, which sent up clouds of steam and set the overheated rubble shrieking in protest. She probably wasn't strong enough to put out the whole town, but that wasn't why Lenis had sent her over there.

As he had expected, everyone in the square turned to see what was going on.

Come on! Lenis snatched his hand from Missy's and lunged for the nearest rope.

His sister followed suit and soon the two were struggling up the side of the hold, Atrum wrapped around Lenis's neck. It took a little over a minute for them to gain the deck, and as soon as they did Lenis grabbed Missy and huddled down against the railing, their hearts beating wildly in unison, sure that someone had glanced over and seen her.

Lenis forced himself to calm down and sensed his sister was also struggling to slow her own rapid heartbeat. Atrum curled up between them, wedged between their heaving ribcages. The small, black-furred Bestia remained as composed as ever and began smoothing down his rumpled fur with his tongue.

I don't think they saw us, Missy said into Lenis's mind.

He nodded. *What's going on in the square?*

They weren't distracted for long. They're still talking. Lenis?

Mmmm?

I think the captain's trying to buy us some time.

That's impossible. Lenis hadn't had time to discuss his plan with any of the others. There was no way Captain Shishi could have known what the twins were doing. Missy hadn't even known until they had started out, but the captain had surprised Lenis several times in the past. Perhaps he had seen them as they climbed the ropes. *Did you scan his mind?*

I can't, Missy admitted. *He never seems to be thinking anything whenever I try, but it's the way he's talking to Karasu. He's not taunting him into a fight and not trying to negotiate for the release of the townspeople. It's like he's stalling.*

Lenis felt himself smile as his heart slowed to a more natural rhythm. The more Lenis got to know the captain, the more of a mystery the man seemed. *We'd better hurry up, then.*

In answer, Missy removed her arms from around Lenis's neck, being careful to maintain contact until she was holding his hand again. Together they pushed themselves up and looked around the deck. With a jarring sense of dislocation, Lenis noticed that Karasu's airship had been constructed using the same design as the *Hiryū*. Airship design was a dynamic industry. Few airshipwrights produced the same vessel year after year, making it rare to stumble across two identical airships. They must have been built almost simultaneously.

It's just like the Hiryū. Missy's thought almost exactly matched his own so that, for a moment, Lenis believed his brain had gone around in a circle.

Yeah, but how did Karasu get his hands on an airship almost identical to the Hiryū?

How many vessels did Pure Land's Ruling Council give Shinzō? Missy asked.

Lenis shrugged. *I don't know. A few? But that still doesn't explain how Karasu got it. If he stole it, why didn't Lord Shōgo tell us back in Nochi when he admitted Karasu wasn't working for him?*

Maybe he was lying.

That wasn't a reassuring thought. They were counting the Warlord of Shinzō as an ally against the Demons now, but Captain Shishi *did* steal the *Hiryū* from him, and the Warlord had spent most of the last year chasing after them to get it back. Or had he?

Something occurred to Lenis. *It wasn't the Warlord.*

What?

In Asheim, Lenis said, *when we were caught. You were in that audience with the prince and the captain, remember?*

Yes, so?

There was an Ostian airship docked next to the Hiryū, *only it wasn't Ostian. It had Ostian flags but a red dragon figurehead, just like the* Hiryū.

And all of the other Shōgo airships, Missy pointed out.

Right! We thought it was the Warlord, and then Karasu showed up.

It was him! Missy saw the thought in his mind before Lenis could articulate it. *That airship was Karasu's. We only thought he was working for the Warlord!*

Lenis nodded. *That still doesn't explain how he got the airship in the first place.*

I guess it doesn't really matter just now, Missy told him. *If this airship is like the* Hiryū *on the inside, too, then we shouldn't get lost. Where do we look first?*

The holds? Lenis suggested, and the two moved to the nearest one.

Lenis took a moment to send his awareness around them, but although Karasu had stationed guards on the ground, there was no one on deck. As quietly as they could, the twins pulled open the door to the first hold a crack, revealing several racks of weapons within. Missy pulled back and shook her head. They moved to the next hold, but this one was full of foodstuffs. The third hold held similarly useful stock, but nothing to suggest Karasu had stored the stones of ebb and flow there.

Lenis suddenly felt his stomach churn. What if Karasu had the stones with him? He pushed the thought aside and screwed up his courage.

Is the captain still stalling? Lenis asked as they moved to the door of the final hold. He figured the most natural place for Karasu to store the stones was in his own cabin. On the *Hiryū*, all of the holds had been converted to storage areas, but originally two of them had been set aside for cabins. It was possible the fourth hold was Karasu's own cabin.

Oh, no!

Lenis didn't need his sister's warning. He had felt it, too. The engines of Karasu's airship had started up.

We have to hurry! Lenis reached for the door to the fourth hold.

His sister pulled him back. *There isn't time! Karasu is heading this way.*

Can't you warn the others? We need more time!

It's no good, Lenis! Karasu got tired of the captain's hedging. He's given the order to move out. We have to get out of here!

Lenis felt frustration flow through him. They were so close! He hesitated, and in that moment they lost their chance to make a clean getaway. The ropes leading down to the ground went taut as someone started climbing up.

The far railing. Missy thought before Lenis could react. She pulled him over to the other side of the airship. They looked over the side at the twenty-foot drop.

Lenis's mouth went dry. At the least they were going to break some bones. *Missy, I don't think –*

Look!

Lenis's eyes followed Missy's finger. He couldn't see anything, just the shadow cast by the hull of the airship, but then something stirred within the darkness and he saw a figure crouched in the lee of the vessel.

Yami! Lenis didn't know why the swordsman was there, but he didn't care. He knew that everything was going to be all right now. *Missy. Jump down. Yami will catch you.*

Lenis –

A shudder ran through the airship. *No time! We're taking off!* Lenis could feel the engines roaring to life. A moment later the airship gave a little lurch. In another second they would lift off the ground and the drop would only get higher. Panicked, he grabbed Missy's hand tight and spun her out and over the railing. He sensed her holding back a cry as he let her go. Missy's sudden appearance overhead had startled Yami, but the swordsman recovered quickly, leaping into the air to catch her.

Lenis! Missy screamed silently as they landed.

Yami placed Missy on the ground and asked her something. She shook her head and pointed upwards, back towards Lenis. Lenis threw one leg over the railing, readying himself to jump. The airship suddenly lurched skywards, sending Lenis sprawling onto the deck as Karasu's airship took to the skies.

◦ MISTAKEN IDENTITY ◦

'**L**enis!' Missy cried aloud, not caring if anyone heard her now.

'Where is your brother?' Yami asked her. His hand was a reassuring weight on her shoulder but couldn't stave off the sinking feeling inside Missy's stomach.

She pointed above her head, to the place at the railing she thought Lenis would be. 'He's on board.'

'*What?*'

Missy had never seen the Shinzōn swordsman so agitated before. Through his grip on her shoulder she felt all of his muscles tense, as though he were about to spring up into the air. He didn't. Karasu's airship was already hundreds of feet above them.

'We must return to the *Hiryū* and give chase,' Yami told her, taking his hand from Missy's shoulder.

The sinking feeling grew worse, until she thought she was

going to vomit from it. 'How? Lenis is the only one who can start the engines!'

Yami was visibly shaking, though whether from rage or fear or pent-up energy, Missy couldn't tell. She couldn't even think straight. Karasu had her brother! Her hand was inside her robe before she even realised it, closing around the hilt of the Quillblade and drawing it out. Her fear and indecision left her as the blade quickened, feeding off her negative emotions.

'We need to talk to the captain.' Her voice was calm and low, and Yami responded to it with a nod.

Together they raced to the southern end of the square. Some of Karasu's guards had been left behind to allow their master time to escape. They pressed close to their captives, menacing the townsfolk with their weapons. Captain Shishi and the rest of the crew were edging closer, their own weapons drawn. Missy strode right between the two groups, Yami close at her heels. She was no longer thinking about what might happen to the people of Fronge. All that mattered was getting her brother back.

'Where has Karasu gone?' she demanded. The Quillblade thrummed in her hands, its power building to match her own rising fury. Electricity sparked along its cutting edge. No one moved or answered. Missy's eyes narrowed.

'Miss Clemens,' the captain began, 'perhaps you should –'

'Lenis is onboard Karasu's airship!' Missy's scream cracked through the tension in the square, and there was the shadow of the Thunder Bird's cry in it.

Everyone took an unconscious step back from her, except for Yami, who remained immobile behind her shoulder. Karasu's airship had long since disappeared behind the black clouds of smoke still hovering above what was left of Fronge. Missy needed someone to answer her question. She needed to know where Karasu was taking her brother. She held the Quillblade aloft. A bolt of lightning arced from its tip up into the smoke-filled sky. The deep rumble of far-off thunder rolled through the square, impossibly long. She could feel Raikō's presence hovering just beyond her reach, ready to be called.

Missy screamed again, and this time there was no mistaking the avian ferocity in it. '*Answer me!* Where is Karasu going?'

Something happened then that Missy couldn't explain. She felt a surge of power, either from the Quillblade or from somewhere deep inside herself, she couldn't tell which. She lowered the *shintai* as her spirit-self suddenly expanded, her awareness going wider than it ever had before. She felt herself spread out until she seemed to envelop everyone in the square. For an instant, she knew what each of them was thinking, their thoughts perfectly clear, but then she was back in the confines of her body, her head spinning, and she was unable to make sense of what had happened. She had seen too many things all at once to be able to focus on any one thing, any one thought. Her mind reeled from the influx of data.

Then everyone started talking at once. Each of them, whether they were one of Karasu's warriors, one of the residents of Fronge, or one of her own crewmates, answered her question, whether they knew the answer or not. Those that didn't told her so, but some of them did. Scattered phrases broke through Missy's discombobulated mind. Most were in Heiliglander and came from the townspeople, but a few came from Karasu's own men, who spoke only Shinzōn.

Missy screwed her eyes shut and tried to focus. Slowly, her brain stopped trying to sort through everything at once. A few phrases remained in the forefront of her mind.

'The temple.'

'The mountains.'

'God of the Sea.'

'The Vision Peaks.'

Whatever Missy had just done, however she had done it, she now knew where Karasu was headed. The mercenary had come to Fronge in search of a temple dedicated to a Sea God and had tortured the townsfolk until they had revealed its location – somewhere in the mountains called the Vision Peaks.

When she opened her eyes Missy noticed that Karasu's men had fallen back behind their captives, placing the people of Fronge between themselves and Missy. She glared at them, her rage building as her mind steadied itself. Missy raised the Quillblade again as Karasu's warriors eyed her over the heads of the cowering townsfolk. More lightning flashed through the sky to strike the blade, and Missy felt its power intensify. Suddenly she could sense the Demon Lord that had once been Raikō nearby, as if he was being drawn towards her. She was caught in a moment of indecision. Could she, *should* she, summon him? Would she be able to control him on her own?

Karasu's men acted before she could make up her mind. They turned and ran, right through the burning ruins of Fronge. Missy watched them go, using all her strength to reign in her anger. *Let them go. They aren't important. Find Lenis.* She realised she was gritting her teeth and forced herself to relax, taking slow, deep breaths until the intensity of her temper ebbed. She noticed the Quillblade was now shining as brightly as Yami's sword did in Gawayn's hands.

'Miss Clemens?' The captain's voice was hesitant.

With an effort, Missy unclenched her fingers from around the Quillblade's hilt and let it fall to the cobbles of the square, where it clanged metallically before curling into its feather form again. As it left her grasp the force of her anger fled, leaving her feeling numb and very weak.

'I'm all right.' Belying her own words, Missy felt her knees give way.

Yami caught her before she could fall. 'You do not seem all right. What happened?'

Weakened as she was, Missy still felt more like her own self now that she wasn't clutching Raikō's *shintai*, more in control. She looked over at the fifty or so townsfolk who had survived

Karasu's butchering. They were staring at her wide-eyed, as if they feared her as much as they had the Shinzōn mercenary who had tormented them.

'I don't know, Sir Yami. I think perhaps it was the Quillblade.' Missy regarded the seemingly innocuous feather lying on the ash-covered cobblestones beneath her feet and wondered if she told the truth. The *shintai* had been a part of what she had done, that much was true, but whatever it was had originated within her. Still, she required everyone's help if she was going to save her brother, and she needed them focused on him, not her. 'I will be more careful in the future. Perhaps Lord Tenjin can explain what happened when we return to the *Hiryū*.'

This seemed to satisfy her crewmates somewhat, for although some still looked at her strangely, no one asked any more questions about how she had compelled them all to speak. They had been privy to the powers of the Quillblade before and witnessed their effects on Missy all too often. Furthermore, they trusted that Kami Tenjin, the one who had given Missy the Quillblade in the first place, would have an explanation for what had happened in the square when they had all felt the compulsion to answer Missy's question.

The captain came over and picked up the Quillblade. 'Perhaps it will be best if you do not handle the *shintai* until after you have spoken to Lord Tenjin. The double-edged nature of this weapon becomes more apparent with each use.'

Missy nodded as he placed the golden feather inside his robe. She could only agree. The *shintai* did give her great power, but she didn't really know how to use it. Although she and Lenis had wielded it to successfully summon and control the Demon Lord that had once been Raikō in the battle with Ishullanu, it seemed that whenever she tried to use it on her own she got herself into trouble. Lenis didn't like the way it drew on her emotions, either, and that worried her more than she liked to dwell on.

She caught sight of Princess Anastasis over the captain's shoulder and felt a prickling at the back of her neck. If she continued to use the Quillblade, would she end up as hollow as the princess, empty of all emotion save the fury that had overtaken her moments before? It wasn't a comforting notion.

'Okay, well,' Kenji said, holstering his pistol, 'where exactly did they say Karasu was going?' The navigator was clearly rattled but was just as obviously trying to carry on as though he wasn't.

Most of Missy's crewmates couldn't speak Heiliglander, so they hadn't heard everything she had during the simultaneous confession. She leant a little more of her weight on Yami and replied, 'He's going to a temple somewhere in a place they call the Sichtspitzen, the Vision Peaks. He told them he was looking for a temple dedicated to the Blue Dragon.'

'Apsilla?' the captain asked.

Missy sorted through the myriad answers she had received. 'I assume so, but the people of Fronge didn't know who he meant. They don't worship any Blue Dragons in Heiligland, but there is an old disused temple near here dedicated to a Sea God. I think they call him Njord.'

The captain looked thoughtful. 'Sea God? I wonder . . .'

'Captain?' Arthur prompted.

'In Shinzōn, the God of the Sea is named Rinjin.'

'And?'

The captain smiled. 'And, Lord Knyght, Rinjin is the father of Seisui, the Blue Dragon of the East.'

Arthur nodded. 'So you think this Sea God has some connection to Apsilla?'

'I do.'

Missy didn't care if there was a connection or not. The temple was where Karasu was headed with her brother, and he already had a strong head start on them. She pushed herself away from Yami and staggered over to the townsfolk. They shied away from her as she approached, which made her wince. They had already seen enough horror today; it had never been her intention to frighten them any more than they already were. She was suddenly glad the captain had taken the Quillblade away from her. The *shintai* fed on her emotions, but it also aggravated them. It wasn't like her to give into anger. She wished she had her brother's empathic gifts just now to help ease the townspeople, but Lenis wasn't here. Missy needed to use her own gifts to get the townspeople to tell her where the Vision Peaks were.

Even without Lenis's empathy, Missy could see the horror and fear that was writ clearly across the townspeople's faces. Missy picked a few at random and scanned their thoughts, bracing herself for fresh memories of what Karasu had done here. She suppressed the images of burning flesh that rose from her own imagination and focused on the task at hand. She was little prepared for what the townspeople were actually thinking. They were, each and every one of them, thinking about a woman. It was clearly the same woman, but each person pictured her in a slightly different way. To some she was tall and slender with blonde hair. To others she was broad-shouldered and carried a hammer. Some pictured her wearing armour; others had her in a white gown. The one thing that linked all these disparate images was the bolt of lightning each person imagined she clutched in her right hand.

For a few moments Missy stood dumbstruck. What could it mean? Who was this woman and why were the townsfolk thinking about her now? And then realisation struck. They were thinking about Missy. They thought she was this lightning-wielding maiden. They thought she was –

A girl of about Missy's age shot to her feet. 'Do not hurt us, great Magni!'

Missy stared at the girl, trying to suppress a groan. They thought she was some sort of god.

'What's your name?' Missy asked, stalling for time so she could delve deeper into the girl's mind. She soon found what she needed. Magni was a goddess with a volatile mood. She was known as the Lightning-Wielder and was rather fond of smiting things with her Storm Hammer. She was a war goddess, which wasn't unusual in the Heiliglander pantheon. They had quite a few war deities.

The girl had long blonde hair in a thick braid down her back, and she wore brown trousers with what must once have been a white linen shirt before the smoke had dirtied it. Over the lot she wore a tan-coloured, ankle-length coat that Missy supposed was made of leather. 'I am Heidi Baumstochter,' she replied. 'Named after my father Heid, who was named for the god Heidrun.'

Missy was thinking fast. Her brother, she was sure, would know what to do. He was always better at planning things than she was. And then Missy had her answer. She *knew* what her brother would do. He'd try and pull a stunt. She didn't really like the idea of tricking the townspeople, particularly after what Karasu had done to them, but she was also aware that the mercenary was getting further away every moment she delayed. She came to a decision.

'Very well, Heidi Baumstochter, daughter of Heid,' Missy intoned in what she hoped sounded like the voice of a goddess, 'hear me. My fellow god, Njord of the seas, has stolen my Storm Hammer. I, the great Magni, seek the Vision Peaks.' Missy cursed to herself – surely Magni would know where the Vision Peaks were! 'I mean, I seek a hidden way into his temple so I can retrieve what he stole from me. There must be a way in that even the gods . . . I mean, that even my fellow gods do not know about.' Missy winced. As a god she wasn't all that convincing. The people of Fronge were looking at her oddly. Heidi had a definite scowl on her face. Time for something desperate. 'In exchange for your help in my most important venture, I will wreak terrible vengeance on the man who has destroyed your town.'

A ripple went through the townspeople. For the first time since Missy had approached, they took their eyes from her and glanced at one another. Heidi regarded Missy with a calculating look on her face. Missy peeked into her mind. The image of the warrior maiden was gone, replaced by roaring flames that devoured faces Missy didn't recognise – doubtless they were loved ones Karasu had consigned to the fires of Fronge.

Eventually, Heidi spoke. 'We have found such a way into Njord's temple, great Magni, beneath the mountains. We are . . . we *were* a community of miners. One day we were digging near the roots of Mount Vorbedacht of the Vision Peaks when we broke through into the lower chambers of the mountain. We mined no further and sealed off the breach, but you should be able to sneak into Njord's temple through there.'

Missy nodded. 'That sounds like it could work. Wait here.'

She drew back to where the crew of the *Hiryū* had gathered to observe the exchange and quickly explained to them what had happened. The townspeople looked on in confusion, most likely wondering why a god needed to confer with mortals. Missy suddenly paused as an awful idea occurred to her. What if they thought everyone on the crew was a god? She shivered despite the heat that still poured off the ruins of Fronge. The towering flames were all gone, but the foundations smouldered.

Missy finished her retelling and her crewmates' faces registered everything from shock and incredulousness to humour, thoughtfulness and even, Missy suspected, respect for how she had handled the situation.

Kenji was the first to break the silence that followed her tale. 'Why don't we just fly after them? It'll be much quicker than going through the mountain.'

Missy shook her head. 'We can't fly the *Hiryū* without Lenis.'

'I've been flying for more years than you've lived, little lady. I'm sure I can work out enough to get us airborne.'

Missy snorted. 'Have you seen the alterations Lenis made to the engines back in Nochi? He's done things to those machines that no one has even *imagined* before. He's invented an entirely new system for powering them. Pull the wrong lever, or the right lever to the wrong degree, and you'll blow us all up.'

The captain crossed his arms across his chest and buried his hands up his sleeves. 'Well, it appears we are to become miners for a while! Lord Knyght, could you please remain behind and help the people of Fronge as best you can? Many of them will need the doctor's ministrations, and you will need to arrange food and shelter for them in the square.'

Arthur also had his arms crossed over his chest, but that was usual for the stoic Kystian. 'You will go alone?'

Missy was about to object when the captain overrode her. 'This will be a stealth mission, Lord Knyght. If, as Miss Clemens tells us, Lenis has Atrum with him, then it is possible they have not yet been detected. I will take Sir Yami with me. His *Eien no Kage-ryū* is ideally suited to this kind of mission. Masters of the Eternal Shadow style of the Yūrei clan can move about unseen by their enemies, which is why Sir Yami was about to sneak aboard Karasu's airship before it took off.'

Missy startled guiltily. That was why Yami had been in the shadow of the airship when Lenis had flung her over the railing. She should have known the captain would have a plan of his own in motion before they all entered the square. No wonder it seemed as though he was trying to delay Karasu. He hadn't been buying time for the twins but for Yami.

'I will also take Miss Clemens along,' the captain said, and Missy felt her heart soar.

Arthur was frowning. 'Is that wise?'

'I doubt Miss Clemens will submit to being left behind.'

'We could use her here as an interpreter.'

The captain shook his head. 'Miss Clemens has told the people of Fronge that she wishes to sneak into Njord's temple. Doubtless her lingering would arouse suspicion.'

Arthur considered this for a moment, glancing over at the townspeople who were only now helping each other to stand. 'You are correct. We will do what we can here.'

'Excellent.' The captain removed his arms from his sleeves and placed a hand on Missy's shoulder. 'Miss Clemens,' he said with only the faintest smile hovering around his lips, 'will you be so kind as to ask your worshippers to show us the way to their sacrilegious tunnel?'

◦ SEPARATION ◦

Lenis sat on the deck of Karasu's airship with his back to the starboard railing and panicked. His calm, methodical mind seemed to have switched itself off completely. They had left Fronge, his sister, his Bestia, the *Hiryū*, the rest of the crew, and even Suiteki, who was probably still curled up contentedly next to Hiroshi's stove, behind well over half an hour ago. In that time Lenis had gone from startled to concerned and was now entering into blind terror. No one would be coming for him. No one *could*. There was no way anyone could work out how to use the engines since he had modified them. Lenis was alone with Atrum on board a ruthless mercenary's airship. If they were caught they wouldn't be punished, or sold.

They'd be killed.

Atrum might be spared – no crew was likely to give up a free Bestia – but Lenis would most likely be thrown overboard. Hung by his neck from the crow's nest. Have his throat slit, just like . . . Lenis began to cry. He made no noise, but his body shook with the force it took to remain silent as the tears came. He swallowed the great sobs that threatened to betray him, but it was only a matter of time before he gave himself away.

◉

Missy felt the temperature drop as soon as she passed the mine's threshold. She shivered, remembering just how cold it was in the mountains of Heimat Isle when you weren't standing in the middle of a burning town. Their guide, the young girl with the long blonde braid, led the way, carrying a makeshift torch. It was little more than a splinter of wood Heidi had pulled out of the remains of a burning building, already alight at one end.

Missy followed directly behind, keeping up the pretence that she was the deity Magni. The captain came next. Yami followed at the rear.

'When we discovered we had breached sacred ground, we abandoned this entire mine,' Heidi informed them. 'That is why this tunnel is so dark. Usually we keep torches burning, or use Bestia light.'

The girl lifted her torch higher, and Missy saw the tube set into the corner where the wall of the tunnel met the ceiling. She cursed silently to herself, wishing she had planned ahead and brought Lucis with them. Her brother would have, she was sure. Lucis would be able to light the tunnels far brighter and with a much steadier glow than the girl's torch, which only lit the way a few feet in front of them and sent shadows dancing up the walls.

Missy shivered. She didn't like these tunnels.

'We also use Bestia to help with the mining.'

'Ah.' Missy figured the girl felt more comfortable talking than she did walking silently through the dark alone with an apparently wronged god and her followers. Missy wondered if she was worried about upsetting Njord by helping them sneak into his temple, even if it was one he no longer used.

'Bestia aligned to the earth can detect mineral deposits and lead us to them.' Heidi went on.

'I see.'

'And flame Bestia can help us blast through difficult sections, though it is dangerous to use them so.'

'I'll bet.' Missy tried to suppress her frustration but was only marginally successful. 'Well, Heidi, how long before we reach the secret entrance to Njord's temple?'

Their guide paused for a heartbeat and then continued on. 'It is not an entrance, great Magni,' she said reluctantly. 'As I told you, we sealed up the passageway.'

Missy swore aloud in Shinzōn.

'What is wrong?' the captain asked quickly.

Missy and Heidi had been conversing in Heiliglander, so the captain hadn't been following their conversation. 'The tunnel is sealed, Captain.' She addressed Heidi again. 'Yes, I remember you telling me it is so, but how?'

'We collapsed the tunnel around it. See?' Heidi stopped abruptly and held her torch higher. Its light penetrated no further than two feet in front of them. The way ahead was blocked by broken earth.

○

Atrum quivered in Lenis's lap, both from his own fear and from the exertion of keeping them both hidden. The Bestia would be able to keep them concealed for longer than he had the *Hiryū*, because Lenis was much smaller than an airship, but he couldn't maintain the cloak of invisibility indefinitely. Lenis didn't know how long they had before Atrum's strength gave out and they were discovered. He couldn't think about it. He couldn't think about *anything*. His brain wasn't working, but somehow some part of Lenis remained focused, churning through the problem while his consciousness was petrified into inaction. The part of him that never really slept, that remained somehow detached from what he felt, beyond his control, was thinking hard. And, he suddenly realised through his panic-induced trance, it had worked out the solution.

Breathe . . . Think . . . Missy will come. She will reach for me telepathically. I can show her how to work the engines. They will come for me. Breathe . . . Think . . .

The loop of thought cycled through the back of his mind, not exactly demanding his attention, but always there, waiting for him to calm down enough to notice. He focused on the thoughts, repeating them to himself like a mantra.

Missy will come. She will reach for me telepathically. They will come for me. Breathe . . . Think . . .

Lenis felt the tears stop and his breathing slowly return to normal. Of course, he should have realised sooner. Missy would communicate with him. That was one of her gifts, part of what made her special. She could send her awareness out further than any other Bestia communicator. She would come to Lenis telepathically, and he would show her how to start the engines, how to monitor the fluxes of Bestia power, how to channel Aeris's power for maximum effect. The *Hiryū* would rise into the sky and chase after them, guided by Lenis and Missy's telepathic link.

Then why hasn't she gotten in contact yet?

Lenis flinched at the unwanted thought and pushed it away. *No! She will come!*

Feeling more in control of himself, Lenis took a long, deep breath. A dull ache pulsed in his side. He winced. Long Liu's pain medication was wearing off. Lenis forced himself to take shallower breaths and considered his situation. Perhaps Missy was even searching for him now. The smoke from the burning town would have hidden them from view, so she wouldn't know exactly which way they were going. It was only natural she would have trouble finding them.

When Missy did find them, it would take a while for the engines to warm up and for the *Hiryū* to lift off the ground. Karasu's airship was already far out from Fronge, and Lenis didn't think he'd be able to direct Missy quickly enough to use the dual-Bestia system safely, which meant they wouldn't be able to catch up with Karasu until he landed or docked at an airdock.

Unless Lenis could slow the airship down. The idea became more promising the longer he mulled it over, and he had to do *something*. Either he had to slow down Karasu's airship, or find a safe place to hide so Atrum could drop her cloak of invisibility and get some rest. If he could do both it would be all the better, and there were still the stones of ebb and flow to find. He couldn't steal them yet, not when he didn't have anywhere to escape to afterwards. As long as Karasu didn't suspect he was on board, though, Lenis had some measure of protection. In fact, he was almost perfectly safe now that he thought about it. Instead of sitting around worrying about what was going to happen to him if he were discovered, he could use this time to spy and plan. Perhaps he could get away with stealing the stones after all. Assuming he survived.

Lenis made sure he had a firm grip on Atrum and then hauled himself to his feet. This airship was so like the *Hiryū* that he shouldn't have too much trouble finding his way around. He decided to start by having a closer look into the four holds on deck. The twins had only had the briefest glimpse inside three of them. They could have easily missed something, and besides they were out in the open so Lenis would have a clear view if anyone came up on deck. He also really wanted to get a look at that fourth hold. There was a good chance it was outfitted for a cabin, and if so it might just be Karasu's. Even if he didn't find the stones, he might stumble across an opportunity for sabotage.

The first two holds held nothing more than the sorts of provisions Lenis and Missy had already seen – barrels of fresh water, fruit, and dried fish, as well as bags of rice. Lenis was suddenly and unexpectedly grateful for Hiroshi's cooking. Whatever the man's faults, he somehow managed to turn airship fare into something palatable.

The third hold, which on the *Hiryū* housed the landcraft and the winch mechanism used to lower it over the side, was the one full of weapons. A closer inspection revealed nothing more than a collection of knives, swords, spears, and bows with barrelfuls of arrows. Lenis frowned. Karasu's airship was stocked to cater for a lot of soldiers, and that was not a good thing. Before leaving, he selected the smallest knife he could find and drew the blade. Grinning despite the tension that was building inside him, Lenis quickly sliced through each of the bowstrings. It wasn't much, but it was something.

As Lenis approached the fourth hold, Atrum started to weigh down his arms. He was not a large or heavy Bestia, but the strain of holding onto him was beginning to take its toll. Lenis silently cursed himself. All this time he had believed he was getting stronger, and here he was complaining that one of his Bestia was too heavy? He adjusted his grip on Atrum, hugging him closer to his chest, and moved on.

Inside the fourth hold, Lenis found what he had been hoping for. It was furnished as a passenger cabin, but a brief look told him it was not Karasu's. Its interior was a haphazard mess of parchment and scientific paraphernalia similar to the contraptions that lined Long Liu's cabin on the *Hiryū*. This had to be Chūritsu's cabin.

Lenis braced himself and stepped inside. It was entirely possible the Shinzōn scientist had the stones in here so he could do whatever it was scientists did with such things. *Experiments of one kind or another*, Lenis thought as he crept around the mess on the floor. He was careful not to disrupt anything. Although everything looked as though it was scattered aimlessly around the cabin, it was entirely possible Chūritsu knew exactly where everything was, and Lenis didn't want him getting suspicious. Then he almost laughed out loud. He was worried about Chūritsu getting suspicious someone had been in his cabin, but he hadn't thought twice about cutting all those bowstrings?

Get a grip, Lenis, he thought to himself.

As he was stepping over an overturned stool, Lenis became aware of people approaching on deck. He wasn't certain if he heard them or sensed them with his special gifts first, but he knew they were there. He held his breath and forced back the panic that flooded through him. Atrum had remained calm since Lenis had begun searching the airship, and the last thing he wanted was for the Bestia to pick up on Lenis's fright and start making noises.

Thankfully, Atrum remained silent. Lenis counted to ten in his head. Whoever was approaching passed by. He waited for another count of ten, every sense available to him searching for signs of anyone else approaching. When he was satisfied he was in the clear, Lenis let out his breath slowly and resumed his search. The strain of remaining immobile had awakened the dull ache in his side. He moved faster now, caring less about making a noise and more about getting done as quickly as possible. When Long Liu's medication wore off, he wouldn't be up to much sneaking.

The search proved futile. There was nothing even made out of stone in Chūritsu's cabin. Lenis scanned the scientist's mess once more before leaving. He waited by the doorway, crouched down with Atrum squeezed tight to him, waiting to see if anyone else would walk by. When he was satisfied he was safe enough, Lenis left the holds and moved into the shadow of the forecastle. The hatch leading below decks was invitingly open, but if he went down there he would truly be trapped if he were discovered. There would be less room for him to manoeuvre down there, more chance of bumping against someone in the close confines of the airship's belly. But what choice did he have? The only other place to go was the crystal-domed bridge, and there was no way he was going to risk that. The rear hatch, too, was out of the question. He wanted to stay as far away from this airship's Bestia as he could. He didn't know if they could sense him and Atrum through their cloak of invisibility, and he wasn't too keen on finding out.

Lenis steeled himself, breathing as shallowly as possible. He could feel people moving around beneath him, but he couldn't be certain where they were exactly. He would just have to hug the wall and hope for the best. Giving Atrum one final squeeze, Lenis entered the hatch.

Missy finished explaining the cave-in to the captain and Yami, then sat down on the cold earth before the sealed tunnel. It had all been a complete waste of time! Karasu had probably already reached the temple of Njord. He might even have discovered Lenis by now! Missy didn't know how long Atrum could keep Lenis hidden, but he had once cloaked the *Hiryū* for most of a day. Surely he couldn't be close to tiring yet. Missy had lost track of time once they'd entered the mine, but judging by how tired she was, Karasu couldn't have been more than a few hours ahead of them.

First Lucis and now Terra. If only she'd thought to bring them both along! The Bestia that powered the landcraft was slight and had long legs and a small, bushy tail. He didn't look like much of a digger, but he had an affinity for earth. Lenis had always told Missy never to judge Bestia by their appearance. Her brother had a knack for drawing out their hidden potential. He had bought and trained Terra for Mistress Kell, a woman with an obsession for racing airships, landcraft, and just about anything else that moved. Under Lenis's nourishing hand, Terra had flourished, but he had been trained for speed, not excavation. Still, it was worth a try.

While she had been thinking, Captain Shishi and Yami had been discussing their options. Finally, the captain said, 'We will have to return to the *Hiryū* and try to work the engines ourselves –'

'Excuse me, Captain,' Missy interrupted, 'but I think the Bestia can dig through this.'

The captain turned to her, his wild eyebrows dancing wickedly in the wavering light of Heidi's torch. 'Are you certain?'

Missy swallowed the lump in her throat. She was sure this was the only way to get to Lenis, but she didn't want to lie to the captain. *Like you aren't lying to the people of Fronge so they think you're a goddess?* Missy pushed the errant thought deep into a corner of her mind, but she couldn't quash it completely. She was suddenly reminded of Lord Butin, the Ostian steward, and how he had used his telepathy to manipulate Crown Prince Alexis like a puppet. The memory caused her to shudder. As always, thoughts of their Ostian foe brought to mind the memory of Namei's last moments, kneeling before Lord Butin as he ordered her throat to be cut.

No! This was different. Missy wasn't Butin. She was only lying to the people of Fronge to get Lenis back.

To get what you want.

With an effort, Missy brought her mind back to the captain's question. 'No, sir, I'm not sure, but I think we have to try.'

Captain Shishi nodded. 'Very well. We will return for the Bestia.'

The idea of walking all the way back to the *Hiryū* only to return to this very spot made Missy chafe. If only there was another way! Then she realised, a little sheepishly, that there was. 'That isn't necessary, sir. I can call them from here.'

Which is exactly what she should have done in the first place! Missy detached her spirit-self and went whizzing back up the tunnel. It was dark, and she passed many openings and turnoffs on her way back, but this was a mine after all, not a maze. It was designed to allow swift access for the miners and equally fast removal of their goods, not to confuse and mislead. After a couple of sharp turns her awareness was back in the main shaft.

Missy raced back to the surface, conscious that the longer she took to reach the Bestia, the greater the chances that Karasu would complete whatever task he had planned for the temple and leave. Would her brother take the opportunity to sneak off Karasu's airship? Would he have a chance? Missy felt her panic rising again and channelled it into increasing her speed.

A moment later she broke out of the mine and into the fading light of evening. They'd been underground longer than she had expected. In passing she noticed that her crewmates and the townspeople had been busy setting up makeshift shelters on the northern end of the square and had even started salvaging what they could from the remnants of the morning's fire. There wasn't much left for them to save. Ironically, they would need fire tonight, for although it was spring the mountains would be freezing come nightfall.

The Bestia were all aboard the *Hiryū*, waiting for everyone to return. Terra was curled up in the Bestia hutch in Lenis's cabin, fast asleep. Missy formed the image-messages she needed to communicate with him and gently nudged him awake, her spirit-self pressing against whatever subconscious dream had claimed the Bestia until he noticed she was there and stirred. She kept the message short and basic, as she always did. Simplification was one of the first things Bestia communicators were taught. Lengthy or complicated messages had a way of getting jumbled.

Three images were enough: Lenis in trouble, the rubble blocking the entrance to Njord's temple, and Terra digging. As the earth-based Bestia leapt up and out of the hutch, the other Bestia looked after him. Missy thought for a moment and then sent similar messages to all of them. She'd lost enough time because she hadn't been prepared with Lucis and Terra in the first place. She may as well bring them all along in case something else sprung up once they were inside the temple. Assuming Terra could dig them a way in.

○

Lenis emerged into the galley, one shoulder pressed against the inside of the airship's hull. It was eerie, stepping out into a place so like the inside of the *Hiryū* and yet strangely different. The layout was the same, but there was a woman standing in front of Hiroshi's stove, and the doorway leading to Long Liu's cabin was open, revealing yet more stored provisions instead of an infirmary.

The female cook had her back to him, so Lenis stepped cautiously out of the corridor and into the mess hall. He could see the mast-shaft through the exit on the other side of the hall. It wasn't that far away, and Lenis was invisible, but dread overwhelmed him as he began creeping towards it. What was he *doing*? How did he think he was going to get away with this? It wouldn't take much – a sharp breath, a scuffed step – and the cook would hear him and turn. She might not notice him immediately, but her suspicions would be aroused and a search would soon follow. It wouldn't take long to find him, even under Atrum's cloak.

Step by slow step, Lenis made his way across the galley, barely daring to breathe. Each movement was agony; each one was carefully considered and precisely executed. Six paces and he was barely into the room. Another six and he was fully committed. There was no way he could retreat in a hurry now without drawing attention. Another six and he was in the middle of the galley. He felt completely exposed. What if Atrum's cloak failed? What if the Bestia tired and left them both standing, completely visible and with nowhere to hide? Lenis willed Atrum to be strong. He put his trust in his Bestia and forced himself to move on. Six more paces. Six more steps. Only six more and he would be safe. Well, at least as safe as he could be, given the circumstances.

The cook said something suddenly in Shinzōn. Lenis froze. Every instinct told him to run, but he didn't. The woman spoke again. Lenis inched his neck around to look back at her. How had she seen him? What had given him away? But she had not been speaking to Lenis. Someone had come down via the forward hatch and was standing right behind Lenis, who had been so caught up in staying silent he had forgotten to keep his awareness alert for anyone approaching. If Lenis had delayed his foray across the galley any longer, he would have been discovered! He was so relieved he nearly broke into a run again, but he forced himself to remain perfectly still. Whoever had come from the fore hatch said something to the cook, who snapped a reply. There was a grunt, and Lenis heard the person retreat. The cook muttered to herself as she turned back to the stove.

The relief made Lenis giddy. He tried to stifle it. He was far from safe, and far from completing his self-assigned mission. He needed to find the stones, and he came to realise the only place where they could be. In Karasu's cabin. In the *captain's* cabin. Lenis forced himself to move on, slower than ever, his heart beating so fast he was afraid the cook might hear it from across the hall.

◉

Missy stared in open-mouthed disbelief as Terra tore through the rubble blocking the passage. She had expected he would use his delicate front legs to dig away at the earth, and she had even prepared to dig right alongside Terra. Instead, he was *eating* the dirt and rock in front of him. His canine mouth snapped at the debris, pulling large chunks of it free and gulping it down. But he was so small! Where was it all *going*? The tunnel was filled with the low thrum of Bestia power Missy had always associated with machinery, but maybe the noise and vibration had never come solely from the machines but from the Bestia themselves.

It was easy enough to see the reactions of the others. Lucis perched in the tube overhead, giving off a bright white light. Yami and the captain watched Terra intently, but they didn't seem surprised. Perhaps because they knew so little of Bestia power in the first place, they just took things as they came, but Heidi seemed as amazed as Missy was. Missy had seen Bestia do all sorts of things. Ignis generated fire. Aeris played with the wind. Lucis gave off light. Aqua could find and even freeze water. Atrum, perhaps most amazingly of all, could make things invisible. But she had never seen a Bestia absorb earth before. She wondered if other Bestia might possess powers she hadn't even considered. Had she become so used to thinking of them only as parts of a machine that she had forgotten they were powerful before machines were even invented? The thought shamed her. Lenis would never think of a Bestia like that, she was sure. Somehow he saw them for what they really were. It was part of what made him such a great Bestia Keeper. It was how he was able to draw out their hidden powers.

Missy looked at the other Bestia, all focused on Terra's progress, and wondered what they would have been like if they had never been hooked up to a machine. Memories came back to her of when she and her brother had first met Aeris back in Pure Land. She had been a wild Bestia and used to play with the twins in the long grass around Blue Lake. She'd make the wind chase them through the tall stalks, or make the leaves dance on the surface of the lake. When was the last time Aeris had played like that? When was the last time any of them had?

'Perhaps it is time we followed the Bestia,' the captain suggested, breaking into Missy's reminiscences.

Missy looked into the opening Terra had created. The Bestia had already disappeared from view. 'I think you're right. We'll have to crawl to fit through, though.'

'What wisdom forbids, Miss Clemens, necessity dictates.'

Missy nodded and reached up to let Lucis out of the light tube. The Bestia climbed eagerly into her arms and then leapt down into the tunnel to follow Terra. They were all suddenly thrown into darkness until Heidi relit her torch.

'I will go first, in case there is trouble,' the captain said over his shoulder as he knelt down. 'Sir Yami, will you bring up the rear to ensure we are not followed?'

As Yami nodded, Missy wondered who the captain was referring to, and then she remembered Karasu's men had escaped into the burning ruins of Fronge. She had thought they meant to escape her and the strange power she wielded, but perhaps they had been sneaking off to ambush them later. They could even be hiding out somewhere in these mines. The thought made her shiver.

Missy followed Captain Shishi into Terra's tunnel. She could see his shadow ahead, a dark blotch obscuring most of Lucis's light. On hands and knees she hurried after him.

◉

It seemed as though Lenis had been below decks for hours when he finally reached the captain's cabin. He guessed that the day had ended while he had snuck, ever so slowly, by the crew's cabins. They were all occupied, their inhabitants sleeping or preparing to. Lenis had been very careful not to draw their attention. He might be invisible to their eyes, but they could still hear his boots on the timber of the deck, or his breathing, or even his heartbeat, which seemed to Lenis to grow louder the closer he came to the captain's cabin. Passing the engine room had been sheer torture. He could sense the thrum of Bestia power, but he couldn't tell if the Bestia could feel him and Atrum. If they could, they ignored them, but it had made for a harrowing few moments as Lenis tiptoed by the doorway.

He had expected to hear his sister inside his mind by now, asking for help with the engines, but no such message came. Lenis pushed his panic far down, unwilling to admit what he knew must be true. His sister wasn't coming for him. He didn't want to think about why. His trust in the *Hiryū*'s crew was still new. Only a couple of months before, Lenis had been plagued by the belief that his captain would sell him off, separating him from Missy for good. He thought such fears were behind him. He wanted so badly to believe in Captain

Shishi and the rest of the crew, but if *they* weren't keeping Missy from reaching out to him, then that meant she wasn't able to. Karasu had left armed men behind in the square to secure his own escape. There must have been a fight, and Missy still had the Quillblade . . .

No! Missy is fine. Something else must have come up! She's probably helping take care of the townspeople. But the hours passed and still no message came from his sister. In that time Karasu's airship had not ventured all that far from Fronge. It seemed as though he was looking for something in these mountains, as Lenis could feel the airship weaving backwards and forwards through the peaks, often circling back on itself. He had no idea what Karasu could be searching for. Every time they turned back towards Fronge, his heart beat even faster and he forgot all about the stones, but eventually they would veer off again and Lenis would continue his search, burying his disappointment down with his panic.

Lenis slipped into the captain's cabin, which was around behind the stairs leading above decks from the engine room, just as it was on the *Hiryū*. He saw the crate instantly and moved to lift the lid. It opened easily, and there, nestled in a bed of straw, was a single orb with a dull grey surface. Suddenly, Lenis remembered the altar back in Seisui's temple in the Wastelands outside of Gesshoku. There had been a depression in that altar that looked as if it could hold a stone like this one. But there had only been one. One altar. One depression. One stone. Back in Asheim, Karasu had boasted to the captain that he had both the stones of ebb and flow. It seemed he had been lying.

Even so, excitement started to build inside Lenis, growing stronger the longer he looked in the crate. Karasu only had one of the stones they so desperately needed, though whether it was the stone of ebb or flow, Lenis didn't know. It didn't matter. The Shinzōn mercenary only had one of them, which meant the other one was out there somewhere waiting for the *Hiryū*'s crew to find. Lenis's enthusiasm dampened as he realised it could be anywhere in the whole world, perhaps even hidden deep within the Wasteland, deeper even than Seisui's temple had been. Or someone else could have it. Someone worse than Karasu. A Demon, or even one of the Demon Lords. Maybe it would have been better if Karasu had both stones after all. At least then they'd only have one foe standing between them and the unlocking of Suiteki's power.

The desire to reach down and snatch up the stone was almost overwhelming. The stone itself, like Suiteki's crystal egg, emitted no energy of its own, or else its force was on a completely different level to anything Lenis could sense, but there was no doubt that this orb was what he had come looking for. Lying right within reach was one of the keys Lenis needed to awaken Suiteki's dormant power, but he could no more take it now than he could leap over the railing with it afterwards. If Karasu came back to his cabin and found it gone, he would order an immediate search of his airship. A single misstep on Lenis's part and he would be discovered.

At the least, Karasu would know someone else was on board. It wouldn't take long for him to discover that none of the crew had stolen the stone.

Lenis was trapped. His only option was to remain hidden and wait for the airship to reach its destination. Once there, he could steal the stone from Karasu and try to hide until he could work out how to get in touch with or return to the *Hiryū*. It was a stupid plan, and a reckless one.

What wisdom forbids, necessity dictates.

He clutched Atrum even closer. The poor creature was quivering from the strain of maintaining the cloak of invisibility around them. He needed a rest. Lenis considered getting him to drop the cloak. Surely they were as safe in Karasu's cabin as they would be anywhere. It was the one place on the airship that wouldn't be receiving a surprise visit from a crewmember. No one would venture here until Karasu retired for the night.

Just as Lenis was bending down to whisper in Atrum's ear, he felt their flight slow and, a minute later, the familiar jolt of an airship docking. He swallowed. They had stopped. This was it. This was his one chance. He reached out a shaking hand to grab the stone.

● APPROACHING THE SEA GOD'S TEMPLE ●

enis heard footsteps in the corridor just as his hand grazed the surface of the stone. He recoiled, pressing himself and Atrum against the wall of Karasu's cabin. It was not a large space. Like the captain's cabin aboard the *Hiryū*, it was bigger than those of the rest of the crew, but that wasn't saying much. There was just enough room for a bunk, a trunk, the crate, and a desk that folded up against the wall. Lenis was hiding in front of the desk, the hinge that held it upright digging into his back. He ignored it, focusing instead on keeping his breathing as quiet as he could.

The footsteps stopped right outside. Hopefully whoever was on the other side of the door was not coming in to use the desk. If not, there was no reason to turn around and . . . Lenis caught his breath. He'd left the lid of the crate open! As soon as Karasu saw it he would know something was wrong. The cabin seemed to press closer around Lenis, growing smaller by the moment as he struggled to hold onto his breath. There was no way Karasu could come inside without touching Lenis, and once the mercenary touched something he couldn't see . . .

The door was thrust open. Lenis could barely stand the ache in his lungs, though if he let his breath out now, Karasu would hear it. But it wasn't Karasu at all. It was a short Shinzōn man wearing thick glasses. He might have been as tall as Missy's shoulder if he wasn't permanently hunched over. It was Chūritsu, the scientist who had been with Karasu back in Seisui's temple. Now that he was up close, Lenis could see the man was unshaven. His receding hair was pulled back in a traditional Shinzōn tail, and there was more white in it than black.

Dots appeared in front of Lenis's vision, and he was covered in sweat. The ache in his side was growing sharper. He'd have to start breathing again soon, regardless of who heard him. Chūritsu was grumbling something to himself in Shinzōn as he stepped into the cabin and reached down into the crate, apparently unconcerned that it had been left open. After he had the stone in hand he turned and stalked out, not even bothering to shut the door.

Lenis let out his pent-up breath slowly and tried to steady the tremor in his hands. That had been *entirely* too close. He waited until he had himself under control and the sounds of hurried footsteps had faded before leaving Karasu's cabin. He moved even more cautiously than before, every sense alert for any sign of life, but the airship seemed deserted. Even so, Lenis wasn't taking any chances. He kept himself and Atrum pressed up against the wall in case anyone walked by, and his footsteps were as light as he could make them. His arms were sore from clutching the Bestia against his chest, and he felt light-headed, but he managed to keep his breathing low and steady. Pausing often to listen for any footfalls or voices, Lenis made his way towards the fore hatch. In the moments he remained motionless, all he could hear over his own breath and the rushing of his blood were creaking timbers.

His progress was agonisingly slow but thankfully free of incident. He emerged on deck into almost total darkness. A few torches had been left burning in the bridge and by the port railing, no doubt marking the location of the airship's gangplank, but these were the only sources of illumination. The sky was blacked out. At first Lenis thought it was full of smoke, and his heart lifted at the notion that they had not travelled far from Fronge, but the brisk breeze was fresh and carried the scent of moisture. Lenis had long since lost all sense of time. Either it was still daylight, and the sun's rays were obscured by storm clouds, or the day had already ended. Either way Lenis figured it would soon be raining or, more likely at this altitude, snowing. He shivered, wrapped only in the thin robe he always wore in the warmth of the *Hiryū*'s engine room. When he left there had been too much going on, and didn't think to grab anything thicker to put on. Now the wind stung his skin. The weather was definitely getting worse.

Lenis had assumed they were stationed at an airdock, but as he approached the portside railing he realised they were loosely moored to a wide shelf cut into the side of a mountain. The shelf looked too straight to be natural, but it hadn't been designed for airships. Usually an airship docked with one wing balloon inside and over the airdock, which meant the deck was higher than the landing site. The shelf was too narrow for that, so Karasu had butted the portside wing balloon against the mountainside, leaving the deck almost level with the shelf. Instead of sloping gently down, the gangplank was stretched horizontally between the deck and the shelf, spanning the entire length of the exposed mast-shaft and wing balloon.

The airship rose and fell gently in place. Lenis couldn't see how the vessel was secured to the rock shelf, but he suspected it had been achieved by tying ropes to hastily erected moorage points. However Karasu had done it, it made for an unsteady berth that caused the gangplank to wobble where it spanned the frightening gap. Crossing it would mean risking a plummet to the very base of the mountain.

Lenis shuddered as he came to understand that was just what he would have to do. The gangplank seemed narrower than most, though he told himself that was just his imagination. Someone had left a torch burning where it rested uneasily on the rock shelf, but there was a stretch in the middle that was in total darkness. An image of Namei running lightly across the *Hiryū*'s mast-shaft came suddenly to Lenis's mind. He remembered his jealousy at the cabin girl's ease and grace. Namei probably would have forsaken the gangplank altogether and leapt up across to the wing balloon and over to the shelf. She probably would have reached the other side by now, too.

It wasn't that Lenis was afraid of heights – he had spent more than half of his life on airships – but he wasn't confident of his balance, and the fact that he would have to cross at least some of the way in complete darkness wasn't helping. Indecision tore at him. The most sensible thing to do would be to crawl across on his hands and knees, but then he'd have to let go of Atrum. Lenis couldn't see anyone on the shelf beyond the lone torch's light, but that didn't mean there wasn't anybody waiting in the darkness. Karasu struck Lenis as the sort who didn't take chances. He'd been willing to murder everyone in Fronge just to find this place.

Lenis wondered if it wouldn't be better just to wait aboard Karasu's airship for another chance to escape, but he was close enough to Fronge that a rescue from the *Hiryū* was still feasible. If only Missy would contact him! He wished that he had her gifts and could reach out over long distances to talk to people. The captain would know what to do, Lenis was sure. He squeezed Atrum to his chest. The captain would probably go after Karasu and try to steal the stone or, if he couldn't do that, find somewhere to hide until the *Hiryū* came. What other options did Lenis have? He had no way of knowing how long Karasu would stay in one place, or where he would be going once he left.

There was nothing to be gained from waiting any longer. Lenis considered taking one of the torches by the gangplank, but he decided that if Karasu had left anyone behind on the shelf they would definitely see a torch coming their way. Besides, he couldn't carry it and crawl at the same time. He would just have to trust his luck that they wouldn't be looking while he was revealed in the torchlight.

Lenis bent down to whisper into Atrum's ear. 'Thank you, boy. You did great. I have to let you go now, so you can drop the cloak of invisibility. We've got to get across the gangplank, okay?'

A shiver ran the entire length of Atrum's body, right down to his extraordinarily long tail. He licked Lenis's cheek, and Lenis sensed the pulse of Bestia power fade. Now perfectly visible, he ducked down behind the railing. As he did so, he recognised a flaw in his plan. Atrum was blind. How was Lenis going to get the Bestia across the narrow gangplank?

Atrum solved the problem for him, climbing over his shoulder and onto his back. Lenis knelt on all fours as Atrum wrapped his long tail tightly around Lenis's waist and spread his weight across Lenis's back. Atrum was shivering. Lenis could sense the Bestia's radiating fear. It wrapped itself around him until he felt his own resolve waver. Lenis steeled himself against it, countering it with an upsurge of confidence he didn't quite feel himself. Atrum stilled, but he dug his claws deeper into Lenis's back. Lenis winced but ignored the pain. He had considered briefly asking Atrum to cloak them again, since they were still going to be in contact for the crossing, but he pushed this aside too. If he asked his Bestia to concentrate on keeping them out of sight, he wouldn't be able to focus on maintaining his grip around Lenis's midsection. A moment of inattention would be disastrous. Better to risk being seen than to witness Atrum falling.

Lenis started to crawl, half-expecting to hear someone cry out from the rock shelf as he left the relative obscurity of the railing and moved out onto the gangplank. No alarm sounded. The first foot or so was easy – the gangplank was secured firmly to the airship – but the further out Lenis crawled, the more precarious his perch became. The wind was not helping. It had picked up considerably since he had come out on deck and was crashing into his side. Atrum gripped tighter, his claws tearing through the fabric of Lenis's robe and into his skin. Lenis gritted his teeth and moved on, inch by inch, worried now that the rain or sleet or snow or whatever was about to start falling would come before they had reached the shelf.

What seemed like an hour later, Lenis's hand plunged down into darkness. He pitched forwards until his hand connected with wood, jarring his entire arm. They had entered the patch of shadow in the middle of the gangway. Lenis's arms and knees were aching, and the sting had returned in force to his ribs. His back was shredded constantly with pain as Atrum clung to him, and he still hadn't reached the halfway mark.

Lenis slowed down, sliding his hands forwards instead of bringing them up, feeling his way along the wood. Splinters dug into his flesh, but he didn't pull his hands away. In his fear he wasn't sure he'd be able to find the gangplank again if he did. Dizziness threatened to pitch him over the side. Up until then he had looked no further in front of himself than his arm could reach, but now he stared ahead, focusing on the torch flickering on the far side of the gangplank. The wind tore at it, making its flame dance. Lenis slid his hand forwards, ignoring the shards of wood that bit into him. He reached out until he could feel the edge of the gangplank, then did the same with his other hand, making sure he knew where the fatal boundaries were so he wouldn't veer too close to them.

The wind grew to a torrent. The torch died. Lenis froze. Every nerve in his body screamed out into the darkness. His head swam, his thoughts tossed around as if by the bluster that slashed at him. A wave of vertigo passed through him, and then another. Lenis leant forwards until his forehead rested against the rough wood of the gangplank. He pulled his legs in close to his stomach, making himself small. As if in response, Atrum pressed lower on Lenis's back, and there they crouched, shaking together in the darkness, suspended out over a fathomless abyss, as the rain started.

◉

Terra's tunnel took less time to get through than Missy had believed it would, but beyond it were still more passageways.

These were straight, tall, and wide, and there was evidence they had been well kept in the past. Those days were long gone, though. The sconces that once held torches were empty, and the dust covering the floor was so thick it was basically dirt. They relied heavily on Heidi's guidance, though Missy wasn't convinced the Heiliglander knew her way through the labyrinthine temple any better than she, the captain, or Yami did. Captain Shishi had cocked an inquisitive eyebrow when he saw Heidi emerge from behind Missy, but the blonde girl had soon taken charge, leading them to the right and then taking turn after turn without any sign of hesitation.

Several times Missy considered skimming Heidi's mind, but she was too tired to concentrate on anything more than moving forwards. They had been underground for hours and hadn't had much of a rest since they had left the airdock at Letzer-Zuflucht on the southeastern coast of Heimat Isle that morning. By Missy's reckoning that was now yesterday morning, though without the open sky above her she couldn't be certain.

The pure light Lucis shed had started to waver in front of Missy's eyes. The shadows seemed to be creeping into the edges of her vision. She stumbled over her own feet and fell onto all fours, skinning her knees and hands. Yami was by her side in an instant, but he didn't try to pull her upright.

'Perhaps we should rest here,' the swordsman suggested.

The captain nodded. 'We will be of no help to Mister Clemens if we arrive exhausted.'

Missy translated for Heidi, and then everyone sat where they had stood. There was nothing to distinguish this stretch of hallway from any of the others they had trodden through, though now that Missy was closer to the ground she saw they had been climbing a slight incline. *I must be tired if I didn't notice that before*, she thought. Her stomach growled; she hadn't brought anything to eat.

Yami reached into his robe and silently offered her something wrapped in a leaf. She recognised it as one of the balls of rice that had become a staple of her diet ever since she had joined the *Hiryū*'s crew. It had been warmed by Yami's body heat, but she was too hungry to care. She bit into it, not even bothering to unwrap the leaf, which turned out to be pretty sour but edible all the same.

Yami took out another rice ball and handed it to Heidi. The Heiliglander eyed the ball suspiciously and sniffed at it before biting into the rice. Her face scrunched up at the taste, but she chewed and swallowed and took another bite. Missy washed down the rice with some water from her canteen. There wasn't much left, but she offered it around anyway. Both the captain and Yami drank but neither ate. Missy thought about asking them if they were hungry but couldn't find the energy to form the words. Her mind felt fuzzy. She closed her eyes, just for a moment, and fell instantly asleep.

She came to as someone shook her shoulder. Her eyes opened so slowly it felt as though she was dragging them up.

Then she had to blink a couple of times as white light blinded her. Eventually her vision cleared, and the blurry outlines of her companions solidified.

Missy brought both hands up to rub her face. 'Sorry. Didn't mean to nod off.'

The captain offered Missy her own canteen. She swallowed the last mouthful it contained. 'I am afraid we must keep moving, Miss Clemens. I fear your brother may need us.'

The captain's words brought Missy more fully awake, and she accepted his hand to help her stand. 'How long was I asleep?'

'Not long,' Yami told her. 'Less than half an hour.'

Missy sighed. *I suppose that's more than I should have taken.*

Yami bent in close and whispered, 'Short sleeps are best. If you sleep any longer your mind sinks deeper into your dreams, which makes it harder to wake. It is an old swordsman's trick.'

Missy was only half-listening to his advice. She *really* had to pee, but where was she supposed to go? She looked around in vain. They were in yet another corridor, like any of the others they had passed through so far. There were no rooms on either side, not even an alcove. But if she didn't go soon she was going to burst.

'Um . . . which way are we going?' she asked, hoping the others didn't hear how desperate she was.

'This way.' The captain pointed off in one direction.

'Could you . . . ah . . . excuse me for a moment.' Missy turned and went the other way, hurrying to get beyond Lucis's light and, she hoped, the range of everyone's hearing.

'Are you all right, Miss Clemens?' the captain called after her.

She half-turned but didn't stop. 'Yes, sir. Won't be long.'

Missy was walking in the dark now, but with Lucis's light behind her she noticed a turning in the corridor just ahead. She almost ran around it and then crouched down next to the wall. The sound of urine hitting stone sounded awfully loud to her, and she knew the others must be hearing it. Her face went warm. She noticed an acrid stench crawling up the back of her throat. Someone had been there before her with the same idea. She tried not to think about the fact she might be crouching down in someone else's urine.

'You're no god.'

Missy screeched and jumped hastily to her feet. Heidi had come around the corner. Missy could see her silhouetted against Lucis's light.

'Miss Clemens?' the captain called out to her.

'It's all right,' Missy replied, though she wasn't sure it was. Heidi was glaring at her. The girl was squeezing her sides and shaking slightly. Missy didn't need her brother's empathic gifts to know the Heiliglander was furious. 'What do you want?' She tried to put force into her words but failed.

'You're no god,' Heidi repeated in a harsh whisper.

Missy stood taller. 'What are you talking about?'

'Gods don't *pee*.' Heidi leaned closer.

Missy took a step backwards, feeling like a fool. She'd led the girl to believe that she was the god Magni so that she would help her find Lenis, but she hadn't bothered to put any effort into her ruse. She was suddenly aware of how dependent they all were on the girl. Heidi had been the one to lead them here. If she decided to abandon them, they'd be lost in the tunnels under the mountain. Missy tried to remember the way back to the mineshaft, but she couldn't. She hadn't been paying attention, relying instead on the others to guide her. Another thought occurred to her – how did Heidi even know her way around down here? She claimed the miners had sealed the tunnel once they realised where it led. Had they had a chance to explore first? Missy needed to focus, but her mind didn't seem to want to work properly.

'I don't know what you're talking about,' she said, playing for time. Should she call the others for help? How would Heidi react to that?

'I saw you,' Heidi hissed. 'You follow the foreigners around like a child. You grow tired like a mortal. You *piss* like a mortal!' Missy wished she'd stop bringing that up. 'Who are you? What are you doing here? What do you want with me?'

Missy hesitated. She had to convince the girl they meant no harm, that they could help each other. Bluffing hadn't worked. Could she make Heidi believe she was a god, like she had compelled everyone in the square to answer her? *No!* She recoiled from the thought. She couldn't. She *wouldn't* do that. That only left one option. The truth.

'No,' she said, looking down at her feet, 'I'm not a god. I'm not Magni.'

'I knew it!' Heidi grabbed Missy's shoulders in a crushing grip. 'You are a fraud! Why? Why did you do it?'

Missy tried to twist away from Heidi's grip, but the girl didn't let go. Missy suppressed the urge to call for help. It was her fault Heidi was here. It had been her decision to use the Heiliglander to guide them to the temple. It was up to her to make it right.

Heidi was gripping Missy so tightly she could feel the girl's worn-down fingernails digging through her shirt and into her skin. Missy forced herself to look into her eyes. Their intensity frightened her. Without even meaning to, she reached into Heidi's mind and was bombarded by memory fragments. The town square. Karasu. The fires. The people of Fronge. The burning. The dying. Missy pulled her awareness away. Heidi's chin was thrust forwards. Strands of blonde hair had escaped their braid and were stuck to her face by sweat, dirt, and ash. This close, even in the shadowed corridor and through the grime, Missy could see the spattering of freckles that covered Heidi's cheeks.

'I'm sorry,' Missy began, choking on her own words. She tried again, 'I'm so sorry. The man in the square – Karasu – he took my brother. I just want to get him back.'

Heidi suddenly released her shoulders. 'Your brother?'

Missy nodded. 'His name is Lenis. We were sneaking on board Karasu's airship when it took off. I escaped. Lenis didn't.'

'You were sneaking onto his airship?' Heidi was peering at her through the gloom. 'Why?'

Missy sighed. 'It's a long story.' Heidi didn't move or say anything. The silence stretched on until Missy felt compelled to continue. 'He has something we need. We've been searching for him. It was only luck we were passing by this way when we saw the smoke . . .'

Heidi sniffed loudly and rubbed a grimy hand across her nose. When she pulled her hand away, Missy saw tears clinging to her eyelashes. 'You have been hunting this man, Karasu?' Missy's throat tightened. She nodded. 'And when you find him, what will you do?'

'Get back my brother, somehow, and the stones. They're the things he has that we need.'

'Will you kill him?'

The words were uttered so calmly it took Missy a moment to react. 'What? I . . . I don't know.'

'You don't *know*?'

'I hadn't thought that far.' Her response sounded lame, even to her. What had she expected would happen when they confronted the mercenary? He wasn't likely to just hand over the stones. Missy shivered and brought her arms around herself. 'I don't know.'

'But you have power!' Heidi grabbed her again, though this time not as hard. 'I have seen it. At your bidding, we all obeyed. The Vaettir do as you command.' Missy instinctively picked the meaning of the unfamiliar word out of the girl's mind. *Bestia.* 'You can destroy the man who . . . the man who . . .' Heidi sagged to the ground, still clinging to Missy's shirtsleeves. Great sobs wracked her frame, and Missy felt tears of her own coming. 'You . . . can . . . avenge . . . them . . .'

Missy gasped. 'I . . . I can't.'

'Why not?' Heidi pulled back. Tears had tracked their progress through the dirt on her face. 'Why can't you?'

Missy thought of the Quillblade she had given over to the captain's keeping. What Heidi said was true. She did have power. Power to read people's minds, to compel them to do as she wished. With the Quillblade she could harness some of the Thunder Bird's power, could even summon him if she had Lenis's help. The thought of her brother pulled her up short. She remembered the look in his eyes when he had first seen her holding the Quillblade. The *Hiryū* had been under attack. There was fighting on the decks and she was going to join in. The *shintai* had somehow reacted to her emotions and the anticipation of battle, but Lenis had regarded her with his sad eyes and had brought her back to herself.

Looking down into Heidi's face, though, it was neither the lust for battle nor the disgust at violence she felt. Instead, she knew a great desire to help the girl Karasu had wronged, and she felt an equally powerful sense of frustration that there was nothing she could ever do that would undo what had been done.

'All right, I'll help you,' Missy said and then glanced aside. 'I don't know how. I don't know what I can do for you, but if I can help you I will.' She disentangled herself from Heidi's grip and helped the girl to her feet. 'I'm *not* promising to kill anyone for you, though. Not even Karasu.'

The Heiliglander wiped at her face with an already soiled sleeve. 'If I have my way, *godling*, I'll kill him before you ever have the chance to make that decision.'

Missy nodded, troubled by the sudden stillness in the girl. Something was happening inside Heidi's mind. Missy could tell by her abrupt changes in mood as much as by using her telepathic gifts. Heidi was building a wall inside her and trying to force the bad memories behind it. She was clutching at her anger, fuelling her will with it to block out the burning and the dying and the suffering. Missy had witnessed such intentional suppression far too often. New slaves did it all the time, cutting their old lives out of them in the hope they wouldn't haunt them in their new ones. It seldom worked perfectly. Such barriers were dangerous. They could give way at any moment, shattering the minds of those unprepared for the fallout, and they affected people in odd and unpredictable ways, too, sometimes warping their personalities.

Missy didn't know Heidi at all, but she knew she didn't want the girl to lose herself because of what Karasu had done to her home, her friends and family.

They rejoined the others in silence. When Captain Shishi and Yami saw them come around the corner, both of them raised inquiring eyebrows. Missy just shrugged. What could she tell them? Heidi had borne witness to something so horrible that Missy shied away from even imagining it, and they had tricked her into guiding them on to a confrontation with the very man who had been the cause of it all. Already, it was having an effect on her, and Missy didn't think it was a good one.

Without a word they continued on their way, following Heidi around whichever turning she seemed to think appropriate. Yami and the captain, Missy knew, didn't mind silence. She had noticed that Shinzōn people in general tended to avoid needless conversations. Except for Jinsei Hiroshi, the *Hiryū*'s cook. He liked to talk so much that Missy suspected he did so whether or not there was anyone there to hear him. For Missy's part, she was happy to shamble along quietly. Her sleep-starved mind settled into a stupor, which she was reluctant to disturb by further conversation with Heidi.

After about an hour of walking, though, Heidi blurted, 'Tell me about Karasu.'

Missy stifled a sigh. The girl had a right to know who her tormentor was, or at least as much as Missy knew about him, which was precious little. It was the only thing Missy could actually offer her. So she told Heidi about the orbs of ebb and flow, and about Seisui and Raikō, which required an explanation of Totem and Demons, which in turn led to a recounting of what had happened in Ost. There was no structure to Missy's story. She was barely able to follow it herself. At one moment she was telling Heidi about Gesshoku and the next she was talking about Namei. By the time she was finished, she had told the Heiliglander all about the voyages of the *Hiryū*, from the time she and Lenis had snuck up onto the deck the night before they left Itsū, right up until they had seen the smoke rising from Fronge.

Missy spoke in a dull monotone, too tired to put any emotion into the retelling, so tired it was an effort to keep her mouth moving. For her part, Heidi listened without interruption. She didn't ask any questions and, when Missy had finished, her throat so dry it ached, Heidi simply nodded. If Missy's story had made any impact on her, had done anything other than break up their silent journey, Heidi gave no sign. She had wrapped her stillness so closely around herself that Missy wondered how deep the mental barrier she had erected went, and how thick she had made it.

Some time later, exactly how long Missy had no way of knowing, Heidi held up a hand. Everyone stopped. The Heiliglander leant so close to Missy's ear she actually brushed it with her lips. 'We are about to enter the temple proper. Ahead there is a sacred chamber.' Missy was shocked by the girl's sudden business-like manner. All signs of her earlier distress had been erased. She might have been telling Missy they were about to enter a public bathroom. Missy glanced at her thoughts, confirming her fears. Heidi was only thinking about the task at hand. All traces of the horrific images Missy had seen in her mind earlier were gone. Heidi had locked them away somewhere deep inside her. Perhaps, if Missy had the time, she could help her come to terms with –

'Njord rests within.'

'*What?*' Missy drew back into herself.

'Shh!' Heidi rebuked her. 'Njord slumbers within, deep in the ice.'

Missy pushed Heidi's problems to one side to worry about later while she translated for the others in a low voice.

The captain listened and then said, 'If this is indeed Njord's temple, it *is* possible the sea god is within.'

'Do you think he could be a Demon?' Missy asked. She was far too tired to deal with Demons.

'I do not think so,' Yami replied. 'Gawayn does not stir.'

Missy still wasn't thinking very clearly. 'But aren't all of the Totem and Jinn corrupted?'

'Silili has not yet fallen,' the captain pointed out. 'He helped Lenis and the Bestia back in Neti's temple.'

Missy had all but forgotten about that. Her brother had told her that a Totem had reached out to him and healed his and the Bestia's wounds. That meant Apsilla wasn't the last Totem to fall. Apsilla . . .

'Wait.' Missy grabbed Heidi's arm as the girl made to move around the corner. She turned to the captain. 'The sea god is Apsilla's father, right?'

'We believe so,' the captain replied, 'though there is as yet no proof of that.'

'But if he *is*,' Missy pressed on, 'that means he's not a Totem or a Jinn at all, but something older, something more powerful.' Missy suddenly felt a moment of clarity powerful enough to banish the fog that had settled over her exhausted mind. 'It means he's a god, a *real* god, like Ishullanu. What did he call himself? A Caelestia?'

The captain drew his eyebrows together. 'It could be as you say, Miss Clemens. Lord Tenjin will have a better idea of how these beings are related.'

'But he's not here.' Missy's mind was still eerily clear. She didn't need Tenjin to tell her she was right. She knew it. She *felt* it. Something settled into place. 'That's why Karasu's here. He wanted the dragon egg. He went to the trouble of finding the stones of ebb and flow, but we beat him to the real prize so he came looking for something even more powerful. Suiteki's grandfather – the sea god.'

The captain remained silent for a moment, considering her words. 'You may be correct.'

'What shall we do?' Yami asked.

The captain looked at each of them in turn. 'I think we should get some sleep.'

Missy shook her head. 'I'm not tired.' She didn't want to sleep now. Her weariness had dropped away from her and she didn't want to risk losing the clarity that had taken its place. She could see things so plainly now. Karasu had come for the god's power. She still didn't know why, or how he planned to do it, but she was confident she could figure it out if the captain would just let her –

'You may not be tired, Miss Clemens,' the captain said, 'but the rest of us are. We are certainly too weary to face whatever is in that chamber. We will set a watch in case Karasu arrives. Until then we should get what rest we can.'

Missy was about to protest, but the preternatural clarity was already starting to slip away. Her fatigue returned. It started in her feet and quickly rose within her. When it reached her head, she yawned. Perhaps she could use some sleep after all. She had just enough time to ask Lucis to dim her light, and then she was falling down into slumber.

◉ CONFRONTATION AT THE SEA GOD'S PILLAR ◉

Move. *Move. Move. Move. Move.*

Lenis repeated the word in his mind as the wind threw the half-frozen rain into his side. The gangplank beneath his hands was now slippery. The wood had soaked up so much water it could take no more. Atrum was plastered to Lenis's back, but Lenis was so cold he could no longer feel the Bestia's claws digging into him.

Move. Move. Move. Move.

If Lenis didn't budge soon he knew he was going to freeze to death. Small tremors were already running through his body, causing his teeth to clash together. He gritted them so tightly his jaw ached. Ever so cautiously he pushed one trembling hand forwards a few inches.

Move. Move. Move.

The other followed, and then Lenis was crawling, slowly at first, but he managed to go faster once he was sure the wind wasn't going to push him over the edge. He realised then that his eyes were screwed shut and forced them open. It made no difference. The night was black around him. If the moon or stars were shining, they were doing so behind the storm clouds. The torches had long since gone out.

Lenis increased his pace, pushing his hands further and further along the gangplank, ignoring the fragments of wood that dug into his palms. He didn't know how far he had come or how far he had left to go. All he knew was that he had to keep going.

In his haste he suddenly overreached, and his hand slipped out into nothingness. Lenis cried out, a small, shrill whine that ended abruptly as his nose connected painfully with the gangplank in front of him. He recoiled. Atrum's claws tensed in his back and this time Lenis felt them deep inside his shoulder muscles and down near his kidneys.

Panic surged through him, carried along by another great shudder. What if Atrum pierced one of his organs? Ridiculous. The Bestia's claws couldn't possibly be *that* long. But when was the last time Lenis had trimmed them? Lenis focused on this thought. The part of him that was a born engineer, that churned through problems with a calm indifference to external stimuli, wandered back through his mind, searching for the time Lenis last sat on the deck of the *Hiryū* with Atrum in his lap as he snipped the Bestia's nails, one by one. Lenis felt a particle of calm as he eased himself into the mental task of remembering. Then, when he was confident his mind was steady, he gripped onto that calm and wrapped it around himself and Atrum until he felt the Bestia's claws retract, just a fraction.

Move. Move. Move.

Lenis started again, once more going slowly. The next time his hand slipped he brought it back to the gangplank and continued on. Eventually he reached the end of the wood and his fingers connected with stone. *The shelf!* He forced himself the final couple of feet onto the rocky surface. Relief raged through him unchecked, shattering the cocoon of calm that had carried him over the final stretch. It didn't matter. They had made it. Atrum let go of him just as Lenis rolled onto his back. A moment later the Bestia was curled up on his stomach, shivering. Lenis gasped in the air, ignoring the icy missiles that rained down on his face.

His celebration didn't last long. He might have reached the other side, but he was no warmer and what little heat his now constant shiver generated was leached away by either the cold rock beneath him or the storm above. Lenis knew there was a way off the rock shelf. Where else had Karasu gone? But finding it in the dark was going to be an ordeal in itself.

Lenis sat up, holding Atrum to him so the Bestia didn't startle and jump over the edge. His feet were still pointing towards Karasu's airship, assuming the orange circles glowing in the darkness were the portholes of the vessel, as Lenis suspected. From what he remembered before the storm had blown out all the torches, the exit to the rock shelf would be behind him to his left. He shuffled backwards before standing up, wanting to put as much distance between himself and the edge as possible. The whole time he kept his eyes focused on the small lights of the airship, his only means of orienting himself.

Atrum was miserable. He pressed up against Lenis's chest as hard as he could; his tail curled around Lenis's body twice. His head was up under Lenis's chin, wrapped in the coils of his tail, but he was completely waterlogged and had probably taken ill already. Lenis opened his robe and pulled its folds around the Bestia. He was in no better shape than Atrum, but hopefully between the two of them they could make enough warmth to keep themselves going.

Lenis resolutely turned his back on the lights coming from the airship. Then he took a nervous step forwards. Then another. At any moment he expected to smash into the rear wall of the shelf. He couldn't assess the damage he'd done to his nose back on the gangplank, but it was throbbing dully. He suspected the cold was numbing the worst of it. Smacking his nose into the mountainside would hardly do it any good.

When he did bump into the wall it startled more than injured him. Leaning against the stone, Lenis rotated until his left shoulder was resting against it. Then he started walking, making sure his shoulder remained in contact with the wall. He stumbled on something in the dark but managed to regain his balance. If anything, he moved slower than he had back on the gangplank. He wasn't sure what lay beyond the edge of the shelf. It could be a doorway, or even a sudden drop. Falling was very prominent in Lenis's mind. The shelf wasn't all that large. On at least one side, there was nothing but open air.

The rain stopped abruptly, causing Lenis to pause. He cocked his head to one side. No, it hadn't stopped. It had just stopped falling on him. He must have walked under an over-hanging in the rock and entered some sort of tunnel. The wind still blew at his back but at least the constant icy shower had ceased.

A moment later Lenis glimpsed a sliver of orange light ahead, like that shed by a torch. He approached cautiously, remembering that he should also be worried about running into Karasu's warriors. As long as he and Atrum remained in the darkness, they were fine, but the Bestia was in no condition to make them invisible if they had to walk through torchlight.

As Lenis edged nearer to the light he noticed it was coming from around a corner. He tried to blot out the noise of the storm so that he could hear if anyone was waiting just around it, but he had no way of knowing if he was successful. Either the downpour was loud enough to drown out whoever was there or the passage beyond was empty. There was only one way to find out.

Steeling himself, Lenis peeked around the edge of the wall. Beyond was a giant hall with a line of torches lighting a pathway through its centre. He could only guess at its size, for though the torches burned brightly they couldn't cast their flames high or far enough to reach the walls or ceiling. Lenis imagined the parts that remained in shadows to be full of Karasu's men. The Shinzōn mercenary couldn't know that Lenis had stowed aboard but would not have forgotten the *Hiryū*. Surely Karasu would expect the vessel to be in close pursuit. He was bound to have left guards behind.

Atrum mewed softly, or had been doing so for a while, and Lenis was only just becoming aware of it now that the sound of the rain quietened.

'Shh, boy,' Lenis whispered, still straining to hear something – a rustle of clothing, a jangle of a weapon's harness – anything that would tell him there was somebody there. 'You'll be okay.'

Lenis wasn't so sure. His own shaking had lessened since they had gotten out of the rain, but Atrum's had not. It seemed no matter what he did, no matter how good his intentions were, Lenis always put his Bestia in danger. Guilt washed through him. He knew he had no right to demand so much of them. It wasn't that he *wanted* to, but somehow what he intended didn't seem to count for much these days.

Taking a deep breath, Lenis rushed around the corner and made a dash for the darkness beyond the corridor of torchlight. No outcry came. Lenis remained hidden in the shadows, pressed against the wall. All he could hear was the pumping of his own blood. He let out his pent-up breath slowly, but to his ear it was still impossibly loud. Suddenly, the adrenaline that had been powering him since he was in Karasu's cabin fled his body, and he felt every hour he had been awake and without food. Atrum wasn't the only one in bad shape. Lenis slid down the wall, just outside of the torches' reach, and pulled his knees up to wrap as much of himself around Atrum as he could.

He knew he shouldn't sleep. He knew that, at any moment, Karasu or some of his warriors might find him, but he was so tired. His stomach and nose hurt. Atrum's misery was pushing against his resolve. And then, without meaning to and against his better judgement, Lenis fell asleep.

◎

Missy woke a heartbeat before Yami touched her shoulder. She looked up at the kneeling swordsman and nodded. She had also heard the voices echoing along the passageway. Without Lucis's light, it took Missy several moments to orient herself. Someone had carried her further down the hallway, back the way they had come. About twenty paces ahead, Missy could see a reddish glow indicating the entrance to the chamber in which Njord slept. The voices were coming from around the corner. They were low but Missy could just make them out.

'. . . him?'

Missy couldn't recognise the voice, but it spoke Shinzōn. Unable to reign in her curiosity, she sent her awareness out ahead of her.

The chamber was smaller than she would have imagined a god's bedroom to be. It was circular, about twenty-five feet in diameter, and twice that high. It had four separate openings leading into it, each set evenly along the outer wall. The walls themselves seemed to be made of ice, though it was hard to tell by the wavering light of a near-dead torch being held by a stooped man with white-streaked hair and heavy glasses. From what the captain had told her, that would be Chūritsu. He stood near a pillar of ice in the centre of the chamber. Another man was with him, carrying a large sword strapped to his back. Karasu. The two men were alone.

Missy nearly returned to her body to get the others. Surely Yami and the captain would be a match for Karasu. The man with the permanent hunch to his shoulders didn't look like much of a fighter. Her curiosity gave her pause, though. If she held off for just a little while, she might learn why the mercenary had come here.

Chūritsu continued his silent inspection until Karasu snapped, 'Is it him?'

'Hmmm?' Chūritsu looked at the mercenary over the rim of his glasses. 'It is hard to say. There is *something* in there. Whether or not that something is Rinjin remains to be seen.'

Missy moved closer to the central pillar. The flames from Chūritsu's torch revealed a smooth, slightly opaque surface that looked a lot like ice, but just at the edge of that light, where it gave way to shadows, she saw a dim blotch within the pillar. At first she thought it was some sort of imperfection within the structure, but the more she concentrated on it the firmer her conviction grew. There *was* something inside it.

It looked small to be a god. It was too indistinct for her to be sure of its true size and shape, but it looked no bigger than a child with its legs pulled up close to its chest. As soon as the image flashed into her mind, Missy knew that was exactly what it was. For a moment she doubted herself, but then she understood the picture hadn't come from her own imagination. It had been an image-message, sent to her by whatever or whoever was in the ice. *Trapped* there.

Missy had been so caught up in examining the ice column that she had all but forgotten Karasu and Chūritsu. The Shinzōn scientist had pulled a pick out of the bag at his feet and was about to smash it into the pillar. Missy panicked. She forgot what state she was in and tried to grab his arm. Her incorporeal form did nothing to stop the pick as it fell against the ice. From around the corner, Missy felt a sharp pain in her temples. She threw her spirit-self back into her body but couldn't stop the gasp that escaped her lips.

'Captain!' she croaked. 'Karasu . . . Chrūritsu . . . Stop them!'

The pain came again, worse now that she was inside her body to feel it. It was as if Chūritsu was slamming the pick into her brain. Somewhere, Missy was aware that Captain Shishi and Yami had left and that Heidi was shaking her arm, or perhaps she was just holding onto her. The blows to Missy's head sent a ringing noise through her mind. She couldn't focus on anything.

As quickly as the pain had come, it was gone. Missy pushed herself upright. Her vision wavered and her head spun, but Heidi had a hold of her and she didn't fall. She had to get around the corner to see what was happening. She dragged Heidi along with her, or perhaps Heidi was dragging her. The pain was gone but Missy's thoughts were still fuzzy. All she knew was that she had to make sure the pillar was intact.

It wasn't until she stepped around the corner that she noticed Chūritsu's torch had finally died. The pure white light that greeted her was coming from Lucis. The captain and Yami stood in front of her, facing Chūritsu and Karasu. The pillar was between them. Missy heard a low growling, so unfamiliar it took her a moment to realise it was the Bestia. She had never heard them make such a noise before. It was low and deep, and they all seemed to be making the same sound so that it came out as a single, rolling snarl. They, too, were arrayed against their enemies. Ignis and Terra on one side of the column, Aqua and Aeris on the other. Lucis was high above them, actually standing on top of the pillar of ice.

The Bestia's anger was shocking in its intensity. Never before under Lenis's care had they seemed so feral. Their tails twitched and their hair stood up all along their backs. Small flames danced at the tips of Ignis's fur, and Missy felt a breeze growing at her back. The earth beneath her feet started to shudder, ever so slightly, and Lucis was generating more light than they really needed and was only getting brighter.

They're gathering their power, Missy thought, awed by what she was seeing. Bestia power thrummed through the entire chamber, causing goosebumps to rise on Missy's flesh. Without machines to channel their energy, Missy didn't know if they could control it. She had never witnessed a wild Bestia exert this kind of force.

'Where did you come from, Lord Shishi?' Karasu asked. The mercenary was projecting a calm demeanour, but Missy saw right through it. His muscles were taut and his eyes darted from the Bestia to the captain and back again. He was tense, not at all like he had appeared back in Fronge, when the numbers were in his favour. 'What do you want?'

He seemed to have given up on his mockery, too. Missy decided that was probably a bad sign.

The captain spoke as calmly as ever, his composure unfeigned. 'We want the stones of ebb and flow, Sir Karasu.'

Karasu's eyes narrowed and his right arm twitched, but Missy saw there was no way he could draw his oversized blade in the close confines of the chamber. It was a massive weapon, taller than the mercenary. It seemed unlikely he could even wield it. Missy had expected Karasu to turn and run, but he seemed reluctant to leave the chamber.

'Delays,' Chūritsu muttered. He was standing behind Karasu's left shoulder, cleaning his glasses. The pick was tucked into the crook of his arm. 'Give him the stone, Karasu, and let us get back to work.' The mercenary looked to his companion, the corner of his upper lip pulled back in a snarl. Chūritsu seemed oblivious to Karasu's ire. 'It's useless to us anyway.'

Karasu's snarl became a smile as he visibly relaxed. He turned back to face the captain. 'Very well, Lord Shishi. A deal. I'm afraid I only have one of the stones of ebb and flow. I cannot tell you which it is, but you are welcome to it if you leave us here in peace.'

Chūritsu replaced his glasses and bent down to place the pick on the ground. He rummaged around in his bag and pulled out a dull grey stone. 'Take it and go.' He sounded bored.

Missy knew the captain would accept. It was why they had come here, after all. That and to save Lenis. With Karasu busy in the chamber with the pillar, they could slip behind him and find her brother. Better to eliminate Karasu as an enemy now by removing the one thing that lay between them, that set them against each other. Captain Shishi might doubt Karasu when he claimed to have only one stone, but having one stone and Suiteki was better than having nothing but a powerless baby dragon.

Heidi still clung to Missy. With everyone speaking Shinzōn, the Heiliglander had no way of knowing what was going on. Missy knew she would recognise Karasu as the man who had sacked her town and murdered her people. What if the sight of him shattered the mental blocks she had put in place to protect herself from her memories? They were still new. If they broke now, if Heidi lost control, there was no way to predict what she could do.

'Forgive me if I doubt you,' the captain said, 'but why would you give us the stone? What is it you do here?'

Karasu snorted. 'What does it matter? You came for the stones I have. I have only one. Take it. Go and fight your war with the Demons.'

Heidi's grip on Missy's arms was solid. Her fingers didn't even tremble. Either she was completely numb, had inhumanly strong willpower, or her fury was operating on a level Missy had never known. Slowly, carefully, she pressed herself into Heidi's mind. Nothing. The girl was doing it. She was keeping herself together. And then Missy felt the slightest quiver run through Heidi's body. Cracks appeared in the girl's mind. A few stray images broke through. Red fire. Blackened skin. Missy panicked. A spasm went through her mind and suddenly Heidi's thoughts were clean again. Missy had somehow reinforced the girl's mental barrier.

'One stone is not enough,' Captain Shishi pressed Karasu. 'We need both.'

'I do not have it!' The mercenary took a step forwards. Everyone tensed, including the Bestia. Small tendrils of flame erupted from Ignis's nostrils, and there was an audible crack in the air above Aeris. Missy drew away from Heidi's mind. She would deal with what she had done later. 'You fall short of your reputation, Lord Shishi. Even a fool, if in your place, would realise the other stone will be in a temple dedicated to Seisui, not Rinjin.'

Karasu's eyes flickered from the captain's face to the pillar in the centre of the chamber. Missy knew he wanted whatever was sealed inside, wanted it enough to give up the stone in his possession. What had changed, Missy wondered, since Asheim? What was the mercenary really after? She knew where the answers lay. Instinctively, Missy sent her awareness out towards him, leaving Heidi to hold up her body. But as she tried to peek into Karasu's mind she encountered the same blur of images she always saw when trying to read the captain's thoughts. It was as if he wasn't thinking about any one thing. Frustrated, Missy returned to her body. Whatever mental training these Shinzōn warriors went through, it made it impossible to scan their minds.

Missy was just wondering if she could somehow force her way beyond these surface thoughts into the deeper reaches of Karasu's subconscious, when there came a noise from the corridor behind Karasu.

'What now?' Chūritsu asked, rolling his eyes.

The noise grew louder as whatever it was drew closer. Soon, Missy was able to make out the sounds of people struggling against each other. And then she heard someone call out, and her heart stopped for the space of three beats. Heidi and Karasu no longer mattered. Missy would know that voice anywhere. It was Lenis!

A moment later he appeared in the doorway behind Chūritsu and Karasu, held up between two of Karasu's warriors. He was fighting them, or trying to, but they had his arms pinned behind his back and there was little he could do against them.

'We found him asleep in the vestibule,' one of the guards said.

The twins cried out in unison.

'Missy!'

'Lenis!'

Karasu glanced over his shoulder, and his smile grew wider. 'Well, Lord Shishi, it seems as though I have found another bargaining chip. Your engineer, I believe? Bring him inside.' The last part was directed at his warriors.

The guards lifted Lenis and carried him forwards. As they moved through the portal and into the chamber, Lucis's light turned blue and grew so bright it was blinding. Missy screwed her eyes shut, then clamped her hands over her ears as a piercing crack tore through the chamber.

In the silence that followed, a deep, booming voice spoke.

KI'AM SU TARU INA KA HARSAG!

◦ THE BOY IN THE PILLAR ◦

Lenis felt the words vibrating through his chest. He had no idea what they meant, but the guards had let him go in their surprise. Lenis dropped to the ground, using his empathic abilities to lead him as he crawled away from the guards and towards his sister. He could feel her more strongly than ever before – a beacon drawing him near. The blue light was so bright it was visible even through his eyelids. It reminded him of when Apsilla had spoken to him in his dreams, and the voice was like hers, too, but louder and more masculine. He could feel the power it contained. So intent was he on crawling through the confusion created by the radiance and the voice of . . . whatever it was that had spoken that Lenis bumped into something. Unwittingly, he opened his eyes. A shadow was outlined by the glow. It reached down to him.

'Mashu?' The voice sounded human enough, though Lenis couldn't place the language. The light began to fade.

Without thinking, Lenis took the offered hand. As his vision cleared he saw that it belonged to a boy, shorter than himself but perhaps a bit older. He had black hair that seemed to hold onto the blue light as it faded, leaving behind odd highlights. His eyes were also a bright blue, but as the light faded they seemed to turn from blue to green and then settled into a light grey. His skin was very pale, a blue-tinged white Lenis recognised as chilled skin, but though the boy's hand was cool, it wasn't cold. There was something odd about his features, too. They were too sharp, his cheekbones too prominent, his brow too heavy, his hands larger than they should have been, his . . . Lenis realised the boy was naked and quickly looked away.

The others were staring at them, apparently stunned into silence. Lenis noticed the Bestia were all there, and they too were regarding him and the boy whose hand he still held.

'Mashu?' the boy repeated, and Lenis knew it was a question, even if he didn't understand what it meant.

'Rinjin?' Karasu stammered from behind them. Lenis glanced over his shoulder. The mercenary had dropped to his knees.

'Rrr-in-ja-in?' The boy enunciated each of the syllables slowly, as if trying them out on his tongue for the first time.

'Seisui?' the captain asked.

Again, the boy repeated the word slowly. 'Say-soo-ee?'

Lenis could feel the boy's confusion. He wondered if Missy was trying to read his mind. Lenis looked quickly at his sister. Her face was blank and she hung limply in a blonde girl's arms, mute evidence her soul had left her body.

Lenis turned back to the boy, knowing he wasn't Seisui and suspecting he wasn't Rinjin either. He didn't *feel* like a Totem or a god. Still, it was worth a try. 'Apsilla?'

The boy's eyes went wide, the irises cycling from grey through green and back to blue. 'Amaru la Apsilla.' And then, more urgently, 'Amaru la Apsilla!'

Lenis sensed the boy's anxiety and tried to calm it. He sent waves of reassurance towards him. 'It's all right. Everything's okay.' He soothed him as he would a frightened Bestia, keeping his tone steady and gently wrapping him in calm.

Keep going, Lenis, Missy said suddenly into his mind. *I think I'm getting close.*

Yami stepped up behind him, so softly Lenis didn't even notice him until he saw the swordsman wrap his own robe around the boy's shoulders. It was odd to see Yami in nothing but a loincloth. It distracted him, and in that moment Karasu stepped forward and grabbed his shoulder.

'You will not –'

The boy let go of Lenis's arm and leapt at Karasu, so fast Lenis couldn't follow the movement. The mercenary was caught off guard and fell back as the boy advanced, hands held forwards as though he was going to rip into Karasu with his nails, which, Lenis noticed, were extremely long and black.

Without thinking, Lenis grabbed the collar of Yami's robe and pulled the boy back. Fast or not, he was no match for a fully armed Shinzōn swordsman. The boy complied without complaint, but the others were already in motion. Yami helped Lenis drag the boy back to where Missy was standing with the blonde girl. The captain and the Bestia moved forwards, forming a blockade across the chamber. It was only then that Lenis realised the ice pillar had vanished, leaving behind a curling strand of steam that rose up into the shadows above them.

In the confusion, Karasu had somehow managed to draw his imposing blade and held it level with the captain's chest. In the restricted space of the chamber the bulky weapon was more hindrance than anything, but its length gave him far greater reach than Captain Shishi's sword, and with that he had the advantage. 'Give me the boy, Lord Shishi, and you shall have your stone.'

Lenis saw more of Karasu's warriors through the doorway behind their leader. He wasn't sure how many of them there were, but they could only enter the chamber a couple at a time and only then if Karasu got out of the way.

'You know I will not do that,' the captain said evenly. 'Give the stone to me, you have –'

Lenis felt Terra's power a moment before he released it. Missy gasped as the whole chamber shook. A second later a spear of rock thrust up from the ground in front of the captain's feet, knocking Karasu's sword aside. Another rose up beside it, and then two more. In the space of half a dozen heartbeats, rock divided the chamber from floor to ceiling, wall to wall, separating the adversaries.

Lenis looked to Terra. 'How did –?'

Missy answered before he could even finish his question. 'It was him. The boy. Kanu. He asked Terra to help.' Clearly Missy had managed to read the boy's mind.

'He spoke to Terra? He's a communicator?'

'He's more than that. I think –'

'Enough,' the captain cut her off. 'We must go.'

'But, Captain?'

'No, Miss Clemens. We must hurry. It will take us most of the day to get back to Fronge. Karasu will be there sooner.'

Missy nodded and then bent her head to whisper to the girl holding her up.

Lenis looked over at the boy, who appeared even paler in Yami's black robes. Missy had called him Kanu. She must have pulled his name out of his mind.

The boy was eyeing him too. 'Mashu?'

Lenis sighed and nodded. 'Mashu.' *Whatever that means.*

Kanu suddenly smiled and looked much younger for it. His nails didn't seem so long either and were more dark blue than black. His eyes were grey again, but Lenis also noticed his teeth were longer and sharper than those of a normal human.

Lenis's stomach rumbled and his legs felt wobbly. He hadn't eaten in almost a day, as far as he could figure. 'I don't suppose anyone has any food?'

No one did, so there was nothing for it but to begin the trek back to Fronge. Lenis hoped they could get there before Karasu.

◉

Missy had never felt this tired before. She and her brother had embraced back in the chamber, and it was a relief to have him by her side again, but her body and mind were too worn out to take any real pleasure in his company. They were all tired, Missy knew. Lenis had to carry Atrum, who was breathing in short, shallow gasps, and Heidi seemed far too calm and composed for someone who had just encountered the man who had slaughtered her kin. Somehow, Missy had strengthened the wall in Heidi's mind. It had probably saved the girl's life, may even have saved all of them, but she felt bad about it all the same. It wasn't up to her to fiddle around with other people's thoughts, and there was no way to tell if she'd done any damage in the process. Not now. Not here. Maybe after she got some rest she could speak with the Heiliglander, try to explain, and then together they could see about taking the wall down. If Heidi even wanted it gone. Maybe she wouldn't ever want to remember what Karasu had done to her. Not the details, at any rate.

The only one who seemed to be okay was the strange boy with the blue-black hair. Missy had managed to pluck his name out of his mind, or at least what she assumed was his name, but Kanu had been too confused for her to get a clear image of what he was thinking.

One thing had been perfectly clear, though. He had known the Clemens twins instantly. He somehow recognised them. Mashu, he had called them, but what did it mean? Was it just a coincidence that he had emerged from his icy cocoon as Missy and Lenis were brought together in the chamber? Surely he couldn't have been waiting for them?

Missy felt a shudder run down her spine. It was too much effort to keep thinking. Whatever Kanu was, he wasn't a threat to them. She saw the way he had lunged at Karasu when the mercenary had grabbed her brother, and the delight in his face when Lenis acknowledged the fact that he was Mashu, and again later when Missy had as well. Whatever Mashu meant, it was important to the boy.

Missy wanted to ask him about it. She wanted to talk to her brother about what had happened in the chamber, about how the Bestia had responded to the boy, and what Lenis believed Karasu was up to. But there would be time for that later, once they had returned to Fronge and gotten something to eat and some sleep. And after she had spoken with Heidi. And after they had dealt with Karasu.

The hours passed in a daze. Missy's brain was numb, her mind frozen into inaction by lack of sleep. She barely noticed when they reached Terra's tunnel and had to crawl back through. A part of her rejoiced at the fact they were almost home. Home? The word seemed to float through her thoughts. She liked the sound of it, the *roundness* of the word, and she loved that when she thought it she saw an image of the *Hiryū*.

They emerged from the mine into the afternoon sunlight so suddenly that Missy was blinded. There were people everywhere around them, all talking at once. Missy couldn't separate thoughts from words. She blinked to try and avoid the brightness but found she couldn't open her eyes again. She felt hands touching her gently, lifting her up. Familiar smells tickled her nose. Sweat, and smoke, and wool.

'I think she's already asleep.'

Missy felt the words vibrate under her cheek. It took her a moment to realise they were in Kystian.

Lenis was somewhere in the dark. He sensed he was safe, but many hands were grabbing at him, pulling him further into shadow, away from the glowing light of the torches. Something gripped his neck. Claws sank into his flesh . . .

Lenis gasped and woke up. 'Suiteki!'

The baby dragon screeched in distress. She must have been sleeping on his chest and was startled as he fought his way out of his dream, clawing at him to keep from being thrown off. It took him only a moment to realise he was back in his bunk on the *Hiryū*, and another to satisfy himself that his Bestia were all nearby.

Atrum was curled up by his side. Lenis's violent waking hadn't disturbed him. That was a bad sign. The Bestia's shivering had subsided, but Lenis could sense he was utterly exhausted. The others were fine, and their water dishes and food bowls were filled in their hutch. Hiroshi must have topped them up. The cook was slowly getting used to the Bestia's dietary requirements, though he still had a tendency to put too much meat in their food.

Lenis lay back down. A bit of extra meat wouldn't do them any harm after the ordeal they had just been through. Still, he knew he should get up and check on them. Besides, for all he knew, Karasu had visited some even more horrible punishment on the people of Fronge while he and the others were traipsing through the tunnels under the temple. Then there was the mystery of Kanu, the boy in the ice. Lenis wanted to talk with him, and for that he was going to need his sister.

Lenis coughed and felt a jab in his ribs. His nose was all blocked up, too. It appeared he hadn't escaped his adventure unscathed after all. Everything just seemed too hard. He closed his eyes and went back to sleep.

Missy woke naturally, having dreamt of flying the *Hiryū* through the skies above Blue Lake. It was strangely soothing to return to her homeland as a free person, to fly above the place she had been enslaved, knowing she could leave whenever she chose. She allowed the calm to flow through her, relishing it, knowing it would soon leave her.

Eventually, she sat up and swung her legs over the side of her bunk. The thought of it made her smile. Her bunk. Her home. She was ravenous, but she knew that just down the corridor there would be food waiting for her. In short, Missy was in a good mood.

As expected, she found Hiroshi in the galley, pressing something into the middle of a ball of rice.

'Morning, girl,' the cook called out, throwing her what he had just been making.

'Morning?' Missy caught the rice ball, her heart suddenly sinking. 'How long did I sleep?'

'All night!' The cook beamed at her. 'And you looked like you needed it, I tell you. It's still early, mind.'

'What about Fronge and Karasu?' So soon her mood had soured. There was just so much to worry about.

'That Demon spawn hasn't dared to show his face back here. As for Fronge,' Hiroshi lowered his voice, 'well, there's not much left. Mark me, we'll be ferrying the people off somewhere pretty soon. Not like the captain to leave people in this sort of state, I tell you. No food, you see.'

Missy nodded. She did see. It was early spring and whatever was left of the foodstuffs the people of Fronge had been surviving on over the winter had probably been destroyed in the fire. Karasu hadn't attacked again, but if anything that only made her more nervous. Where was he, and what did he want? It was bad enough they had to worry about Lord Butin and the Demon King. They still had to find the mercenary and somehow get the stone from him.

'You are awake.'

Shujinko was standing by the stairs leading to the forward hatch. He was wearing an apron like the one Hiroshi habitually wore, and he held a scrubbing brush in one hand and a bucket in the other.

Missy caught herself staring and said, 'Yes, I'm awake.'

The cabin boy nodded. A few strands of hair had come loose from his tail and fallen across his face. He brushed at them with his forearm. 'I think the captain wants to see you.'

'Let her finish her breakfast in peace, young Shujinko,' Hiroshi admonished. 'Have you finished scrubbing the figurehead?'

The cabin boy blushed. He ducked his head to try and hide it, but it was all too apparent. Missy thought it made him look younger, closer to her own age. 'Yes, Mister Hiroshi.'

'And did you feed the Bestia?'

'Yes.'

'You didn't wake young Lenis, did you?'

'No, sir.'

'Good! That boy needs all the rest he can get, let me tell you. He caught a cold or worse up in those mountains, if I'm any judge.'

Missy knew Shujinko wasn't happy with his role on the *Hiryū*. She was vaguely aware he was much higher in the Kami clan's hierarchy than Namei had been. Namei had wanted nothing more than to fly on an airship, and though it had cost her life, she had been happy to be the *Hiryū*'s cabin girl. Missy got the impression that Shujinko was more used to giving orders than following them. He kept mostly to himself, answering when spoken to directly but not seeking out the companionship of any other crewmembers. Not at all like Namei.

Missy realised she was staring at him again and looked down at her half-eaten rice ball. What was it about him? Every time he showed up Missy couldn't help looking at him. Maybe it was because she knew what it was like to be sent somewhere without having a say in whether or not you wanted to go. There was also something about his eyes. They were such a light brown they looked like rich, amber honey, and they were kind of sad . . . Missy shook her head and shoved the rest of her breakfast into her mouth. Who cared about his eyes?

'I'd better go see the captain,' she said through her mouthful and hurried out of the mess hall, her face inexplicably burning.

When next Lenis woke it was more calmly, though he felt worse. A headache lurked behind his eyes, and his nose was even stuffier. Worse, he thought the weight on his chest was too heavy to be Suiteki. He probably had some sort of infection. He was also desperately hungry and thirsty. There was nothing for it. He'd have to go visit the doctor.

Suiteki rode on his shoulder as he left his cabin, nuzzling him behind the ear with her snout.

In the hallway outside his room he met the last person he wanted to see. Shujinko inclined his head slightly in greeting, and Lenis returned the gesture.

'Good to see you out of bed,' the older boy said.

'Thanks,' Lenis muttered and walked by. Inside he was seething. Shujinko was always outwardly polite, even while pummelling Lenis during their training bouts, but Lenis didn't have to rely on visual cues to know what the cabin boy really felt. He sensed it perfectly. Just beneath Shujinko's stoic Shinzōn façade was a great deal of anger and resentment. Lenis had been aware of it from their very first meeting, though then it hadn't been directed at him.

Shujinko had been chosen as Namei's replacement, but he hadn't wanted to fly on an airship, much less be a cabin boy. If Lenis hadn't made that one little mistake when they first met, Shujinko might have found another target for his repressed anger. It had been an honest mistake. The boy wore his hair long and, from behind, he *looked* a great deal like his cousin Namei. If he'd turned around a moment sooner, or if Lenis had approached him from a different angle, Lenis never would have welcomed him aboard as the new cabin *girl*. Trying to pass off his mistake as a translation error had only earned Shujinko's further contempt. The cabin boy had not been convinced, and the damage had been done. There was nothing Lenis could do about it now. Besides, he had other things to worry about.

As soon as he'd had something to eat and drink and visited the doctor, he was going to go and have a talk with the captain. Then he needed to sit down with Missy and Kanu and try to work out what exactly was going on.

'Well, well!' the cook boomed as Lenis stepped into the galley. 'What have we here? A couple of hungry dragons! You've just missed your sister, boy!' With a flip of his wrist Hiroshi lobbed something at Lenis. He caught it awkwardly, squishing the ball of rice too tight. Hiroshi laughed good-naturedly. 'Get that down, and then you'd best be off to see the captain too.'

Lenis nodded as Suiteki ran down his arm, her claws digging into his flesh for grip, and started biting at the rice ball. 'Thank you,' he tried to say, but his nose was so congested he ended up mumbling.

'I knew it! I told them you'd caught a cold, boy!' Hiroshi seemed more pleased that he had been right than concerned for Lenis's health. 'Don't you worry. I'll fix something up for you that'll have you fighting fit in no time, I tell you.' He suddenly grinned. 'And don't think I've forgotten you, little lizard!'

Hiroshi flipped something else into the air. Suiteki left off nibbling Lenis's rice ball, raced back up his arm, and climbed the side of his head to catch it in her jaws. It was a sliver of meat. Some sort of rabbit, from the smell of it. Lenis grimaced as Suiteki scuttled back down to his shoulder to gorge herself on the offered tidbit. He never would have fed a Bestia so much meat. In fact, he had done some reckoning and figured that Aeris, the Bestia that had been with him the longest, had eaten less meat in her lifetime than Suiteki had in hers. Lenis had to remind himself that Suiteki was not a Bestia but the child of a Totem, and though she was small enough to sit in his hand she might one day grow to be larger than an airship. Besides, she enjoyed the meat and didn't suffer for eating it.

Hiroshi disappeared behind his bench and popped up a moment later with a large mug, which he handed to Lenis. 'Drink that down, boy. Do you good.'

Lenis accepted the mug, sniffed at it, and then took a sip. Sometimes Hiroshi's idea of what was good for him didn't extend to his sense of taste, but this proved delicious. It was a thick, rich soup that tasted heavily of garlic and ginger. Lenis thanked the cook again, forwent his visit to the doctor, and carried his rice ball and mug of soup up to the bridge, accompanied by the sound of Suiteki's gnawing right by his ear.

● THE MANY FACES OF THE LADY OF RAIN ●

Missy had just finished presenting herself to the captain when Lenis walked in. It was still early. The sun was up beyond the eastern mountains, but it would take hours to get high enough in the sky to be seen. The bridge was all but deserted at this hour, though not because her crewmates were still abed. Most were in Fronge, helping the survivors as best they could. Tenjin remained behind, seated in a chair with his injured leg up on a short stool.

When Missy arrived the captain had been speaking with a representative from the destroyed town. He was a tall man with curly brown hair and broad shoulders, who had bowed low to Missy before departing. Clearly Heidi hadn't yet managed to convince her fellows that Missy wasn't a god.

'I am glad you are both here,' the captain said after Lenis had bowed, much to Suiteki's distress. The poor thing nearly dropped her breakfast as she clutched Lenis's robe to keep her perch on his shoulder. After he straightened, she nipped him on the ear, put the strip of meat she had been picking at in her jaws, and slipped down his collar into his robe. 'I wished to discuss certain matters with you. Things have taken a surprising turn since we diverted to Fronge.'

'Yes, sir,' Lenis replied, hunching his shoulder to rub his ear since both his hands were full.

'However, our mission remains the same. We must retrieve the stones of ebb and flow to unlock Suiteki's power. We know Karasu holds at least one stone. Also, for whatever reason, he wants the boy we found in the temple.'

'Kanu,' Missy said.

'Yes. This means Karasu will eventually come to us. I believe we should therefore focus our attentions on the second stone. I have decided to follow Karasu's advice and seek the unclaimed stone in temples dedicated to Seisui. Lord Tenjin believes he knows of such a temple here in Heiligland.'

Tenjin coughed and adjusted his foot on its rest. 'I cannot be certain. The theory that the Totem are worshipped by different names in different countries – the World Tree philosophy – has yet to be proven, but we must remember it was the connection between the Totem Apsilla and the Blue Dragon Seisui, which Lenis drew back in Gesshoku, that led us to the dragon egg.'

'Yes, sir,' Lenis repeated. Missy sensed her brother was in a bad mood. He obviously wasn't well and probably should have stayed in bed.

'Well,' Tenjin continued, 'if we assume Rinjin and Njord are the same entity – the god of the sea – it follows logically that Apsilla's Heiliglander guise would be a daughter of Njord.'

'Because Apsilla is the sea god's daughter?' Missy asked.

'That is correct, Misericordia.'

Missy nodded. 'Does Njord have any daughters in Heiligland?'

Tenjin stroked his beard before placing his hands inside his sleeves. 'He has several. We know Apsilla is the Lady of *Rain*, so I have ruled out those of Njord's offspring who share no such affinity with water. That leaves three possible candidates: Ran, a vengeful ocean deity; Jormungand, a slothful deep water goddess who invokes feelings of regret; and Kolga, a gentle goddess renowned for guiding lost sailors to safe havens.'

'It's Kolga,' Lenis said, his voice muffled by his cold. 'It has to be.'

Tenjin nodded. 'I suspect you are correct. Kolga is the most compassionate of the three. The captain and I have discussed this and we believe Kolga corresponds most closely with what we know of Apsilla.'

Missy found their reasoning to be pretty thin. Even if the World Tree philosophy was correct and Apsilla was known as Seisui in Shinzō and something else in Heiligland, that didn't mean she was benevolent in both cultures. Perhaps Heiligland was where she went to vent her frustration by wreaking vengeance on sailors.

'It is likely Karasu will draw the same conclusion,' the captain said.

'He's the one who suggested we find her temple,' Lenis mumbled. 'He knows we need the stones. It could be a trap.'

The captain nodded. 'Indeed. Karasu may try to take the boy from us by force, or he may seek the second stone to gain a greater position from which to barter. In the temple he attempted to trade the boy for the stone in his possession. He may try again. Either way, a confrontation seems likely.'

Missy stared out of the crystal dome of the bridge at the walls of Fronge. Tendrils of smoke still curled up out of the ruins. The captain's words brought back memories of her conversation with Heidi. Is that really where all this was leading? Was violence the only way to resolve the problem of Karasu? Didn't they have enough to worry about with Ishullanu and his growing Demon army?

'Kanu.' Missy hadn't realised she'd said the name aloud until she felt the others watching her. She turned back to them. 'He's the key to whatever it is Karasu is up to. He wanted the dragon egg. Now he wants Kanu. We need to speak to him. Maybe he can tell us what all this is about.'

Captain Shishi smiled. 'A wise suggestion, Miss Clemens. We do not know who or what Kanu is, nor do we know what Karasu wants with him. Perhaps he believes the boy is the sea god. The boy seems to be who he was looking for in the temple. Kanu may hold some clue to Karasu's motivations.'

'You want us to talk to him?' Lenis asked.

'I do. You are both extremely gifted in various methods of communication. The boy speaks a language no one else can understand, but he seems to have some sort of connection with you both. If possible, I would like you to try and converse with him. Find out as much about him as you can.'

'Where is he?' Missy asked. She had her own reasons for wanting to talk with Kanu. A quick glance at her brother told her that he was having similar thoughts.

'He is down by the water,' the captain told them.

'The water?' Missy hadn't noticed any water during their mad flight to Fronge, but then she had been a bit distracted and there had been a *lot* of smoke.

'Over that rise to the west.' The captain pointed to a series of low-lying hills set between two towering peaks. At their summit was a stone wall, blocking any further view in that direction. 'There is a gate in the wall and a path that will take you through the mountains and down to the shore. The people of Fronge have a jetty there for loading their minerals and shipping them to the mainland.'

Missy forgot about Kanu for a moment. 'By sea? Can they do that? What about the Demons?'

Lenis answered her. 'Metal ore is too heavy to transport via airship unless you keep the loads too small to make the voyage worthwhile.'

The captain turned to her. 'There are those who still sail the oceans, Miss Clemens, despite its dangers. The members of Miss Shin's family have been sailors for many generations. Her nautical skills are what earned her the post of helmswoman on the *Hiryū*.' He saw the doubtful look on Missy's face. 'I have been to the wall myself. It is quite defensible.'

'Yes, sir,' Missy said, though she wasn't thinking of defending Fronge from Demons. She had known that Shin had been a sailor before joining the *Hiryū*'s crew, but somehow she had never really dwelled on it. The Shinzōn woman had spent most of her life on waters infested with the Wasteland taint. *That takes a special sort of courage,* Missy thought.

The twins bowed to the captain and left the bridge. As they passed by the stairway leading below decks, Lenis turned to head down into the hull. 'We'd better grab warmer clothes, and I'll leave Suiteki with Hiroshi. She won't like going out into the cold.'

Once they were attired in heavier gear, including gloves and padded boots, they met at the gangplank. Although both had been given new Shōgo uniforms in Nochi after the Warlord had legitimised their theft of the *Hiryū*, Missy preferred to wear the clothing Andrea had given her. She felt more comfortable in breeches and shirts than she did in Shinzōn robes. It was closer to what she used to wear back in Pure Land. She still wore her hair tied back in the Shinzōn fashion, but where once she had done so to emulate her owners, now it was to keep her hair out of her face. The coat she wore was another gift from Andrea. It had a large hood and was heavily padded with wool.

Her brother seemed to prefer Shinzōn clothing. He had fallen into the habit of wearing his Shōgo uniform, which consisted of black, wide-legged trousers and a black robe embroidered with a red dragon motif, tied with a red belt. He had complained that they were poorly suited to the high winds of airship travel until he had learned to layer other robes on top of and beneath his uniform. No one had bothered to teach the twins how to wear Shinzōn clothing when they were just slaves, but Lenis had picked it up from watching the captain and Lord Tenjin.

Both wore Shinzōn boots, which were little more than sealed casing of hard leather that fitted over their regular boots. It took a while to get used to them, but Missy had to admit they were very warm. They also both wore the red scarves Namei had given them back in Gesshoku.

The walk to the foothills was uneventful. They went in silence, both concerned with thoughts of their own and both, Missy realised, anxious about their upcoming conversation with Kanu. When Lenis had confronted Ishullanu at the World Tree, the Demon King had told him that the Clemens twins were different, that they weren't even supposed to be human. They could do things no other Bestia Keeper could do. Missy was telepathic. Lenis was empathic. They could communicate not just with Bestia but also with Totem and humans and who knew what else. Somehow Kanu had recognised that difference in them. Missy was anxious about what that might mean.

Two guards met them at the wall. Missy felt her face flush as she drew near. She had tricked these people into believing she was a god. She had frightened them, too. It had all been to get her brother back, but that thought didn't help her feel any better after the fact. Doubtless, Heidi had told her kinfolk what a liar Missy was. She didn't relish having to talk to any of them.

As they came closer, Missy suddenly realised that the guards looked more like shopkeepers than warriors. They wore aprons over their clothes and carried no weapons. Karasu had probably killed off the fighters before torturing the other townsfolk. What was going to happen to the people of Fronge now? They had few possessions and almost no food. Worse, if Demons rose out of the sea to strike them they would be almost defenceless.

Missy bit her lip as she prepared to face the guards' scorn, but the twins were waved through silently. The guards lowered their eyes as the two passed, as though they still believed she was Magni. Missy hesitated only a moment and then scanned their minds. They *did* still think she was a god. She didn't know if she felt relieved or sickened. Being treated like a god had gotten her what she wanted, but deep inside she knew that what she had done in the square was wrong, even if she hadn't meant to do it. She didn't want people to be afraid of her, to do what she asked whether they wanted to or not. She had been a slave too long to ever want to enslave anyone else.

'You okay?' Lenis whispered, and Missy knew he had sensed her turmoil.

'I think so,' she replied, wondering why Heidi had not told the guards about her lie. Perhaps the Heiliglander hadn't had a chance yet.

Missy stepped through the gate and into a corridor leading between the mountains on either side of them. Ahead she could see the ocean about half a mile away, but there didn't seem to be any sand. It was as though the rock gave way directly to the sea, which was a slate-grey colour where it wasn't whipped into low white peaks by the errant breeze. The path beneath their feet was straight and well maintained. At first Missy mistook it for a naturally formed rock shelf, but then she noticed a perfectly straight crack cutting across their path and she realised it was made up of slabs of worked stone fitted tightly together. It must have been carefully laid to stand up to generations of traffic that consisted mostly of cartloads of metal ore.

'Are you sure?' Lenis prompted, which Missy knew to mean *no, you're not*.

She sighed, pushing back her hood. The exertion of their walk was making her sweat. 'I don't know. It's just . . . I don't know.' How could she explain it to him? 'First there was Fronge, and then I thought we'd lost you! It was hard, you know?'

'Yeah,' Lenis muttered. 'It wasn't any fun for me either.'

'I guess not. Just another grand adventure for the Clemens twins, right?' Missy nudged her brother with her elbow; Lenis remained silent.

They reached the edge of the road and stepped onto a stone jetty that projected out into the ocean. At the end of it was the silhouette of a small boy. It was Kanu. He didn't turn as the twins approached, but Missy knew he had noticed them. He was dressed almost identically to Lenis, in a black robe and trousers, though he wore no winter gear at all and his feet were bare. The cold obviously didn't bother him.

When the twins were a pace or two behind him he spoke up. 'Ki'am Tamtu adi la basialaku.'

'He's very sad,' Lenis whispered.

'Sa-da,' Kanu repeated, turning to face them.

Missy reached out to his mind. Trying to understand another language was slightly different than skimming someone's thoughts. You had to piece together what they were saying with the general flow of what they were thinking, as well as hope that what they were saying matched up with what they were thinking. If they were lying it could lead to all sorts of false interpretations.

'Can you understand us?' Missy asked, speaking slowly. She repeated the question in Heiliglander, Shinzōn, Tien Tese, Ellian, Lahmonian, Kystian, and even Garsian. Kanu made no reply. 'Who are you?'

Kanu indicated the ocean behind him with a sweep of one arm. 'Tamtu.'

'The sea? Tamtu means sea?'

Kanu cocked his head to one side, and a moment later Missy felt something she had never felt before. Kanu had somehow gripped her spirit-self. He had felt her in his mind and held on to her. After her initial panic, she relaxed. His hold wasn't strong, and there was nothing threatening in his manner. It felt more like a handshake than anything else, an acknowledgement that she was there.

Then Kanu looked to her brother and suddenly Lenis was there with her, inside the boy's mind.

What's going on? Lenis asked. Like her, he wasn't afraid. What they were experiencing was new, but it didn't feel like it. It felt *right*.

Alka, Kanu said to them, and then Missy's mind went blank.

⊙ CONNECTIONS AND MEMORIES ⊙

Lenis and Missy had joined once before, back in Nochi when they had used their combined wills to control Raikō the Demon Lord. This felt like that, only now that they weren't in imminent danger, the twins could examine their bizarre transformation. Their physical bodies still stood beneath them, holding hands at the end of the stone jetty. Kanu stood across from them, his own hand resting on theirs, his strange skin and nails looking even more alien against theirs. Their hands. Somehow their gloves had come off. They were connected, skin to skin.

What is this? the part of them that was Missy asked.

I'm not sure, the part that was Lenis replied.

Now I understand, a third voice added. They looked up and saw Kanu floating with them, above their bodies. They could understand him now. They had entered a state of being beyond language barriers. *You are you but not you.*

Sorry? Missy asked.

You are split, but here your halves can join.

The Clemens twins' spirit-self quivered. Kanu's words had echoed Ishullanu's and woken something uncomfortable in them.

It was the portion of them that was Lenis that broke the silence. *Who are you?*

One who serves, Kanu replied. *I have been waiting for you for a long time, but you have not come as you should have come. Something has gone wrong. Come.*

Where are we going? Missy asked.

Home.

The twins felt themselves pulled along behind Kanu's spirit-self. As they flew, the colour seemed to leach out of the world. The sky filled with dark clouds. The Lenis part of them recognised where they were going. They were flying back to the temple of Njord.

An instant later they were there, as if naming their destination had been enough to make them reach it. Only this time they didn't enter via a rock shelf or a long tunnel. They had descended to sea level and arrived in front of a set of doors that looked a thousand feet high. Inscribed on the door was a series of glyphs and runes that Lenis recognised from Neti's temple. It was the stylised representation of the World Tree. He wondered then as he did now how the carving came to be where it was.

They passed through the doors without them opening.

They were at least ten-feet thick, though it was hard for even Lenis's mind to calculate accurately in the state they were in. Once inside they noticed that the ocean flowed in under the doors, and that the place was brightly lit, though to them it still appeared in shades of grey.

There were people everywhere. Kanu pulled them closer. They were all like him, with large cheekbones and heavy brows. Their hands and feet seemed strangely disproportionate to the rest of their bodies. They were mostly naked. Only the older ones were wearing loincloths.

What is this? Missy asked.

This is my memory, Compassionate One.

The Clemens twins shivered again. That was what Ishullanu had once called Missy.

How long ago was this? Lenis asked. His mind was always the most practical out of the two. Their combined-self maintained that aspect of him.

Long before the Nintunaki died.

As if a dormant memory of their own had stirred, the Clemens twins saw the Nintunaki as they were. Spirits. Beings of pure energy that flowed through this world and kept it connected with the World Tree. But what had happened to them? How had they died?

Kanu went on, *When the Enkidalla and the Ereshkigalla were still young.*

And the twins knew that he meant the Totem and the Jinn, and that he was using their True Names, the names given to them by the gods in the language of the gods.

But Kanu hadn't finished, *And the Kidal and the Shigal and the Marduk were but buds on the World Tree.*

He was speaking of the Bestia and the Lilim and of humanity.

And Mashu was but a promise of the gods.

The Clemens twins pulled free of Kanu's hold. He let them go. They floated above the cavern filled with beings like Kanu. Some were swimming, others reclining on the rock shelves that lined the giant atrium. Some few were weaving together the seaweed their fellows pulled up from the ocean floor. There was calmness all around them, but something inside the twins was frightened. Already they had felt something had changed. They knew that if they followed Kanu any further, something even greater would shift inside them. Maybe it was already too late. The connection between them had grown much stronger. When they returned to their separate bodies something would be lost. They wouldn't feel whole any more.

But neither Lenis nor Missy could resist the desire to know. To know who they were and *what* they were. Kanu was the key. He could show them. Hesitantly, they reached out and took a hold of his spirit-self and were whisked through the mountain again.

They passed through solid rock and winding passageways, through chambers and caverns, until finally they reached a door identical to the one that marked the entrance to the temple, though this one was much smaller. Leading up to it was a large hall that Lenis half-remembered. There! He saw a crack in the wall and knew that if they went through there they would come out on a narrow rock shelf you could dock an airship alongside. This was the same place he had come to with Atrum. Only now the hall was not dark. The torches that lined the walls gave off more light than their small flames had a right to. The floor was covered in kneeling forms and each of them held a candle so that there were no shadows in the vestibule.

Kanu didn't stop. He dragged them straight through the door and into the darkened chamber beyond.

And there was Kanu, standing alone, holding a candle that cast a small ring of illumination, the only source of light in the chamber, making it impossible to see how large it was, or what may be hidden in the darkness. Their spirit-self shivered again.

Then something spoke, and even through the filter of Kanu's memory, the twins knew that it was a god.

DO YOU UNDERSTAND YOUR TASK, YOUNG SERVANT?

The Kanu in the memory replied, 'Yes, Great Apsu, God of the Sea. I will wait for Mashu to appear and I will serve him when he comes.'

LONG AFTER YOUR PARENTS HAVE DIED, YOU WILL WAIT. LONG AFTER THE TITANS HAVE

PERISHED, YOU WILL WAIT. LONG AFTER THESE HALLS STAND EMPTY, YOU WILL WAIT. PERHAPS EVEN LONG AFTER I HAVE CEASED TO BE, YOU MAY HAVE TO WAIT. DO YOU UNDERSTAND?

The Kanu from long ago held aloft his torch. 'I understand and obey.'

Something stirred at the edge of the candlelight. As it passed into the circle of light it glinted. The twins saw it was a claw and knew that it belonged to a dragon, though one much older and larger than Apsilla had ever been. This was Apsu, who was also known as Rinjin and Njord and many other names besides. This was one of the Firstborn, a True Dragon, a Caelestia, the God of the Sea, and that made him Ishullanu's brother.

But who are the Titans? Lenis demanded. *What is Mashu? What is it you have waited for all these years?*

You are Mashu, Kanu replied calmly. *I have waited for you.*

But why? the twins asked together.

To serve you.

Lenis blinked and was back in his own body. He felt dizzy. His head was still blocked up from his cold, which only made things worse. Kanu was standing in front of them, smiling as only the truly content can smile. Missy was still holding Lenis's hand. He pulled his own away. Something between them snapped, but he didn't want to think about that. He had so quickly adjusted to feeling and thinking things with her, to being joined with her. Now he was alone again. They were separate. It left him with the vague impression that a part of him was missing. He didn't like it at all.

'I still don't understand,' Missy mumbled. She sounded miserable. A moment later Lenis realised that she *was* miserable. Whatever he felt at their disconnection, she felt it too.

'I don't either.' Lenis found their gloves by his feet and bent to retrieve them. 'I was convinced he'd have some answers. I thought he would *know*.'

'Know what?' Kanu asked in flawless common tongue.

Lenis and Missy stared at him.

'You can speak the common tongue?' Missy asked.

'You taught me.' He didn't even have an accent.

'Do you know anything else about us?' Lenis asked slowly. At any moment he half expected Kanu to vanish right in front of their eyes. He seemed unreal, like a phantom conjured up by the fog of the Wastelands.

'You are Mashu,' Kanu said.

Lenis fought back his anger. 'But what does that *mean*?'

Kanu cocked his head to one side. 'Mean?'

Missy grabbed her brother's arm. 'Lenis, calm down.'

He let out a long breath. 'Sorry. It's just frustrating.'

'I know,' she said.

'What are we going to do?'

Missy looked into his eyes, but he couldn't tell what she was looking for. Perhaps she was trying to see some evidence of their recent connection, or she was trying to confirm to herself that they really were two different people. 'He says he wants to . . . help us.'

Lenis knew she was about to say 'serve us' but had stopped herself. 'Help us do what?'

Missy squeezed his arm and then let go. 'Don't tell me you've forgotten about Ishullanu?' She knew he hadn't, of course. She also knew that he didn't want to think about the Demon King right now. 'We still need the stones of ebb and flow if we're going to unlock Suiteki's power.'

'So, what? We use Kanu as bait, or did you just want to trade him to Karasu for the stone and be done with it?'

'No, of course not! I didn't mean –'

'Whatever.' Lenis turned and strode off down the jetty, back towards the artificial shore. 'I need to be alone.'

He increased his pace until he was almost jogging. Anger roiled inside of him, mixed with an overwhelming frustration. Kanu had been no help at all. He'd only made things even more complicated than they already were. That, and he'd somehow brought the twins together. Thinking about it made Lenis's skin crawl. They had fused so totally that Lenis hadn't been Lenis any more. He became a part of whatever it was they were, whatever Mashu was supposed to be. He had thought things with his sister, *felt* things with her, and he didn't like it. People weren't supposed to get that close to one another. It wasn't natural.

I'm not natural.

He pushed the thought away. He was gifted, that was all. Special. He wasn't a freak. It was bad enough he'd had to listen to the Demon King's madness, as if Lenis could trust him anyway! Whatever the gods thought the Clemens twins were, or were *supposed* to be, they weren't. It was as simple as that. Maybe they were going to be this Mashu thing, whatever it was, but that wasn't how things had turned out. Lenis was Lenis, Missy was Missy, and that was that.

Lenis stalked back down the stone road towards the wall of Fronge, glad he had left Suiteki behind when he went to fetch his winter coat. He needed to be alone, to be *himself* for a while. He wasn't angry with Missy. That wasn't it. After all, this wasn't *her* fault, but being with her at the moment was the last thing he wanted. He needed to put as much distance between them as possible. Lenis had never feared the connection between them before, never even thought about it really, but now it loomed up like some terrible fate, waiting to dissolve who he was and make him into something the gods wanted him to be.

Lenis liked being himself. He liked the way his mind worked, the way a part of it was always calm and rational, able to mull over complicated problems on its own. He liked the way he could sense the feelings of others. He didn't want to give that up and, he suddenly realised, he didn't want to share it, either. It was what made him unique.

The wall came and went, and Lenis didn't even notice the guards that let him through. As he emerged on the other side his feet took him to the north, away from the remains of the town, away from the *Hiryū*. A stiff wind had come up. Lenis bent his head as he walked into it. He entered a stand of trees. The breeze cut off abruptly. He kept walking, head still down, avoiding trees by watching for their roots.

So it was that he nearly ran right into Anastasis.

Lenis jumped back. He hadn't even felt her presence, which meant Disma wasn't with her, and that was odd. 'Oh, sorry,' he stammered. 'I didn't see you there.'

The princess said nothing. She just looked at him. Her stare as blank as always, with eyes that never seemed to reflect any light. Her hair lay flat against her skull and may once have been almost yellow but was now so dull it just looked like dirty straw. She was wearing the same dress she always wore, the crimson one with the fancy cuffs, but it was little more than a rag now. It had once been pristine, but Ostian court attire could not long withstand the harsh conditions of airship travel. Lenis had never seen her in anything else. He wondered if she ever washed her clothes. He had been on airships for so long that the smell of unwashed bodies was too familiar to be repulsive, but Anastasis didn't seem to have a scent. Perhaps she had given that part of herself to her Lilim as well as everything else.

Well, *almost* everything else.

'There is now no reason to return directly to Asheim, the captain has said.' The princess's grasp of the common tongue was almost perfect, but sometimes her phrasing was a little odd, as if she was trying to make what she said fit into the rhythms of her native language.

Her abruptness was a bit of a shock. Lenis had been so wrapped up in his own worries that he had forgotten Anastasis only cared about one thing – killing Lord Butin. It was the one aspect of herself she had not given to Disma in exchange for the Lilim's power.

'We were only going there to pick up Karasu's trail,' Lenis told her, his desire to be alone greater than ever. Talking with the princess always made him uncomfortable. He could feel just how *empty* she was, and she only ever said things that related to her single-minded desire. It was even worse when Disma was near, and he could feel the connection between them. It reminded him too keenly of the strange connection he had just shared with his sister, each half having to give something up in order to form the bond. 'We know where Karasu is now, and we know what he wants . . . sort of.'

'Butin is in Asheim.'

Lenis sighed. 'Yes.' He lowered his head again and tried to walk past her.

She barred his way. 'The captain promised me he would help me kill Butin if I gave you the dragon's egg.' There was no accusation in her voice, no emotion of any kind, but underlying it all was the single, pure desire for vengeance.

'Where's Disma?' Lenis asked. As unnerving as it was to have the Lilim around, she could usually keep Anastasis quiet.

'She is with the captain. They are talking about going north. Asheim is to the –'

Lenis's impatience gave way to his anger. 'Look, I don't care about Butin. Nobody does! We've got more important things to worry about. Listen to yourself! "I want to kill Butin. I want to kill Butin." We get it, okay? Just shut up! You're not even a real person any more. You're no better than a Demon!'

The princess flinched, ever so slightly. It was the barest tensing of muscles, so faint Lenis almost missed it. If Anastasis had been normal, had been filled with the usual whirling of human emotions, Lenis probably wouldn't have noticed the slight spark that ignited somewhere deep inside her. It lasted only briefly, to be drowned out by the strident chord of hatred she kept curled within, but it had been there, he was sure of it. Even in its brevity it had been intense, some profound fury so innate it had flared up when Lenis had snapped at her. She was a princess, after all, used to getting her own way, and here was an airship's boy, a former slave, trying to tell her what to do.

'Just leave me alone,' Lenis muttered, the vehemence gone from his voice. As extreme as Anastasis's response had been, it was short-lived and buried far too deep. Lenis had troubles enough of his own without worrying about a spoilt Ostian princess, one who had willingly given up so much of herself in the pursuit of power. He pushed past her and continued on his way.

◦ NECESSARY DECEPTION ◦

Missy watched her brother go, stung by his rejection. Kanu remained silent. His presence unnerved Missy. He had witnessed what had happened between the twins, had perhaps even *caused* it and its aftermath. Lenis had spurned their connection. Missy became aware of the cold biting her hand. She slipped her glove back on and flexed her fingers. As her brother disappeared from view she was left all but alone to contemplate what had just happened.

It had felt so natural at the time, just like when they had joined to take control of Raikō, but now that she was back in her own body she felt wretched, raw, as if her spirit-self had been wrung out, stretched thin, pulled apart. She didn't seem to sit right in her own body. She had to get her mind off it, so she focused instead on the strange boy standing beside her.

'Kanu.' Her voice sounded strange to her own ears. 'Do you know what that man, Karasu, was doing in the temple?'

'No,' he replied. 'He tried to hurt Mashu.'

Missy sighed. 'He did. You stopped him.'

Kanu grinned as he nodded. His mouth extended a little wider than a normal human's. 'I will protect Mashu. I will serve Mashu.'

'Thank you for helping Lenis, but you don't have to serve anybody.' Missy wondered again what Kanu was. He wasn't human, or Totem, or Jinn, or Bestia, or Lilim, or anything else she knew about. He had once served the sea god, Apsu, and now he served the Clemens twins. The thought made her head spin. For some reason the god of the sea had charged Kanu with serving the Clemens twins. There was no way to know how long ago that was or how long Kanu had been trapped in that pillar of ice. What did Karasu want with him? More disturbing, how had the mercenary known he was there?

Kanu drew his heavy brows together. 'I am a Titan. I will serve Mashu.'

Missy sighed. How was she supposed to respond to that? 'Come on, Kanu. The captain will probably want to speak with you now that you can . . . um . . . talk back.'

Kanu nodded and fell into step behind Missy as she made her way back down the jetty. It felt odd, having him follow along behind her. She kept craning her neck to look at him.

Eventually, she snapped, 'Why don't you walk next to me?'

'I will.' Kanu obeyed as though Missy had given him a direct order, which only made her feel worse. It was the town square all over again. She didn't *want* to tell people what to do. What right did she have to order anyone around? The fact that Kanu seemed perfectly happy to follow her commands made her feel no better. She had seen slaves like that back in Pure Land. She had *been* a slave too, eager to please, to prove she was worth something. No, not just *something*. To show them all that she was worth more than they had paid for her. She didn't like being reminded of that, and she hated that someone was acting that way towards *her*, as if she were no better than a slave owner. Nothing had gone right since she had seen that smoke!

As they approached the gate Missy saw Heidi leaning against the stone wall, clearly waiting for her. She didn't want to deal with the Heiliglander just now, but she knew she couldn't put it off. Missy needed to make sure she hadn't harmed Heidi when she helped bolster her mental defences, and there was also the question of whether or not Heidi would want her assistance taking them down. Missy *had* promised to help her however she could. Maybe this was all she could do for her.

The guards averted their eyes as Missy walked through and Heidi fell into step beside her. At least the girl hadn't told everyone the truth about Missy not being Magni yet. That was something else Missy would have to deal with eventually, but the longer that was put off the better.

For a long time the three walked in silence. Kanu seemed perfectly content with it, but Missy grew increasingly agitated. How was she going to explain to Heidi what she'd done inside the girl's mind? Would she understand what Missy had done to her? Missy didn't even really know herself. She'd always considered her telepathy to be a tool for communication, but hadn't she used it to coerce those people in the square? Maybe that had nothing to do with the Quillblade after all. Perhaps it was a part of her gift to make people do things. Missy shuddered inside her thick clothing. That wasn't the sort of power she wanted.

'You can't keep moping around like that,' Heidi suddenly whispered.

Missy stopped in her tracks. 'What?'

'You don't look or act anything like a god, much less the great Magni. If you're going to convince anyone you're the Lightning-Wielder you're going to have to do a better job of it. *I* was able to figure it out fairly quickly. The others will too if you aren't careful.'

Missy was stunned. She couldn't believe what she was hearing. Heidi was actually encouraging her to trick her own people into believing Missy's lie! But why?

'I said stop that!' Heidi chided. 'You think Magni would stand around in the middle of the road with her mouth gaping open like that? You're supposed to be a goddess of war!' Missy clamped her mouth shut. 'That's a bit better.'

'What are you talking about?' Missy whispered, fearful someone would come by and overhear them.

Heidi looked at her for a long moment. 'There's this war coming with the Demons, right?'

Missy wracked her memory. Had she told Heidi that? Yes, she'd told her all about Ishullanu and his plans for the Demons. 'That's right.'

'And Karasu is working for the Demon King? That's what you said.'

Now Missy was really confused. Had she really? She couldn't recall. All she knew was that she had tried to tell Heidi about the *Hiryū*'s voyage, and that she had been too tired to really pay attention to her own story. Had she somehow implied that Karasu and Ishullanu were connected?

'Don't you get it?' Heidi demanded. 'If this Demon King starts a war with humanity, it's going to affect *all* of us!'

'Yes, but –'

'Didn't it ever occur to you to *warn* us about it?'

Missy felt her mouth hanging open again and closed it. 'But we're going to stop it.'

Heidi snorted. 'And if you don't? Look, all of a sudden I'm starting to see things clearly, you know? And what I see is that Karasu is working for the Demon King by trying to stop you from getting these orbs or stones or whatever they are that you need so you can fight against him, but what about the rest of us, Missy? This war isn't going to wait for you to get these magic rocks. Karasu already started it when he destroyed –' a blank look flashed across Heidi's face and vanished just as suddenly '– the war has already begun!'

Missy knew she had to put a stop to this. She didn't remember telling Heidi that Karasu was working for

Ishullanu, but it wasn't fair to let her keep thinking there was a connection. Whatever the mercenary was after, Missy doubted it had anything to do with the Demon King and his coming war, and Heidi's sudden clarity was disturbing, too. Missy thought she knew where it came from. 'Heidi, wait, I think you should –'

'I don't know what's going on here.' Heidi turned aside and started pacing backwards and forwards across the road. 'I don't know who Karasu is. I don't know who Ishullanu is.' With each point she gesticulated more wildly with her arms. 'I think Fronge just got caught up in the middle of something. Something big. Whatever it is, we're not ready for it.'

Missy was trying to follow the girl's thoughts, but they were all over the place. She was drawing connections, making plans, fitting her ideas together in various combinations. What she wasn't doing was factoring in the horrors of what she had seen in Fronge. Those images were absent from her mind, and with them the emotional connections Heidi should have been making but wasn't. It was as if they didn't factor into her thinking, which, Missy realised with a sickening feeling, they probably didn't.

'Me. Fronge. Heiligland. All of us!' Heidi continued her rant. 'None of us are ready. Look at what happened to Fronge. There was no resistance. Karasu took the town in a single morning. We aren't ready to fight this, but *you* are.'

'Heidi, please –'

'They'll listen to you!' Heidi stopped pacing and rounded on Missy. 'Don't you see? They think you're Magni, the goddess of war. If you call them to arms, they'll listen. They'll prepare for war!'

Missy was finally starting to make sense of the girl's raving. 'You want me, as Magni, to tell your people to prepare for war?'

'Of course!' Heidi grabbed her shoulders, just as she'd done back in the tunnels under Njord's temple. Missy glanced at Kanu, but the boy stood, silently watching the exchange. 'Please! They'll listen to you. They have to!'

There was no mistaking Heidi's sincerity. Once more Missy found herself staring into the girl's eyes. The feeling of hopelessness began to rise in her again, but this time she thought about Heidi's words. Could she do it? *Would* they listen to her? The Warlord of Shinzō was preparing for the coming war with the Demons, but he could do little alone. If they had any hope of defeating Ishullanu, they were going to need more allies.

The idea was tempting, but to pull it off Missy would have to keep deceiving people, to make them believe that she was a god. She would have to pretend that what Karasu did to Fronge was part of Ishullanu's plan. She would have to keep lying to Heidi, to make her believe that the Demons were ultimately responsible for Karasu's actions. It was tempting, so very tempting, but there was something wrong about it. Missy was filled with doubt. How could she do such a thing?

How could she take advantage of Heidi's pain like that? But there was no pain. Heidi had blocked it out, forgotten it, sealed it deep inside herself. Missy knew the girl would never be talking like this if she hadn't. To Heidi's new way of thinking, Fronge was little more than a strategic misstep. And Missy was at least partially responsible for that.

'You're not thinking clearly,' Missy said to her, staring into her eyes, trying to make her see.

'I've never been able to think so clearly in my life.'

'And you don't see that as a problem?'

Heidi shook her head. 'Not really. Ever since you helped me in that chamber I knew –'

'What?'

'I was there, Missy. It happened in my head. After what Karasu did to Fronge, I was destroyed. Can't you understand that? I couldn't function. I was shutting down. The grief was so strong I felt as though my throat was going to close up and suffocate me. I tried to block it out, to be strong, and when you came, great Magni,' Heidi chuckled, 'I drew strength from you, that you would choose me to lead you. But you aren't a god, and when I found that out my resolve faltered. In the chamber I could feel myself crumbling again, but god or not you were still there and somehow made me strong again. And now it's just . . . gone. I don't have to fight so hard to block it out. You did that for me.'

Heidi hadn't released her this whole time. Missy felt trapped by her gaze. 'B-but we can take down the barrier and –'

Heidi gave her a little shake. 'Don't you dare. I don't want to take it down. Not ever. It's not hurting me and I don't want to have to deal with what's behind it. I like the fact you took that pain away from me. I *thank* you for it. But will you help me now, like you promised? Will you lend Magni's power to the people of Heiligland?'

It was a good plan. Missy could see how it could work. They had to stop Ishullanu, after all. They couldn't do it alone. If they could stir up the Heiliglanders' outrage, convince them that Magni was calling them to war to avenge the people of Fronge, then they would gain a valuable ally in the coming war. Wasn't it worth it?

'All right,' Missy said, and Heidi's grasp tightened. 'I'll do it.'

But a part of Missy quailed inside her.

Heidi stepped back abruptly, and Missy rubbed her shoulders. The girl had already left bruises there the last time she had grabbed her.

'Good.' Heidi turned and kept walking as though nothing had happened.

'Are you sure you're all right, though?'

Heidi glanced back over her shoulder. 'Definitely. Now come on. We need to get you ready. You can't speak to everyone dressed like that. You look like a child.'

Missy blushed and hurried to catch up with the Heiliglander. 'Wait a minute. We have to speak to the captain about this.'

'Why?'

'Because he's my captain. I can't just go off on my own.'

'Fine.'

Half an hour later Captain Shishi stood on the bridge and looked at the two girls in silence. He had listened to Heidi's plan without comment and was now considering it. A part of Missy hoped he would spurn the idea and give her an excuse to pull out. He would demand she reveal the truth to Heidi, that Ishullanu had nothing to do with what Karasu had done. Heidi would be furious that Missy had manipulated her, but she would understand. She had to. The whole thing was madness! No one would ever truly believe Missy was a god. Not for long, anyway.

Her desire to come clean warred with the knowledge that the people of Heiligland *had* to be warned about the coming war. Would they believe her if they didn't think she was Magni? Would they turn to face the Demons if they knew the truth, or turn their attentions to hunting down Karasu? The deception was the only way of making sure they were prepared.

'The idea has merit,' the captain said at last. Missy translated for Heidi, who grinned in response, but Missy's own heart sank. What would the captain think of her for manipulating the Heiliglanders? She suddenly realised that what he thought of her was pretty important. 'I have perhaps been too focused on our own mission to consider the wider repercussions. With Apsilla now gone, Ishullanu could launch his offensive at any time and from any quarter. Humanity must be prepared to meet him when the time comes. Miss Clemens, when we reach Erdasche you will have your chance to convince Duke Freyrsson that you are Magni.'

'Erdasche?' Missy asked.

'To the north. It is the capital of Heimat Isle,' the captain replied. 'We have decided to ferry everyone there. The duke must be informed of the destruction of Fronge. It is well known that Karasu is a member of the Shōgo clan. We must take steps to convince Duke Freyrsson that Karasu was acting independently of the Warlord to ensure blame is not laid on Shinzō. Miss Baumstochter's plan will aid in that. You must persuade the duke that Karasu's attack was the vanguard of Ishullanu's invasion.'

More lies. The whole thing felt wrong, but Missy knew the captain spoke wisely. If she could pull off the deception it could save people's lives. It would be worth it.

'Yes, sir,' Missy said. 'I will try my best.'

'Good. Miss Baumstochter can assist in your preparations.' The captain paused and then pulled something out of his robe. It was the Quillblade. 'I have my misgivings, Miss Clemens, but perhaps you will need this to complete your guise. I suggest you speak with Lord Tenjin before attempting to use it again.'

He handed Missy Raikō's *shintai*. She took it reluctantly. The thing had some sort of power over her, and she didn't like that. She tucked it quickly inside her coat and tried to forget about it.

'Is there anything else, Captain?' she asked.

'Have you and your brother had a chance to speak with Kanu?'

How had she forgotten about *that*? Kanu had remained so silent during their discussion of Heidi's plan that Missy had all but dismissed him from her mind. 'Yes, Captain. He can speak the common tongue, it seems.' She didn't tell him *how* he had learned it. 'But I'm afraid he doesn't know anything that can really help us.'

The captain cocked an eyebrow at the strange boy. 'I see. We shall let this go for now. The situation here should be our primary concern. I suggest you begin your preparations.'

'Yes, sir.' Missy bowed and left the bridge, Heidi trailing along after her. Kanu followed them both.

○

Lenis returned to the engine room in a foul mood. He considered going through the galley to fetch Suiteki but decided against it. She might have been able to make him feel better, but he didn't want to inflict his bad temper on her. His walk had done little to ease his frustration. He had seen Missy, Heidi and Kanu speaking with the captain up on the bridge as he crossed over the deck but hadn't wanted to join them. When he entered his room the sight of the engines stilled his inner turmoil. They needed checking. He hadn't had a chance since they landed. He had to be sure the first use of the dual-Bestia system hadn't caused any damage.

That was far more important than whatever was going on up on the bridge.

'Looks like things are back to normal,' Lenis muttered under his breath as he began to check the pressure valves. 'No one tells me anything.'

'No one tells you anything about what?' a voice asked from the doorway, causing Lenis to jump so high he nearly banged his head on a pipe. It was Shujinko. The cabin boy was the last person Lenis wanted to see. In fact, Lenis didn't want to see *anyone* just now.

Lenis ignored his question. 'Did you want something?'

The cabin boy was peering around the engine room, taking in the Bestia hutch, the engines, and Lenis's unmade bunk. No doubt *his* bunk was perfectly made up. 'I have come to see when you wished to resume your training. You have done nothing for several days.'

Lenis had to grit his teeth to keep from snapping something back. It wasn't as though Lenis had been doing *nothing* for the past few days. He'd stowed away on an enemy's airship and crept into a frozen temple, all with little sleep and no food. Not to mention being captured, and then everything that had happened with Kanu and his sister.

'Well?' Shujinko prompted.

'I'm a little busy,' Lenis growled. It was true, too. It's not as if he could just drop everything he was doing because the cabin boy wanted him to. Besides, he probably just wanted the pleasure of knocking Lenis to the deck again.

The other boy made a small noise in his throat. 'A true warrior hones his skills every day.' He turned to go but looked over his shoulder. 'A true warrior does not make excuses.'

Lenis felt his anger flare up and had to struggle to hold onto it. If he let it get the better of him, allow it to get out of control, he didn't know what it would do. *Smash the little brat against the wall*, a small part of him said. *Throw him overboard. Show him that* he's *the weakling for being afraid of heights.*

A sound broke through Lenis's raging thoughts. One of his Bestia was whimpering. Suiteki wasn't the only one attuned to his feelings. Lenis's anger subsided as he moved around the engine block to check on his charges. Shujinko left without another word. Atrum was sleeping in one corner of the hutch, his tail wrapped around himself several times. He was slowly recovering but still pretty weak. Lenis was happy to let him remain where he was, curled up between the other Bestia. As long as he was kept warm he'd be okay.

Ignis was the one who had whimpered. He was standing up in the hutch, resting his paws on its lip. His stubby tail shook as he wriggled around in distress. When he saw Lenis approach he jumped out of the hutch and up into Lenis's outstretched arms, where he continued to tremble. The flame Bestia had been scared by Lenis's temper, but even though he now had it under control, Ignis was still concerned for him. Lenis held Ignis close and allowed the Bestia to lick his face. In Ignis's excitement his tongue burned hotter than normal.

'I'm sorry, boy,' Lenis crooned. 'It's okay now. It's okay.'

But another part of Lenis wondered if it was.

◉

'There, that's a bit better,' Heidi said, running a critical eye over Missy's new outfit.

She didn't sound too enthused, but the girls hadn't had much to work with. Missy was wearing a leather jerkin over a loose-fitting, ankle-length dress. The dress had probably once been white, but even a thorough wash hadn't been enough to restore the smoke-damaged garment to its former lustre. Heidi had torn it to give it a more battle-ready look, or so she said, but Missy was self-consciously aware of how much leg she was showing.

Missy's teeth chattered together. 'I'm freezing.'

'Gods don't get cold,' Heidi noted unsympathetically.

'I'm not going to look much like a god if I'm shivering to death,' Missy countered. So far all of their conversations went like this. Missy couldn't tell if the other girl was trying to torture or help her.

'Hmmm. Good point.' Heidi handed her a thin woollen garment. 'Wear this underneath. It'll help warm you up. A bit.'

Missy clenched her teeth against the cold and took off the jerkin before pulling the dress off over her head. She stood practically naked behind the burnt remains of a small cottage as she struggled into the woollen shift Heidi had given her. Then she put the dress and jerkin back on.

She didn't feel any warmer. 'This isn't going to work.'

'Okay,' Heidi said, and held out another piece of clothing. 'Put this over the top.'

It appeared to be some sort of long skirt made out of strips of leather. 'What is it?'

'It's a battle kilt,' Heidi told her. 'It'll block some of the wind.'

'Why didn't you give this to me before?' Missy demanded as she tied the leather cord that held the skirt on. Her fingers were so numb she could barely form the knot, much less pull it tight enough to hold the kilt on properly. It proved to be heavy. With an impatient hiss, Heidi grabbed the ends of the cord and yanked them tight. Missy yelped as the leather cut into her waist.

'Shush.' Heidi crossed her arms and scrutinised Missy again. 'Gods don't carry on like little girls. And I didn't give you the kilt before because Magni wears a white dress into battle. I told you. Gods don't feel the cold, or pain for that matter.'

'Well, this one does.'

'You aren't a god.'

Missy gritted her teeth to keep from retorting. Heidi had a right to be angry with her, she supposed. Better just to let it pass. 'Well, how do I look?'

'You've got it on backwards.' Heidi stepped forward, grabbed the waistband and gave it a tug, nearly pulling Missy off her feet. 'That's a *little* better.'

'Great.' Missy suppressed a sigh. Maybe this wasn't such a good idea after all. She felt completely ridiculous, and she was still freezing! There was no way this was going to work.

'We'll have to find you some thicker boots,' Heidi noted, more to herself than to Missy, who agreed that this was an extremely good idea. 'And we'll have to do something about your hair.'

'My hair?' Missy reached up and grabbed her tail.

'Magni wears it loose, secured by a golden circlet. I suppose we'll have to improvise.' Heidi reached back and grabbed the cord from around Missy's hair. Missy squawked in protest. 'What did I say about carrying on like a little girl? Do you want someone to hear you?'

Heidi ran her fingers through Missy's hair, separating the strands.

Missy bore the administrations as best she could. 'I don't look anything like Magni, do I?'

'How would I know? I've never seen her.' Missy opened her mouth to say something, but Heidi went on, 'I'm sure no one else has either. The last war was hundreds of years ago. I'm just going by what the priests say, and by the tapestries.'

'So you're making it up as you go?' Missy demanded.

'At least you look less like a foreigner!' Heidi countered. 'Where were you born, anyway?'

'Pure Land.'

'With your colouring you must have some Heiliglander blood in you.'

Missy had never thought of that before. For most of her life she had been a slave, and no one cared where a slave came from as long as they did what they were told. 'Do you think?'

Heidi nodded. 'And you speak without an accent, which will help. It's your manner that's the problem.'

'My manner?'

Heidi nodded. She was still staring at Missy in that disconcerting way that made her feel as if Heidi wasn't really looking *at* her. A quick peek into her mind revealed an image of a fierce warrior-maiden in a bloodstained white dress. This must be the great Magni of Heidi's imagination. She was much taller and *older* than Missy was. There was no way this was going to work.

'You lack confidence, Missy. You need to be more assertive.'

Missy hugged herself and tried to rub some warmth into her shoulders. 'What do you mean?'

'You keep looking to others for advice or permission. Look at how you're standing. You're all hunched over like a child out in the snow.'

'I *am* a . . . I am standing out in the snow!'

'I keep telling you. Gods don't feel the cold. You need to stop acting like a little girl pretending to be a god. You're not very good at it.'

'Thanks,' Missy muttered.

'You need to start acting like a god. You have to start thinking you *are* a god.'

'How do I do that?' Missy demanded. Her shivering had intensified, and she was starting to worry about catching a cold like her brother. She wouldn't sound very divine with a stuffed-up nose.

Heidi snorted. 'You have power. I know you do. I've *seen* it. You called down lightning and thunder back in the town square.'

Missy looked at the Quillblade lying by her feet. 'That wasn't me. That was Raikō.'

'I didn't see any Raikō. I just saw you.'

'I don't –'

'Yes, yes, you *don't know*! You're hopeless, do you know *that*?' Heidi turned away and stalked off, her hands clenched into fists by her sides. She spun around and strode back, stopping right in front of Missy. Their faces were only inches apart. 'Look.' Heidi's jaw was clenched tight. Missy could see the veins in her temples throbbing. 'This isn't about you. You fly in here on your airship and you chase away Karasu, and I'm grateful for that, all right? But this whole "save the world" quest you and your captain are on isn't a game. Demons are real. Karasu is real, and I don't know what he wants from you or you want from him, but he came here, and that means *we're* involved. Fronge. Heimat Isle. Heiligland. All of us! Do you think someone can come and destroy one of our towns and we won't do anything? Did you think you could just fly off and we'd just sit around and wait for you to fix everything? The world doesn't work that way. So I'm asking . . . No. I am *telling* you that you are going to do this. I don't care how hard it is for you. You *will* do it.'

Missy forced herself to remain upright, to stare into Heidi's eyes without taking a step backwards, when what she really wanted to do was run away. She was on the verge of tears. It ached to hold them back, but she couldn't, she *wouldn't* let them go. Her lip quivered and her muscles ached from being held motionless in the frigid air, but Missy stood fast in the face of Heidi's tirade. She withdrew as far into herself as she could.

Heidi fell silent, clearly waiting for Missy to say something in return, to answer her challenge. Missy tried to speak, but her throat was too tight from trying not to cry. She swallowed painfully and tried again. 'I'll try.' It sounded thin and weak, even to her.

Heidi snorted again. She turned around and walked away, pausing by what remained of the cottage's front wall long enough to say over her shoulder, 'Not good enough, little girl.'

As soon as she was gone Missy crouched down on the cold stone and wept. She scrabbled across the ground until her fingers tangled in her overcoat and clutched it around herself, pulling the hood up over her head. Hugging herself, Missy let the tears flow. She was shaking now from more than the cold. It wasn't fair! Why was Heidi treating her like this? It wasn't Missy's fault Karasu had come to Fronge. It wasn't Missy's fault everyone had believed she was a god. She had nothing to do with Ishullanu and his Demon war. None of it was her responsibility! She was just a slave girl caught up in Captain Shishi's wild pursuit of his Way.

Except she wasn't. Not any more. She hadn't been a slave for a long time, long enough, she knew deep down, to choose her own Way. As Missy knelt in the cold, burnt-out remains of the cottage, she finally started to understand what the captain meant when he spoke of the Way. A path she chose for herself in spite of what others did around her or to her. A part of Missy knew that Heidi was right. It was time she stopped acting like a slave, waiting for others to decide what was to become of her, seeking their permission or approval. Perhaps Missy hadn't meant for any of this to happen, but it *had* happened, and now she had to decide how she was going to deal with it.

Even as Missy reflected on these things her resolve faltered. But how could she? If she couldn't even stand up to Heidi when the girl knew the truth about her, how was she going to fool an entire nation into thinking she was a god? How was she supposed to stand up to their scepticism and demand they prepare for war? She already felt guilty about fooling Heidi into thinking Karasu was working for Ishullanu to help him stage his Demon war. Could she stand the guilt that fooling an entire nation would bring?

Missy knew she wasn't ready for this. She wasn't strong, like the captain or Arthur. She wasn't even as daring as her brother. But what would happen if she failed? Would Ishullanu and his Demon armies overwhelm the whole of Heiligland? And what about the other nations? What about Lahmon, and Ellia, and Kyst, and . . . it was all too much. If only she hadn't fought with Lenis, she could share this burden with him, but he was still avoiding her.

Missy was alone. Even when she had been bound to the ailing Lord Raikō, she somehow knew that Lenis was there for her, that he would come for her. Now, for the first time in her life, she doubted that he would. He was *repulsed* by the connection between them. There was no other word for it. What had always been a constant in their lives, the most cherished part of what made them special, had become something to be shunned.

Missy cried on. She could sense the Quillblade beside her, calling out for her suffering. It fed off her emotions, off her fear and anxiety and even her anger. She felt its hunger and reached down to place a hand on its hilt. The sword thrummed beneath her fingers.

◦ MAGNI THE LIGHTNING-WIELDER ◦

They spent another night in Fronge getting things organised, but it was apparent they could wait no longer to ferry the fifty or so survivors to the island's capital of Erdasche. There was simply not enough food left to go around. The *Hiryū*'s stores were all but depleted, and there was nothing left in Fronge, which had the dubious benefit of lightening their load as the townsfolk had nothing but the clothes they were wearing to take with them.

Missy stood in the forecastle, in the outfit Heidi had dressed her in, trying not to fidget as her loose-flowing hair tickled her neck and face. It had been so long since she had worn her hair out of its braid that she'd forgotten how irritating it could be. The urge to push it back behind her ears was constant, so she gripped the railing instead, looking out over the clustered faces filling the deck with what she hoped was a regal and dispassionate air.

I am a god. I am Magni. I am a great warrior.

The thoughts spiralled through her mind but gave little comfort. Missy could feel her knees shaking, and the tears in her eyes weren't from the bitter wind, though she hoped the people of Fronge believed they were. The Quillblade was pushed through a loop of the ridiculous leather kilt she wore. It was in its feather form, and it took surprising effort to keep from stroking its hilt. Just a touch and it would drain away some of Missy's nerves, but she was still wary of the *shintai*'s power.

The deck was overcrowded with people, and most of them were looking at her. There was standing room only, the people of Fronge crammed into any safe available space for the flight to Erdasche. It was difficult to move around on deck and this, Missy told herself, was why she hadn't seen Lenis since his outburst yesterday. She wasn't avoiding him, but of course she knew she was. His anger was the result of his frustration, she was sure of it. They were both frustrated. They had both expected Kanu to give them the answers to . . . what? Everything, Missy presumed. Who the Clemens twins were, who they were *supposed* to be. Why they were so different from everyone else. Why Ishullanu the Demon King had taken such an interest in them.

The strange boy was standing to Missy's left. The Heiliglanders seemed to accept his presence as a matter of course. To them he was some monstrous servant she had summoned from the underworld.

'This is good,' Kanu said to her suddenly. He was looking out over the crowded refugees and smiling his too-wide grin.

'What do you mean?' Missy asked without turning her head.

'You are Mashu. It is only right that people see you as a god.' The boy laughed. It had an odd screeching quality to it that shocked the nearest Heiliglanders into pressing against the mass of their fellows in an effort to move further away from him. 'Although it would be better if they knew you as you are and not as Adad.'

'You knew Adad?' Adad was Raikō's true name.

'I saw him once, flying over Apsu's temple. His cry hurt my ears, but I didn't look away. In his wake he trailed lightning, and the sky greeted him with calls of thunder.'

Missy glanced at Kanu out of the corner of her eye. 'Well, I'm not a god,' she whispered as low as she could so he would be the only one to hear, 'and I don't like people treating me like one.'

Kanu just laughed again. 'Given enough time, Mashu, I'm sure you'd come to enjoy it.'

Missy made no reply to that. She didn't have one. Worse, she thought that maybe he was right, and that made her as uneasy as his presence did. Kanu's determination to serve the twins was unsettling enough without the knowledge that the sea god had foreseen the twins' existence countless centuries ago and knew that they would need his help. Last night she had told Tenjin, Arthur, and the captain everything that had happened when she and Lenis had spoken with Kanu, but not even Tenjin had heard of the Titans. Whoever they were they had perished long before humanity had started keeping records, or at least long enough ago that all records about them had either vanished or been destroyed. They were gone nonetheless, just as the god Apsu had predicted, and that left them with more questions than answers.

Lenis had already started the engines. They had been on the cold ground so long that they needed some warming up. While they waited for the *Hiryū* to launch, the captain had suggested to Missy that she might address the crowd to let them know that everything was going to be all right, that they were going to be safe in Erdasche, and that something would be done about the horrors that had been visited upon them. Magni, goddess of war and wielder of lightning, would avenge them.

A deep chasm had opened up inside Missy's stomach. Her mouth and throat were dry. As she stood there, gripping the railing in the forecastle and looking down at the countless expectant faces, she felt as though she was going to faint. Her carefully rehearsed speech, which Heidi had prepared for her, was all but forgotten. The townsfolk were beginning to mutter amongst themselves. It was time. She should have started already.

Missy caught Heidi's eye. The girl was waiting at the bottom of the stairs leading up to the forecastle, her hands in her pockets as she leant against the railing. She might have looked perfectly at ease, but Missy knew how tense she was. Heidi was waiting for Missy to keep her promise.

Missy's fingers twitched on the railing, and before she was really thinking about it her hand strayed to the hilt of the Quillblade. The result was almost instantaneous. Her nerves died, her fear vanished. The weapon stiffened at her side. A hush fell over the gathered crowd as a low rumble of thunder echoed through the mountains. Missy didn't *think* she'd done that.

'People of Fronge, hear me!' she called out in perfect Heil-iglander. 'Know that I have heard your prayers. The atrocities you have endured will be avenged!' A rough cheer rose up from one side of the deck. Missy ignored it. 'The time of war has come again, and the armies of the homeland must once more gather to meet the threat.' There was more rumbling from the crowd. She allowed a small tendril of command to enter her voice. 'We will meet this threat!' she repeated, and as she did so she *compelled* them to listen to her. She did it automatically, as she had done in the town square when she had demanded and they had obeyed. Missy felt a slight connection to the minds of those gathered before her. It was tentative, not as powerful as it had been in Fronge where she was able to see what any one person was thinking clearly, but it was encompassing enough to give her a general sense of the crowd's thoughts. 'The man who did this to you was an agent of Ishullanu, the Demon King.' Missy saw it ripple through their collective minds. Of course, they didn't *know* who Ishullanu was. And without any effort at all, Missy placed a memory in their minds. It was indistinct, nothing more than a shadowy outline of a great and menacing serpent, but she buried the image deep, and from out of their minds she drew a name they could recognise and hung it on him. 'The Demon King Idunn is gathering an army of Demons. He struck first here, in Fronge, but soon his army will be large enough to threaten the whole of Heiligland. And we will meet the Demon threat!' This last part she shouted, and the people of Fronge cheered and Kanu threw back his head and roared, more beast than child.

Just then the *Hiryū* launched itself into the air. It was only Missy's long experience on airships that kept her upright. Many of the townsfolk fell against one another as the vessel soared skywards. Missy kept her eye on the eastern horizon and, just as the airship rose high enough to allow the sun to peek over the furthest mountaintop, she drew the Quillblade and held it aloft. The rays of the early morning sun were caught in the golden metal of the *shintai*. Missy concentrated and a small pinprick of electricity appeared on the Quillblade's tip. There was a moment of stunned silence, and then the people were cheering again, chanting her name over and over.

Except they weren't chanting Missy.

'Well done, Mashu,' Kanu whispered, just loud enough for her to hear.

Below decks, alone with his Bestia in his engine room, Lenis heard the animation from above. So, Missy's plan was working. As Lenis ran his eye over the pressure valves mounted on the engine block he pressed his lips into a thin line. He didn't like it. Not one bit. Whatever the reason, whatever her motivations, Missy was *manipulating* people. It wasn't right. The Puritans found ways to justify slavery too. Missy should have known better.

Worse, he could feel the Quillblade feeding on Missy's negative emotions, even amidst the mass gathered on deck. He didn't know if it was just that he could always sense his sister, that she was always *there*, or if it was the power of the *shintai* that drew his attention. Whatever it was, Lenis knew when Missy used the Quillblade, and he feared for her. Was the *shintai* like a Lilim? Would it eventually drain Missy completely, leaving her an empty husk possessing not even the desire to breathe, to go on living? The thought of where that would leave both of them made Lenis shudder.

He was glad he could remain in the engine room. He didn't want to go up on deck and see his sister playing god, to witness firsthand the leechlike effect of the Quillblade on her, and of her power on the refugees of Fronge. *What you're really frightened of*, a small part of him whispered, *is seeing silvery lines running from the Heiliglanders to your sister, just like the ones that connected Butin to his Ostian minions.*

'The people certainly seemed to appreciate your performance,' Arthur noted as Missy entered the bridge. After her speech the people of Fronge had melted away from her, pushing and shoving in their efforts to make way for her to cross the deck.

Missy smiled at the first officer and sheathed the Quillblade at her side. Its effects on her ceased as quickly as they had begun, leaving her feeling drained and extremely tired. A vague sense of unease settled over her, and she shook her head to rid herself of it.

Missy took her seat. 'It's a start.'

'You did better than I expected you would,' Heidi whispered into her ear. Missy jumped. The Heiliglander must have followed her, and she hadn't even noticed! 'It will be more difficult in Erdasche. The people there weren't in Fronge to see what Idunn and his followers are capable of, and Demons have only ever been a distant threat to Heimat Isle.'

Heidi had said 'Idunn'. Had Missy stripped the name Ishullanu out of her mind in her attempt to reach the others? Missy's stomach gave an uncomfortable lurch. Her nerves returned in force. She had been so caught up in her success with the people of Fronge that she hadn't even considered how she would handle things in Erdasche. If the weather remained steady they would reach the capital by nightfall. Missy didn't have long to figure out a plan of action.

'I think you should let me take the lead in Erdasche,' Heidi said suddenly. 'You don't know what you're doing, but if you appoint me as your emissary, I can talk to the duke for you.'

'An emissary?' Missy asked. 'Don't you mean acolyte, or a priestess or something?'

Heidi snorted through her nose. 'Whatever. You need to do it now, in front of my people, or they will be suspicious.'

Missy hesitated. She turned to the captain and translated Heidi's newest plan. As she did so, she tried to ignore the Heiliglander's frown. Here she was again, looking for someone else's approval, someone else's permission. Well, the girl could think what she liked. The captain was still in charge on the *Hiryū* regardless of who or what Missy was or pretended to be.

'It is a good idea,' Captain Shishi replied. 'We cannot be delayed in Erdasche for long. We can leave Heidi behind to rally the duke while we continue on our own quest.'

Missy was far from reassured. There was something nagging at the back of her mind. Not guilt. Oh, she felt that all right, but that wasn't what was bothering her now.

You've claimed another servant.

Missy looked quickly at Heidi. 'All right. Go and tell your people that I have appointed you as my agent, or whatever.'

Heidi nodded and left. Missy watched her go and then turned to look at Kanu, who was still by her side. *You've claimed another servant.* The thought kept floating through her mind. She couldn't quite banish it. But they *weren't* her servants. She wasn't like that, was she?

'Why don't you go and see if Lenis needs any help in the engine room?' she suggested to the boy.

'Yes,' Kanu said, and scampered below decks. She was as glad to see him leave as she was ashamed she'd told him to go.

◉

'I need to talk to you.'

Lenis knew without looking up from the engines that it was the princess. He could tell from her wooden monotone. But why would she want to talk to him? As far as he knew, she never sought anyone out unless it was to talk about going after Lord Butin. He sighed. He could already sense that Disma wasn't with her. This was going to be an awkward conversation.

'Of course, Princess,' he said as politely as he could. 'What do you need?' Lenis straightened up from behind the engine block.

She took one step into the engine room and then stopped. 'Before. You said I was like a Demon.'

Lenis felt a little ashamed at that. He hadn't really meant it. He had just been so . . . *angry* over what Kanu had done to him and his sister, and the princess had gotten in his way. It was hardly fair of him to take out his frustration on her, but she was just so, well, *frustrating*!

'Oh,' he stammered. 'About that. I'm sorry. I just –'

'Why?'

'Sorry, what?'

'Why?' Anastasis repeated.

'Why did I call you a Demon? Um . . .' Lenis faltered and tried again. 'Well, I didn't, really, I said you were *like* a Demon, because, you know, they're empty, and you're . . .' His voice trailed off.

'No,' the princess said. 'I don't want to know about that.'

Now Lenis was really confused. 'You don't? Look, I –'

'Why do I care?'

Lenis was dumbstruck. He opened his mouth to say something and then closed it again.

'I shouldn't be able to care,' Anastasis went on. 'I shouldn't be able to *feel*.'

'But you do?' Lenis asked.

'Yes.'

'I'm sorry,' Lenis repeated. 'I don't know. I don't understand.'

'Neither do I.'

They remained standing there, considering one another for several moments before the princess turned and departed without another word. Just after she left, Kanu came charging into the engine room. Lenis suppressed a sigh. Why couldn't people just leave him alone?

'Do you need any help, Mashu?' Kanu asked. He reminded Lenis of a newborn Bestia, all nervous energy and eager to please.

'Not really,' Lenis said, more shortly than he'd intended.

For a moment this didn't seem to affect the boy, and then he sort of deflated, the exuberance melting out of him.

'Oh.' Kanu sat on the edge of Lenis's bunk. 'Mashu, why am I here?'

'I'm sorry?' Lenis moved around the engine block to stand near him.

The Titan child looked up at him. 'Why am I here?'

'I . . . I'm not really sure, Kanu,' Lenis admitted. 'I don't understand it any more than you.' All this time he'd been so frustrated Kanu didn't have any answers it had never occurred to him that the boy might have questions of his own.

'I understand,' Kanu said, surprising Lenis. 'I am here to serve Mashu.'

'Um, okay?'

'But *how* am I meant to serve you, Mashu? What do you need me for?'

Lenis had never felt such a depth of longing as he did in Kanu. The Titan boy wanted, he *needed*, an answer, but Lenis didn't have one. He didn't want to be Mashu, or anything that came with it, and he definitely didn't want anyone serving him. But how was he supposed to say that to the boy when he was sitting there feeling so miserable and useless?

'Look,' Lenis said eventually, 'why don't you go and fill the Bestia's water dishes for me? When you get back I can show you how to brush them, and then maybe you can feed them.'

It was such a small thing, but it was apparently enough. An impossibly large smile spread across Kanu's face, and he literally leapt off Lenis's bunk to obey. When he was gone, empty water dishes in hand, Lenis did sigh. It seemed he had another small creature to take care of. As if in response he felt a questing from Suiteki, a tugging at his empathic awareness. It took all his effort to find a sense of calm to reassure her with.

● MEETING WITH THE DUKE OF HEIMAT ISLE ●

Missy tried to concentrate on only one of the Bestia housed in the Erdasche airdock. Some idiot had decided it would be a good idea to use a whole team of them to receive incoming messages. That was all good and well in theory, but they kept them together in the same hutch, which made it extremely difficult to get through to one particular Bestia, especially when none of them were trained very well. She finally settled on one with an affinity for earth, as they tended to be less flighty. They were seldom used in airdocks as they had the habit of keeping their attention focused on the ground below instead of the air around them, but this one seemed to be pretty steady.

To make matters worse, though, there was only one Bestia communicator on duty, and he was trying to listen to what each of the Bestia was relaying to him simultaneously. It was one of the most inexperienced and inefficient examples of Bestia communication Missy had ever dealt with, but deal with it she did. Eventually, the *Hiryū* was able to dock and unload its fifty plus passengers onto the unprepared airdock authorities.

For several minutes Heiliglanders milled around aimlessly on the airdock, with most of the *Hiryū*'s crew watching from the bridge, until a man easily seven feet tall with a bald head and an impressively long, blond moustache strode out of the authorities' office and began bellowing orders. In a matter of minutes the people of Fronge were loosely corralled into one corner of the airdock while the tall, bald man stomped up the *Hiryū*'s gangplank.

'I think it's time you went to work,' Missy whispered to Heidi, who nodded and squared her shoulders.

The two girls followed the captain and first officer down to the deck to meet the official.

The man drew in a deep breath and cried, 'What by Freyr's beard are you –'

But Heidi strode up to him and shook a finger under his nose. 'You can't talk to us like that!'

Missy groaned inwardly. It seemed her doubts about appointing Heidi as her spokeswoman were proving well founded. The girl was going to get them all into trouble.

'You listen to me, you little . . .' Missy didn't recognise the word the man used to describe Heidi, but she knew the tone of an insult when she heard one.

'No, you listen,' Heidi insisted, her finger waggling backwards and forwards, 'Fronge has been destroyed –'

'*What?*'

'– and we haven't got time to be standing around talking to an insignificant airdock administrator. Take us to the duke at once!'

The man's whole head turned purple.

Missy stepped up behind Heidi. 'Ah, Heidi –'

Heidi turned and scowled at her. The message was clear. She wanted Missy to stay out of it. Heidi addressed the official again. 'My name is Heidi Baumstochter. The great Magni, wielder of lightning and goddess of war, has anointed me as her chosen herald. The news I bring is grave. There is a Demonic horde gathering within the Wastelands, poised to strike into the very heart of Heiligland. We must see the duke *immediately*.'

The airdock official looked as though he had been stunned into speechlessness. He kept opening and closing his mouth, but no words came out, just a sort of gasping noise. Then all of the survivors of Fronge started talking at once, describing the horrors that Karasu had inflicted upon them in service to Idunn the Demon King. Missy tensed, ready to lay hold of the Quillblade and use her powers to convince the airdock official to let them see the duke, but whether it was Heidi's speech or the excited babble of the people of Fronge that convinced him, it didn't matter. 'You had better come with me,' he muttered and turned to stalk back down the gangplank.

Missy translated for the others and then followed along

behind him as he led them down to the airdock and over to a large stone tower that was built adjacent to it.

Missy grabbed hold of Heidi's hand. 'What are you *doing*?'

Heidi snatched it away. 'What we came here to do. Now play your part, *Magni*.'

Missy fell silent and trailed along after the daunting figure of the airdock official. Once in the tower they were led down a series of tightly spiralling steps and eventually out onto the cobbled street. They passed a number of people dressed in trousers and shirts and leather coats who, just like the people of Fronge, stopped to stare at the strangers with their foreign features and odd clothes.

Arthur was in his navy-coloured short coat with the gold buttons, and the captain was wearing his black Shinzōn robes. Missy was still wearing the outfit Heidi had chosen for her. Her curly hair had become all knotty from the wind, and the leather kilt was beginning to chafe her skin raw through the flimsy dress she had on underneath. She was so cold she didn't think she'd ever be warm again and longed for Andrea's heavy woollen coat. Most of the Heiliglanders in the streets had bright yellow hair, but a number of them had brown or even dirty-blond hair like hers. Their eyes, too, were light like Missy's, though there was far more blue and grey than green.

As they were led further into Erdasche, no doubt towards the duke's residence or the local town hall or something like that, Missy fretted over their plan. Her nerves grew more fraught with every step. Heidi seemed to exude confidence, but none of it rubbed off on Missy. She wanted to read the Heiliglander's mind so badly, but she didn't attempt it. All she would see in there would be images of Heidi's plan, which Missy already knew enough about. Besides, she'd lied to and manipulated the Heiliglander as it was without betraying her privacy any further.

Eventually they reached a small square with a stone fountain set in the middle of it. Behind that was an impressive looking structure, built out of stone and wood. Its walls were painted white, offsetting the dark timber that made up the support columns spaced evenly along its length. The roof was also made of wood, unlike so many of the other dwellings and businesses they had passed, which were thatched. If Fronge had been built in a similar manner, it was no wonder the town had burned down so readily.

There were no guards at the doors, which Missy found both odd and a little unsettling. She was so used to places of governance being guarded that this one felt vulnerable. Karasu was still out there, after all, and if he had pursued the *Hiryū* instead of going on to Kolga's temple in the north, as they were guessing, he could easily do here what he had done in Fronge. Missy tried to reassure herself that Erdasche was much larger than Fronge, a city more than a township, and probably safe from the Shinzōn mercenary, but still . . . She wouldn't feel truly safe until they had both the stones of ebb and flow in their possession.

Their bald guide with the enormous moustache thrust open the wooden doors and strode into the building, leaving the others to follow along behind him. Inside was a large empty hall. It had a hard-packed mud floor and was lined with racks of weaponry. Beams of the same wood used for the pillars supported the ceiling. It was no wonder there were no guards on duty. There was nothing to steal inside except for some dusty, rusty-looking weapons. Missy noticed there was a hole in the middle of the ceiling, and directly below this was a fire pit ringed by shirtless men. Each one had an animal skin draped over his shoulders and wore leather trousers.

Their guide moved straight over to the fire pit. 'Hail, Ajat Freyrsson, I have brought emissaries from the gods to speak with you.'

One of the men stood up. He was taller than their guide, and his hair and eyes were black. His chest and knuckles were as hirsute as his head. Across his shoulders he wore a pure white pelt of some animal Missy didn't recognise. Whatever it had been in life it must have been huge. 'Hail, Olav Olafsson. What did you say you have brought us?'

'Emissaries,' their guide, Olav, repeated, 'claiming to be sent by the gods.'

The ring of men burst into laughter. Olav purpled again.

'It is true.' Heidi's voice rang out clearly in the mostly empty hall. 'We bring grave tidings from the gods!'

The silence that greeted her words lasted only a moment, and then the men were all laughing again.

'Child,' Ajat said, the giant of a man wiping tears of mirth from his eyes, 'what jollity is this?'

Heidi turned to glare at Missy. 'Do it,' she hissed. 'Now.'

Once again, Missy's throat went dry and she felt nauseous. This was it. This was why they had come here. She was going to have to pretend to be Magni again. All she had to do was convince these men she was a god and then they could return to the *Hiryū* and get out of here.

'We have no time to waste with you.' Ajat waved a dismissive hand at them and sank back to the ground.

Heidi was still glaring at Missy. She was waiting for Missy to step in and take charge of the situation, just as she had done back in the square in Fronge, but Missy hesitated.

Heidi waited another moment before crying out, 'Fronge has been attacked!'

'What?' Several of the men jumped to their feet this time.

Heidi went on. 'Fronge is destroyed! Ajat Freyrsson, you are the Duke of Heimat Isle. You *must* hear us out.'

'What are you saying?' Ajat demanded, once more on his feet. This time he strode around the fire pit to confront them. Missy fell back to stand beside Arthur and the captain. Heidi held her ground.

'What is going on?' the captain asked, his hand resting on his sword hilt.

Missy remained dumbstruck as Ajat bore down on them. Arthur had tensed beside her, and though the captain appeared at ease, she knew that he was getting ready to draw his blade.

'Miss Clemens?' the captain whispered in Shinzōn.

'What is this nonsense?' Ajat demanded, spittle flying from his lips and spraying Heidi's face.

Heidi somehow managed to maintain her composure. 'I speak the truth.' She looked back at Missy but went on, 'Fronge is destroyed. Consumed by fire.'

'Who did this? Who dares attack what belongs to Ajat Freyrsson?'

For a heartbeat, Heidi said nothing and thoughts whirled through Missy's mind. The girl had done it now. She had committed them to their lie. There was no telling what the duke would do. What was it Heidi had said? *Do you think someone can come and destroy one of our towns and we won't do anything? Did you think you could just fly off and we'd just sit around and wait for you to fix everything? The world doesn't work that way.*

'Fronge was destroyed by Demons,' Heidi said quietly.

Ajat's response was immediate. He grabbed Heidi by both shoulders and shook her. 'There are no Demons on Heimat Isle!'

Missy swallowed the lump in her throat and grasped the Quillblade's hilt. The situation was getting out of control. It was now or never. 'Enough!' she cried out, her voice magnified as it had been back in the town square in Fronge. 'Release my herald *now*!'

Ajat all but dropped Heidi, who exaggerated her fall and turned it into a grovelling bow. Sprawled on the compacted mud, her forehead pressed to the ground, she called, 'All hail Magni Lightning-Wielder!'.

'What is this?' Ajat demanded. 'Some joke? You expect us to believe that this slip of a girl is the Lightning-Wielder?' He threw back his head and laughed.

Whether it was his contempt for her or a result of the Quillblade's effects, Missy didn't know, but suddenly she was angry. Really angry. She didn't even want to be here in the first place and this man was wasting their time!

'Listen to me, Ajat Freyrsson,' she cried, using her power to force the words into his mind, to make him believe her. 'I *am* Magni, and I have come to ready your people for war!'

Missy had been so intent on convincing the duke that she had forgotten about the others in the hall.

'What is this, Ajat?' one of them scoffed. 'Do you take orders from children, now?'

The hide-draped men laughed and Missy turned her ire towards them. 'Do you *dare* to mock me?' She felt the Quillblade respond. The throbbing in the *shintai* intensified as it fed on her emotions. Its power grew with her fury. She needed to do something to show them she was serious. Missy directed her mind to the fire pit. There was already a hole in the ceiling, if she could just . . .

Her brow furrowed as she concentrated, and a moment later a bolt of lightning burst out of the clear sky overhead, through the hole in the ceiling of the hall, and crashed into the pit between the duke's men. They cried out and fell back. Missy pushed herself into their minds, altering their images of the war goddess. She became younger in their imaginations, shorter, thinner. The bolt of lightning she held in her hand became a golden feather. And suddenly, as one, they saw her as Magni the Lightning-Wielder.

'Great Magni,' one of them grovelled, scrabbling towards her on his knees. 'Forgive us.'

'We have known peace too long,' another said, holding out his hands to her in supplication. 'We had forgotten you.'

Missy considered the hide-draped men for a moment, satisfied she had them where they needed to be. A very small part buried deep inside was crying, but a larger part was gloating. She had done it. She may not have been Magni but she *was* the Lightning-Wielder, and these men would listen to her now.

'Arise, my herald,' Missy said to Heidi, who was looking at her with something akin to awe in her face. 'Arise and deliver my message.'

'Thank you, oh great Magni,' Heidi stammered as she got to her feet. The girl was shaken. *Good*, Missy thought, *let her see what has come from her god forging.* 'Hear me now, Ajat Freyrsson,' Heidi went on, her voice growing steadier. 'The great Magni has come to us from Vanaheim, the home of the gods, to warn us about a Demon army gathering within the Wastelands.' The duke raised his head and stared from Heidi to Missy. Missy kept her face impassive. 'A Demon King has arisen, who is more powerful than any Demon known to us. I speak of Idunn! He seeks nothing less than the destruction of humanity. He has already razed Fronge.' Heidi's voice caught at the mention of her hometown. Missy thought it was a bit overdone. 'It is too late for my home. The warriors of Heiligland must unite to repel this Demonic invasion or we will suffer the same fate. It falls to you, Ajat Freyrsson, to ready Heimat Isle, and then to travel to the mainland and speak with the other rulers of Heiligland. All must stand united against this coming threat. So speaks the great Magni, goddess of war and wielder of lightning.'

As the echoes of her words died, Heidi collapsed. Missy wasn't sure if it was because the captain had somehow followed the conversation, or if it was just his well-trained reflexes, but he caught her before she hit the ground.

'Ajat Freyrsson has heard your words, great Magni,' said the duke, his voice trembling. He rose to kneel on one knee. 'I will do as you command and prepare the whole of Heiligland to meet the Demon threat.'

Missy nodded as regally as she could manage, but inside she was exulting. She had done it. Heiligland would ready itself for war. They would prepare to fight Ishullanu and his Demon army. The taste of victory was sweet.

● THE ORIGINS OF ZENAKU ●

As much as Shujinko's words about Lenis's lack of training had rankled, Lenis had to admit the cabin boy was at least partly right. Lenis needed far more practice if he was ever going to be able to defend himself, much less defeat Shujinko in a fair fight. So once the *Hiryū* was docked and the passengers unloaded, Lenis went in search of Yami. He found the swordsman on the forecastle watching the happenings on the airdock. As Lenis climbed the steps to join him, he looked over the railing and saw that the people of Fronge were being led down the airdock.

'Did they pull it off?' Lenis asked without preamble.

Yami nodded. 'Captain Shishi, Lord Arthur, and your sister have gone with Heidi to see the duke.'

'Oh.' Lenis crossed his arms along the railing and rested his chin on top of them. 'Do you ever get the feeling things have gone awry?'

The swordsman chuckled. 'I have felt that way often since I joined this crew. What in particular are you concerned about?'

Lenis sighed and straightened. He turned so he could lean his back against the railing and stared out at the open sky beyond the *Hiryū*'s portside. 'Everything,' he muttered. 'I don't know. When we left Shinzō it was all so clear. We find Karasu. We get the stones. Suiteki's power is unlocked. And then . . .'

Lenis's voice trailed away. He could feel the baby dragon's contentment rising from below decks. Suiteki was in her nest by Hiroshi's stove, her stomach full, and the warmth from the cook-fire seeping into her side. It took an effort to extricate himself from the dragon's cosy, comfortable world, but Lenis managed it.

'And then what?' Yami prompted.

The feeling of frustration came rushing back. 'I don't know! Defeat Ishullanu. Stop the Demons.'

'Save the world?'

Lenis stared at Yami's immobile features. 'Well, yeah, I guess.'

'That is quite a heavy burden to carry, Lenis.'

'You don't think we can do it?'

Yami laughed softly again and turned away from his scrutiny of the airdock to look into Lenis's eyes. 'What has changed?'

'What?'

'You said everything was clear when we left Shinzō. What is it that has changed?' When Lenis didn't reply, Yami went on. 'We now know where Karasu is, or at least have a good idea of where he is heading. We will find him and retrieve the stones.'

Yami was right. Nothing had changed. Their goals were the same. As the swordsman had said, if anything they were a little closer to achieving them. Then why did Lenis *feel* as if something had changed? Something important. It hadn't felt the same since Kanu had come along. What had he done to the twins back on the jetty? He had brought them together, like when they had fought Ishullanu, but maybe that wasn't what they were supposed to be after all. It was what the Demon King wanted, maybe even what the sea god Apsu wanted, but it wasn't what Lenis wanted. If that was what it was going to take to ultimately defeat Ishullanu, he wasn't sure he could do it.

And something was happening to his sister. She was leaning more often on the Quillblade, allowing it to take more and more of her away. Every time Missy used it he felt a bit of her slip away from him, and there was nothing he could do about it. Not while she was intent on this ridiculous farce with that Heiliglander girl. There was something else there, too – he wasn't ready to deal with it yet. Why hadn't Missy sought him out while he had been trapped on board Karasu's airship?

'Would you like to hear about the origins of Zenaku?' Yami asked suddenly.

'Zenaku?' Lenis asked. 'What's that?'

Yami drew his sword out of his sheath. The black blade came free silently, with not even the slightest rasp of metal. 'This is Zenaku. My family sword.'

Lenis had never examined the weapon up close before. He had seen Yami use it and had wondered how it could pass through flesh but deflect blades. As he looked at it now, he saw that it didn't reflect any light. It was as though it wasn't even made out of metal. Somehow, Lenis knew not to reach out to try to touch it.

'It looks . . . odd,' Lenis said at last.

In one smooth motion, Yami sheathed Zenaku. He made a sort of grunting noise that almost could have been another laugh. 'It is most definitely odd, Lenis. It is a Lilim.'

'*What?*'

'It is true. Although, I had never heard the term Lilim until I came aboard this airship. In Shinzō, we call them *oni*. Magicians summon them from the netherworld to do their bidding. Once, a long time ago, there was a master weapon-smith named Masamune. He forged bows that could be drawn by children, staves that would never break, and spears that would never dint. His swords were the stuff of legend, even before he died. He was a magician, and it was said he forged *oni* into the blades of his swords. The cost of such a weapon was unimaginable. He demanded payment not only in gold and jewels, but in the very souls of those who sought his services.'

Lenis gulped. 'Their souls?'

'Zenaku has power beyond a normal sword. It takes on the properties of whoever wields it. When I draw the blade –' he drew Zenaku again and slashed through the air before returning it to its sheath '– it takes on the properties of shadow. The Yūrei clan train their warriors in stealth. When Gawayn holds Zenaku . . .'

'It becomes a sword of light,' Lenis finished, remembering the Kystian's battle with the ocean Demon when the *Hiryū* had fled Yukitoshi.

'Just so.' Yami sighed. 'I wonder, Lenis, if knowing the truth is worth the price of belief.'

This took Lenis aback. 'I'm not sure I understand what you mean.'

'Since joining this crew I have discovered more about the Lilim. I have learned something of what they truly are. I once thought this blade –' he rested his hand on Zenaku's hilt '– was an *onitai*, a weapon forged with the soul of an *oni*.'

'And now?'

'There must have been a pact, of course,' Yami said. 'The Lilim who made that pact with my ancestor manifested in the physical world as this sword. When the pact was complete –'

'When your ancestor was sacrificed?' Lenis felt a shiver run through him.

Yami nodded. 'Yes. When he gave the last of himself to the Lilim, the sword remained.'

'So now you know how the blade was really forged.'

Yami nodded.

'But Zenaku itself hasn't changed.'

'The sword itself is as it ever was, Lenis, but my idea of it is no longer the same. My *belief* in Zenaku is what has changed. This sword has not left my side since my father entrusted it to me, but I had no idea of its true nature. None of my ancestors knew, except perhaps for the one who sold his soul to Masamune. If I could be so mistaken about Zenaku's nature, what else may I have misjudged?'

'Your curse.' Lenis knew it was true before he even said it.

Yami nodded again. 'I believed myself cursed by an *oni*, by a creature of the netherworld. But if Bakeneko is just another Lilim, then why did she curse me? How? Did she once make a pact with Gawayn? Does his soul now belong to her? And mine to Zenaku?'

They fell into silence. Lenis marvelled that Yami was being so open with him, that he trusted Lenis enough to share his doubts. He thought about what he knew of Bakeneko, the Lilim who had cursed Yami all those years ago. She was bonded to the Emperor. Was that it? Was that the connection? Maybe it wasn't Bakeneko who wanted to curse Yami but Emperor Botanichi. Though why would the Emperor of Shinzō want to do that?

'Show me your technique,' Yami said.

The abrupt change in direction left Lenis at a loss. A moment ago Yami had been confiding in him, and now he was asking for Lenis to demonstrate his form? Yami moved away from the railing. Lenis shook his head and followed. This was why he had come looking for Yami, after all. Whatever had elicited the swordsman's confidence had vanished as quickly as it had come. He was once more his usual closed self.

When Lenis was in the centre of the forecastle he planted his feet squarely on the deck. He took a deep breath and let it out slowly as he straightened his spine and placed his arms into the neutral position.

'Begin,' Yami commanded, and Lenis moved into the first defensive stance and on into the second. As his body flowed from defensive positions to attack postures, his arms moving in steady, sweeping movements and his weight shifting from foot to foot as he manoeuvred around the foredeck, Lenis's mind slowed. The constant churning that always occupied it quieted and stilled almost completely, waking only when Yami moved in to correct the position of his various body parts.

'You have not been practising,' Yami noted as Lenis settled back into the neutral position. It was a statement, not a question.

Lenis bit back the excuse that jumped to his lips. Yami wasn't Shujinko. Where the cabin boy enjoyed pointing out Lenis's faults, his teacher only did so to help Lenis learn from his mistakes. 'No, sir.'

Yami passed no judgements. He moved back out of the way. 'Again.'

So Lenis went through the forms Yami had taught him for a second time, and then a third. By the fourth attempt Lenis needed almost no correcting, for his mind knew the forms even if his body wasn't entirely used to them yet.

'You have improved,' Yami said as Lenis finished his sixth set of movements.

Lenis nodded. His body ached as his muscles readjusted to the unpractised actions. He never would have imagined moving so slowly could tire you out, but he felt as though he'd been working all day. His body was sore, the exercises reawakening dormant bruises and the pain in his side, but his head felt clear. For the first time since Fronge, Lenis felt calm.

'Come,' Yami said. 'Attack me.'

Lenis couldn't stop a grin from spreading across his face. Finally he would get to spar with Yami instead of Shujinko. His first strike was aimed squarely at Yami's chest. The swordsman stopped it with a forearm, moving so fast Lenis's eyes couldn't register the block, and then Yami grabbed Lenis's wrist and used his own momentum to pull him off balance. As Lenis was dragged forwards, Yami thrust up with his other arm, his fist stopping just before it connected with Lenis's chin. He helped Lenis regain his footing.

'Again,' Yami commanded, and Lenis tried the same move. Yami countered it the same way. 'Again.'

Lenis was already breathing hard. He had to move faster. He had to find a way to move in under the block, or maybe go around it, or maybe –

This time Yami's fist tapped his chin, ever so lightly. The swordsman held him where he was and reached up to poke Lenis's forehead. 'Stop thinking.'

Lenis nodded and tried again. And again. Each time, the tap on his chin grew a little harder, his own movements a little slower.

Finally, Lenis threw his hands up in the air. 'I can't do it! I'm not fast enough!'

Yami smiled, but where the same smile on Shujinko's lips would be mocking, Yami's was a sign of his pleasure. 'Correct. Is your arm sore?' Lenis nodded. 'Good. With each blow, your muscles are working. The more they work, the stronger and faster they become.'

'They don't feel stronger,' Lenis noted, rubbing his forearm, 'and they certainly aren't faster.'

'In time,' Yami told him. 'How are your ribs?'

'Okay,' Lenis lied. The pain in his side was growing stronger, sharper, but he didn't want to stop now.

Yami nodded. 'Again.'

Lenis focused all of his energy into his arm and swung as hard as he could. Yami blocked him easily.

'Strike faster, not harder,' Yami told him.

Lenis had no idea how to do that, but he tried anyway, only to be blocked again. 'I don't understand, Yami. What's the point of just mindlessly trying to punch you? I'm never going to hit you.'

'We are toning your body, Lenis.' Yami shifted his

stance. 'Try and block me.' Yami punched him right in the stomach.

Lenis doubled over. His ribs sliced into his side. It had been a hard hit. 'Ow!'

'Again.'

At Yami's word, Lenis instinctively swept his arm up wildly to try and block the incoming blow. His arm connected with Yami's and pride welled up within him. He'd done it! Then Yami struck again, and this time Lenis was too slow.

'Focus,' Yami rebuked him, and for the next few minutes Lenis swept his arm up to block until it grew so tired he could barely lift it, but something inside made him throw his arm up anyway, even if it was little more than a spasm of movement. Sometimes Yami hit him and it hurt. Other times he blocked Yami's fist, but the swordsman ended up hitting him anyway, and that hurt too. And every once in a while, Lenis actually blocked the blow.

'Good,' Yami said eventually, and Lenis sighed, relieved to be finished for the day. 'Now, the other side.'

It turned out Lenis's left side was much weaker and slower than his right, and he got hit with greater frequency. But his damaged ribs were on the other side of his body, so at least they didn't pain him as much this time around. When he switched to left-hand punches, it was all Lenis could do to lift his arm, let alone put any force behind his strikes.

'Good,' Yami said again after about an hour of blocking and striking.

The sun had already set. Lucis had come up on deck and curled up on the railing, and it was by her light that they were practising. Lenis's arms ached, and his chest, side, and stomach hurt from the punishment Yami had dealt him. If anything, his body was worse than after a training session with Shujinko, but overall Lenis felt *better*. He felt as though he had really achieved something.

But Yami wasn't finished with him yet. He went from basic strikes and blocks to teaching Lenis how to grab his opponent's arm, just as Yami had done earlier. From this technique, Lenis learned how to pull an opponent forwards and off guard, against his strong desire to push them away from him, and also how to jab the opponent's chin.

And then, when Lenis felt as though he could do no more and Lucis had begun yawning from her perch on the railing, Yami taught him what to do if you had been pulled off guard and there was a fist coming for your chin. Yami showed him that you had to lunge forwards, even though your body instinctively tried to pull back against your opponent's leverage, and then you sort of twisted your body a bit so your front leg was behind their leg, and if you did it right you could counterattack with your free hand. Of course, if you did it wrong your opponent could also twist and throw you over their shoulder. Lenis only got to try it once. Yami recognised immediately that this particular exercise was too hard on Lenis's ribs and put a stop to it.

When the ordeal was over, Yami made him go through his forms again. He said it was to make sure his body didn't seize up after the training, but at that point Lenis was convinced beyond all reason that it was just a fresh wave of torture.

Finally, after Yami had excused him and Lenis had thanked his teacher for the lesson, Lenis was able to stagger below decks. He was in more pain than he had ever been in before, even counting the time he had burned and bruised his body during the *Hiryū*'s escape from Yukitoshi, but he also felt strangely euphoric. The frustration that had plagued him for the past couple of days was gone. He was too tired to dwell on it.

'What happened to you?' Hiroshi asked as Lenis entered the galley. The cook picked up a handful of what he was chopping and dumped it into his pot.

'Training.' It came out as a mumble, and Lenis drew in a deep breath and tried again. 'Training.'

'Good lad!' Hiroshi laughed. 'Training is dedication, I tell you. Soon you'll be looking back and thinking, "What a weakling I was!" Don't you doubt it.'

Lenis nodded, too tired to try and form any more words. Suddenly he felt dizzy, so he sat down on the nearest chair and cupped his head in his hands. Nausea rose up in him, and he felt as if he was going to faint. He didn't even flinch as Suiteki ran up his leg and began nipping at his fingers.

Hiroshi's laughter drew closer and there was a small thud as the cook placed something on the table in front of him. 'Here, get that into you.'

Lenis peeled open his eyes and lowered his hands as Suiteki stopped biting him to sniff the contents of the bowl. For a moment his vision turned white, but then he caught the scent of noodle soup, or perhaps it was Suiteki's sudden craving for savoury things rubbing off on him, and his stomach growled. His head stopped spinning and his vision cleared. Gently, in case any sudden movement brought back the dizziness, Lenis picked up his spoon and started eating around Suiteki, who watched his movements closely with her glinting dragon eyes so she could dip her head into the bowl when he wasn't looking. He didn't mind. There was something about their shared hunger and the satisfaction in seeing it fed that revived him as much as the food itself. Together, they devoured the noodle soup Hiroshi had brought them.

'Thatta boy!' Hiroshi slapped him on the back. Lenis winced but kept eating. 'We'll make a warrior out of you yet, I tell you!'

● THE PRICE OF POWER ●

Missy had never quite believed that anyone could truly mistake her for a god. She was only thirteen years old and up until a few weeks ago had been a slave. Heidi had soon lost her awe of Missy back in Fronge, and Missy suspected Ajat Freyrsson would too if they lingered too long in Erdasche.

Magni was a thunder god, just like Raikō. They were probably the same Totem, the one who had captured Missy's soul and ordered her to find a cure for his sickness. Adad the Thunder Bird. Now he was just another Demon. The only thing left of him, of the *real* him, was the Quillblade, and that was clasped firmly in Missy's hand. There was no way she was letting go of it until the *Hiryū* was on its way again. The weight of it was reassuring, and it kept her fears at bay.

It didn't seem as though she was going to make it back to the airship before dawn. The people of Erdasche had turned out in force to catch a glimpse of the long absent war goddess once word had spread that Magni had returned. Missy suspected Heidi's hand in this. She was taking her role as the goddess's personal herald to heart, calling out to anyone who would listen that war was coming with the Demons. Missy was given a place of honour by the duke's fire pit. The men who had been with him when they had arrived, the ones dressed in animal hides, clustered around her, keeping the other folk back at what they deemed to be a respectful distance. Missy sat cross-legged between Arthur and the captain, thankful they had remained by her side while this whole thing played out. She wanted nothing more than to sneak off and return to the *Hiryū*, but she knew that would have to wait until the last of the Heiliglanders left her in peace.

Missy's grip tightened on the Quillblade's hilt, every sense alert for trouble. The hall was full of people now. Some knelt as close to Missy as her makeshift honour guard would allow. Others stood in clusters and whispered amongst themselves. Missy didn't need to be telepathic to know what they were thinking. *Who is this child claiming to be Magni?* Her mind was ready to pounce on any who doubted her, to instill in them an image of herself as the Lightning-Wielder, but this proved largely unnecessary. It seemed that people were already altering their perceptions of what they thought Magni looked like to mirror the girl sitting before them. Perhaps the word of Ajat Freyrsson was enough to quell any disbelief as to her identity, or perhaps it was a lingering effect of Missy's telepathic manipulation of the duke and his men. Certainly it seemed as though the Quillblade amplified her own powers. Maybe she was somehow radiating a sense of herself as Magni without even realising it.

A flicker of unease itched at the back of Missy's mind only to be absorbed by the Quillblade a moment later. She was glad when it left her. She didn't want to deal with her doubts and guilt right now. All that mattered was that she had done it. Her deception had worked. The Heiliglanders would be ready to confront Ishullanu's army of Demons. That was all that mattered. Besides, whatever her reservations had been about her actions, the worst of it was over. It wasn't as if she could go back and change things. Soon she would be back on the *Hiryū* and far away from here. She may as well try to relax.

If Missy had ever wondered what gifts the people of Erdasche believed would please a war goddess, she didn't have to any more. As they arrived at the meeting hall, they presented her with gift baskets full of chunks of red meat and earthenware jugs Ajat told her were filled with honeyed ale. There were also flowers. They looked like the white snap-dragons Missy remembered from back home in Pure Land, but these ones were rose-pink verging on red, and they were called loewenmaul in Heiliglander, which meant 'mouth of the vicious beast'. Missy supposed that was close enough to snapdragon anyway.

'Miss Clemens,' the captain whispered to her in Shinzōn, 'I understand that you are enjoying yourself, but how long do you intend to allow this to continue? Karasu is getting further ahead of us.'

Missy startled. Was she enjoying herself? Yes, she supposed she was. She wasn't used to being the centre of attention, much less on the receiving end of so many presents. And it wasn't as though she was hurting anybody. Another wisp of unease curled around inside her, but it too vanished into the Quillblade. If she had to pretend to be a goddess, she could at least have some fun. 'Sorry, Captain,' she whispered back. 'I'm not sure how to make it all stop.'

'You are the goddess here, Miss Clemens.' His face remained impassive, but she thought he sounded more amused than angry. 'It will end when you decide to end it.'

Missy swallowed and nodded. It was probably time to go. She was tired and the captain was right; they had to go after Karasu. She stood up awkwardly. The hall fell silent as everyone turned to her. The Quillblade quickened in her grip, vibrating gently as it absorbed her nerves. Heidi scowled at her from where she was greeting the new arrivals – and accepting their gifts, Missy noted. No doubt the Heiliglander was worried Missy was about to ruin everything.

Missy cleared her throat. 'People of Heimat Isle.' No. That wouldn't do. 'My people! As you know, I have come to warn you to prepare for war with the Demon King and his army. I charge you to gather your forces and rally the rest of our people. I have to leave you now.' A murmuring rose amongst the crowd. 'I must go north,' she went on quickly, 'to a temple dedicated to, er . . .' What did Tenjin say Apsilla's Heiliglander name was? '. . . to my cousin Kolga. She has been . . . um . . . holding onto a weapon for me. One of great power. With it, we can defeat many Demons.' Missy faltered. The murmuring had turned to whispering. 'I will be leaving. Now.'

Ajat Freyrsson cleared his throat and rose to his feet. 'You will not stay and lead us into battle, oh great Magni?'

'Magni has much to attend to,' Heidi called across the hall. 'It is not for us to question her actions.' Missy saw many of the hall's occupants nodding in agreement. 'With the goddess's permission, I will remain behind so that she may speak to you through me.'

Missy wasn't sure she liked that idea at all. She understood the logic behind the girl's plans to mobilise her country, but now Missy detected something else in her. Ambition. If Missy allowed her to remain here to speak for Magni, what would Heidi do in her name? Suspicion blossomed inside her, and this emotion the Quillblade did not take.

Everyone was looking at her, and Missy realised they were waiting for her decision. It occurred to Missy that she could make Heidi come with her. She could even make her happy to do so. They could be friends. All it would take would be a suggestion, planted deep in her mind, a shared memory or two, and then the erasure of Missy's deception and manipulation of the girl. Missy was already reaching out to Heidi when she brought herself up short.

What was she *doing*?

She shook her head to clear it. 'Yes. Of course my herald should remain amongst you in my absence.' Missy saw the triumph in Heidi's face and turned away from it.

Both Arthur and the captain had risen to stand behind her. Arthur was eyeing her closely. 'Are you all right?'

'I want to go home,' she whispered in Kystian. Snatches of feelings were flaring up inside her, only to be dragged down into the Quillblade so fast she couldn't register what they were. She didn't dare let the *shintai* go. Not here. Not now. 'I want to get back to the *Hiryū*.'

The Kystian nodded and began pushing through the crowd. Missy followed along behind him, trying to feel something. Anything. She had been planning to manipulate Heidi's mind, to *force* her into liking her. How could she have even considered such a thing? A few hours ago even reading the girl's mind without her knowledge had seemed repulsive. What had changed? Missy tried to hold onto the feelings these thoughts evoked. Uncertainty. Fear. Anger. Self-loathing. But the Quillblade devoured them all. She felt the captain moving close behind as they approached the exit to the hall, and Arthur's back was a reassuring mass in front of her, but inside she knew that something was desperately wrong, for as the unsettling emotions were sucked out of her the Quillblade bolstered contradictory ones within her. Instead of fear she felt reckless. Instead of uncertainty she felt determination. And instead of hating herself for what she had done to the men in the hall, for what she had been about to do to Heidi, she felt only an overwhelming sense of self-righteousness that was building close to fury.

How dare Heidi claim to speak for me! How dare she shun my friendship! She should be grovelling before me!

The familiar tingling in the Quillblade had turned to an incessant throbbing. Sparks of electricity arced down its length. Missy's hand ached from holding its hilt so firmly. Her jaw ached from being clenched so tightly. The only thing that kept her moving was the desire to return to the *Hiryū*, to *her* airship. It was where she belonged. Why was it taking so long to get there? Didn't these people know who walked amongst them? What was the delay?

At the doorway Heidi made to touch her hand but pulled back when Missy looked into her eyes. There was fear there. Missy could see it riding at the forefront of Heidi's mind. Well, this was what the girl had wanted. Magni the war goddess. Implacable. Battle-ready. Wielder of lightning. She had no idea how right she was. Magni was all but dead. What remained of her was held firmly in Missy's hand. Her wrist twitched and the Quillblade screeched. Heidi backed away, her head bowed. The rest of the Heiliglanders fell back as well.

'I wish to leave,' Missy said, and even her voice didn't sound like her own any more. It was higher, and beneath it she seemed to hear the shrieking of the Thunder Bird. 'Do not get in my way.'

Finally they were out of the hall and alone. The Heiliglanders, who had been so eager to cluster around her, now left her to venture into the night without them. Missy broke into a run. She was dimly aware of Arthur and Captain Shishi beside her, behind her, falling ever further back as she outstripped them. Her muscles were working harder than they ever had before. She could feel the Quillblade's electricity coursing through her. Her feet barely touched the ground. The distance between strides grew longer until she wasn't running but leaping. Higher. Further. Faster. The frigid air tore through her lungs. The pain was exquisite. The Quillblade whirled in her grasp. She could see sparks.

And then Missy was at the airdock. A leap and she was on the *Hiryū*'s deck. For a moment she stood there, exulting. She *was* the Lightning-Wielder. She was the Thunder Bird. The Lord of Storms. She was Magni! She was Raikō! She was Adad and all of his incarnations! Let Karasu try and stand against her. Ishullanu would fall to her blade.

Suddenly Kanu was kneeling before her, and it was *right*. Here was a servant worthy of her. Heidi was nothing. A mere human. Kanu was a Titan. He was born to serve her. He had been chosen for her eons past. Missy reached out to place a hand on his shoulder but then, over Kanu's bowed head, Missy saw her brother. He was standing at the top of the stairs leading below decks, holding Aeris. It was good. He had finally come to speak to her.

Except Lenis wasn't looking at Missy. He was staring at something in her hand. Missy followed his gaze. Where once she had held the Quillblade she was now gripping a bolt of lightning. It crackled like strands of blue fire. Missy looked from it to her brother. Panic assailed her.

What was she doing?

What had she been doing?

It vanished. But the terror returned, sharper than before, cutting through the feelings of triumph, through the strength, through the shield the Quillblade had formed inside her. It pierced deep inside her, and this time when she looked down at the lightning bolt in her fist she felt revulsion. What was it doing to her? What was it making her into? She had to get rid of it, had to get away from it. She had to get *it* away from *her*.

Missy tried to throw the Quillblade away, but it was stuck fast to her hand. Then Lenis was there, and he was pulling at it, gripping the writhing lightning bolt in his bare hands.

'No, little brother,' Missy whispered as she felt something tearing in her palm. The light died. The world went dark. She heard the metallic clang of the Quillblade hitting the wood of the deck. Then she felt everything. All of the fear and anxiety and unease the Quillblade had taken from her came rushing back. Bile rose in the back of her throat. Missy vomited. Her stomach muscles clenched and unclenched and clenched again. Every muscle burned. She became aware she was crying even as her guts heaved.

And through it all her brother held her. She threw up all over him, but he didn't let her go. Vaguely, as if from a great distance, she heard others speaking. There were pinpricks of light in the darkness. They stung her eyes and added to her nausea.

So this is what remains of Adad's power? a voice whispered inside her mind. *Oh, my compassionate one, they should never have been allowed to use you so. Do you not see? You and your brother will never know peace until they are gone.*

It wasn't that Ishullanu had so easily reached into her mind that so unnerved Missy. He was a Caelestia, one of the most powerful beings in the world. She already knew he was a dangerous enemy. What scared Missy the most was knowing that, for the briefest of moments, she had believed his words.

● THE MAROONING OF ANDREA FLORONA ●

Lenis looked down on his sister, numbed by exhaustion. It had taken every ounce of his strength to awaken her fear of the Quillblade and use it to pierce through the barrier the *shintai* had formed around her heart. Even then, the weapon had not wanted to give up its grip on Missy. Lenis's bandaged hands were evidence of that. He was developing an unhealthy talent for damaging his hands. Not a good trait in an engineer.

Missy was worse off. She had passed out in his arms and slept through the night in the doctor's cabin. This, too, was becoming an unhealthy pattern – Lenis watching over Missy's comatose body. The energies of the Quillblade had torn through her system, stripping away her muscles and flesh. She looked haggard. The skin sagged on her frame and there were dark circles under her eyes. There was no telling what harm had been down to her psyche. Lenis shook his head. He'd *told* her the Quillblade was dangerous. Why hadn't she *listened* to him?

Suiteki was a quivering ball inside his robe, pressed up against his skin. The baby dragon hadn't been present up on the deck, but she was so in tune with Lenis's emotions that she couldn't help but feel what had happened with him and his sister and the Quillblade. He reached inside his robe and placed a hand over her. Suiteki gave a little squawk. It was the sort of noise a Bestia might make if you left it out in the rain to get all sodden and miserable. From somewhere deep inside, he found a pool of reassurance and cupped it in his hand, around the little dragon. Eventually, she relaxed. Her breathing slowed; her shuddering stilled. Finally she slept and dreamt tranquil dragon dreams, and it was his turn to draw peace from her.

Lenis heard someone yelling in Heiliglander in the galley behind him, and on reflex built a bastion of calm around the dragon dozing in his robe, nestled against his heart. He thought he recognised the voice. Turning away from his sister, he looked down on Kanu, who was crouched by the doorway. Lenis had seen him grovelling in front of Missy the night before, but the sight of her vomiting and damaged in the aftermath of her arrival had shaken the boy deeply. Lenis felt sorry for him. Destined to serve Mashu, the Titan had woken to a very different fate. Fate. Lenis almost laughed at the word.

'Look after her while I'm gone,' he said.

Kanu bobbed his head, imitating a Shinzōn bow. 'Yes, Mashu.'

Lenis drew his hand out of his robe and stepped out into the hall, closing the door firmly behind him. 'What's going on?' he asked in a hushed tone. As he'd suspected, Heidi was the one making all the noise. The Heiliglander was glaring at the *Hiryū*'s lookout, fists clenched at her sides, jaw set, face crimson.

'She says she needs to speak with your sister,' Andrea told him, pushing back her wild hair. 'Something's come up.'

'Well, obviously she can't speak to Missy right now. What's the problem?'

'The duke wants to send an escort with us.'

Heidi snapped something in her native language, and Andrea fired back a reply.

'You can speak Heiliglander?' Lenis asked.

The Ellian lookout shrugged. 'A bit. It was a Heiliglander airship that dumped me in Shinzō. Look, what do you want me to tell her?' She jutted her chin in Heidi's direction.

Lenis sighed. 'What does the captain say?'

'An escort could prove useful, Mister Clemens,' the captain replied from under the mast-shaft. He was just making his way into the mess hall, drawn, no doubt, by Heidi's ruckus. 'It will give us a numerical advantage if we run into Karasu.'

Lenis nodded. 'So what's the issue?'

'It may be difficult for Missy to keep up her charade as Magni in front of the crew of these other vessels, given her condition.'

Heidi was glaring from one of them to the next. She said something in Heiliglander that sounded more like a command than a question. Andrea ignored her.

'She's supposed to be Magni's herald,' Lenis said. 'Why doesn't she just tell everyone the goddess wants some privacy?'

Andrea shrugged again and spoke to Heidi. The girl didn't look pleased, but she nodded and strode out of the galley.

'That one is going to be trouble,' Lenis muttered. The captain chuckled and Lenis blushed. He hadn't really meant to say that aloud.

'We'd better go and keep an eye on her,' Andrea said and followed the Heiliglander up on deck, the captain close behind.

Gently, Lenis extricated Suiteki from her cave inside his robe and placed her in her nest by the stove. She twitched in her sleep and made a little noise that was more like one of Aeris's mews than her usual caws. Then she wrapped herself into a tight ball and settled back to sleep.

Lenis hurried above decks. When he reached the open air he made his way to the railing between Andrea and Captain Shishi. Heidi was speaking with Duke Freyrsson on the airdock. Lenis couldn't hear what she was saying from here and couldn't understand it even if he could, but she was gesticulating wildly.

'She's really taking this whole herald thing seriously, isn't she?' Lenis asked without taking his eyes off her performance. A couple of people had appeared on the airdock. One was a woman who looked to be in her fifties with steel-grey hair and a deeply lined face. The other was a boy Lenis's age. He had blond hair and looked vaguely familiar.

The captain answered Lenis's question, 'I am sure her motives are pure, Mister Clemens. The Demon threat is –'

'Demon's wings!' Andrea hissed and leapt over the railing onto the airdock.

'What's that all about?' Lenis asked as he followed the captain to the gangplank.

Andrea strode across the airdock, passed a startled Heidi and the duke, and went right up to the couple that had just arrived. Without any warning Andrea pulled back her arm and slapped the boy squarely across the face. Lenis heard the smack clearly across the airdock. The boy's head snapped back. He reached up to rub his cheek but made no move to defend himself or retaliate.

'Hey, sis,' the boy mumbled around his swollen cheek.

Andrea slapped him again. '"Hey, sis"? Is that all you have to say to me?'

'Well, nah,' the boy retorted, 'if you gimme a minute without smacking me.' Andrea raised her hand again. The boy shied away, but the *Hiryū*'s lookout restrained herself. 'Uh, how you doin'?'

'Angelus Draconus Florona, you miserable son of a –' She reverted to her native Ellian tongue, and Lenis was sort of glad he didn't understand the string of invectives she hurled at the boy.

'Calm down, Andrea,' the woman with the grey hair said. 'It's not *his* fault you missed the airship.'

'Ursula,' Andrea almost spat the name. 'What are *you* doing here?'

The woman shrugged. 'The usual.'

The captain cleared his throat quietly. 'Do you all know each other?'

'Captain Mayonaka Shishi,' Andrea said, 'may I present Ursula Klinge, captain of the *Geschichte*. And this Demon spawn is my brother, Angelus.'

That explained why the boy looked so familiar. He was even dressed like his sister, in a loose-fitting white top and brown pants. He wore an oversized coat open over his clothes and had the sleeves bunched up by the elbows, making him seem shorter and younger than he actually was. Lenis looked from the boy to Andrea and back again.

'Hey,' Angelus said when he caught Lenis staring.

'Oh, hey,' Lenis replied.

The boy pointed behind Lenis. 'You the cabin boy on that airship?'

Lenis glanced over his shoulder at the *Hiryū*. 'Um, no. I'm the engineer.'

Angelus whistled through his teeth. 'Wow. Epic. You must be, like, a genius or something.'

Lenis blushed and looked down at his boots.

'The *Geschichte*?' the captain asked. 'Was that not the airship you came to Shinzō on?'

'It was, Captain,' Andrea replied. 'They abandoned me in Yukitoshi.'

'We had to leave early to miss an incoming storm front,' Ursula interjected.

'Funny. Usually the cabin boy is sent out to round up the crew when that happens.' Andrea looked pointedly at her brother, who flinched again.

'Give the boy a break, Andy,' Ursula said. 'It's not his fault he couldn't find you in time.'

'Don't call me that, *Lucy*.' Andrea crossed her arms over her chest.

Before they could get into a real fight, Heidi came over and started talking to them in Heiliglander. Soon Andrea, Ursula, Heidi and the duke were all in deep discussion. Captain Shishi and Lenis stood by helplessly. Neither could understand what was being said. Lenis was used to not knowing what was going on around him, but it must have been a new experience for the captain.

'They're talking about taking you to Kolga's temple,' Angelus said suddenly. 'That's what you wanna know, right? Neither of you can speak Heiliglander?'

The captain inclined his head.

The boy pushed his sleeves back up. 'My big sis made me learn when we left home. "We ain't never goin' back," she said, "so get used to it".'

'You're both from Ellia, right?' Lenis asked.

'Yeah, from up north near the Wastelands' border. Except the border's way further south since the Demons ran amok up there.'

'The Demons attacked your home?'

'Yeah.' Angelus kicked at the decking of the airdock with his giant boot. 'Wastelands got bigger. That's why me and Andy left. She said it was safer in the air. Not so many Demons.'

Lenis had heard this sort of story before. It seemed almost everyone in the western lands had lost someone to the Demons. Growing up in Pure Land, Demons had just been scary monsters in tales. They couldn't really hurt you. They weren't quite *real*. Over here it was different. You actually had to live with the Demons on your doorstep. There was no way of knowing when they would attack over the Wastelands' borders. There was no way to predict when the Wastelands themselves would expand into healthy land. And now Ishullanu was bringing the Demons together. All of them. Lenis wondered how even Pure Land could remain safe when faced with such a threat.

'It'll be okay,' Angelus interrupted Lenis's thoughts. 'Andy can get real mad, but she'll settle down. It's good to see her, you know?'

Lenis did know. He didn't understand what was happening between him and his sister, but the idea that they could be separated was too much to bear. It had been a constant threat when they were slaves. The fear of it clung to Lenis still, even now that they were free.

'So you really just left your sister in Yukitoshi?' Lenis asked.

Angelus glanced backwards and forwards and lowered his voice. 'Sort of. You see, Charlie, he's our engineer, he and Andy had a bit of a thing goin' on and then he finds out that she –' Andrea snapped something at him in Ellian and Angelus grinned. 'Well, let's just say it wasn't exactly an accident.' Lenis found himself smiling back. 'So, you got Bestia and stuff?'

The abrupt change in direction caught Lenis by surprise. 'Um, yes. On the *Hiryū*.'

'Can I see 'em?'

Lenis looked to Captain Shishi. 'Captain?'

'Of course. Just be sure to leave Magni to her rest. The goddess does not like to be disturbed.'

'Yes, sir.' Lenis had almost forgotten they were supposed to be carrying the Heiliglander lightning god. Still, as long as he and Angelus stayed near the engine room there was no danger of him stumbling across Missy in the doctor's cabin, or of him waking up Suiteki.

'Epic.' Angelus had a large smile on his face. 'Charlie almost never lets me play with our Bestia. How many you got? We only got two, but the *Geschichte*'s only half that big. Are they real powerful? I bet they'd have to be to lift that thing off the ground. I once saw an airbarge lift off and it had, like, fifty Bestia powerin' it. I swear! You can call me Drake, by the way. Short for Draconus. That's my middle name. Only Andy calls me Angelus. I don't like it. It's, like, too formal, or something.'

'I'm Lenis.'

'Come on, Len.' Drake grabbed Lenis's hand and all but dragged him towards the *Hiryū*. Andrea shouted something after them in another language, but if Drake heard her, he gave no sign.

'You must really like Bestia to be an engineer,' Drake went on, seemingly inexhaustible. 'I love 'em! Charlie says I might be an engineer one day, but he says I'm too young. I bet once he sees you, he won't say that no more. Wait till you meet him. He's a bit stiff, but he's orright. Gustav's the one you gotta watch out for. Cook and doctor. What's with that? Don't know if he's carving you up for dinner or stitching up your insides.'

The boy kept up his monologue all the way to the engine room. He never seemed to run out of breath, and he never paused long enough for Lenis to answer any of his questions. And he asked a *lot* of questions. In spite of himself, Lenis found Drake's enthusiasm infectious.

So did the Bestia. As soon as Drake spotted them he dropped Lenis's hand and raced to their hutch. Ignis jumped up into his arms and began licking his face.

'Careful,' Lenis cautioned. 'He's a flame Bestia.'

'Aw, it's orright,' Drake laughed, as he held the squirming creature at arms length. 'I'm used to it. Blitzer's a flamie too.

We're good pals. And who's this?' He put a disappointed Ignis down and ran a hand down Atrum's back, all the way down the length of his tail. The boy whistled. 'That's some tail!'

Lenis found himself grinning. 'That's Atrum, and that's Aqua. She doesn't really like –'

Too late. Drake had already picked her up and swung her into his arms. He was rewarded with a nip on the chin. Drake squealed and let her jump down. The water Bestia stalked off back to the hutch and leapt silkily over its edge.

Drake whistled again. 'She's feisty! Who's this one?'

For a time, Lenis allowed Drake's good-natured affection for the Bestia to flow around him. He forgot about his sister and their mission. When Ignis and Lucis both nipped Drake's ankles and sped off down the corridor, Lenis followed the boy as he chased them through the airship.

'What's this?' Hiroshi demanded when they broke into the galley. Ignis ran along the top of his stove, and Lucis jumped onto one of the tables. The boys leapt after them, and Lenis knocked over a rack of Hiroshi's utensils. Suiteki awoke with a pitiful cry but soon sensed there was no danger about. She started out of her nest, half-wanting to be part of the game, but then decided she'd rather be warm and re-curled herself up to sleep. 'Get out of here, you little rapscallions. I'll have both your hides, I tell you!'

Hiroshi brandished a ladle at them, but despite the cook's grim expression Lenis could sense that he was amused. Suiteki peeked out from between her coils, snorted, and closed her eyes again. The Bestia and the two boys chased one another up the stairs and out onto the deck. As they emerged into daylight Shujinko appeared before them. Ignis leapt over his head and Lucis dashed between his legs. Lenis was laughing so hard he couldn't stop himself in time and nearly crashed into the cabin boy. He would have if Shujinko hadn't shifted his own weight and thrown Lenis over his shoulder to land heavily on his back on the deck. The pain in his ribs came back in force.

Lenis heard a high-pitched whistle.

'What did you do that for?' Drake demanded.

'Who are you?' Shujinko countered. Lenis propped himself up on his elbows and saw the *Hiryū*'s cabin boy was in a fighting stance.

'Shujinko, it's all right,' Lenis began. 'This is –'

Drake cut him off. 'Drake Florona's my name. What's your problem?'

'Florona?' Shujinko turned his head slightly so that he could see Lenis. 'A relative of Miss Florona?'

'That's my big sis,' Drake went on. 'Why did you have to knock Len over like that for?'

'Len?'

'If you want trouble, fella, you found it.' Drake raised his hands and coiled them into fists.

Shujinko regarded him for a moment and then said to Lenis, 'You and your bodyguard should stop playing around.' He relaxed his stance. 'We're scheduled for departure in fifteen minutes.'

'*Dorns!*' Drake snapped. 'I'd better go. Lucy'd leave me behind in a wink. Later, Len!'

The boy ran over to and down the gangplank before disappearing from view. Lenis got to his feet. 'Nice throw.'

'You should have dodged it.' Shujinko moved below decks.

Lenis turned to make his way to the rear hatch. Why did Shujinko have to take the fun out of *everything*?

⚙ DETERMINATION ⚙

Missy came awake slowly. Her eyelids were sticky, and it took her a moment to pry them open. She felt . . . something. It took her a moment to realise it was pain. For some reason it felt very far away. She tried to swallow but her throat was raw. Her whole body ached, and she was so tired she closed her eyes and tried to go back to sleep. She couldn't. The nagging sensation of soreness became more insistent. It seemed to draw closer.

Not now, she thought, but her body gave her no respite. A moment later it was wracked by a spasm of agony. She cried out and began to struggle feebly.

'Tcha.'

Something cool was pressed to her lips. The doctor held a wet rag to her mouth. Long Liu squeezed, and a tiny trickle of liquid seeped out of it. It wasn't enough to drink, just enough to moisten her tongue. She lapped feebly at the rag. Long Liu took it away and brought it back. There was more moisture in it this time, and Missy sucked at it greedily.

'Slowly now,' the doctor soothed. With his free hand he brushed the hair back from her face. 'Slowly.'

Finally, Missy tugged her mouth away from the offered water. 'What happened?' she tried to ask. It sounded more like a croak, but the doctor seemed to hear her.

'Magic. Or as close to it as we're ever likely to see. The energy of the Quillblade.'

Missy shuddered as last night's events came back to her. Last night? How long had she been asleep? She tried to ask Long Liu but he shushed her.

'Sleep now.'

Missy tried to keep her eyelids open but they were growing heavier. Reluctantly, she allowed the rocking of the airship to lull her back to sleep. She had just enough time to realise they were flying again before her dreams claimed her.

'Mister Clemens, you are needed on the bridge.'

Lenis heard the captain's command echo through the speech tube and jumped to obey. They had left Erdasche in the middle of the morning, and it was now almost evening. Suiteki had made the move from the galley to the Bestia hutch, but had otherwise spent the entire day sleeping. This wasn't all that unusual, but Lenis was aware that the more she slept during the day, the more likely it was that she was going to wake him up that night.

As Lenis came out on deck he could see the southern coast of Heiligland approaching fast. He had been here before, during their flight to and from Asheim. The lights of a familiar airdock winked on the horizon.

Lenis turned from the sight to climb the steps to the bridge. The captain was standing with Tenjin near Kenji's chart-filled table. All three men looked as though they were in deep discussion, but they were speaking in Shinzōn and Lenis couldn't understand them. Shin was at the tiller, but Arthur was nowhere in sight. That was unusual. He was normally always on the bridge while the *Hiryū* was underway.

'Ah, Mister Clemens.' The captain looked up and beckoned him over. 'I am glad you are here. Your sister is still indisposed and we will need you and Lucis to help coordinate our docking procedure.'

Of course. Without their communications officer, the *Hiryū* would have a hard time finding a berth. Lenis could transmit messages using flashes of light from Lucis. It was a cumbersome way of communication, but it was the only option they had at the moment and it had sufficed the last time Missy had lain comatose in the doctor's cabin.

'Are you discussing our course?' Lenis asked, nodding towards the map table.

'Indeed. We are almost directly south of our destination. Come and see.' The captain motioned Lenis over to the table. On top of it was a map of Heiligland, weighted down in one corner by Kenji's pistol and at two others with metal rulers.

The fourth corner was pinned down by a half-filled mug of tea. 'As you can see, Kolga's temple is only a short flight north.'

Lenis scanned the map. He found Erdasche easily and tracked their course north with his eyes. They were headed to an airdock directly across the straight. Above that was a line of mountains, and beyond these, circled in red, was a small X. Lenis should have guessed. It was in the middle of the Wastelands. They'd have to fly over the infested mountains to reach it. Lenis did a few calculations. The flight wasn't impossible, but it would put a strain on Aeris unless they landed during their flight. He was just wondering if he should use the dual-Bestia system to get them over the tainted ground faster, when the captain tapped a spot far to the west of Kolga's temple.

'You see here?' the captain asked. 'This entire stretch of land is healthy ground. It is almost entirely encircled by the Wastelands, but the Heiliglanders have a settlement here.' He then tapped a spot on the western edge of the clearing. 'We could land here and take the landcraft along this terrain, though it is rather mountainous and may prove difficult. If we follow this river here, it will lead us directly to Kolga's temple.'

'How bad is the terrain?' Lenis asked. He couldn't make out what the markings on the map meant.

'It's bad,' Kenji told him. 'Almost impossible for a landcraft to get through, I'd say.'

'So, what do we do?' Lenis asked.

Kenji looked at the captain, who nodded. 'There's a small settlement to the southwest of the temple. It's not on the map, but it's free of the Wasteland taint.'

'How is that possible?' Lenis wondered. The map showed only Wastelands in the area Kenji indicated.

'We do not know,' Tenjin answered. 'I have never heard of such a thing before. Mister Jackson assures us it is uncorrupted, however.'

'Trust me,' the navigator said. 'It's clean. I've been there before.'

'What sort of place is it?' Lenis asked.

Kenji glanced at the captain and then focused his attention back on the map. 'It's a safe haven. Of sorts.'

'What does that mean?'

'It means we can land there and take the landcraft to the temple.' Kenji hadn't avoided Lenis's question, but he sensed the navigator was holding something back. He remembered how Kenji had found them in the streets outside of Asheim's prison, and how he had facilitated their escape from the city. The navigator had already demonstrated he could be quite resourceful when he needed to be.

The captain didn't seem to notice Kenji's hedging. 'It is not uncommon for places to be left off a map.' Before Lenis could figure out what sorts of places might be ignored by cartographers, the captain added, 'This is especially the case when the people in those places wish to remain undiscovered.'

Kenji coughed and hastily took a swig from his teacup, causing that corner of the map to roll up.

'What about our escort?' Lenis pointed out of the bridge's crystal dome at the *Geschichte* trailing along in their wake.

Kenji laughed. 'Oh, something tells me Captain Klinge is fully aware of this particular settlement.'

More puzzled than ever, Lenis opened his mouth to ask what the navigator meant, but realised how close they were getting to the Heiliglander airdock. 'I'd better go and get Lucis.'

'You do that,' Kenji told him, smoothing the corner of his map back down.

○

The airship bumped into something and woke Missy up. Her head was spinning a little, but the pain was all gone. She reached up to rub at her eyes and caught sight of her hand. There was a nasty gash through her right palm. It was scabbed over, but the skin around it was tight when she flexed it. The Quillblade. It had somehow turned into a lightning bolt in her hand and –

The Quillblade! Where was it? She patted herself down but didn't find it. She was wearing only the thin dress Heidi had given her. She panicked. What had she done with it? Lenis had pulled it out of her hand and thrown it . . . where? Not over the side! She swung her legs over the edge of the bunk. Her limbs moved slowly, but there was no real pain. Just a slight soreness deep under her skin.

'Extraordinary.'

Missy glanced over at the doctor. He was sitting on the edge of his own bunk, looking at her.

'Have you seen the Quillblade?' Missy asked. She had to find it! The last time she had lost it, Lenis had taken it from her. Did he have it now?

Long Liu ignored her. 'How do you feel?'

'Fine, I guess.' Missy wasn't interested in the doctor's questions. How could she have lost the *shintai*?

'Hmm . . .' The doctor stood up and came over to poke her in the leg.

'Hey!'

'No pain? Any tenderness?'

'A bit. Look, I'm sorry, but have you seen the Quillblade?'

Long Liu poked her in the shoulder, and then in the forearm near her damaged hand. 'The boy has it. And you really feel all right?'

'Yes! Can I go now?'

'I suppose so,' the doctor said. 'What an extraordinary thing.'

Missy groaned. What was the crazy old man going on about now? 'What is it?'

'The water the captain brought back from Neti's temple, where they found the Bestia. Do you remember?'

'Of course.' Missy's spirit-self had followed along behind her brother and the small party that had ventured into the

Wastelands on the southern coast of Heiligland. The Bestia had run off and the crew found them in an old temple. Missy hadn't gone inside with them, but Lenis had told her about how there was a pool of water that had healed them all, and about Silili the Totem. She hadn't given it much thought after that. Both she and her brother had decided it had been the Totem who had healed Lenis and the Bestia, not the water. 'Are you saying the water cured me?'

'It would appear so,' the doctor told her. 'Extraordinary.'

'Why do you keep saying that? It healed Lenis and the Bestia, right?'

'But it is just water,' Long Liu said. 'I have tested the sample Captain Shishi brought back. I've tried it on burns and cuts and bruises. Nothing. It's just water.'

'But it healed me?'

'Just so. Quite extraordinary.'

'Look, I really need to find the Quillblade. Can I go?'

'Of course. Extraordinary. Extra. Ordinary. Extra. Extra. Extra. Ord. *Inary*. Or. *Dinary*. Ordi. *Nary*.'

Missy remained silent as she opened the doctor's door to leave. Sometimes he was so coherent he seemed almost normal, but his madness was always lurking just beneath the surface. For the first time Missy wondered what had made him like that. She had heard that Long Liu had trekked across the Wastelands dividing Tien Ti and Shinzō all by himself. Perhaps what had happened to him during that time had affected his mind.

Missy pushed all thoughts of the doctor's past aside and stepped out into the galley. She had to make sure the *shintai* was safe. Long Liu had said 'the boy' had it. That meant Lenis or Shujinko. Or Kanu. It was easy to forget Kanu was there. He was usually around but didn't do much to draw attention to himself.

'You are well?'

'Argh!' Missy clutched a hand to her chest as Kanu came up from behind her. He must have been crouched down beside the doctor's door; Missy hadn't even seen him. 'Kanu, yes, I'm all right.'

'Good.'

Missy tried to steady the fluttering of her heart. 'Were you waiting for me?'

'Yes.'

Missy nodded. The boy definitely had a way of blending into the background. 'Um, have you seen the Quillblade?'

She might just have offered him a treat. Kanu's eyes went wide and his lips curled up into what would have looked like a grimace on someone else's face. He kept bobbing his head as he reached inside his robe. One of Lenis's old ones, Missy noted.

Just as he began to pull his arm out, though, Missy shook her head and placed a hand on his shoulder. 'Wait.'

Suddenly Missy didn't want to touch the Quillblade again, not since its power had torn through her. There was no way to know how much damage would have been done, *had* been done and healed by Silili's water. The *shintai*'s powers were too potent for her. That much was now obvious. Tenjin had his big book of spells that somehow drew on Raikō's power, but Missy had never quite got around to asking him to teach her how he did it. Now she wondered why she hadn't.

Something had always come up, she supposed. First there was Fronge, then the whole thing with Lenis and Kanu, and then Heidi and her whole Magni scheme. Was that it, or on some level did Missy not want to learn? Her brother had warned her about the Quillblade. The first time she had used it, Raikō had stolen her soul. Then there was the square back in Fronge, where she'd used her powers to control everyone, even if only for a moment. And then there was Erdasche. She'd been out of control, she knew that now, and the Quillblade had lashed out at her because of it. Why risk that again? Who knew what would happen the next time she tried to wield the Quillblade?

But what choice did she have? They had so few weapons to use in the coming war with Ishullanu. Even if Suiteki gained her full powers she would still be just one Totem. Their hopes rested on her succeeding where other Totem had failed. They couldn't afford to discard what could prove valuable in the coming conflict. It might be the only thing standing between them and the Demons. But what use was the *shintai* if Missy couldn't even handle it properly? What if it killed her next time? What if she killed someone else?

No. She wouldn't use the Quillblade again. Not yet. Not until she learned how to do so safely. She needed to speak with Tenjin. It was time to start her training. The next time she picked up the Quillblade, she would know how to use it.

'Kanu, can you do something for me?' Missy asked. 'Can you, *will* you hold onto the Quillblade and keep it safe?'

The smile shrank on Kanu's face until his lips were pressed into a thin line. He cradled both arms across his chest as though to shield the *shintai* within his robe. Then he bowed low to her in the Shinzōn fashion.

'I will do so, Mashu,' he said, still doubled over.

'Thanks. Um . . . thank you.'

Kanu straightened. 'Thank you, Mashu.'

He looked so solemn, so earnest, that Missy just couldn't stand looking at him. She had only meant it as a request, as a favour of sorts, and Kanu had turned it into a decree from Mashu and *thanked* her for it.

Missy turned her face away from the Titan child. 'Look, I need to talk to Shujinko for a moment. Alone.'

Kanu nodded, only it appeared more like another bow out of the corner of Missy's eye, and backed away from her. Missy bit her lip and walked out of the galley. She didn't really need to speak to Shujinko now that she knew Kanu had the Quillblade, but his was the first name that came to her. She wanted to be away from Kanu for a while.

Just as she was wondering if maybe she would like to speak to Shujinko after all, she knocked heads with him while ducking under the mast-shaft. They both recoiled and swore, the cabin boy in Shinzōn and Missy in Heiliglander, of all languages.

'My apologies,' Shujinko said in the common tongue, stepping clear to allow Missy to pass under first. He always spoke so formally, as if he'd learned the common tongue from a textbook rather than a fluent teacher, but sometimes he rounded off his words like a native, which made Missy think he was only trying to sound formal. 'Are you hurt?'

'Oh, I'm fine,' Missy said, a little more flippantly than she'd intended. 'How are you?'

'I am also fine,' he replied. 'Shinzōn men have hard heads.'

Missy giggled. She *actually* giggled and then covered her mouth with her hands to stop herself. Shujinko looked offended. The corners of his mouth twitched down, and his eyes narrowed fractionally.

'I wasn't . . . I mean, I didn't . . .' Missy floundered as the blood rushed to her cheeks. 'I thought you were joking,' she blurted.

Shujinko seemed to consider this for a moment. 'I was not.'

'Oh, sorry.' Missy found herself staring at his chin to avoid looking into his eyes. 'So . . . um . . . you're from Nochi?'

Shujinko nodded once. 'Excuse me. I must report to Mister Hiroshi.'

'Oh, of course,' Missy mumbled.

The cabin boy ducked under the mast-shaft. Missy hurried above decks, suddenly wanting to feel a nice cold breeze on her face.

◦ TENSIONS ◦

'How did *you* hear about Haven?' Ursula asked. She was sitting, with her feet up on the table, in the Heiliglander airdock officials' office. The Heiliglanders had reluctantly vacated it to give them all somewhere to meet. After Lenis and Lucis had guided the *Hiryū* into a berth, Arthur and Kenji had taken him along to discuss their next port of call with Captain Klinge.

Two men had entered with Ursula and now stood behind her. One was tall and thin with a long, pointed nose. He was dressed in a grey Kystian dress suit, complete with bow tie. He wore a crimson waistcoat beneath his coat, and his boots were so shiny Lenis could see his reflection in them. The other man was short and broad. He had a big bushy moustache and curly black hair. His brows were thick and his nose was wide. He was wearing black leather trousers, a tan-coloured shirt and the largest boots Lenis had ever seen.

'I get around,' Kenji drawled. Not to be outdone, the *Hiryū*'s navigator also had his feet on the table, and he was leaning back so that he was looking at the ceiling rather than at the captain of the *Geschichte*.

'It doesn't matter how we heard of it,' Arthur interjected. He was sitting next to the navigator with his elbows on the table and his hands clasped together. 'Haven will provide us with a safe berth for our airships while we visit Kolga's temple, yes?'

Ursula turned from Kenji to Arthur. 'I wouldn't call it *safe*, exactly. What has he told you about the place?'

'All I need to know.'

'Really?' Ursula tried to catch Kenji's eye, but the navigator was steadfastly ignoring her. 'You told him *everything* he needs to know?'

Kenji abruptly kicked his feet off the table, planted them firmly on the ground, and rose to his feet. 'Doesn't matter. That's where we're going. Just thought you should know.'

Ursula regarded Kenji coldly before addressing Arthur again. 'Haven is a place for fools and madmen. There is no authority there. None that you would understand. The strong take what they want from the weak. The smart take from the stupid. Your airship. Your boy.' She nodded her chin in Lenis's direction. 'Whatever they want. Honest people don't end up in Haven.'

If Arthur was surprised or concerned by her words, he betrayed no hint of it, even to Lenis's senses. 'We have Magni with us. What is there to fear?'

'Gustav,' Ursula said over her shoulder to the squat man. 'Show them.'

The man grinned wickedly and pulled up one of his trouser legs. Where his own leg should have been there was only a thick wooden club running down into his boot. 'Lost it in Haven, mates. Lost a good shoe with it, too.' The man's grin widened, and Lenis saw he was missing a few teeth. The ones he had left were crooked and yellow. 'Ain't no place for noble folk such as your good selves. Goddess or no goddess. The folk in Haven ain't the pious type.'

'Put it away, von Zauberei,' the tall man said. 'I think they understand well enough without your crudeness.'

The short man laughed and let his trouser leg drop back down. Lenis swallowed. He'd seen people being maimed before in the slave pens, but he never got used to it.

'*Von* Zauberei?' Arthur asked with genuine curiosity. 'You're a noble?'

'At yer service, guvnor,' Gustav said and tugged a forelock of his hair.

'You seem surprised, Lord Knyght,' the tall man interjected. 'I would have thought that you of all people would be able to sympathise with poor Gustav here. After all, the higher a person rises, the farther they have to fall.'

Arthur's shoulders tensed. He unclasped his hands and laid them flat on the table. Very deliberately he pushed himself up and faced the tall man squarely. 'I don't believe I know you.'

'Charles Mild, at your service.' The tall man bowed stiffly from the waist. 'A fellow Kystian adrift on the currents of fate.'

Arthur scrutinised the man up and down as if committing every detail of him to memory. Lenis had seen that look on the first officer's face before. If it had ever been directed at him he would have cowered before it. Charles Mild faced it head on, a slight smile playing at the corners of his mouth.

'It's not my place to question the Lightning-Wielder,' Ursula interjected, 'but I can't understand why she wants us to change course, much less why she would want to go to Haven.'

'Who can understand the whims of a goddess?' Kenji drawled.

'You should show more respect for the divine,' Captain Klinge snapped. 'I'd feel more comfortable if Magni was aboard the *Geschichte* instead of riding with a bunch of heathens.'

'You have our destination,' Arthur said suddenly. He glanced at Ursula. 'Magni has made her decision. It is not open for debate. You may follow if you wish.'

Arthur turned and strode out of the room. Kenji followed, and Lenis was quick to fall in behind. The trio remained silent as they returned to the *Hiryū*. It wasn't until they were back on board and standing before the captain that Arthur spoke.

'She's suspicious.'

The captain sighed. 'It is to be expected, Lord Knyght. What need would Magni have to make such a detour? I fear our charade will not last much longer, even now that Miss Clemens is awake.'

'Missy's awake?' Lenis asked.

'She appears to have made a full recovery, Mister Clemens.'

Lenis nodded, relieved. 'What do you think Captain Klinge will do?'

The captain glanced over the railing in time to see Ursula, Gustav and Charles leave the airdock official's office. 'We cannot know. We must continue as we are for now.'

'Do you think Missy should speak to her as Magni?' Lenis's heart sank, even as he said the words. She had barely survived her last encounter with the Quillblade.

'I do not believe that will be necessary,' the captain said. 'Or wise. Miss Baumstochter was able to see through the deception easily enough. Given time, anyone would. It is better if your sister remains out of sight for the remainder of this voyage. Miss Clemens is with Lord Tenjin on the bridge, if you wish to check on her.'

'Oh, thanks.' Lenis was strangely reluctant to see his sister. He was glad she had recovered, but where once he would have rushed to her side, now something held him back. His own hands were still sore, though it was hard to say exactly what was wrong with them. They weren't burnt, or cut, or bruised, but the palms were red from where he had grabbed the Quillblade and the skin on them was still raw.

As the others went about their business, Lenis moved below decks. He would see his sister later, after she had spoken with Tenjin. He wasn't avoiding her. He just didn't want to interrupt whatever it was she was doing with the records keeper. He knew that was a lame excuse even as he thought it up.

◉

Missy saw her brother speak with the captain. She knew Captain Shishi would be telling him that she was all right. She knew that Lenis would come and see her, and she would apologise for being so stupid, and show him what Tenjin was teaching her. He would see that she wasn't going to even touch the Quillblade until she knew what she was doing with it. He would understand and everything would be all right again, like it was before they met Kanu.

Only Lenis didn't come up to the bridge to see her. He didn't even look in her direction as he went below decks. Missy frowned. He was being so childish! He could only avoid her for so long. They were on an airship! There weren't all that many places to hide.

'Is something the matter?' Tenjin asked gently, and Missy turned to look into his wrinkled face.

'No, Lord Tenjin, I'm sorry. What were you saying?'

The records keeper was pointing at something in one of his books. 'The Quillblade is still linked to Raikō, even though the Lord of Storms has turned into a Demon Lord. His power is still intact. It is still there for you to access, as you have seen, but you must prepare yourself for it.'

Missy nodded and tried to concentrate on what he was saying. Thoughts of her brother kept distracting her. What was his problem? He hadn't been acting like himself for quite some time. If he'd just stop being so silly about everything, they could sort out whatever was bothering him and move on. It wasn't like she was *entirely* to blame for everything that had happened. She had her own stuff to deal with when it came to the Quillblade, but she was doing something about that! He was just moping around like a . . . like a boy!

'. . . electrocute yourself.'

Missy startled. 'What, sorry?'

Tenjin smiled at her. 'It is a lot to take in, I know. These simple exercises will help prepare your body for the influx of Raikō's power. I will leave you to study them in your own time. Now, as for the . . . ah . . . *negative* effects of the Quillblade, that is much harder to control. You must learn to direct only a small amount into the *shintai* and learn how to draw out only what you need. We won't even begin talking about that until you've read through these.'

Tenjin reached under his desk and pulled out three large volumes. There was a blue one, a green one, and a red one. Each was as thick as her wrist.

'It'll take me forever to read all that!' Missy cried, and then hurried on, 'I mean, I've never learned how to read Shinzōn.'

'Truly?' Tenjin stroked his beard before placing his hands inside his sleeves. 'I had not considered that. Still, given your talents as a communicator, I am sure you will pick it up quickly.' He opened the green volume and pointed to the first symbol. 'This character represents *shi*.'

Missy groaned inwardly as she bent down to follow Tenjin's finger, which ran down the page, pointing out each squiggle as he explained its meaning. Learning to use the Quillblade was going to take more effort and a lot more time than she had thought.

◉

After Lenis checked on the Bestia and Suiteki, who was of course hungry but not quite starved enough to leave the pool of warmth shed by the Bestia, he sought out Yami and asked if they could continue his training. He tried to time it so that Shujinko would be busy helping Hiroshi in the kitchen, and in this he was successful. Yami agreed to his request and they spent the next couple of hours sparring together on the *Hiryū*'s forecastle. It was literally the furthest place away from Missy that Lenis could get on the *Hiryū*, but he tried not to think of it that way. Instead, he lost himself in the rhythms of striking and blocking, dodging and counterstriking. It wasn't a relaxing way to spend an evening, but he felt better for it.

'Might I suggest, Lenis,' Yami said after he had finished his last set of movements, 'that we take this opportunity to avail ourselves of the hospitality of our Heiliglander hosts?'

'Sorry?'

'You smell, and I would like a bath.'

Lenis wrinkled his nose and tried to remember the last time he had taken one. Surely it hadn't been as long ago as Nochi. Why was it he could remember the exact moment he had last washed the Bestia or cleaned out their hutch but couldn't quite seem to recall his last bath? When he caught a whiff of himself he supposed it had been at least as long ago as Nochi, and he *was* a little rank. 'Oh, okay.'

He followed as the Shinzōn swordsman walked down onto the airdock and asked after a bathhouse. They were told there weren't any public bathhouses in town, but there was an inn on the next street over where they could probably find some hot water.

Together they moved down the airdock and crossed the street. Lenis hoped Shujinko had washed out the crews' clothes. The last thing he wanted was to have to wear filthy robes once he got back to the *Hiryū*. When they reached the inn, Yami handed over a few coins, which bought them some clean towels and an escort from the landlord himself to the back room. There were three tubs inside. One was already occupied.

'Shujinko!' Lenis cried. 'What are you doing here?'

The cabin boy looked as if he was about to snap a reply, when he noticed Yami standing behind Lenis. 'Mister Hiroshi granted me an hour of shore leave.'

Lenis suppressed a sigh. The last thing he needed while he was trying to relax was Shujinko's animosity battering at his senses. He selected the tub furthest away from the cabin boy, turned his back, disrobed, and climbed quickly into the tub. The water was hotter than he had expected, and he had to stifle a shout, but once he settled in it felt good on his chilled skin. Lenis closed his eyes and dunked his head under before scrabbling furiously at his hair. It was so knotted he could barely untangle his fingers from it. He'd have to brush his hair out before he went to sleep.

Yami was standing next to his tub, pouring water over his head. For reasons Lenis could never quite understand, it was the custom in Shinzō to wash yourself *before* bathing. He thought it rather defeated the purpose. If you were already clean, why get in the tub at all?

Lenis grabbed a hank of soap and a rough brush and scrubbed himself until his skin was pink. The grind of the bristles felt incredibly good on his stiff muscles. When he was done he lay back and closed his eyes, trying his best to block out Shujinko's simmering resentment.

Shujinko, it seemed, wanted to talk. 'Did you train today?'

Lenis sighed. 'Yes. We just finished.'

The cabin boy grunted. 'Have you seen your sister since she woke?'

Lenis was all too conscious of Yami resting in the tub between them. 'Not yet.'

'You should. We are all worried for her.'

Lenis made no reply. Maybe if he remained perfectly still and silent, Shujinko would forget he was there. No such luck.

'How does Suiteki fare?'

'She's fine.' What did the boy want to know? She was a baby dragon. She ate and she slept. That was pretty much it.

'Is there any sign of her power emerging on its own?'

Lenis scowled and leant his face against the edge of the tub. 'No. Why would there be?'

'I do not know such things, but I thought *you* might. The captain told me you have a gift for drawing out a Bestia's power. If the Totem's power could be awakened naturally in the same way, we would not need the stones and there would be no reason for us to face Karasu.'

'She's not a Bestia,' Lenis snapped. 'Are you scared of Karasu or something?'

Shujinko didn't rise to the bait. 'Of course. He is one of Shinzō's most powerful swordsmen.'

'Humph.' Lenis reverted to his original tactic, and for a time it seemed to be working. Shujinko kept quiet and Lenis felt himself relaxing.

'What are you going to do about Kanu?'

Lenis suppressed a curse. Why couldn't Shujinko just be quiet? 'I don't know.'

'Will you release him from your service?'

Lenis sat up in the tub, sloshing water over the side. 'What are you talking about?'

Shujinko was regarding him levelly. His resemblance to Namei was even more pronounced with his hair wet around his face. They might have looked the same, but Shujinko was nothing like his cousin.

'Neither you nor your sister seem to know what to do with him,' the cabin boy said. 'It would be better to release him, I think.'

Lenis felt the blood rush to his face. 'Is that what you think?'

'Yes.'

'Well, it wouldn't do any good.'

'Why not?'

Lenis tried to decide how to phrase it. Shujinko could probably never understand how important the Titan boy's role as Mashu's servant was to him. Maybe no one could without Lenis's empathic gifts. Finally, he said, 'Because he wouldn't leave. He can't. And even if he could, where would he go? All of his family – all of his *people* – are long dead.'

'So he's your slave.'

The water in Lenis's tub suddenly felt icy. 'What did you say?'

'If you won't release him and he cannot leave, that makes the boy your slave.'

Lenis surged to his feet, unmindful of the fact he was stark naked. 'You don't know anything! Kanu isn't a slave. He's . . . well, he's not like you or me. He isn't *human*. He's something else. But he isn't a slave. You don't know anything about slavery, you spoilt little –'

'Lenis.'

Lenis had completely forgotten about Yami. 'Sir Yami, I –' As he turned to face the swordsman he slipped and fell backwards out of his tub, sending water flying across the room. His legs caught on the edge and he banged his head painfully against the wall behind him before sprawling on the floor.

'Are you all right, Lenis?' Yami called.

Lenis heard him rising out of his tub and groped desperately around for a towel. He was all too aware he was lying naked on the floor. His hand found his robe, which he wrapped awkwardly around his waist, then he scrambled to his feet. 'I'm fine.'

Yami was about to step out of his own tub. 'Are you sure?'

'Yes, I'm fine.' Lenis stalked out of the bathing room, his cheeks burning with embarrassment and anger, Shujinko's amusement washing through him.

● DEMONIC FURY ●

L enis felt the tension building within the *Hiryū* throughout the whole of the next day. It seemed to pack the close confines of the airship, pressing in on all sides of him. The Bestia were worried, but they kept their distance from him, choosing instead to remain in their hutch. Suiteki stayed with them, buried beneath a pile of their fur with only occasionally a blue scale peeking through. It was as if they could all sense that trouble was brewing, and the only thing the Bestia could think to do to help was somehow shield Suiteki from it.

It had begun to rain even before they left the airdock. The moisture in the air only increased the stifling atmosphere below decks. Lenis felt suffocated. The heat from the engines made the engine room humid.

They had passed into the Wastelands in the late afternoon. The *Hiryū* was high above the tainted ground, but even from this distance Lenis sensed the corruption of the Demons spreading out beneath them. He felt their now-familiar sorrow and the resonance of their rage lingering in the hollows of the lands where they dwelt, as though these were the only emotions left within the empty creatures. The same sensations had assaulted him back in Gesshoku, when he had seen his first Demon.

So many of them were gathered in the Wastelands below him now, and so close to the Heiliglander border, that Lenis couldn't help but wonder if this was a part of Ishullanu's army. Despite the fact that he had seen more of the Wastelands than was good for anyone, his experience with them was still limited. He didn't know what constituted normal Demonic activity, so he had no way of gauging if the Demon population here was denser than it should have been.

Lenis hadn't seen Shujinko or Yami since the incident in the inn's bathhouse. In fact, he hadn't seen anyone, which suited him just fine. He didn't want to have to deal with them. He'd made a fool of himself, and he knew it. The last thing he needed was to feel their mockery, or worse, their sympathy.

Suiteki had been spending more time in the Bestia hutch and less time in her nest by Hiroshi's stove, and a part of Lenis knew she was trying to stay close to him, to offer him whatever support she could give. Instinctively, she knew how much he needed her just then. They shared a bond, one that was somehow deeper than the one he had with the Bestia.

Lenis had held Suiteki when she hatched, at the moment of her mother's death. For weeks afterwards she had clung only to him. Lenis cared for all of his charges, but he knew the Bestia could survive without him if they ever needed to – they had proven that back when the *Hiryū* had washed up on the southern coast of Heiligland – but Suiteki needed him, *really* needed him, and that made all the difference.

But even his connection with Suiteki couldn't cheer him up. Lenis was tired. He had contusions all over his body. His muscles were sore. His ribs hadn't healed yet. His palms had started to itch from where he had grabbed the Quillblade. He was lonely. He didn't have anyone to talk to. He missed Namei now more than ever. He missed her laugh. He missed the way she tied her scarf.

Suddenly, Lenis wanted to be in the forecastle. Once the thought entered his mind, the urge grabbed hold of him and, almost before he knew what he was doing, he was racing up the stairs and across the deck. Namei. She was gone. She had been gone for months now, he realised. But there was something of her left behind. There was a stain in the wood right where Namei had been killed. Her blood had seeped into the decking, and no one had tried to remove it, even when the *Hiryū* had undergone repairs in Nochi. Once, just after Suiteki had been born, Lenis had gone to the forecastle and felt . . . *something*. A connection. A bond between himself and the rest of the crew. He desperately wanted to rekindle that bond, to feel a part of the *Hiryū* again.

The rain beat down on his face. It was harder than he had thought it would be. Almost torrential. He slipped as he climbed the stairs up to the forecastle and grabbed the railing to steady himself. This section, he remembered, had been replaced, but there was still a part of his friend up above, behind the dragon figurehead. He stopped when he saw the discoloured wood. This was where Namei had died. This was the last piece of her. Lenis groped after some sense of connection. He opened himself as wide as he could, using his unique gifts to pick up on something, on anything.

A great sob wracked his whole body. Nothing. There was nothing here. Just the simmering tension that had so suffocated him in the engine room. If anything, it was worse here. Here where he should have been at least partially free of it. Below him, the cook was scolding Shujinko for something. On the bridge, Shin and Kenji were sniping at one another. Even his sister was out of sorts, barely holding in her frustration with Tenjin as the old man tried to teach her something. Lenis had sensed such things before. The crew had spent too long confined on the airship together. The stress was getting to all of them. Petty grievances and small annoyances were festering, feeding upon themselves, growing out of all proportion until something caused them to snap.

Lenis was too sensitive to such things. The emotions of everyone pushed in on him, *infected* him, until they became his own. He felt a headache brewing at the front of his skull. He had to get away from it all. He had to be alone, *truly* alone, but there was nowhere for him to go. Nowhere he could escape it.

It was almost a relief when he saw the Demon. All of his attention focused on it. The maelstrom of the crew's emotions was forgotten. There was only the swiftly growing shadow on the horizon, silhouetted against the thin strip of light visible between the clouds above and the mountains below. A flying Demon. From what Lenis had seen and heard they were rare. Perhaps most winged Demons simply lacked the faculties to fly any more.

As the creature approached, Lenis saw that it was indeed a giant bird. His thoughts turned instantly to Raikō, Lord of Storms. That was one Demon Lord Lenis was keen on facing. All of his pent-up frustration bubbled to the surface now that it had a target. The Thunder Bird and his *shintai* had caused nothing but trouble, and if this weather was the Demon Lord's doing, well that was just one more reason to do something about it.

Dimly, through the roar of the downpour, he was aware of Andrea shouting a warning. He felt the others moving onto the deck. The Demon Lord grew closer. Lenis turned his attention inwards, focusing on the fury that was building inside him. He concentrated it, squeezing it down into a tight ball deep within him, his eyes following the Thunder Bird's approach. The ball of fury grew stronger, reinforced by Lenis's frustration. Sweat broke out on his forehead as he concentrated, waiting for the Demon Lord to move closer.

The others were approaching the forecastle. Perfect. He drew their simmering resentments into himself, adding them to his seething mass of hatred. Just a little longer. Just a little closer.

The Demon bird shrieked, but no lightning arced from its wingtips. Instead a great blast of wind swept across the deck of the *Hiryū*. Lenis staggered back into the railing. He couldn't see what had happened to the others. His vision had narrowed so much that he could only see the Demon Lord. But something wasn't right. It didn't look like Raikō at all. No matter. It was almost within range. Just a little more.

The Demon Lord stopped, hovering in the air just beyond the reach of Lenis's power. It opened its beak and shrieked again. Another blast of air. Lenis was already propped against the railing. He let it sweep over him. It stung his eyes and caused them to water, but he didn't blink. He might only get one chance. Deep inside him, the roiling emotions pushed against his control. What had once been a small ball was beginning to bulge in places as Lenis's control slipped.

'I am Etana, Lord of Fury!' the Demon Lord cried. Its voice pierced Lenis's eardrums like a sharp wind. 'I am the Warden of Retribution!'

Etana beat his wings and the air around him gathered together into a tempest that swept towards the airship. Lenis reacted on instinct. He drew the surging emotions up and out of himself and threw them at the Demon Lord. They passed through the onrushing hurricane and smashed into Etana. The Demon Lord screeched again, this time in fear, and plummeted out of the sky. Lenis's victory was short-lived. The mass of tempestuous wind the Lord of Fury had sent towards them struck. The crewmembers were swept up in it and tossed around the deck. Lenis gripped the railing as hard as he could, but he was thrown up and over it to hang suspended in the mighty winds above the deck. He felt as if his arms were being pulled out of their sockets, but he didn't dare loosen his grasp. Out of the corner of his eye he saw someone heaved into one of the holds, and someone else nearly went over the portside railing but managed to clutch it just in time. Below him he saw Missy and Shujinko huddled within the captain's outstretched arms in the lee of the forecastle, at least partially shielded from the Demon Lord's blast.

And then it stopped. Lenis fell heavily on top of the trio beneath him, his arms too weak to hold onto the railing any longer. For a moment he lay where he was, trying to get air into his lungs as the others scurried out from under him. The whirling winds had settled, but it was still raining heavily. When he could take long, steady breaths, Lenis hauled himself to his feet.

'Is everyone all right?' the captain shouted. He had climbed up to the forecastle.

'I'm fine!' Lenis heard Andrea call from up in the crow's nest. Ironically, even though she was the most exposed of them, she had been safely above the Demon Lord's attack.

'Me too,' Shin shouted from where she lay against one of the holds.

Lenis heard the others call out that they were okay, then looked up at the captain and nodded.

'What about the *Geschichte*?' Kenji asked. The navigator had been the one Lenis saw almost thrown over the side. His left hand was clamped over his right shoulder, which fell at a sharp angle that made Lenis think he'd dislocated it. Lenis had come close to that himself.

'No sign of her,' Andrea called out.

'And the Demon Lord?' the captain asked.

'No sign yet. Whatever Lenis hit him with got him good.'

The captain looked down at Lenis. 'Mister Clemens?'

Lenis took a shaky breath. 'I –'

'Spoke too soon!' Andrea shouted. 'He must be right below us, hiding himself beneath the airship. I just caught sight of a wingtip. He's rising fast!'

'Mister Clemens, can you get us away from here?' the captain asked.

Lenis nodded. 'Yes, sir. You all better hold onto something.'

'He's actually giving us warning this time!' Lenis heard Kenji shout, but he was already running across the deck. At the top of the stairs Lenis reached out and grabbed the railing before leaping the rest of the way down. He dashed into the engine room and scooped up Ignis as he passed the Bestia hutch. The rest of the Bestia crowded around Suiteki, pressing her down and back as she tried to wriggle out of their protective huddle. She kept crying out, but Lenis didn't have time to stop and comfort her.

He moved around to the other side of the engine block. 'Here we go again, boy!'

Ignis launched himself into the second compartment and was ready to go before Lenis closed the hatch. He rapped on the outside of it. 'Hold on, Ignis.' He forced himself to slow down and adjust the necessary levers, preparing the engines for the combined powers of Aeris and Ignis. Air and fire. He could feel Etana rising up beneath him and tried not to think that there was only the hull of the airship between him and the Demon Lord. Suiteki's panic pushed against Lenis, and as much as he wanted to ease her fear he had to focus first on getting the engine settings right.

When everything was ready, he pulled the second ignition lever and the *Hiryū* surged forwards. Lenis steadied himself just as another detonation of air shattered into the rear of the airship. At this point Etana's fury did more to speed them on their way than to slow them down. The Demon Lord's cries rang out behind them but faded as the *Hiryū* sped onwards, and Lenis was finally able to run to Suiteki, snatch her out of the Bestia hutch, and wrap her in the protective folds of his robe. He crouched down and wrapped his arms around himself and the baby Totem as Aqua, Atrum, Lucis, and Terra jumped out of their hutch to gather around them, mewing gently to reassure Suiteki that they were there, that she was safe.

Lenis could feel Suiteki's tiny heart fluttering through her ribs, right against his own. 'It's all right, baby girl, it's all right,' he kept repeating, as much to reassure himself as her or his Bestia.

○ THE WAY TO HAVEN ○

For half an hour, everyone was on high alert. Missy sat in her chair on the bridge and scanned the surrounding sky, but Etana's pursuit had fallen away behind them almost as soon as Lenis had engaged the dual-Bestia engines. The encounter with the Demon Lord had reminded them all of how dangerous the Wastelands could be, even if you were flying high above them. Even so, after a while the crew began to relax. Hands were taken off sword hilts. Eyes wandered from scanning their wake.

Kenji went to see the doctor. He hadn't said anything, but he'd clearly hurt his shoulder badly. Shortly after he left the bridge, Missy heard his cry reverberating up through the airship's hull. Then nothing.

'The doctor has most likely reset his shoulder,' Tenjin said into the silence.

A few minutes later, after Missy had reopened the book

she and Tenjin had been going through, Kenji reappeared, looking extremely pale.

'Should you not be resting?' the captain asked him.

Kenji shook his head – once – and then answered in a series of grunts. 'No time. Moving too fast. Need to find Haven.'

Shujinko stepped forward and helped Kenji over to his map table.

The captain turned to address Missy. 'Miss Clemens, have you been able to contact the *Geschichte*?'

She replied, 'No, Captain. It's as though they've disappeared.'

Or fallen out of the sky, Missy thought. It was what they were all thinking, but no one said anything and so neither did she. Missy wondered how Andrea was handling things. She'd only just been reunited with her brother, and now . . .

'They know where we are headed,' the captain said. 'Let us hope they meet us there.'

Missy nodded and returned to her studies. She had been completely helpless when Etana had attacked. Her first instinct had been to grab the Quillblade, and she was glad it hadn't been there for her to touch. She had vowed not to use it again until she could do so safely, and she was intent on sticking to her vow.

Her determination remained firm, even though it seemed to be taking forever for her to learn how to read Shinzōn. This was a new frustration for her. Missy usually picked up languages so swiftly, but she was finding reading was completely different from speaking or listening. She constantly had to ask Tenjin what certain symbols were, even ones he had already tried to teach her. It was a little easier if she thought in Shinzōn while she read, rather than trying to translate into the common tongue, but her progress was still painfully slow.

'What are you reading?' Shujinko's voice came from behind her shoulder.

Missy snapped the book shut, her cheeks warming. 'Nothing.' And then, because she realised there was no point lying to him, 'Just something Tenjin loaned me.'

'It must be important.'

Missy looked over her shoulder at the cabin boy. The very corners of his mouth were turned down, and his eyes had narrowed just like they had the last time they had spoken. Did he disapprove? It wasn't like she was wasting her time. She was studying!

'It's so I can learn how to use the Quillblade properly.' She heard the defensive note in her reply, looked back down at her desk, and began running a finger along the Shinzōn characters stamped into the cover of the book. Why should she even care what Shujinko thought about what she was doing, anyway?

'That is good,' the cabin boy replied. 'Your brother should follow your example.'

'What?' It came out even sharper than she'd intended.

Shujinko leaned past her to flick open the book's cover and whispered, 'Your brother claims he wants to be a warrior, but he makes any excuse to neglect his training.'

Missy slammed the book shut again, nearly catching Shujinko's fingers between the pages. The cabin boy snatched his hand back.

'Leave Lenis alone,' Missy whispered, self-consciously aware of how close their crewmates were. 'He's doing his best.'

Shujinko made a noise in the back of his throat. 'Now you are making excuses for him.'

Missy swivelled in her chair to glare at him. 'It isn't like that!' she hissed.

Shujinko remained silent for a moment. When he spoke it was to change the subject. 'Where are you from?'

Missy turned around and clasped her hands over the book on her desk. 'Pure Land.'

'I know that much already,' Shujinko pressed. 'Where in Pure Land?'

Missy wondered what difference it made to him. 'I . . . we don't know where we were born exactly, but we grew up in a place called Blue Lake.'

Shujinko was silent again, and then said, 'Ah, the Blue Lake iron refinery.'

How could he possibly know *that*? Missy turned around to ask him, but the cabin boy had already returned to Kenji's side. Shinzōn or not, he was one of the oddest boys Missy had ever met.

Lenis had switched off the dual-Bestia system as the sun set. He left Ignis powering the airship so Aeris could take a break. Their progress had slowed down as a result, but the avian Bestia had been working hard ever since they had left Nochi. It was good to lie down with her on his chest in the crisp evening air. They were on the forecastle, and though the rain had stopped, the sky was still heavily overcast. It blocked out any stars, leaving Lenis and Aeris alone in the dark. She was curled up on his chest, asleep, the steady rhythm of her breathing lulling Lenis towards calm. The chill, fresh air was soothing after the muggy heat of the engine room.

The battle with Etana was still fresh in Lenis's mind. Somehow, he had done it. He had driven the Demon Lord away. And he was able to do it without the use of a *shintai*. If he could only get strong enough, learn to master his powers, then they wouldn't need to rely on the Totem any more. His sister wouldn't need the Quillblade, and Suiteki wouldn't need the stones of ebb and flow.

They were close to their confrontation with Karasu now. The Shinzōn mercenary had had ample time to get ahead of them and reach Kolga's temple. Chances were he now had both stones. If only Lenis understood his empathy better, if only he was a great warrior like Captain Shishi or Yami.

Lenis drifted closer to sleep. His thoughts turned to Kanu. The boy in the ice. The Titan. Kanu was strong. He had shown that when he tried to defend Lenis back beneath Apsu's temple, and he had forced Lenis and his sister to merge. A shiver ran through Lenis, causing Aeris to stir. He reached up to pat her back in long, soft strokes until she settled.

Lenis tried to think of something else, but he knew it was no use. He was going to have to face this once and for all. He and his sister were one. He shivered again. They had come together so effortlessly, so *naturally*, blending their minds into a single entity, but afterwards . . . it had felt so *wrong*. It seemed that Ishullanu had been right about them. Lenis couldn't hide from that any more. The Demon King had claimed that he and his sister weren't human, that they weren't *meant* to be human. It was only due to Ishullanu's intervention that they were even partly human, but there was a part of each of them that wasn't. And that part was what connected them. Missy's telepathy. Lenis's empathy. They had always believed that they were just gifted Bestia Keepers. Now Lenis knew the truth, and he hated it. He wasn't gifted. He was a freak. Half human. Half something else. Half *of* something else. He would never be whole. Not really, and he couldn't bear the thought of what it would take to bring the two halves of whatever it was the Clemens twins were together.

Just then, something tingled at the edge of Lenis's awareness. He dismissed it as some stray emotion from one of the crew. It certainly felt like one of them. It brushed against his senses again. He sat bolt upright. Aeris mewed in protest and jumped off him. The Bestia glared at Lenis before retreating below decks. It came again. Stronger this time. Lenis felt his heartbeat quicken. It was a sensation so familiar that it stirred a deep longing in him. But it was impossible. Then it was there, all around him, and he knew it was true. It was *real*.

'Namei,' Lenis whispered the cabin girl's name, frightened of dissipating the sense of his lost friend's spirit. It grew stronger. His conviction that it was truly her solidified. Soon it felt as if she was standing right next to him. But how? Namei was dead and gone. Ignis had burned her body to ashes.

Lenis felt a tingling in his palms. He looked down. They were both pressed flat on the deck. He had been lying in the middle of Namei's bloodstain and was now sitting up. He marvelled at the sensations of Namei sweeping through him, gliding over him, engulfing him. It was impossible, but it was happening. His senses had never been wrong before. Namei was here, on the *Hiryū*. She was a part of the airship. Here at last was the connection he had been groping after when Etana had attacked. Here was the bond. Namei. The Heart of the *Hiryū*. As real and solid as if she were still alive.

'What are you doing?'

Shujinko's words crashed into Lenis like a blow, whipping away the sense of Namei's soul. The last vestiges of her were overwhelmed in the all too familiar sting of the cabin boy's contempt. Lenis felt fury ignite deep inside him.

'Leave me alone,' he growled, not trusting himself to look at Shujinko.

'You should be training.'

'Leave me alone.' Lenis's teeth were clenched. He could feel tears already falling from the corners of his eyes.

'What's the matter?'

'I said leave me alone!' Lenis shouted.

He stood and rounded on Shujinko in one swift movement, unwittingly unleashing his fury at the same time. The cabin boy took the blow squarely in the middle of his chest and was knocked back down the stairway to the deck. Lenis heard him hit, hard, and then someone was shouting, but he didn't care enough to figure out who it was. There was a roaring in his ears like a strong wind. His clenched fists were extended before him. Everything around him was etched into sharp relief.

The cabin boy had gone too far this time. He had taken Namei away from him, just as Lord Butin had done all those weeks ago. Lenis was suddenly aware of a low growling emanating from somewhere. It took him a moment to realise it was coming from him. He moved to the top of the stairs and then took the steps, one by one. Shujinko was scrambling away from him across the deck. The boy's fear was palpable. It had always been there, lingering under the surface, but it was stronger now, and it wasn't reserved for heights.

And then Shujinko said the most stupid thing he could have said. 'What *are* you?'

Lenis screamed a bestial cry and leapt on the cabin boy, battering him with his fists. In a fair fight, Shujinko would have been able to counter such a clumsy attack. A part of Lenis knew this, but in his rage Lenis wasn't fighting fair. He lashed out at the boy with every insecurity, every ounce of fear that the cabin boy possessed. Lenis's blows were fuelled by a controlled fury. His mind, that part of it that never quite slept, that always watched and analysed and weighed outcomes, found every hole in the cabin boy's hastily erected defences, every weakness in his guard. He saw every counter before it happened. Lenis felt the satisfying crunch of damage being done but, strangely, felt no pain himself.

'Lenis, that's enough!'

He looked up and saw his sister standing over him.

Missy was horrified. She'd never seen him lose it like this before. It was so unlike him. 'Lenis, that's enough!'

It was like he didn't even recognise her.

'Leave me alone!' he barked.

'Lenis, look at yourself!' She took a step closer but stayed out of reach. She glanced down at Shujinko. He was unconscious but still breathing. The crew had formed a ring around them. They were all staring at her brother. Lenis snarled, baring his teeth at Missy. 'What's wrong with you?'

Lenis's chest was heaving. His fingers were curled into claws. He was kneeling over Shujinko's prone form. There was spittle at the corners of his mouth. Missy locked eyes with him. There was something deeply wrong there. His eyes were wild, their pupils dilated. There was something savage about him. Bestial. Out of control. Missy knew what she had to do.

'Bring me the Quillblade,' she said to Kanu, not daring to break the stare she shared with her brother. It seemed to immobilise Lenis, and she couldn't risk losing him again.

'Miss Clemens, I –'

'Please, Captain. Please.' Missy could hear the pleading in her own voice. She hoped he could too. Kanu stepped into the ring of crewmembers, the Quillblade a limp feather in his arms. 'Give it to Lenis, Kanu.'

The Titan boy nodded and pressed the *shintai* into Lenis's curled fingers. His hands twitched as he instinctively grasped the hilt. The weapon stiffened in his grip. Missy could hear its vibrations from across the deck. Slowly, intelligence returned to her brother's eyes.

Missy let out a pent-up breath. 'Lenis, we were –'

'Leave me alone.' He spat the words out.

'Lenis, what –'

'You heard me.'

The captain took a step forwards, his hands held out before him. 'Mister Clemens –'

Lenis didn't even look in his direction. 'Stay out of this.' Several crewmembers gasped. Missy was shocked to her core.

Lenis had *never* spoken to the captain, to *any* captain, like that. She couldn't work out what was going on with her brother. Shujinko groaned suddenly at his feet. Lenis looked down at him, his mouth twisting cruelly.

'Lenis!' Missy was moving before she could stop herself. She reached out, over Shujinko, and grabbed Lenis's wrist. Missy could feel something moving just beneath his skin – the power of the Quillblade moving through his veins. 'What are you doing? Why did you attack Shujinko?'

Lenis laughed. It was a short and ugly sound. 'You don't know? I've had to put up with his disdain ever since he came on board. Do you know what it's like to have to *feel* that? To have it always there, nagging at you?'

Missy tightened her grip on him. Their faces were so close she could smell his ragged breath. 'So you thought you'd beat him up? That's a petty excuse, Lenis.'

'He had it coming.'

'No, he didn't.'

'You don't know what he did!'

Missy stopped herself from cringing away from his shout. 'No, I don't! But I know he took care of the Bestia while you were gone. Did you know that? He cared for them while you were away.'

If she thought mentioning the Bestia would bring her brother to his senses, she had completely misjudged the situation. 'While I was gone?' Lenis laughed again. 'Oh, yes, I remember. Tell me, Missy. Tell me why?'

Missy hesitated. 'Why what?'

'Why didn't you come for me?'

'What? I couldn't. You're the only one who can fly the airship!'

'You could have reached out to me. I could have *told* you what to do. For a telepath you don't use your brain very much.'

'Lenis, I –'

'What? You had something more important to do? *You left me up there!*'

'That wasn't *my* fault! You were the one who wanted to sneak on board in the first place!'

'So I got what I deserved?'

'Lenis, no! That isn't what I meant!'

'You abandoned me!'

'No, I didn't! I did everything I could to come after you.'

'Everything?'

'I didn't think of *that*, okay? And what about you? You were the one who ran away after what happened with Kanu!'

'So? I just wanted to be alone! Can't you understand that? You're always *right there!*'

'Just stop it! Stop acting like a child!'

'*I'm* acting like a child? What about *you*? Did you have fun playing dress-ups, *oh, great Magni*?'

'That isn't fair! I was just trying to help!'

'Oh, really? And I suppose I'm not doing anything?'

'I didn't say that!'

'You didn't have to!'

'That's enough!' The captain snapped. He had approached during the twins' fight and was now almost close enough to touch them.

'Yes, Captain,' Lenis said simply. 'It is enough. I'm sick of this airship, and I'm tired of all of you. Do you know how hard you are to be around?' Lenis turned away from Missy and scanned the gathered crew. 'No. You don't know, do you? Everything you feel, I feel. Everything! Your emotions radiate off you like a stench, and you don't even realise that I can sense them, that I *have* to sense them. Every one of them. All of it. It's so *draining*. I just want some peace!'

Missy felt his hand waver. The tip of the Quillblade drooped. She couldn't tell what it was doing to him. She had hoped it would draw off some of his rage, but now she was beginning to worry it would go too far and he would end up like she had the last time she'd used it.

Missy reached up with her free hand and placed it on Lenis's shoulder. 'It will be all right, little brother.'

He shook his head. 'No, Missy. It won't.' He looked into her eyes. 'She can read your minds.'

'Lenis!' Missy cried.

'It's true.' Lenis looked around at the crew again. Missy didn't take her eyes off him. 'That's how she fooled everyone into thinking she was Magni. It wasn't the Quillblade. It wasn't her costume or her acting abilities. She *made* them think she was a goddess. She manipulated them with her brain.' He caught Missy's stare again. She could see herself reflected in the tears that filled his eyes. 'We're both freaks. We aren't even human.'

'Lenis,' Missy whispered. He had said it. The thing that had sprung up between them, that had kept them apart ever since the incident with Kanu on the jetty. He had said it, and now it was out in the open and there was no denying it. It was true, and now the others knew it too. Missy bowed her head as she started crying. Her forehead rested against Lenis's chest, but he didn't move to put his arms around her, to comfort her.

For a while, nobody spoke or moved, and then Missy became aware that they, too, were crying. Hiroshi was sobbing noisily behind her brother's shoulder. Even Arthur, the stoic Kystian noble, was sniffling. The sound made Missy snap her head back. They *were* all crying.

Missy shook her brother's shoulder. 'Lenis, stop!'

'What?' He looked down at her blearily.

'It's you! It's coming from you!'

Snot was running out of his nose. 'What is?'

Missy's hold on Lenis's wrist had slackened. She gripped harder now. 'The sorrow. It's not ours. It's yours! Calm down. Relax. Let go of the Quillblade.'

Missy had to use both of her hands to pry the *shintai* out of her brother's grasp. It fell to the deck with a metallic clang and then reverted to its supple feather form. Missy instantly felt better. She heard the others stirring behind her. Noses were being blown. Faces were being wiped on sleeves.

The captain cleared his throat. 'I believe we need to have a discussion.'

◦ A TIME FOR EXPLANATIONS ◦

Shujinko returned to consciousness in the doctor's arms. The cabin boy hadn't been moved. They were all still standing there, encircling Lenis and his sister. Lenis felt raw. Trapped. Exposed.

'What just happened?' Kenji demanded. His right arm was in a sling. Lenis stared at it while all the others began asking questions.

The captain silenced them with a sweeping gesture of his arm. 'Let us give Mister Clemens a chance to explain.'

Captain Shishi turned to Lenis and waited. Lenis stayed silent. What was there to say that he hadn't already said? Let them pass judgement on him and be done with it.

Lenis felt tiny claws dig into his leg through his pants. Suiteki climbed up his clothes and buried herself inside his robe. The baby dragon pushed herself hard against his ribcage. He could feel the beating of her heart and something else.

She was reaching out to him as she always did, although this time she wasn't seeking comfort but offering it, pushing it against Lenis's frayed emotions just as he had so often wrapped his own sense of calm and reassurance around her. Was this some manifestation of Totemic power, some skill passed down to her from her mother or grandfather that she was just now trying for the first time? Or had she learned it from him, by watching and feeling what Lenis did so often and so instinctively?

'Mister Clemens?' the captain repeated, but it was Missy who answered him.

She told them everything, while Lenis allowed Suiteki's presence to soothe him. Missy told them about how the twins had combined their wills to control Raikō once he was a Demon. She told them about Fronge, and Kanu, and Apsu. She told them about everything Ishullanu had said about them. About who they really were. About Mashu. She told them about how the Quillblade had affected her, and how she had abused her powers to get what she wanted. Her voice was hoarse by the time she was done. Part way through her story she pulled away from her twin and sat down heavily on the deck. When she finished, she leant against one of the holds and pulled her knees up to her chin.

The crew listened in rapt silence. Missy suspected that at least some of them had known the twins were different ever since the *Hiryū* had first left Itsū, but they couldn't possibly have guessed how different they were. She couldn't tell them now. She didn't really know.

'I don't think I like the idea of being around a couple of kids who can steal my thoughts and play with my emotions,' Kenji said into the quiet that had greeted Missy's tale.

'Shush, Kenji,' Shin admonished.

'I'm just saying what we're all thinking.' He stepped towards Missy. 'Am I right?'

Missy didn't look up at him. She just shook her head. 'It doesn't work like that. I don't just "see" what you're thinking. It takes effort to go into someone's mind.'

The navigator snorted and turned away.

The captain tucked his arms into the sleeves of his robe and made a noise in the back of his throat. 'You have given us much to ponder, Miss Clemens.'

'What's to think about?' Kenji demanded. 'I say we put them off the *Hiryū* the first chance we get.'

'And then who's going to fly the airship?' Shin snapped.

'We can hire new Bestia Keepers in Haven,' Kenji countered.

'And what about Suiteki?' Shin asked. 'The Totem has a bond with Lenis. All of the Bestia do. We need them.'

Lenis felt a stirring of gratitude towards Shin for her support, but it couldn't dispel the despondence that had settled over him since his outburst. Neither could Suiteki's aura. Not completely. As he reflected on the past couple of days – had it only been days? – he realised that his frustration had been building for some time. Ever since Fronge. Ever since Kanu had forced Lenis and Missy to merge and then taken them through his memories. Lenis glanced over at the Titan boy. He was looking at the twins oddly, his head cocked to one side as if he was puzzled by something.

'Let us not be hasty, Mister Jackson,' Captain Shishi said. Lenis avoided looking directly at him. He couldn't meet the captain's eyes. 'The Clemens twins have proved to be valuable allies. I have suspected for some time that their abilities were extraordinary.'

'Yet you said nothing?' Kenji's tone was pleading. 'Captain, can't you see how dangerous they are to have around?'

'Might I point out, Mister Jackson, that if Miss Clemens wished to, she could *make* you decide to keep her around? The fact that she has not speaks well of her character.'

Missy looked up at this. A smile curled her lip but died when the navigator said, 'How do we know she isn't manipulating you right now, Captain? How do *you* know?'

Lenis felt a chill run through him. The crew would never trust them now. They would never believe that the twins weren't controlling them. Suiteki suddenly poked her head out of Lenis's robe and nipped him on the chin. He threw his head back, more startled than hurt, and when he looked back down it was straight into her eyes. Had they always been so blue? And so bright? The more Lenis looked into them the older Suiteki seemed to grow. For the briefest of moments, she wasn't his baby dragon any more. She was a Totem, and there was more wisdom and compassion in her stare than Lenis felt he could bear. He knew that no matter what happened here on the *Hiryū*, she would stay by him. They would have each other. Always.

Then the captain spoke and the moment fled, and Suiteki was his little dragon once more. 'I know this because Miss Clemens cannot enter my mind.' Lenis and Missy both stared at the captain. 'Nor can she penetrate Sir Yami's mental defences, or Mister Hiroshi's, or Lord Tenjin's. Shinzōn swordsmen are trained to cloud their thoughts. Those of us who know this skill will teach the rest of you.'

'What about him?' Kenji pointed at Lenis with his uninjured hand.

'I can't control it,' Lenis mumbled, holding Suiteki gently against his chest. 'Emotions aren't rational. They're subconscious. I can't help myself from sensing them any more than you can stop yourself from feeling them in the first place.'

'It almost seems as though you've got something to hide, Kenji,' Shin interjected.

The navigator glared at the helmswoman. Lenis could feel the tension beginning to build again. It made him nauseous. He needed to sit down. No, lie down. He needed sleep. Lenis reached up and rubbed at his eyes.

'Let's not forget our enemy!' Arthur said out of nowhere. The first officer had remained still and silent for so long that Lenis had almost forgotten he was there. 'These children are not our enemy. They are on our side. We should be considering how best to utilise their talents in the coming conflict instead of speaking of abandoning them.'

'Lord Knyght is correct,' the captain said. 'We face so many foes that we cannot begin to fight amongst ourselves.'

'But he attacked me!' Shujinko interjected. A swollen cheek and a cracked lip muffled his voice. The cabin boy surged to his feet and advanced on Lenis, who didn't make any move to defend himself but hunched over a little to protect Suiteki. He deserved whatever Shujinko did to him, but the baby Totem was innocent.

Kanu leapt in front of Shujinko with a snarl, his black claws extended. 'Leave him alone.' His words echoed Lenis's eerily, and Lenis felt a sense of foreboding. *Please, not again.* He hadn't realised he'd spoken aloud until he noticed Kanu ease back from his fighting stance, his claws retracting into fingernails again, turning from black to blue.

'I'm sorry,' Lenis mumbled. 'I don't know what came over me. It all just got to be too much, and you . . .' He couldn't tell them about Namei. They wouldn't understand. '. . . you caught me at a bad time. I didn't mean to hurt you.'

Shujinko hadn't backed off. 'You will not take me by surprise again.'

The captain stepped in front of the cabin boy. 'Tensions have been high for all of us. It is difficult to be confined in such close quarters for so long, and the pressure of our quest weighs heavily upon us. We must *all* make an effort to remain calm, for the sake of our cause and each other.'

'But what about him?' Shujinko demanded. 'What about what he did?'

'Do not carry on like a child, Shujinko,' Yami chided. 'You have defeated Lenis on many occasions in the past. It was only a matter of time before the balance shifted. Being beaten is a natural component of training. Perhaps in future you will hold your sparring partner in greater respect.'

'This wasn't training!' Shujinko protested. A purple bruise was forming above his left eye, swelling it shut.

Yami was relentless. 'For a swordsman, everything is training. It seems Lenis has been holding back during your bouts. He is stronger than either of us believed.'

'No he isn't! He has no skill!'

'Do not whine! When you face an opponent in battle, they will use every one of their abilities and all of their strength to destroy you. If they are strong they will seek to overpower you. If they are smart they will try to outwit you. If they are skilled they will outmanoeuvre you. Your training and skill are superior to his, and yet Lenis was able to defeat you. Learn from it. Train harder.'

Shujinko glowered and seethed, but he said no more. Lenis wished he could take pleasure in Yami's chastisement of the cabin boy. This was what he had always wanted, to put Shujinko in his place, but not this way. He had aspired to defeat him in hand-to-hand combat, not by destroying him emotionally. After Lenis had fought the Warlord off in Nochi he had decided he didn't want to use his powers like that, but when it came down to it he was unable to control himself. Instead of triumph, all he felt deep down, within the cocoon of Suiteki's love, was shame.

○

Missy followed along behind the captain and Arthur as they made their way back to the bridge. It was hard to describe how she was feeling. A part of her was actually relieved that she had finally told the rest of the crew all about the twins' powers, even if it had cost her their trust. One day she would win it back. Missy would do whatever it took to show them that she was on their side.

The matter with her brother was far more serious. Whatever had caused him to go into a rage, whatever reason he had for attacking Shujinko, in the end he had turned on her. They had never fought. Not like this. They had disagreed any number of times, but they had never thrown accusations at each other, never tried to wound one another. He had as good as called her stupid. Worse, he had accused her of abandoning him. There was just enough truth in that to sting. Missy hadn't abandoned him, but she hadn't sent her spirit-self after him either. And why hadn't she? She hadn't thought twice about hurling herself into the inferno of Fronge. Why hadn't she gone after her brother? The fact that it simply hadn't occurred to her did little to ease her conscience. It made no sense, even to her.

There was nothing to be gained from dwelling on the matter. She'd made a mistake and now they would both have to find a way to live with it. As Missy settled into her chair she had to admit to herself that the argument hadn't been all one-sided. She had called Lenis a petty child, and she'd done it to hurt his feelings. That wasn't at all like her any more than Lenis's violent outburst was like him. Perhaps they *had* spent too long on board together. With everything the crew had to deal with, someone was bound to snap eventually. Missy just never imagined it would be Lenis. He was always so controlled, and she'd come to rely on that more than she realised.

Captain Shishi cleared his throat. 'Are we far from Haven, Mister Jackson?' Missy could tell from his tone that the fight and the twins' revelations had unsettled him.

'Give me a minute to work out where we are,' Kenji replied.

The navigator avoided her stare. Missy wondered why he of all the crew seemed so concerned to hear about the twins' abilities. Perhaps Shin was right and he did have something to hide. Missy was briefly tempted to find out what it was and cursed herself for it. That wasn't the way to go about winning someone's trust. Always in the past she had told herself her telepathy was harmless. It wasn't until she was confronted by someone's outrage at the idea of it that she was forced to consider how much of a violation it really was. She wondered how Lenis dealt with feeling their emotions. Missy could choose not to use her gift, but he had no way to stop sensing the feelings of others.

Kenji turned to face the captain. 'We're close. There won't be any lights, so we're going to have to move carefully.'

The captain nodded and picked up the speech tube. He hesitated before calling down to Lenis. 'Mister Clemens, please decrease our speed.'

'Yes, sir.' Lenis's voice sounded hollow, devoid of any emotion. Missy tried to convince herself it was just an effect caused by the speech tube.

For the next few moments, Kenji kept looking from his charts and maps through the crystal dome of the bridge and back again. It seemed like a pointless exercise. Night had fallen during the events on deck, and the sky around them was illuminated only in brief flashes as Lucis ran through her pipes.

Missy gathered her courage. 'Do you want me to search for you?'

Kenji glared at her. Missy thought for a moment that he was going to refuse out of spite. Eventually, he said, 'You're looking for a Bestia called Pog.'

Missy nodded and detached her spirit-self from her body, glad to leave the bridge behind. Her spirit-self didn't need eyes to see, so she wasn't bothered by the darkness. She felt the mountains around her and the sky above her and made wide, sweeping searches of the valleys around them. She was only halfheartedly trying to locate Pog. The sensation of being free of her body was refreshing. The cares that plagued her were left behind, shed along with her physical husk, and so it was with some disappointment that she found a rather large Bestia who responded to her call. Pog had four short legs barely long enough to carry his barrel-like body. He had almost no nose or tail and his ears were long and floppy. He was one of those rare Bestia whose elemental affinity was so rigid he couldn't leave it behind. For an earth Bestia that meant he spent most of his time submerged in mud.

Pog didn't like new people. At first Missy thought he was going to ignore her altogether, but she battered away at his mind until he was forced to acknowledge her. She kept the message short. Just a picture of the *Hiryū* and an airdock. She also threw in an image of Kenji Jackson. The navigator had been here before, so the airdock officials might recognise him.

'All done,' Missy said once she had returned to her body.

'You found Pog?' Kenji asked.

'Yes, and I've arranged a landing. If we edge around the shoulder of that mountain there,' she pointed to portside, where Lucis had just illuminated a rock face, 'we'll see a signal. We have to fly in pretty low. From what I can gather, the city is sort of under the mountain.'

'You've already spoken to them?' Kenji demanded. 'Why did you do that?'

Missy was taken aback. 'I thought –'

'Demon's wings!'

'What is it, Mister Jackson?' the captain asked.

'I don't suppose you kept me out of it?' Kenji snapped.

Missy swallowed. 'Um . . .'

'Oh, that's just great!'

'What's the matter?' Shin demanded from the tiller.

'Nothing,' Kenji muttered, then scrutinised one of his charts. 'Nothing at all.'

○

Lenis received the order to land and began making the necessary adjustments to the engine. He vented some of Aeris's power, making sure the airflow was even between each wing balloon. There was something infinitely soothing about working the *Hiryū*'s engines. He could forget all about whatever else was going on and focus completely on the business at hand.

But then the Ostian princess spoke, shattering his calm. 'You can feel things.'

It wasn't a question, but Lenis answered anyway. 'Yes, I can feel things.' He didn't bother to soften his tone; it wouldn't make a difference to her if he did.

'Can you feel me?'

'Excuse me?' Lenis forgot all about the engines. 'What?'

'Can you feel me?'

The princess stepped around the engine block, right up to Lenis, and grabbed his hand. She placed it on her chest, between her breasts. Just because the girl was empty didn't mean Lenis was. His cheeks flushed crimson as he tried to snatch his hand back. Anastasis was too strong for him, though, and she kept his hand firmly where it was.

'I have to get back to the engines.' Lenis looked longingly at the Bestia compartments, hoping Anastasis would get the hint.

Of course, she couldn't. 'Can you feel me?'

'Well, um, yeah,' he mumbled.' Yes. I can feel you.'

The princess frowned. 'You can feel me?'

Lenis realised what she was asking. He sighed and concentrated on her. As usual, she was just empty. Disma was nowhere nearby, so Lenis couldn't sense anything other than her hatred for Butin, but that was always there. Then he remembered their brief encounter back in the woods near Fronge. That time, he *had* felt something. He focused his powers and pushed deeper, past the tumult of Butin-directed rage. But there was nothing. He started shaking his head, but then he felt it. A wisp of longing. Nothing more. It was so small, but in her it was immense.

'There *is* something . . .' Lenis tried again, and there it was! Deep in her core Anastasis longed for something besides Lord Butin's destruction. But what was it? He couldn't tell. It was too faint. 'You want something. I can't tell what.'

Anastasis nodded, but she wasn't looking at Lenis. While she was distracted, Lenis pulled his hand away and made several non-essential adjustments to the engines.

'There is more,' Anastasis said. 'I did not realise there could be more.' She turned to walk out of the engine room.

On impulse, Lenis ran after her and grabbed her arm. 'Wait!' he whispered, looking around to make sure her Lilim familiar wasn't nearby. 'Promise me something.' She gave him her usual blank look. 'Promise me you won't give this to Disma. Keep it for yourself. Please! Promise me!'

He didn't know why he asked this of her, and why it suddenly mattered to him. Perhaps it was because Anastasis's bond to her Lilim reminded him so strongly of the negative effects the Quillblade had on his sister. Whatever his reasons, Lenis felt something else stir deep inside Anastasis.

The corners of her mouth twitched up and then back down. 'Very well. I will keep this, just for me.' The princess shook free of his grasp and headed towards the galley.

Lenis stared after her for a moment. When he heard the captain's voice through the speech tube, he hurried back to make the final adjustments for landing.

◦ SEEKING SANCTUARY ◦

The airdock was nothing more than a long, raised shelf almost at the bottom of a narrow ravine. The *Hiryū* had no problem descending through the cleft, guided by the lone light-shedding Bestia waiting on the airdock's lip, but there was no way an airbarge could have made it through. It turned out that Haven wasn't actually under the mountain but roofed in tight netting the inhabitants had covered with brush and scrub.

The first thing Missy noted was that this was not a Heiliglander settlement, at least, not entirely. The people who had come out to meet them were all wearing long, flowing gowns in dark shades covered in black overcoats. The gowns looked Lahmonian to Missy, but the coats were definitely Kystian. The people wearing them were of differing nationalities.

The second thing Missy noted was that the air was fresh.

For a settlement in the middle of the Wastelands, this was unusual. There was no green fog, and there didn't seem to be any Demons about. Missy followed Arthur and the captain out onto the deck and over to the gangplank. The black-coated people of Haven waited in a ring below.

'Why are you here?' one of them called up in the common tongue. Missy tried to place his accent. She thought it was Lahmonian but couldn't be sure.

'We are just passing through,' Captain Shishi replied. 'We seek Kolga's temple, just to the northeast of here.'

The group bent their heads together and whispered amongst themselves. Finally, their spokesperson called up. 'You have a man with you. We saw him in your message.'

Missy tensed. What had she done now?

'We have several men with us,' the captain called down. 'You will have to be more specific.'

'Do not play with us, Captain.' The spokesman raised an arm and a number of Bestia emerged from behind rocks and within crevices. 'Kenji Jackson is aboard your airship. Bring him to us.'

'What do you want with him?'

'He knows what he owes us.'

Kenji appeared at the *Hiryū*'s railing. 'All right, Michael, here I am.'

'Hello, brother,' the spokesman, Michael, called up. 'It has been too long.'

'*Brother?*' Missy asked.

Kenji rolled his eyes at her. 'Not literally. It's a form of address.'

'Only if you're a . . . you're a *priest*?'

'Is that so hard to believe?' He looked over the railing. 'I'm coming down, Michael. Don't stab me with anything. Oh, and I have a pistol.'

'Thanks for the warning,' Michael replied. 'Are your friends joining you?'

Kenji looked at the captain. 'Probably. Don't stab them either. They haven't got anything to do with us.'

'Their safety is assured.'

'Mister Jackson, could you tell us what is going on here?' the captain asked.

'It'll be all right, Captain.' Kenji jumped onto the gangplank. 'They won't kill *you*.'

'That is hardly reassuring,' Arthur noted, his arms crossed over his chest.

'It'll be fine. You'll see.' Kenji held his pistol ready as he began walking down the gangplank. 'You'd better come along. She'll want to meet you all.'

'She?' Arthur asked.

'The Cunning Lady,' Kenji replied. 'Welcome to Haven, home of the Brotherhood of the Nine-Tailed Fox.'

Missy looked to the captain and then to Arthur. The Kystian shrugged. 'We had better go with him. Fetch the others.'

She nodded and ran below decks. Missy passed through the galley, stopping only to tell the doctor, the cook, and Shujinko what had happened before hurrying on to the engine room. Her brother was waiting for her in the doorway.

'What's going on?' he asked. He was holding Suiteki close to his chest.

Missy was suddenly reminded of a much younger Lenis standing in the doorway of their hut in the slave pens. 'I don't know, but you'd better come along. They want us all to meet the Cunning Lady.'

'The who?' Lenis asked, following her up the stairs.

'Don't know. She must be the one in charge.'

The twins were the last ones to leave the *Hiryū*, save Princess Anastasis and Disma, who were waiting by the railing.

'You aren't coming with us?' Missy asked.

'There's nothing here for us,' Disma told them. 'You'd better hurry up.'

Missy and Lenis ran down the gangplank to catch up to the others, who were being herded along by the figures in the large coats. As they moved through Haven, Missy saw that the buildings were a mismatch of different designs. They passed small stone huts, larger wooden buildings with heavy foundations, and lines of canvas tents. There was no fire. The only light came from the many Bestia scattered about. Missy hadn't seen so many Bestia gathered together in one place since she'd left Pure Land, but these ones weren't in cages. They were running free.

Missy was aware that they were being watched from inside the various dwellings around them, but no one came out onto the street. She realised then that their silent guides were more likely guards from the town. She had the distinct impression the crew was under arrest.

Eventually they came to a wide paved area, across which was a wall of rock. Set into the rock was a rectangular opening Missy found hauntingly familiar. Like something she had encountered before . . . the entrance to Neti's temple! Missy looked up and saw what appeared to be a starburst design carved above the doorway. The star had nine points.

'Well, here we are again, Kenji,' Michael said. 'You want your friends to wait outside?'

Kenji seemed to consider it. 'No. They better come with me. They might be able to convince the Lady not to eat me.'

Michael laughed. 'Oh, she wouldn't really eat you. At least, I don't think she would. She might bite you a bit.'

'How do you bite someone a bit?' Kenji asked.

'An intriguing question. Be sure to ask the Lady before the end of your trial.'

'Trial?' The captain raised an eyebrow and looked at the *Hiryū*'s navigator.

'Nothing to worry about, sir,' Kenji told him. 'Just a formality. I'm sure the Lady plans to kill me either way.'

'Mister Jackson,' the captain barked. 'This is not funny.'

'Oh, but it is, Captain. It's absolutely hilarious. You'll see.'

The crew was ushered inside. Missy couldn't quite work

out if they were in trouble. It was hard to tell if Kenji was joking. He certainly didn't seem too worried for a man who was about to be condemned to death.

They passed through a darkened corridor and emerged into a hall festooned in burgundy bunting. Billowing orange cloth hung down from the ceiling, and there were red cushions edged with gold tassels strewn around the interior of the temple, if it really was a temple at all. Bestia of every shape and size lounged upon them. Most were sleeping. A few looked up as the crew entered. At the far end of the hall Missy saw a massive divan with a woman draped across its length. She had mousy brown hair down to her waist and was wearing a flimsy gown of pink gauze. Missy almost gasped. The fabric was so thin she could see right through it in places.

'Kenji Jackson has returned, my Lady,' Michael called from behind them. He hadn't entered the hall but remained cloaked in the shadow of the entryway.

The woman propped herself up on one elbow. The neckline of her gown drooped, revealing most of one of her breasts. Missy caught her brother staring. His face was as red as the bunting.

'Kenji Jackson?' the woman asked in a sleepy voice. Her tone made it hard to place her accent. Missy detected hints of Lahmonian in it, and maybe some Ellian. 'What's he doing here?'

'I won't be staying long, my Lady,' Kenji called across the hall.

The woman squinted over at them. 'Oh, this is silly. Come here, all of you.' She motioned with both her arms, and her gown fell down to her waist. Missy poked her brother in the ribs as the woman absently adjusted her outfit so that she was covered. 'Well, come on. Now.' On the last word her lethargic demeanour vanished, and there was no doubting the note of command in her voice.

As one the crew looked to Kenji, who shrugged and began picking his way across the hall through the clusters of reclining Bestia. The others had no choice but to follow. By the time they had reached the other side, the woman was sitting fully upright, facing them.

'Kenji Jackson.' She looked down on him from her perch atop the raised divan. 'Kenji Jackson. What am I going to do with you?'

'Michael thinks you might bite me,' Kenji offered. If he was actually concerned, he gave no sign of it.

The woman tilted her head to one side, as if considering it. 'I'm not sure I'd like how you'd taste.' Kenji laughed and rubbed the back of his head. 'How's Pure Land?'

'The same,' said Kenji.

'Pity.'

The captain cleared his throat.

The woman turned to stare at him, unblinking. 'Yes? What do you want?'

'I am Captain Mayonaka Sh –'

The woman cut him off. 'I asked you what you wanted.'

'We only wish to moor our airship to your airdock for a time,' Captain Shishi told her. 'We have business –'

'That is a simple enough matter. I'm sure Michael can arrange for some sort of fee. You can pay, can't you?'

The captain bowed his head slightly. 'Of course.'

The woman waved her hand. 'Then it's settled.'

'Um, my Lady?' Kenji asked.

'Yes, Kenji, what is it?'

'There was just the small matter of –'

The woman sighed. 'Oh, yes, your sentence. I had almost forgotten. I suppose I'll have to kill you.'

Kenji gulped. The sound was audible throughout the hall. 'Is that really necessary?'

'It seems appropriate. Don't you think?' She tilted her head to one side, and Missy got the distinct impression that she was actually interested in Kenji's input.

'Well, I was sort of hoping . . .' His voice trailed off.

'You would.' The woman smiled, showing her teeth. It seemed to Missy that her eyeteeth were quite a bit longer and sharper than was normal. 'You always were clever, Kenji, and sneaky. Dishonest too. And shrewd. Oh, and manipulative.'

Kenji bowed low. 'Thank you, my Lady.'

The woman inclined her head. 'You're welcome. However, I never suspected you were disloyal.'

'Never that, my Lady.'

'No?' The woman arced one perfectly shaped eyebrow.

'Then the reports I received were false? You aren't working for the Puritan Ruling Council?'

Missy glanced at the navigator. He was an agent of the *Council*? But why? What did he want? What did *they* want? As she contemplated the possibility, she realised the answer was simple. A spy aboard Warlord Shōgo Ikaru's new airship. It was so obvious she couldn't believe she hadn't thought of it before. That was why he alone had remained of the Puritan crew who had flown the *Hiryū* over to Shinzō. He was working for the Ruling Council all along. Another piece fell into place. His pistol. Missy had always wondered how he had managed to smuggle one out of Pure Land, not to mention how he had gotten his hands on a working one in the first place. Now she knew. The Council had probably given it to him.

Kenji spread his hands wide in supplication. 'I don't suppose you'd be willing to trust me.'

He isn't denying it! He is a Puritan spy!

The woman just laughed. 'You are always such fun to have around, Kenji. I shall miss you.'

'How about a trade?'

The woman's eyebrow shot up again. 'What sort of trade?'

'My life, naturally.'

'I had assumed as much. What do I get in return?'

Kenji grinned. 'Another Totem artefact to add to your collection. And a quill from the Thunder Bird.'

Missy gasped.

'Makes a pretty good sword. Or a pen, I suppose. Oh, and I'll include a baby Totem into the bargain.'

● IN THE FOX'S LAIR ●

Swords were drawn. The crew moved to circle the navigator. Missy stood by, mouth hanging open, unable to believe what Kenji had just said. He was selling them out to save his own life! How could he even *consider* it?

'Do we have a deal?' Kenji asked, ignoring the crew-members arrayed against him.

'A baby Totem?' The woman on the divan clapped her hands together. 'I have to see it!'

Kenji pointed at Lenis. 'The boy has it with him.'

'No!' Lenis shouted, clasping his robe closed and hunching his shoulders, no doubt shielding Suiteki from the man. In an instant both Yami and Captain Shishi were standing between them, swords levelled at the navigator's chest.

'What is this, Mister Jackson?' the captain asked in a low voice.

'Don't bother killing me,' Kenji said. 'If you do, the

Brotherhood will destroy the *Hiryū* before you set foot outside the temple.'

'You do not disappoint me, Kenji!' the woman cried. 'Tell me, what game are we playing today?'

Kenji shook his head. 'No game, my Lady. I want to live. You like powerful objects. Seems like a fair trade to me.'

'Kenji!' Shin cried. 'You cannot do this!'

Somehow, Missy found her voice. 'I can stop you, you know.'

Kenji turned to look at her. 'Yes. I know.'

Missy shook her head in disbelief. 'Then why?'

Kenji shrugged. 'I'm glad you asked.'

Just then Michael shouted from the entryway, 'Demons are attacking Haven!'

The woman flicked her wrist towards the back of the hall. 'Deal with it.'

'There's a Demon Lord with them,' Michael called back. 'We think it's Etana.'

The woman pushed out her bottom lip. 'Him again. What a shame. I was having fun. You.' She pointed at the captain. 'Captain Whatever-Your-Name-Is. You have weapons. Go and defend my Haven.'

'Lady, you're crazy,' Andrea said. Her knives were drawn and held at the ready.

'Etana has to go through your airship to get here,' the woman pointed out.

'She's right.' Arthur looked to the captain. 'We can deal with Kenji later.'

The captain nodded, once, and relaxed his stance. His eyes never left Kenji's face. 'Mister Clemens, please bring Suiteki and stay behind me. Sir Yami and Miss Clemens, please remain here with Mister Jackson. Everyone else should come with me.'

Slowly, the captain turned away from the *Hiryū*'s navigator and moved beyond the ring of crewmembers. Lenis followed him so closely he was almost stepping on the captain's heels. One by one the others fell into step behind them.

Missy was still staring at Kenji. 'Why? Why are you doing this?'

The navigator remained where he was, standing before the woman on the divan, between Missy and Yami. 'You're the telepath.' He turned his head and smirked at her. 'You tell me.'

She was tempted, so very tempted, but something held her back. It wasn't that she felt she owed this man anything. During their time together on the *Hiryū*, Missy had never fully trusted him. Besides, he'd just proven that any trust in him was misplaced. It occurred to Missy just then that he had planned this all along. He was their navigator. They relied on him to plot the right course for them. He had known the Brotherhood wanted him dead for turning against them. It would have been so simple to convince the captain to come here, to lure them to Haven so he could barter the only weapons they had against Ishullanu for his own life.

The man's treachery was appalling. Missy had never encountered such betrayal before. Not since her father . . . she felt her fury rising, her fingers twitching, yearning for the Quillblade. Why was she holding back? Why *now*, after everything, did she not enter the man's mind, find the truth, force him to . . . He deserved it! He had tried to sacrifice them, their *mission*, just to save himself. And he was acting as though it didn't even matter! Anything Missy did to him, anything she *made him do*, would be small punishment for that.

But Missy didn't even attempt it. This wasn't about him. She had decided not to manipulate anyone ever again. There was no excuse for it. Not even if that person was now her enemy. Nothing gave her the right to force him to think as she desired. What was it Lenis had said to her? *For a telepath you don't use your brain very much.* Well, she would show him. It didn't matter what Kenji had done, Missy could still get them all out of this. There was more at stake than their own lives.

She turned to the lady on the throne-like divan. 'So, you like *shintai*?'

The woman tilted her head towards Missy. 'What's a *shintai*?'

Missy cursed. First mistake. Tenjin had once told Missy that there was no word for a *shintai* except *shintai*. She'd have to do better than that. 'It's a weapon. A gift from a Totem. It holds some of their power.'

'Oh, those. Yes, that's right. I have a . . . fondness for them.'

Okay. This was better. 'What do you know about them?'

The woman chuckled. 'This seems like an odd time for a lesson in arcane paraphernalia.'

Missy shrugged and hoped she looked nonchalant. 'We've got nothing else to do until the Demons are taken care of.'

'I like you,' the woman said. 'You may call me Vixen.'

Missy raised her own eyebrow, attempting to mimic the woman's manner. 'That's a ridiculous name.'

'Who said it was my name? If you'd prefer, try Füchsin. Or what about Kitsune? There's always Volpe. Every word for fox is beautiful.'

'How about *renarde* or *hu li*. There's also *lisitsa*. That's Garsian.'

The woman clapped. 'I *do* like you!'

'Why are you called "Fox"?' Missy countered. She needed to get her talking about *shintai* again. Kenji had mentioned she had a collection, and a plan was quickly forming in Missy's mind.

Fox placed a hand over her heart. 'I am the High Priestess of the Fox God.'

'And you have a *shintai* given to you by this Fox God?'

Fox's eyes narrowed momentarily, and Missy thought she had misjudged the woman. She felt sweat starting to gather at her brow but resisted the urge to wipe it away. Equally strong was Missy's desire to read the woman's thoughts. She'd never had to do this before, to assess someone based solely on what she could see and hear and guess. To distract herself, she deliberately turned away from the divan and began examining a pair of Bestia lounging nearby. They looked a bit like foxes themselves, except their red fur crackled with fire.

'I may have something of the sort lying around here,' the woman said eventually.

Missy knelt down and began running her hand over the Bestia's fur. It was hot to the touch but didn't burn. As she'd guessed, these Bestia had been around humans for a while. Missy wondered just how long Haven had been out here. Parts of it had seemed very old, but she had noticed newer bits on the way in. How had it managed to repel the Wasteland taint?

She glanced at Fox out of the corner of her eye. 'You aren't sure?'

The woman clicked her tongue. 'Kenji was right about you. How bothersome. Why do you care if I have one of these . . . *shintai*?'

Missy straightened and looked Fox in the eye. 'Because I want to know if you can use it.'

Lenis followed along behind the captain, clutching Suiteki close to his chest. It was impossible to tell whose heart was beating faster. Never before had Lenis sensed such distress in the baby dragon, not even when the Demon Lord had attacked the *Hiryū*. Whether she was reacting to Lenis's own shock and fear, or because she could sense the mass of Demons descending on Haven, the tiny Totem wouldn't hold still.

Lenis was used to her squirming around in his grip and managed to keep hold of her, ignoring the welts her claws raised in his flesh.

Kenji had betrayed them. Lenis had always found the navigator to be insincere. His empathic gifts meant he could always tell when someone was being false. Still, he had never suspected Kenji would, that he *could*, deceive them all so horribly. Not like this. Somehow, Lenis had always believed, despite how wary he was of the man, that Kenji shared the same goals as the rest of the crew.

His head reeled. If he had been wrong about Kenji, whom else might he have misjudged? How much did he really know about the other members of the crew? He suddenly realised it might now be too late to find out any more about them.

As the crew rushed through the indiscriminate buildings of Haven, Lenis could feel the Demons closing in. He could sense them, as surely as he could feel the crew's growing anticipation. Maybe it was because Lenis was stuck at the bottom of a ravine with the Demons up above him, but it was as though their aura was bearing down on him, suffocating his empathic senses in the collective fugue of their sorrow. And above them all was the raging hunger of a Demon Lord. Etana. Lord of Fury. Former Jinn. Warden of Retribution. He was up there, and he was coming closer.

As they emerged from beneath the netting that covered Haven and caught sight of the *Hiryū*, Lenis had to bite back a sob. His airship was safe. His Bestia were safe. His relief was short-lived. The settlement of Haven was at one end of a narrow ravine. It was not much wider than the *Hiryū*'s wingspan, but it was very deep. Bestia lit the darkened crevice brighter than daylight ever could. The fierce whiteness of their illumination cast equally sharp shadows up the walls on either side of them. The airdock was a narrow shelf built along one wall. Dark-robed figures moved along it, towards the far end of the ravine. The crew made to follow. And then Lenis felt –

'Stop!' He shouted.

'Mister Clemens –' The captain began.

'No!' Lenis pointed above them.

They all craned their necks back to see what Lenis was trying to show them. There was nothing visible beyond the Bestia's light. They couldn't even see the lip of the ravine wall. It was far too high.

The captain placed a hand on Lenis's shoulder. 'I do not see –'

Lenis shook his head. He could *feel* them.

'Wait,' Andrea said. 'Did anyone else see that?'

'What?' Shin asked.

'They're climbing down the walls.' Andrea's voice was hushed, as if she couldn't believe what she was seeing. 'That must be over five miles high . . .'

'Higher,' Lenis mumbled. He knew from the *Hiryū*'s descent that they were almost twice that high. This was mountainous country and the ravine ran deep.

Andrea cupped her hands to her mouth. 'They're climbing down the walls!'

If any of the dark-coated defenders of Haven heard her, they didn't seem to believe her. None of them stopped or turned back, leaving the *Hiryū*'s crew to face the incoming wave of Demons alone.

'And if I can use this *shintai* thing?' Fox was leaning forwards with her elbows on her knees and her chin resting atop her clasped hands. 'Not that I'm admitting I have any such item in my possession, of course, but if I *did*, why do you want to know if I can use it?'

Missy straightened from her scrutiny of the Bestia and took a deep breath. This was it. She turned back to the woman and noticed Yami had not so much as twitched a finger out of his original position. Somehow the fact that he was there gave her courage.

'I need to know if you can use it because I want you to teach me how,' Missy said. '*Something* has been keeping Haven safe from the Wasteland taint. I'm willing to bet it's you and your *shintai*. If you have that sort of power, I want you to teach me how to wield it.'

The woman leant back and tapped her lips with one finger. 'And what makes you think that I can, or *will*, do such a thing?'

Missy swallowed. 'I was sort of hoping you would do it because it's the right thing to do. I need to learn if I'm going to help stop the Demon King and his army from overrunning the world.'

Fox curled her lips into a smile, once again revealing her extra-long eyeteeth. 'Your hopes mean little to me.'

Missy hesitated. She could feel Kenji watching her. Now that she knew what he was capable of, he was making her more nervous than ever. With an effort, she ignored him. She had to focus on Fox. Missy was probably only going to get one chance to convince her. 'Then I'll make a bargain with you. I don't want your *shintai*, and I'm certainly not going to give you mine, but if you know how to use them then you can teach me. That's what I want. Teach me how to wield the Quillblade.'

'I know what *you* want. What are you offering to pay *me* for these lessons?'

Missy licked her lips. She had to force the words out before she stopped herself. What she was offering was madness. She knew she couldn't deliver, yet she could think of nothing else the woman might want that she couldn't just take. 'You serve the Fox God. Assuming this god of yours exists, he's probably a Totem or a Jinn or something like that, and that means he's been turned into a Demon by now. If not, he soon will be. If you teach me how to use the Quillblade properly, I'll find a way to heal him.'

Fox threw her head back and laughed. There was a touch of madness in her mirth that reminded Missy of Long Liu. 'No one can do such a thing, foolish child. You had better –'

'I know there is no cure,' Missy interrupted her. 'I know that no one can do such a thing, but I believe there might be a way.'

'Oh? I suppose you have access to some sort of magic elixir? Some potion no one else has ever concocted before?'

If only she knew how close to the mark she had struck, Missy thought. She said, 'I do not have access to such a potion.' Fox smirked at her. 'Not *yet*. But I think I may know where to find one.'

Fox chuckled. 'Oh?'

Missy took a steadying breath. 'Have you ever heard of Silili the Peaceful Guardian?'

◦ FACING IMPOSSIBLE ODDS ◦

Lenis saw the Demons long before they reached the ravine floor. Everyone in the crew did. There were so *many* of them clinging to the rock face with their hideous claws. More than Lenis had seen from the walls of Gesshoku. There, they had been on the fringes of the Wastelands. Gesshoku marked and protected the boundaries between the two worlds. But Haven was in the middle of the Wastelands, surrounded on all sides by diseased ground.

The Bestia lighting up the area cast their illumination high enough to see the waves of decaying forms descending on them. As in Gesshoku, the Demons came in all shapes and sizes. There were a number of large cat and goat Demons, and more than a few bear Demons too. There were small lizard-like Demons, no bigger than Suiteki, but too numerous to count, swarming throughout the Demonic mass.

As the Demons came they made the horrid noises of

enraged beasts, the sounds made all the worse by their wounded throats. As with other Demons Lenis had seen, these ones seemed to be decaying, their blackened skin peeling back to reveal the rotting flesh beneath. The stench from their hides pressed down upon him. Rancid meat and something like rotten eggs. In Gesshoku he had been too far away to notice it, but there was nothing between him and the beasts now.

As the undulating mass continued its descent, moving ever closer to the ravine floor, Lenis saw that not all the Demons wore the shape of animals. Scattered throughout the multitude were even more fearsome creatures. Something with three long arms and three impossibly stretched legs picked its way down almost delicately, from rocky perch to rocky perch, moving like a spider. Its body was tiny with a child-sized torso and skinny waist, but its head was a perfect, featureless sphere. Behind it came a squat, almost human figure. Its shoulders bulged, and its feet were slabs of stone. It shouldn't have been able to find purchase on the mountainside, but its massive hands had many fingers. Lenis counted as many as fifteen on each hand, and these dug into the wall and clung to the thinnest outcrops of stone. This pair weren't alone. In all Lenis counted six Demons who had all the trademarks of tainted Lilim. He remembered Akamusaborikū, the Demon who had accosted them in the Wastelands near Seisui's temple. Decapitation hadn't been enough to kill him.

Lenis felt a tingling at the back of his neck and heard a roaring in his ears. Strange lights played across his vision. He leant against a nearby mooring post and tried to steady his breathing, willing himself not to pass out, for Suiteki's sake as much as his own. What possible hope did they have against so many? The crew couldn't hope to hold out for more than a few moments. Captain Shishi, Arthur, Shujinko and Shin each held their swords. Andrea had sheathed her daggers and was aiming her automated crossbow above their heads, waiting for the Demons to come into range. Long Liu was sitting cross-legged on a block of stone, his sack nestled in his lap. Lenis remembered the sorts of things the doctor kept in there. Weapons capable of maiming and disabling human opponents. Hiroshi stood by Princess Anastasis, swinging his *kusarigama*. The princess was leaning against her war hammer, its barrel-sized head planted solidly at her feet. Tenjin was there, too, with his book of spells and – Lenis remembered – the Quillblade. The records keeper was still favouring his ankle, but his determination was palpable. Kanu was standing behind Lenis. He was looking up at the Demons, just as the rest of them were, but all Lenis could sense from him was sadness.

They were, each of them in their own way, warriors. Each had their strengths, their power. But what could even they do against so many foes? Lenis wished that Yami was by his side, even if his curse transformed him into Gawayn, the long-dead Kystian swordsman.

A high-pitched shriek pierced Lenis's eardrums and interrupted his thoughts. A moment later a blast of wind shattered against one wall of the ravine, scattering Demons and sending them sprawling to the ground. They didn't move again. Lenis recognised the cry. Etana. Lord of Fury. Suiteki had curled herself up into tight coils inside Lenis's robe, pressing herself as far down as she could go. Lenis cradled her through the fabric, but he had no calmness to offer her, no hope, no reassurance. All he could do was hold her.

'Captain?' Arthur held his sword loosely by his side as he craned his neck back to regard the approaching Demons. They would soon be low enough to attack. Lenis sensed Andrea tense, readying to release her first volley.

'We cannot run, Lord Knyght,' the captain said. 'The *Hiryū* would be overrun long before we cleared the top of the ravine.'

'Then we fight.'

'Yes, Lord Knyght. I am afraid we must become Demon slayers for a time.'

○

'The Totem have fallen,' Fox said carefully. 'All of them.'

'No, they haven't.' Missy had to fight to keep her voice steady. 'Not all of them. My brother has spoken to Silili. The Peaceful Guardian healed him and his Bestia, and we think he protected the Bestia from the Wasteland sickness.'

'You *think*?'

Missy nodded. 'No promises. I'm only offering you a chance. I don't know where Silili is, or how to contact him, but I know how to track Totem. I can find him, though I'm not even certain if he can cure the Wasteland sickness, or why he hasn't done so already if he's able to.'

'Then why would I strike such a bargain with you?' Fox hissed between her teeth and waved a hand dismissively in Missy's direction. 'I'm bored with you. Go and die alongside your friends.'

Missy ground her teeth together. She couldn't lose control now. Not like she had back in Erdasche. She had to keep her mind where it belonged. 'So you won't even consider my proposal?'

The woman crossed her arms over her chest and leant against one of the divan's armrests. 'I don't see why I should.'

'So your god doesn't mind that you're a coward?' Missy snapped.

Fox's eyelids narrowed so her eyes were mere slits. They seemed to glint in the rosy light in the temple. 'Be careful, girl.' It almost came out as a growl.

'Why should I?' Missy had one more shot at this. There was no point holding back now. 'We're all about to die anyway. If not today, then soon, once the last of our defences has been stripped away, once the Demon King has an army large enough to invade the untainted lands. I haven't got the time to be careful. You're stuck in this hole in the middle of nowhere and you do what? Serve your god? Hardly! I'm offering you a chance. It's a slim chance, I'll grant you that, and it might come to nothing, but I'm willing to bet it's the best offer you've ever had. And what do you say? You're bored! I'm sure the Fox God appreciates your devotion –'

The woman's hand was suddenly around Missy's throat, squeezing so tightly Missy could barely breathe, much less speak. She'd moved impossibly fast. Missy hadn't even seen her tense. Even Yami, her silent protector, was too slow. An instant later he was behind Fox, his sword resting against her neck, but the woman ignored him.

'What do you know of devotion?' Fox hissed. She gripped harder and Missy began to gag.

'Release her!' Yami shouted.

The woman turned her head just enough to be able to glare at him. 'Your Lilim blade is of no concern to me.' She lifted Missy up by the neck, high off the ground. Missy choked, kicking her feet. Her vision darkened. 'Do you want to learn how to use a Totem's gift, brat?' Fox lowered her voice to a whisper. 'Come. I'll give you your first lesson.'

The woman released her hold and Missy fell, gasping, but before she hit the ground she was caught around the waist and yanked to the side so fast she felt her stomach heave.

◉

The first Demons fell to Andrea's volley of bolts, but there were more just behind them, reaching the ravine floor almost as quickly as the bodies of their fallen companions. The crew rushed to meet them. Lenis watched them go, Suiteki shivering in his grasp. Their panic mingled and fed off each other. Lenis couldn't move. As his crewmates reached the front ranks of the Demonic onslaught, his legs gave out from beneath him. He collapsed against the mooring post, wrapping both arms around his dragon. His mind churned on. *Is this what all your training has been for? To give in to fear at the first sign of real trouble?* Lenis shook his head, unable to seize control of his own body. All he could do was watch and offer Suiteki the meagre shelter of his limbs, setting as much of his body between her and the Demons as he could.

Everything moved so slowly. The captain's first thrust took a bear Demon in the eye. He recovered his weapon and spun on the spot, the sweep of his blade taking the horns off a goat Demon coming at him from the side. The captain flowed onto his back foot and then shifted momentum to strike at the goat creature's neck. There was a flash of blue light as a bolt of lightning exploded amongst a group of lizard Demons off to the side. Tenjin was waving the Quillblade as if it were a wand and reading from his book.

Arthur stepped up to the captain's side. The first officer parried a swipe from a cat Demon. The beast's claws rang against the metal of his sword, but then Arthur stepped forward and impaled it through the chest. His blade jammed in its ribcage. An instant. Two. His shoulders heaved as he tried to disengage it. The three-legged Lilim stepped down into the ravine and flicked one of its arms, catching Arthur in the chest. The first officer flew backwards, leaving his sword still sticking out of the cat Demon's carcass.

The Lilim stepped over the cat and bore down on the first officer, and then Hiroshi was there, wrapping Murasaki, his *kusarigama* weapon, around the thing's legs. The sharpened links of the chain tore into its flesh even as Hiroshi tightened his hold, drawing its limbs together. Lenis could see the sweat on the cook's forehead as he struggled to bring the Demon down.

Behind him, Andrea hacked and slashed at a dozen or more tiny lizard Demons, her crossbow lying forgotten at her feet, her daggers once more in her hands. Even now, Lenis could see her energy draining, her movements slowing. She cried out when one grabbed hold of her pants and scurried up her leg. Without thought for her own limb, she swiped at it with both blades. The thing was cut in three, but she'd left herself open on her right side and one of the Demons leapt onto her shoulder.

Meanwhile, Shujinko jumped over Hiroshi and swung his sword, detaching the orb-like head of the Demon Lilim looming over Arthur's prone form. The cabin boy landed awkwardly and staggered backwards, right onto the horn of another goat Demon, puncturing his side. The captain appeared by him and slew the beast.

'No,' Lenis whispered. Or had been whispering. Over and over again. 'No no nononononono . . .'

Not like this. It couldn't end like this. He saw the brute-like Lilim, the short one with the overpumped muscles and the large, heavy feet, turn to him. They locked eyes. It was so *human*, save for its disproportionate limbs and multiple digits. The Demon flexed its many fingers and started towards him with long, ponderous strides. He heard Andrea scream, her cry filled with equal parts anguish and outrage. The Demon reached Lenis. It raised one massive foot above the boy's head. It brought it down. Lenis stared, wide-eyed, open-mouthed, unable to comprehend what was happening, thinking only that he had failed Suiteki, that she would be crushed because his flesh was not solid enough to protect her from what was descending on them, that she would die before growing into the magnificent Totem she was destined to be.

There came a sound like a howling wolf. Another Demon barrelled into the one above him, knocking the thing back, slashing at it with its own claws. The new Demon was over seven feet tall and had a mane of stiff black hair running down its spine, which curved like a cat's. It leapt back and planted itself before Lenis, facing the brutish, many-fingered Demon. The new Demon's tail twitched backwards and forwards, and Lenis caught glints of blue in its black fur. Its toes were spread wide as the thing dug its long, black talons into the ground. A moment later the newcomer sprang forwards, once more lashing out at the other Demon, shredding the thing's torso and face.

Its savagery flowed into Lenis, igniting something deep inside him. Slowly, grabbing the mooring post for support with one hand and maintaining his grip on Suiteki through his robe with the other, Lenis pulled himself to his feet. The many-fingered Demon clutched the wolf-like Demon's oesophagus, and Lenis's defender went from slashing to scrabbling as it sought to free itself. A whine escaped its throat, and Lenis felt himself overwhelmed with pity. Whatever the creature was, it had saved Lenis's life. He couldn't just stand there and watch as the life was crushed out of it.

The many-fingered Demon was as empty as Lord Raikō had been when Lenis and Missy had combined their wills to control the Demon Lord, but it was nowhere near as powerful as the fallen Totem. Instinctively, Lenis wrapped his power around the creature, inundating it with his own pity for the wolf Demon and his strong need to protect it. Slowly, Lenis's desires filled the empty vessel of the many-fingered Demon until it, too, wished to preserve its prey. One by one, its fingers loosened and let the wolf Demon go. With a snarl, the wolf Demon lunged forwards and slashed his adversary's throat. Lenis, still connected to the creature, felt its animalistic panic and hastily drew his awareness back. It staggered away and Lenis caught a glimpse of his friends behind it.

They were losing the fight. Arthur and Andrea were already down. Shujinko was kneeling with one hand pressed against his side, which was red with his blood. His other hand still clutched his sword, but Lenis could tell he no longer had the strength to wield it. The princess swung her hammer ceaselessly, but the massive weapon was ill-suited to fighting the smaller Demons, which were scurrying in under her guard. Disma did her best to keep them away from Anastasis, but the princess's already ragged dress was hanging off her in shreds, and she was bleeding from several small lacerations. Hiroshi had lost his *kusarigama* but had somehow managed to free Arthur's sword from the cat Demon's body. He held it in one hand and had one of Andrea's daggers in the other, but the Kystian weapon was bigger than a Shinzōn blade and heavier than the cook was used to. He was almost spent. The captain was still fighting, but he had been separated from the others and was now facing two Demonic Lilim on his own. Lenis couldn't see Long Liu, but he saw Tenjin step backwards to dodge an incoming blow, only to catch his foot on the lip of the airdock and go down. The Demon that had swung at him moved forwards to finish the records keeper off.

Lenis glanced away, unable to witness Tenjin's death. It was only then that he noticed Kanu wasn't there. When had he left? Where had he gone? Lenis scanned the battleground for any sign of the boy. Panic threatened to overwhelm him. How could he have let the boy out of his sight? As Lenis was looking back towards his friends he caught sight of a flicker of blue-black hair in the tail of his defender. It took him a moment to place its significance. Blue-black hair. Blackened nails. The wolf Demon was no Demon at all.

'Kanu?' Lenis whispered.

The creature growled low in its throat. 'We have to get everyone to the *Hiryū*.'

Kanu. The small, silent child they had stumbled across in the temple of the sea god. Kanu. The young boy who had been charged with serving the twins so long ago. It was so easy to forget he was even there. He was always in the background, never drawing much attention to himself. The boy's voice was deeper now, his shoulders broader than Arthur's. The angles of his face didn't seem as sharp, either. They had settled into a blending of canine and feline features. His heavy brow overshadowed blue eyes with slit pupils. His pointed ears swept back from his skull. The tattered remains of a Shinzōn robe still hung from his waist, the same one Lenis had given him back aboard the airship. But the boy who wore it . . . this was no boy. *This* was a Titan.

Lenis shook his head, trying to clear his thoughts. 'It won't help, Kanu. Even if we could get everyone to the *Hiryū*, it would soon be overrun. There are just too many of them.'

And they kept coming. For each one the crew felled, two or three or four more came down off the walls. Most of the fighters from the *Hiryū* were injured. All were tired. Dimly, Lenis was aware of the sounds of fighting coming from the far side of the ravine, where the defenders of Haven were stationed. The cries were growing fainter. There was less light in the ravine too, as if the Bestia who were generating it were growing weaker, or fewer. It wouldn't be long now. It was almost over.

Lenis turned back to the transformed Titan boy. 'We've lost, Kanu.' He couldn't believe he was saying it. Couldn't believe it was *true*. 'Ishullanu's won.'

Kanu threw back his head and howled again. His bestial yowl reverberated around the ravine. Suiteki began to screech too, a reptilian ululation that pierced Lenis's ears and burned his heart. There was such depth to her sorrow that Lenis thought it was going to claim him completely, obliterating everything else that was not despair.

Their calls were answered by another cry filled with outrage and fury. Lenis thought it was Etana, the Demon Lord come to finish them all personally, but then he realised the noise was coming from a human throat. It was impossibly loud, but it was definitely human, and it carried a message.

'*Get out of my Haven!*'

● THE POWER OF THE CUNNING FOX ●

enis watched in awe. Where his fear had petrified him only moments before, now he was simply stunned into immobility. A woman was running along the ravine's *wall*. It was the woman from the temple, still wearing that flimsy see-through gown, and she had something . . . no, *someone* thrown over her shoulder, but she was running horizontally along the wall. And she was moving so *fast*. Lenis had been in a few races before. Mistress Kell, one of the Puritans who had owned the twins, had a love of speed, but no Bestia, landcraft, or even airship could move this fast.

She had raced past them, dumping whoever she was carrying at Lenis's feet and then leaping from one side of the ravine to the other to land in the midst of the fighting. It took Lenis a few seconds to realise it was his sister lying on the ground before him.

'Missy!' Lenis crouched down next to her. She seemed a bit dazed but otherwise unhurt.

'Lenis!' Missy grabbed his arm and hauled herself upright. 'Look!'

The woman was fighting the Demons *barehanded*. It was too much to take in. 'What is she doing?'

'She's using a *shintai*,' Missy said breathlessly.

'Where?' Lenis demanded. 'I don't see it!'

'On her hands!' Missy pointed. 'Her gloves!'

Lenis hadn't noticed them until Missy had drawn his attention to them. As he watched, they seemed to grow larger, transforming from leather gloves into metal gauntlets. They shone silver in what remained of the Bestia light bathing the ravine. At the tip of each finger was a golden claw. These were getting bigger too.

The woman tore through the ranks of Demons besieging the *Hiryū*'s crew. She moved so fast that the Demons couldn't defend themselves from her. Her blows broke horns and shattered bones. Her slashes removed limbs and heads. The Demon that was menacing Tenjin was suddenly torn in half mid-strike. The ring of Demons surrounding the captain simply fell where they stood. In less than a minute, she had annihilated every last one of the Demons that had almost destroyed the *Hiryū*'s crew.

She didn't stop there. With a jump and a midair somersault, she landed on the wall and ran up it, sending the bodies of vanquished Demons crashing down into the pit beneath her.

'How is she *doing* that?' Lenis shook his head.

'It's the gloves,' Missy said, her own awe evident. 'They're *shintai* from the Fox God.'

Lenis turned to his sister as the woman disappeared beyond the reach of the Bestia light, heading off towards the mouth of the ravine. 'Fox God?'

Missy shook her head. 'Not sure. I think it's one of the Totem. Lord Tenjin might know which one.'

Lenis shook his head again. Demonic bodies were still raining down from above. 'We'd better go help the others.'

Missy came reluctantly; her gaze turned skywards as if she could pierce the gloom above.

Things were worse than Lenis had feared. Arthur was breathing raggedly. The doctor, who himself had a large gash across his left temple, was inspecting the Kystian's chest. With the sack hanging off his belt now empty, Long Liu wiped absently at the blood pouring down his face as he continued his examination. Hiroshi was trying to get Shujinko to show him the wound in his side. Lenis remembered seeing him gored on a goat Demon's horn. If the cabin boy had damaged any of his organs, there was little anyone would be able to do for him.

The captain and Shin had found each other. Both looked pretty haggard and had several cuts and bruises on their faces and arms, but they seemed otherwise to have escaped serious injury. Princess Anastasis was standing alone with Disma, apparently unaware that she was bleeding from various gashes. Her hammer showed signs of heavy use. Lenis turned away from the gore that clung to it. Until then he had been pushing his nausea down, but the sight of the princess covered in Demon blood and guts was enough to make him gag. The smell had grown worse, too, and more than anything Lenis wanted a breath or two of fresh air.

Tenjin and Kanu, who had reverted to his near-human form, were both kneeling next to Andrea. Dismay hung heavy about them. Lenis braced himself for the worst and moved towards the trio. She was lying on the ground, very still. As he came closer he saw the blood covering her head. A coldness welled up inside Lenis as he crouched down next to her, but then he saw her chest move and relief flowed through him. She was alive! There was a lot of blood, but hadn't Yami or the doctor once told him head wounds always bleed excessively? She would be fine. She had to be.

The pool of sadness solidified around him, and Lenis saw that Andrea was sobbing. Her grief was sharp in his chest. The ache of it brought tears to his eyes.

'Where is she hurt?' Lenis asked Tenjin.

Before the records keeper could respond, Andrea reached up blindly and cried out, 'My eyes! I can't see!'

The force of her pain knocked Lenis backwards. His mind reeled from it.

'Lenis!' It was Tenjin, kneeling over him now.

'I'm all right.' Lenis sat up and pushed Andrea's emotions away. It took all of his will to shield himself from them.

'Oh, Andrea.' He touched her outstretched hand, but she snatched it away. 'Shh,' he soothed and placed a hand on her shoulder. She shied away from even that contact. Lenis closed his eyes and looked deep inside himself. He found a memory of the twins playing with Aeris on the shores of Blue Lake. It had always been a source of comfort to him. He tried to recall that solace. It was difficult. Most of his strength was devoted to keeping Andrea's grief from overwhelming him. Then Suiteki moved inside his robe, uncoiling from the ball she had wound herself into. He felt the questing from her again, a drawing and a yielding. Her fear of the Demon attack was still fresh, but through that she knew he needed her. A small kernel of hope blossomed inside Lenis. He shielded it from the chaos that surrounded him, nurtured it with more thoughts of his sister and his Bestia, and cocooned it in Suiteki's aura. As it grew, he drew it up out of himself and wrapped it around Andrea.

Slowly, her sobbing quieted. She let Lenis place a hand on her shoulder, and then he took her hand. He pushed harder, willing his own comfort on the grieving woman, smothering her panic, her sense of loss and hopelessness and horror. Sweat broke out all over his body. His teeth were clenched so tightly he thought they might crack, but he didn't ease up until Andrea settled down into sleep.

Shaking from his efforts, Lenis fell back and stared into the blackness of the night. The night? No, faint traces of dawn had appeared over the lip of the ravine far above them. Suiteki poked her head out of the folds of his robe and nudged his chin and cheek with her snout. Her claws pricked the skin on his chest, but the sensation brought more comfort than pain.

'Lenis?' Tenjin asked softly.

'I'm okay,' he mumbled. 'Just tired. I made her calm. Should get the doctor.'

He felt Tenjin pat his shoulder. 'You have done well, Lenis.'

Lenis nodded, marvelling at the changes in the sky above him as the Bestia light gave way to the sun's rays, and Suiteki pressed herself into his neck. The only Demons he could see were dead ones.

◉

Missy wandered away from the others, following Fox as she butchered her way towards the far end of the ravine. The woman showed no signs of slowing or tiring. She fought as well on the wall as she did on the ground. Better, in fact, as the Demons clinging there were at an obvious disadvantage.

Missy was terrified and excited in equal measure. This was the true power of the *shintai*. Even Tenjin hadn't known the full force of the Quillblade. If he had, there was no way he would have just given it to her. If Missy could learn to wield it safely she would have the strength she needed to defeat Ishullanu. But how was Fox using it without losing control? How did she learn to master it? And could she, *would* she teach Missy the secrets of the *shintai*?

By the time the sun had risen enough to pour some meagre light down over the lip of the ravine, the Demons had been repelled. Some had fled. Others had fallen to the defenders of Haven and the crew of the *Hiryū*. Most had died by Fox's hand, by the hand of the *Fox God*.

As Missy approached the cluster of black-coated defenders, who had gathered around their Cunning Lady, she knew that somehow she would convince this woman to teach her. There was simply no alternative. She pushed through the people of Haven until she could see the woman. Fox was laughing so hard her head was thrown back. There wasn't so much as a scratch or a bruise on her.

Fox caught sight of Missy out of the corner of her eye. 'So, little girl, what did you think of your first lesson?'

Missy pushed her sense of awe aside and ignored the ring of people surrounding them. If she couldn't convince Fox to teach her, there was no hope of defeating Ishullanu and his Demons. Missy weighed her words carefully, judging them based on what she had witnessed since meeting the woman, resisting the urge to simply take what she needed from her mind. Missy crossed her arms over her chest and tilted her head to one side. 'Not bad.'

Fox snorted. '"Not bad," she says.'

Missy nodded. 'You might just be up to the job after all. I have to admit I had my doubts.'

Fox glared at her for a moment and then started laughing again. Missy was once more reminded of the half-crazed Tien

Tese doctor. 'I *do* like you, girl. I tell you what. We'll give it a go.' Missy felt her hopes rise, but unease pierced her as Fox returned her stare. 'Just remember your side of the bargain.'

Missy swallowed and nodded. 'I will.'

Fox threw an arm around Missy's shoulders 'Ha! One way or the other, girl, the Fox *always* gets what it wants.'

Missy shivered. 'I want you to let my friends go, too.'

Fox shrugged. 'We'll see. I have to do *something* about Kenji.' She spun Missy around to present her to her followers. 'My Brotherhood! This cub is now my pupil. Let's go and celebrate!'

The people of Haven cheered as Missy was pulled along after their leader back towards the relative safety of Haven. She had done it. For whatever reason, Fox had agreed to teach her. Missy should have felt triumphant. Instead, a deep pit of grief had opened up within her. There was one part of her hastily constructed plan that she hadn't allowed herself to think about, but now that it was happening there was no avoiding her dilemma. If she was going to learn from the High Priestess of the Fox God, she was going to have to leave the *Hiryū* and her brother.

◦ NO TIME TO RECOVER ◦

The people of Haven were celebrating. The crew of the *Hiryū* had retreated to their airship, leaving the inhabitants to their festivities. Lenis supposed today had been a good day for them. They had repelled a major Demonic assault and suffered only minor losses. For Lenis and the rest of the crew, there was little to rejoice in. The galley had been converted into a hospital ward, where the tables became beds. Kanu and Lenis were put to work helping the doctor. Suiteki, finally freed from Lenis's protective grasp, was coiled in her nest by Hiroshi's stove. Even so, Lenis was always aware of her reaching out to him, both seeking and offering comfort. She craved it as much as the heat coming from the stove, but more and more she was aware of what Lenis needed. He felt her shielding her hunger from him, as if the baby dragon knew he had more pressing concerns and didn't want to pester him. Lenis let his tears fall.

The crew was in pretty bad shape. Arthur had broken several ribs. Shujinko had a large hole in his side, which the doctor was worried would soon become infected if it wasn't already. Demon scratches were nasty at the best of times, but to be gored by one . . . It was a miracle he hadn't punctured any of his organs. Even so, Long Liu insisted the cabin boy remain on bed rest to ensure he escaped serious infection. Tenjin had broken the same ankle he had sprained back on Heimat Isle. Shin, Hiroshi, Captain Shishi, and Princess Anastasis were swathed in bandages. They, too, were in danger of infection but only from lesser cuts.

Andrea was a different matter. Lenis had been there when the doctor had cleaned the wounds on her face. It had not been a pleasant experience, but Lenis had smothered his revulsion and forced himself to help. There was little he could do other than hand Long Liu clean swabs and pass the soiled ones on to Kanu for the Titan child to dispose of. Andrea remained comatose throughout. Lenis wasn't sure if the doctor had somehow kept her asleep using his medical skills, or if she were still under the effect of Lenis's empathic enforcement of calm. Either way, it was a mercy she didn't wake up. When the doctor was finished, she still looked a fright. Long Liu had stitched up several gashes on her face, including one that ran from under her nose down through her lips. She had lost one earlobe and chipped a couple of teeth. When Lenis asked about her eyes, the doctor shook his head and asked Lenis to hold Andrea up while he bandaged her face, placing a heavy wad of cloth over each eye.

Missy was nowhere to be seen, but Lenis didn't have time to wonder where she could be. Long Liu kept him busy caring for the others. At least he could take comfort knowing that Yami was with her wherever she was. The Shinzōn swordsman hadn't returned to the *Hiryū* since the battle. Lenis hoped he was still keeping an eye on Kenji. The *Hiryū*'s navigator had remained with his companions in the Brotherhood of the Fox. Lenis didn't mind if he never saw him again.

Eventually, Lenis had to sit down. His legs were all wobbly and thinking of Kenji brought on a peculiar draining sadness. The man had been a member of the crew. If not a friend, he had at least been a comrade, someone Lenis had come to count on in the crew's quest to unlock Suiteki's power and, ultimately, defeat Ishullanu. When had he come to rely on them all so explicitly? Their journey was difficult enough without having to worry about their allies as well as all of those arrayed against them. Suiteki left her nest and coiled herself up in Lenis's lap. He absently scratched her under the chin, and a ripple ran through Suiteki's scales from head to tail tip.

'You look troubled.' It was the captain. He came to sit next to Lenis on the bottom step of the stairway leading up to the fore hatch. In one hand he carried a bowl, which he offered to Lenis. The other was pressed to his side, mute evidence of his own injuries.

Lenis simply nodded and took the bowl. The smell of broth rose out of it, but he had no appetite. He cradled it in his lap within the loops of Suiteki's body, enjoying the heat that soaked from it into his hands. The little dragon was also pleased by this and twisted her head around to lap at the thin soup. Lenis hadn't realised how cold they both were until he felt the warmth radiate inside her belly. Winter seemed to be clinging to the mountains of Heiligland far longer than it ought to.

'I do not know where to begin.' The captain's admission took Lenis by surprise. He'd never known the man to show doubt before. He didn't even bother to whisper, and the rest of the crew were right there in front of them. 'It seems that every time we turn around, we face a new danger, a new obstacle. We no sooner deal with one than another two take its place.'

Lenis nodded again. It appeared Kenji's betrayal had hit the captain hard too, and that had been followed so quickly by their defeat at the hands of the Demons. No wonder the man was distressed. 'It does seem like that sometimes,' Lenis mumbled.

'Already I fear that Karasu has beaten us to Kolga's temple.'

'There's really only one thing we can do,' Lenis noted, trying to put some strength into his words.

The captain turned to him, one eyebrow cocked. 'And what is that, Mister Clemens?'

'Our best.'

The captain smiled. A moment later he laughed. 'You are quite correct.' He stood up and addressed the rest of the crew, who were still gathered in the galley. 'I understand that we have all suffered today, and that we are injured and exhausted, but we must continue in our pursuit of the stones of ebb and flow. The Demons have withdrawn for the time being, and the people of Haven are busy with their merriment. We must take this opportunity to push on to Kolga's temple. Miss Shin, please work with Mister Clemens and Mister Hiroshi to ready the landcraft.'

'Is this wise, Captain?' Lenis could hear the fatigue in Shin's voice. 'None of us is in any condition to make such a journey.'

The captain chuckled and glanced at Lenis. 'What wisdom forbids, Miss Shin, necessity dictates. We must make haste while the Demons are still in disarray and before the Cunning Lady decides she will take Mister Jackson up on his offer.'

'Yes, sir,' Shin replied, though her voice lacked conviction. She nodded to Lenis and Hiroshi. As Hiroshi followed Shin above decks, Lenis tried to place Suiteki back in her nest, but she gripped fast to his robes and, rather than tearing them, he just sighed and allowed her to slither into their folds. He had to admit he was grateful for the warmth she shed when he was up on deck.

Lenis stumbled through the next half hour in an almost trance-like state. He was beyond tired. His entire body was in pain and his muscles ached as he tried to force them to keep going. His eyes were full of grit. It took an enormous amount of effort to keep from constantly yawning. Hiroshi and Shin were, if anything, in worse shape. They didn't seem as lethargic as Lenis, but their injuries, however minor, still slowed them down. He could tell from the way the cook limped that he was favouring his left leg, and Shin couldn't lift one arm above her head. Still, together they were able to set the winch and manoeuvre the landcraft over the side. There was barely enough room for it on the ravine floor, but soon they were ready to go.

Lenis went down to the engine room to fetch the Bestia. They were in quite a state. Although they had remained safe on board the *Hiryū* throughout the battle, Lenis could tell they had been almost frantic with fear and concern. Their relief at seeing him safely return flooded over him when he entered the engine room. The sensations were so comforting they lulled him dangerously close to sleep. Ignis jumped all over him. Aeris and Atrum both wound themselves around his feet. Atrum's tail nearly tripped him up as he crouched down to pat and embrace his Bestia. Their presence drew Suiteki out of Lenis's robe, and the baby dragon scrabbled down into their hutch, squawking away as though regaling the Bestia with a recounting of her adventures.

Terra was huddled in the far corner of the Bestia hutch, with his nose hidden under his tail. The most sensitive of Lenis's Bestia, he had coped the worst during the Demon attack. Lenis reached down and scooped him up, holding him close against his chest and rocking backwards and forwards as the earth Bestia pushed his nose into Lenis's neck. Guilt washed through him as Lenis thought about what he was going to ask of the Bestia now. He looked down at all of them and wondered, not for the first time, how he could place them all in such danger.

Aeris stood up on her hind legs and placed her forelegs on his thigh. He reached down to run a hand between her ears, drawing her understanding up and wrapping it around himself.

Lenis hugged Terra even tighter. 'Come on, boy. It's time to go.' He looked down. 'You too, Atrum. Let's get this over with as quickly and quietly as we can.'

The other Bestia stood in the doorway, barring Suiteki from the exit while Lenis, Atrum, and Terra climbed the stairs to the deck. Hearing the baby Totem's protests, Lenis wanted nothing more than to go back down to his bunk, pull all of his charges around him, and sleep. But that would have to wait.

'Have you seen your sister?' Shin asked as Lenis emerged on deck.

Lenis shook his head. 'I think she's still with Yami and Ken–' He stopped short.

The corners of Shin's mouth turned down, the harsh lines carved into her face by a lifetime sailing the infected oceans were set, turning her countenance into a horrible mask. 'Someone has to keep an eye on that traitor in case he tries anything else.'

Lenis nodded and fell into step behind her. Shin's presence had a way of putting Lenis at ease ever since their encounter in Neti's temple. Hiroshi, the captain, and Kanu were waiting for them by the landcraft.

'We must make haste,' the captain reiterated as they all mounted.

Lenis placed Terra in the engine block and climbed up into the pilot's seat. Atrum jumped up into his lap and, a moment later, Lenis felt the Bestia's power spreading around them, wrapping them in his cloak of invisibility. The engines rumbled to life and Lenis steered them down the airdock towards the far end of the ravine.

There were Demonic bodies everywhere, too numerous to count even if Lenis had wanted to. The Cunning Lady had done her work well, protecting her Haven with the power of a *shintai*. A part of Lenis was grateful, but another part was not. If she had acted sooner, no one would have been hurt. Andrea would not have lost her sight.

Despite the fact that the Demon force had been routed, Lenis kept his senses alert for their presence. For one thing, the Demon Lord, Etana, had not been defeated. Perhaps the Fox Lady had scared him off, or maybe he was simply waiting for them to leave the safety of Haven. Either way, Lenis was vigilant. Atrum's cloak should protect them, but it was possible a Demon Lord like Etana was powerful enough to pierce such a veil.

Reflexively, the crew pulled their scarves up over their mouths and noses as they drove through the cleft in the rock face that marked the entrance to Haven and left its bubble of protection behind. Lenis's scarf had been a gift from Namei. Thinking about her brought a fresh wave of grief, and he was reminded of the sense of her he had felt up on the forecastle before his fight with Shujinko. He longed to try to form that connection again but so far had not had the opportunity. Once they were done here and underway, he would try again. For now, as the sickly sweet stench of the Wastelands tickled the back of his throat and the familiar greenish mist rose up to swallow them, Lenis had to focus on driving once more into the Wastelands.

◉

Missy sat on the step below Fox's divan with her elbow on her knee and her chin resting on her palm. She longed to return to the *Hiryū*, to find out how the others fared, but Missy feared leaving the woman's side in case she reneged on their agreement. Missy couldn't risk that. Not now.

Missy was also afraid that seeing her brother would make her change her own mind. The enormity of it could not be confronted head on. Things hadn't really been right with them since their experience with Kanu on the jetty of Fronge, and now she was going to leave him. There was no way to know if she would ever see him again. Once the *Hiryū* left, Missy would be stuck in Haven with the Fox Lady. *If* the *Hiryū* left. Who knew what Fox would decide to do with them? With the amount of power she could wield, Fox could do whatever she wanted.

And then there was the problem of Kenji Jackson. What would Fox do with him, *to* him, and how would that affect the *Hiryū*? The navigator was now lounging against one wall of the temple, being ignored by everyone except Yami, who maintained his guard.

'Brighten up, cub,' Fox said as she bent down to mess up Missy's hair. 'This is supposed to be a party.'

Missy did her best to put a smile on her face but worried it looked more like a grimace. She turned to Fox. 'I'm fine.'

The corners of Fox's mouth turned down. 'No. You're not.' Missy opened her mouth to object but Fox cut her off. 'They don't call me the Cunning Lady for nothing, you know. I tell you what. If you relax a little, I'll agree to let your friends go when they get back from the Wastelands.'

Missy surged to her feet. 'The Wastelands!'

Fox shrugged. 'Of course. Isn't that why you came here? Now try to enjoy yourself, just a little. Okay?'

◦ THE TEMPLE OF THE GENTLE MAIDEN ◦

L enis tried to shake the feeling that they were lost. The captain seemed confident he remembered the way to Kolga's temple, but Lenis wasn't sure he trusted him on that. It was easy to lose your way in the Wastelands, even more so when those Wastelands were in the mountains. After leaving Haven, Lenis had been forced to steer the landcraft along a narrow rocky ledge between a towering mountain and a vast roiling world of greenish mist. The edge of the shelf on which they drove was all too evident, but beyond that there could be anything – a drop into an even deeper gorge, the roots of another mountain, or even an inland sea. Whatever was there was shrouded in the vapours of the Wastelands.

After about an hour of driving, however, the ledge broadened out into a plateau. This was even more disturbing, as the world around them became flat and empty. The mountain wall they had been following disappeared as the fog encircled the landcraft. There were no trees, no outcrops of stone, no features at all. Suddenly locating Kolga's temple was the least of Lenis's fears. Without any landmarks and surrounded by mist, he was starting to worry that they were never going to be able to find their way back to Haven.

'Try to keep us moving straight ahead, Mister Clemens,' the captain said, his words muffled by his scarf and the oppressive air.

Lenis did try. He was exhausted, his eyes were so dry it hurt to keep them open, and his hands were stiff and sore from clutching the steering shaft and his earlier encounter with the Quillblade, but he persevered. At any moment, they would reach Kolga's temple, and then . . . Lenis didn't know what would happen. Either they'd find one of the stones of ebb and flow, or they would discover Karasu had already beaten them to it. He didn't want to consider that maybe there was no stone out here at all, that it lay hidden in some other temple in some other country where Apsilla was known by some other name. Or worse, that someone else besides Karasu had already found the stone and taken it. In Seisui's temple, in Shinzō, they had found engravings that led them to Asheim in Ost. If an adventurer or an explorer had been to Kolga's temple before them and taken the treasure the *Hiryū*'s crew were seeking, there was no guarantee that they had left behind similar clues.

A familiar headache began building in Lenis's skull. The tainted air played tricks with his mind. A low buzzing had been building just inside his range of hearing. He did his best to ignore it, but it seemed to grow louder. Then he realised what it was.

'That's an engine!' Lenis cried out.

The captain reached forwards to place a hand on his shoulder. 'Softly, Mister Clemens,' he whispered in Lenis's ear. 'Sound can carry strangely in normal fog, more so in this tainted atmosphere. That is indeed an engine. I dare to hope it is the sound of Karasu's own airship.'

As the captain sat back, Lenis felt his heartbeat quicken. If it really was Karasu's airship, then they were almost at their destination, but it seemed impossible! How could they both arrive here at exactly the same time?

The sound grew stronger, and Lenis found himself holding his breath. Slowly, he exhaled. Even if it were Karasu, he would not be able to see them as long as they remained absolutely silent. It was likely the sound of his airship's engines would drown out the noise of the landcraft, but they could only mask so much.

Lenis lost all track of time. This, too, had happened to him before in the Wastelands, but now he was distracted by the increasing whirr of engines calling out to them, drawing them onwards. So focused was he on the sound that it took Lenis a moment to notice there was something looming up ahead of them. He strained his eyes, trying to make out what exactly it was. One moment, he was sure it was an airship. The next, it looked more like a building or tower. Lenis felt his frustration build, which he discovered was being fuelled by his companions' emotions. By concentrating, Lenis was able to block out their impatience and tension, but that still left him dealing with his own.

The fog broke and the shape came into focus. It was an airship, and it looked just like the *Hiryū*, right down to the red dragon figurehead. Behind it was the now familiar squat shape of a Totem's temple. Lenis could not believe their luck. Not only had they found Kolga's temple, but Karasu was here as well. If they could somehow get both stones away from him, the one in the temple and the one already in the mercenary's possession, then their quest would be over! They would finally be able to unlock Suiteki's powers.

Lenis brought the landcraft to a stop. For a while no one said anything, and then the captain motioned them all closer.

'It appears our timing is fortunate,' he whispered. The words were so low they were barely louder than his breathing, but Lenis could sense Captain Shishi's controlled excitement. 'We must decide whether to attempt to sneak aboard Karasu's airship and retrieve the first stone, or confront him in the temple for the second.'

Lenis remembered back to their near-encounter with Karasu in Seisui's temple and their confrontation in the chamber with the ice pillar. He didn't want to face the mercenary in a direct fight, but back in the Wastelands of Shinzō, Karasu had gone into the temple with only Chūritsu for company, leaving his warriors aboard his airship. Had he done so now?

'We could split up.' Lenis tried to speak as low as he could. 'I could take Atrum and sneak on board the airship. I know where the stone is kept.'

'It is possible Karasu will have it with him,' the captain countered. 'I will not risk you facing him alone, Mister Clemens. Pull the landcraft around to that side –' he pointed to a spot between Karasu's airship and the temple '– and let us see if we can gain a clearer assessment of the situation.'

Lenis nodded and, as slowly as he could manage, he manoeuvred to the place the captain had suggested. There was no sign of movement either on board the airship or near the entrance to the temple, except for the flickering of torches.

The captain motioned Lenis, Kanu, Shin, and Hiroshi in close again. 'We must make haste. That Karasu still has his engines running suggests he means to leave soon and in a hurry. The fact that he hasn't departed yet makes me believe he is still in the temple.'

Hiroshi's attempt at a whisper was awfully loud. 'So, which is it, then? The temple or the airship?'

Lenis could feel the captain's indecision. At first he thought the man would never be able to make up his mind, but then Captain Shishi said, 'The temple. It is the better option. At worst, he has left the stone he already possesses on the airship. If we can disable Karasu, we can use him as a hostage to barter with his crew for the stone.'

The others nodded, content to let this decision be the captain's.

Lenis moved the landcraft around the temple's corner so that it would not be easily spotted once Atrum's veil of invisibility moved away from it. Then he quickly explained Atrum's power, telling them all that they would each have to remain in physical contact to be affected by it. It was awkward, climbing down out of the landcraft whilst holding each other's hands, but they managed. Lenis held Atrum and Kanu's hand. Next came the captain, then Shin, and finally Hiroshi. In an uneven line they moved around to the temple's entrance.

Like the other temples Lenis had seen, this one had a gaping rectangle for a doorway. On either side, Karasu had placed torches, and the crewmembers moved around them warily, not quite believing their invisibility. Lenis had an advantage here, as he could sense Atrum's power at work, while the others just had to trust him. Once they were inside the temple, Lenis could hear voices. He moved in deeper until he was able to make out the interior.

Kolga, it seemed, took the form of a maiden. The walls of her temple were covered in carvings of a young woman holding an overly large jar. According to the engravings, the jar held many wonders. It could pour fresh water for people to drink, douse fires, sooth injuries, and water crops with, or, as in the one that drew Lenis's immediate attention, it could repel the ocean's waves. His excitement grew. This was it! It *had* to be.

And then he noticed who was speaking. It had not been Karasu and Chūritsu, as Lenis had hoped. They were both there, but they were speaking with another figure that had greenish skin and large tusks protruding from its mouth. Its hair was a tangle of dry tree branches, and Lenis could see a single horn rising out of the top of its head. It was girded in a reed skirt, and its hands and feet were webbed. Lenis knew at once that it was a Demon, but he could also tell it had once been a Lilim, its physical presence a clear indicator that it had completely devoured the human it had been bonded to.

'Well, here is your precious stone, Lord Karasu.' The Lilim waved at something behind him, out of Lenis's line of sight. He felt Kanu grip his hand, hard. The signal to stop and wait.

'Is that mockery I hear in your tone, Akandoji?' Karasu snapped, and it occurred to Lenis that they were speaking in the common tongue. Why would they do that? Akandoji sounded like a Shinzōn name. Surely . . .

'Of course not, master.' The Demon performed a stiffly formal bow. 'I would never dare to mock you.'

Something tickled at the back of Lenis's mind. It was something, he now realised, that he had been pondering for some time. Akandoji reminded him of Akamusaborikū, and not just because they had met in similar circumstances – seeing Karasu in or near a temple in the Wastelands. Lenis wondered why he hadn't thought of it before, but of course, he *had*. He had been thinking of it ever since Gesshoku. Akamusaborikū could talk. And so could Akandoji. How were they able to do that? Demons were mindless vessels. They lost their souls to the Wasteland sickness. Yet here was a Demon conversing with Karasu, just as Akamusaborikū had been taunting them back near Shinzō. It should not have been possible. The Lilim Demons they had just fought in Haven hadn't been this intelligent. What was the connection? Was it the temples? Surely it could not have been Karasu?

'It hardly matters,' Chūritsu said, then scooped up the stone from behind the Demon, depositing it in the sack he carried over one shoulder. 'We aren't going to be *using* it. Not as anything more than a bargaining chip, at any rate. Let's just get out of here. This tainted air does terrible things to my allergies.'

Karasu snorted. 'So be it. The attack on Haven should be at an end by now. Let us go and pick through the debris.'

All three figures turned and started walking towards the entrance. Chūritsu asked, 'You don't think the Mayonaka brat could have been killed, do you?'

Karasu gave a bark of laughter. 'Not that one. Besides, the witch will probably protect him. There's no way she'd let the Demons get their hands on the baby Totem. Isn't that right, Captain Shishi?'

The mercenary stopped halfway to the doorway. Akandoji and Chūritsu walked on for a few more paces before they, too, paused. The scientist scratched the back of his head. 'What are you –?'

Karasu said something in Shinzōn. Lenis felt the captain pull away from Kanu's hold. He, Shin and Hiroshi were no longer cloaked under Atrum's power – they were no longer invisible.

The captain drew his sword. 'Very perceptive, Sir Karasu. Out of curiosity, might I ask what gave us away?'

Karasu reached behind his back and drew his own large sword. A Lilim blade, Lenis now surmised, forged when a Lilim chose to exist forever in the form of an inanimate object rather than face death as a living thing. 'I have been expecting you, Captain Shishi, for some time now.'

'Oh?' The captain raised one eyebrow.

'Your engineer taught me a few new tricks.' The mercenary grinned and looked straight at Lenis. Lenis's heart thudded in his chest. How could he see him? Atrum was still cloaking him. 'I would never have thought to use a Bestia so. You can come out, boy. I can see you. The torchlight flickers around the edges of your cloaked form.'

Lenis blinked. He hadn't even thought of that. If Atrum made them invisible by refracting the light around them, then *shifting* the torchlight would . . . He pushed the idea to the back of his mind to churn through on its own. Lenis pulled his hand away from Kanu's and squeezed Atrum, who jumped out of his arms and dropped his veil of invisibility.

'That's better,' Karasu said. 'We are all here.'

'Give us the stones, Sir Karasu,' the captain said in an even voice.

The mercenary laughed. 'Of course. You may have this one now.' He reached into Chūritsu's sack and pulled something out. It was the size and shape of the stone Lenis had seen in Karasu's cabin, when he had snuck onto the mercenary's airship in Fronge, but there was something *different* about this one. Karasu bent down and placed the stone on the ground at his feet. 'Now, step aside. We will leave peacefully. You get one of your little stones. No one needs to die.'

Captain Shishi was implacable. 'Both stones.'

Karasu shook his head. 'I will give you this one as a sign of my good faith. The other, I will keep.'

'Are you working for the Demon King?' the captain demanded. The question took Lenis by surprise, but if Karasu was working for Ishullanu his refusal to hand over both stones made sense. Then again, why hand over either of them?

Instead of replying, Karasu turned his gaze on Kanu. The boy regarded him calmly in turn. 'You had me fooled, boy. I mistook you for your master.' He turned back to the captain. 'Stand aside, Shishi, and I will make you a deal. Allow me to leave and you may follow along behind me. When we reach our destination, I will give you the second stone. As a further sign of my good faith, I will even tell you we are heading to Kaltheim in Ost. There, you see? Fighting will accomplish little. Look at you! You're wounded and exhausted. I am offering you an alternative to violence. One where we all get what we want.'

The captain remained silent for a moment. 'What is the catch?'

Karasu smirked, eyeing Kanu once more. 'Bring this boy with you.'

'Why?'

'You will see when we get to where we're going.'

'Captain?' Shin interrupted.

Captain Shishi nodded. 'Very well.'

'Captain!' Hiroshi cried. 'We can take them all, I tell you!'

'No, Mister Hiroshi.' The captain raised his arm to one side. 'We have been offered a peaceful alternative to fighting. We shall take it. Stand aside, all of you. Allow Karasu and his . . . companions to leave.'

Karasu nodded. 'Wise decision, Shishi.'

He, Chūritsu and the Demon Akandoji started walking again. Lenis grabbed Kanu's hand and pulled him to one side as Karasu approached. When they drew level, the mercenary looked Lenis in the eye and said, 'You really are a remarkable Bestia Keeper, boy. I will remember you once this is done.' He turned to go but then paused. 'A true master of his craft must first be tested,' he said over his shoulder. 'Can your *Hiryū* catch my *Ryōshiryū*? Such a task would be a fitting trial for an airship engineer's skills, do you not agree? The winner shall claim the dragon's heart.'

'What does that mean?' Lenis demanded, shaken.

'If you can catch me you will be worthy of an answer.'

Saying no more, Karasu led his two companions out of the temple.

As soon as they were gone Lenis rushed towards the discarded stone, pushing Karasu's challenge to the edge of his thoughts. Finally, they had retrieved one of the stones of ebb and flow! For whatever reason, and Lenis had no doubt he *had* a reason, Karasu had given them what they had come for. As he knelt down to retrieve the stone, triumph surged through him, only to be doused as his hand closed around the long sought after orb. A large crack marred its otherwise smooth surface. It was broken.

◉ THE DEMON OF THE NORTHERN ISLES ◉

'**C**aptain!' Lenis shouted, cradling the stone in both hands. 'Captain, it's broken!'

They all rushed to where Lenis was kneeling, demanding to see the stone for themselves.

'He tricked us,' Shin said.

'After him!' Hiroshi shouted and took off out of the temple.

The others were quick to follow, their wounds and tiredness forgotten. To have come so close only to walk away with nothing . . . they would take their fury out on the Shinzōn mercenary! Lenis felt himself buoyed along by his crewmates' outrage. He drew it into himself, feeding his own anger, allowing it to burn away his fatigue. He found his own fingers twitching for a weapon he had never held.

And then they were outside, where Karasu was already

on board his airship, giving the order to get underway. But before them, barring their way and frustrating their drive for vengeance, was Akandoji the Demon.

Lenis expected the captain to attack immediately, as he had done back in the Wastelands outside of Gesshoku, where the captain had leapt up and decapitated Akamusaborikū in one swift motion. Either his encounter with that Demon had made him wary – not even chopping off his head had been enough to stop the Demon – or the captain was in a worse state than Lenis had thought, because instead he stopped and raised a warning hand to the others.

Akandoji laughed. It sounded like the gurgling of water over stones. 'So, you are the mortals who bested Akamusaborikū?'

Lenis had been right. There *was* a connection between the two Demonic Lilim!

The captain crouched into a fighting stance, his sword held low but at the ready. 'I am Mayonaka Shishi of the *Uchū no Shinpan-ryū*. Break off your horn and surrender to me.'

As Akamusaborikū had done before him, Akandoji threw back his head and laughed all the harder. This time it came out like a torrent. 'Well, *I* am Akandoji, Demon of the Northern Isles and Servant to Lord Aitō the Water Demon, and I do not submit to the judgement of *any* mortal.'

'Except for Shōgo no Akushin Karasu?' the captain countered.

The Demon looked over his shoulder to where Karasu's airship had just begun to lift off the ground. 'Ha!' Akandoji muttered. 'Me? Serve *him*? Foolishness!'

'You serve Lord Aitō?' the captain pressed.

Lenis wondered why he was wasting time talking to the Demon. Every second they delayed gave Karasu a chance to get further away. Already it would take time to return to Haven, deal with the Brotherhood of the Nine-Tailed Fox, and then get the *Hiryū* in the air to give chase. What was the captain *thinking*?

Akandoji was considering the captain carefully. 'What do you know of Lord Aitō?'

The captain replied, 'I know that he was once the *Onishu* who brought tsunamis and floods to Shinzō. His tears could drown a whole village.'

'Indeed!' The Demon chuckled. 'I had misjudged you for a fool!'

'I also know that Aitō has many names, and that his power stretches into distant lands.'

'True! True!'

'And that the only thing he fears in this world is Akuma, Lord of the Underworld.'

'Yes,' Akandoji said with less enthusiasm. 'All fear the King of the *Onishu*.'

Lenis's mind was working furiously. He didn't have his sister's head for languages, but he remembered Tenjin had once told him *Onishu* was a Shinzōn word meaning 'Demon

Lord'. Something clicked into place. Akuma, King of the *Onishu*. Just like *Ishullanu, the Demon King*!

'My crew and I,' the captain went on, 'are on a quest to destroy Akuma.'

'You *are* a fool,' the Demon scoffed. 'His power is too great for any mortal to overcome.'

'Perhaps,' the captain conceded, 'but I do not see why a servant of Lord Aitō would seek to thwart Akuma's enemies.'

Akandoji took a while to process this. Eventually the Demon shrugged, tossing his gnarled hair about. 'Neither do I, mortal. You may be a fool, but you are a wise one. You may go.'

The captain relaxed his stance, but only by a bit. 'You will let us pass?'

'Of course.' Akandoji gave another bow and waved his hand to one side, motioning for them to go ahead. 'I sought only to delay you long enough for Karasu to leave. Besides,' he added as he straightened, 'I'm not all that hungry for human flesh just now.'

'Captain?' Shin asked, her eyes never leaving the Demon.

'Return to the landcraft,' the captain said. 'I do not believe Akandoji will try to stop us now.'

The Demon smirked. 'Quite so.'

The others turned and walked around to the side of the temple, where the landcraft was waiting. Each of them kept their necks craned around so they could watch Akandoji in case he tried to attack their backs. He remained where he was.

So did the captain. 'Why are you working with Karasu?'

Akandoji looked to his left and then to his right, as if afraid of being overheard. It was such a human gesture that it made Lenis shiver. As alien as the Lilim were, there was always something *human* about them. It was unnerving, even more so when that Lilim was a Demon – a Demon that was also somehow *still alive*.

'That man is also a fool, mortal,' Akandoji said in a stage whisper. 'But he is a useful one.'

The captain paused for another moment before walking over to the landcraft. He didn't once look over his shoulder to ensure the Demon wasn't about to pounce on him.

'What was *that* all about, Captain?' Hiroshi asked as they all mounted.

'I am not sure, Mister Hiroshi,' the captain replied. 'It seems there is even more going on in the world than I had suspected. Mister Clemens, please get us back to Haven as quickly as possible. We must try and catch up with Karasu.'

Lenis settled into the pilot's seat and started the engines. 'I'm not sure I *can* find our way back,' he admitted. 'Every direction looks the same out here.'

'Can you not sense the Bestia as you did back in the Wastelands near Neti's temple?' the captain asked. 'There are many of them in Haven.'

'Oh, I forgot about that,' Lenis admitted and, feeling a little sheepish, he sent his awareness out into the Wastelands around them.

Missy stood at the entrance to Haven and stared out into the Wastelands. Not that she could see far, but she was determined to meet her brother as soon as he returned. They really needed to talk. Missy had to tell him that she was staying in Haven, that she was sorry, and that she didn't want them to be mad at one another when they parted ways. Dread filled her. She feared how he would react. Would he see this as just another attempt to claim power for herself? Would he look at her with those sad blue-green eyes of his?

She shivered. No. He would understand. He *had* to understand. It wasn't that she wanted to leave. There was no choice. Even with Suiteki at full power they would need more than one Totem to stand against Ishullanu and his Demon army. Even if all she wanted was to stay with her brother aboard the *Hiryū*, and the thought of leaving them tore her up inside, it didn't matter. She would do it. As her brother always said, *what wisdom forbade, necessity dictated*, or something like that.

Missy's resolve did nothing to ease her growing guilt, nor fill the hollowness opening up inside her. She was so caught up in her own turmoil that she hadn't noticed the sound of engines riding the wind. Her heart skipped in her chest. This was it. The time had come.

Only it hadn't. What she heard was not the engine of a landcraft, but those of an airship. Her body tensed. Who could it be? Leaving off her vigil, she raced down to the airdock. Ahead of her she could see the black-coated members of the Brotherhood coming out to greet the new arrival. Missy tried to tell herself to relax. The signal Bestia were lighting the way, so whoever it was had probably contacted Pog before coming in to land.

After what seemed an age, the airship settled into the berth next to the *Hiryū*. Missy recognised it immediately. It was the *Geschichte*, their lost escort. Ursula Klinge, the airship's captain, was at the railing before the vessel touched down.

'Did they arrive?' she called as she came storming down the gangplank. 'Are they safe?' Ursula caught sight of Missy and strode up to her. 'You're all right! After that Demon attack I was wondering . . .' Her words trailed off as she took in Missy's appearance. She must have looked a sight. Tear-stained cheeks. Sweat-soaked clothing. Shivering like a *child*. What was it Heidi had always told her? *Gods don't get cold.* Ursula was frowning down at her. 'You aren't Magni.' She sounded uncertain, as if she was asking rather than stating.

Missy shook her head, shame flooding through her. 'I'm not Magni,' she began in a small voice, 'but I can explain.' And she did, as fast as she dared. She told Ursula about Ishullanu and the *Hiryū*, and about Fronge and Heidi and the Quillblade, the words rushing out of her in her haste to be heard and, she had to admit to herself, to justify what she had done. All the while Ursula remained unmoving, her brows pulled together and her mouth set. The crevices etched into her face seemed to grow deeper, too, casting her features into unreal lines of shadow. 'We didn't have a choice,' Missy finished.

Ursula opened her mouth, then she pressed it close again. Finally, she let out a long breath through her nose and said, 'You may not be a god, girl, but you move in some pretty divine company.'

Missy wasn't sure how to take that. When Ursula didn't say anything more, Missy ventured, 'Are you mad?'

Captain Klinge looked grimmer than ever, but then she gave a bark of laughter and reached out to push a curl of hair back from Missy's face. Missy looked down, strangely embarrassed by the woman's gesture. 'It's hard to be mad at someone who's trying to save the world. What's your name? Your *real* name?'

'Misericordia Clemens. Missy.'

'Well, Missy, I don't like being lied to, I'll say that straight up, but I've been flying long enough to know that the Demons *are* multiplying, and I've seen more than a few safe ports enveloped by the Wastelands. I don't fully understand what you're doing or what's going on, but I believe you when you say you were only trying to help. Way I see it, the Demons will come as you say, or we'll end up having to go after them. Either way, Heiligland needs a war goddess, and since the real Magni seems to be hiding somewhere, I guess you'll do.'

'Do you mean that?' Missy's throat was so closed up she croaked the words.

Ursula shook her head. 'Demon's wings! You're just a child.'

Missy felt the tears prickling behind her eyes. She didn't know how to respond to the woman's kindness, but then Michael, the man who had first greeted them in Haven, started shouting, 'They're back!' and she didn't have to.

He was pointing towards the entrance to Haven. Missy looked up and saw the landcraft pull into the crevice that marked the beginning of the ravine. Her brother was in the pilot's seat, looking haggard but apparently unharmed. She raced up to meet them and nearly dragged Lenis off the machine as she reached up to embrace him, choking on her sobs.

'What's the matter with you?' Lenis mumbled. He was completely worn out.

'I was so worried about you!' Missy cried. 'Did you find it?'

Lenis sighed. 'Not exactly.'

He held something out to her, and she took it from his hand. It was a smooth orb, marred by a single, savage crack. 'What happened?'

'Karasu.'

And then everyone was gathering around them, demanding explanations, shouting accusations. Missy ignored them all. She only had eyes for her brother, who was so weary he could barely stand without her support. Pulling his arm around her shoulder, she began leading him towards the *Hiryū*. With a pang inside her chest, Missy looked back at Ursula, but Captain Shishi had approached the *Geschichte*'s captain and was talking earnestly with her.

Lenis. Focus on Lenis.

She felt her burden lighten and glanced across Lenis's semi-prone body. Kanu had taken her brother's other arm. Together they got him up the gangplank, below decks, and into his bunk. He was snoring softly even before the Bestia clustered up and around him, welcoming their Keeper home.

'I think I know now,' Kanu said.

The words caught Missy off guard. 'Know what?'

'I understand why I am here.'

Missy felt her heart catch for a moment. Not this *servant of Mashu* thing again. 'And why is that, Kanu?'

'I am here because he needs me to be here.'

Missy suppressed a sigh and studied her sleeping brother's face. He always managed to appear so peaceful when he was asleep. The creases that so often marred his forehead when he was troubled smoothed themselves out. The tightness around his eyes lessened. His mouth went slack, and a spot of drool dribbled down his chin. Absently, she used the corner of his blanket to wipe it away. Lenis. Her little brother. When he woke up she would have to say goodbye to him. Tears formed at the corners of her eyes and then began to fall. Kanu left them in peace.

◉

Lenis woke from what he thought might have been a bad dream, but he couldn't remember what it had been about. The Bestia were all over him, and Suiteki was looped over his neck, but he resisted the urge to pull himself free of them. Instead, he settled deeper into his bunk and tried to fall back asleep. There would be time enough to deal with reality when he was properly awake. He placed his hand over his pocket to make sure the stone was still there. For now he was content to let his body rest and his mind drift back into his dreams.

A moment later his eyes flew open. Karasu. He didn't have the time to lie around in his bunk. He tried to disentangle himself from his Bestia without waking them, but of course they stirred as soon as he moved. Lenis placed a hand over Suiteki and transferred her into the space inside his robe she loved so much. Aeris mewed at him before curling up on his pillow. Lenis scratched her between the ears, gave Ignis a quick pat, and then headed up to the bridge. It was empty. Lenis went back down to their makeshift infirmary. Shujinko was the only one there. The cabin boy was lying on one of the tables, wrapped up in blankets. He didn't seem too happy about it, either.

'Where is everyone?' Lenis asked.

Shujinko glared at him. His left eye was still discoloured

from the beating Lenis had given him. 'They have gone into Haven.'

Lenis nodded, moving around Hiroshi's bench to place Suiteki back in her nest. She didn't want to, but Lenis tapped the baby dragon gently on the nose. She snipped at him, her hunger pushing against his senses until he rummaged around in the cupboard and found the jar of tidbits Hiroshi kept for her. Suiteki snapped up the kernels of dried meat and sent a blast of recrimination at Lenis for tapping her on the nose. He grimaced and nudged her with remorse.

Lenis was surprised when he sensed her satisfaction. 'Well, my lady, aren't we growing up into quite the little princess?'

'What did you say?' Shujinko snapped.

Lenis stood up to see the cabin boy straining up from his makeshift pallet to look over Hiroshi's bench. 'I was speaking to Suiteki. Shouldn't you be lying down?'

'I am fine.'

'You don't *look* fine.'

The two glared at each for a moment, and then Shujinko looked away. 'You did nothing.'

Lenis felt coldness spread through his chest. 'What?'

'During the battle, you did nothing,' Shujinko repeated. 'Ever since you beat me, I have wanted to challenge you again, to test myself against you. Two warriors using their full power without holding back. But I no longer wish for that. There is no honour to be won or lost in challenging a weakling.'

Lenis's heart beat faster. His surging blood warmed his whole body. 'Just a min –'

'You have power, Lenis, but you do not use it. Shinzōn swordsmen spend all of their time training. Every moment of every day. It is their purpose, their focus. Everything they do and everything they are is their sword. You do not even possess a weapon. Your sister is more of a warrior than you are. No matter how much you may wish it, you will never be one. You are not a fighter.'

Lenis stood there dumbfounded, resentment boiling inside him, but he couldn't refute Shujinko's words. The cabin boy had been badly wounded fighting the Demons, protecting their crewmates, while Lenis had cowered behind Kanu.

'I doubt the dragon can even understand you,' Shujinko said, and lay down again to gaze at the ceiling.

'She understands enough,' Lenis mumbled, his voice made hollow by the cabin boy's casual dismissal of his prowess. With a few small statements Shujinko had shattered Lenis's illusions of himself as any sort of warrior. He made mockery of all of Lenis's training. How pathetic his few practice bouts must have seemed to the fully trained Shinzōn boy. No, not boy. Swordsman. Shujinko was a swordsman, just like Yami and the captain. He would be the one fighting Demons alongside them. Not Lenis. In light of the cabin boy's words such private dreams were made vainglorious and childish, and his words weren't even the worst of it. Shujinko no longer hated Lenis. He no longer resented him. If Shujinko felt anything for Lenis it was pity, the same pity he reserved for any helpless creature.

Lenis turned from the cabin boy and crouched down next to Suiteki again. The little dragon was still gorging herself on treats. Blinking through tears, Lenis pulled the marred stone from his pocket and offered it up to her.

Suiteki gulped down her mouthful and looked at the stone with her head tilted to the side. Lenis pushed it a little closer, and Suiteki scrabbled out of her nest to sniff it. She cawed and then licked the orb's surface. Lenis felt nothing from the stone, but the sadness that welled up inside the baby Totem was so intense he hastily put the thing back in his pocket. So, he had been right. There was something wrong with it.

'. . . are you even listening to me?'

Lenis rubbed at his face before standing. 'Sorry, what?'

'I said,' Shujinko repeated slowly, 'you should probably get to the temple in Haven. The captain wanted you at the meeting.'

'What meeting?'

Shujinko sniffed and looked away. 'The one they're having to decide the *Hiryū*'s fate. Without me.'

◦ PREPARATIONS ◦

Missy sat on a chair next to Fox's divan and tried to avoid the questioning looks her crewmates were directing at her. *Former* crewmates, she reminded herself. They were soon going to find out that she had decided to leave them. She hoped they would understand. She knew that they would, but that didn't stop her from feeling guilty for abandoning them without a communications officer.

The Bestia had been cleared from the temple, which was now ringed in divans occupied by the crews of the *Geschichte* and the *Hiryū*. The doctor had forbidden Shujinko from leaving his pallet in the galley, so the cabin boy wasn't there. He had given the same order to Arthur and Andrea, since their injuries were just as severe. Both had ignored him. Arthur needed to be carried in, but he now sat stoically next to the captain, his chest rising and falling in an unsteady rhythm. Andrea was sitting rigidly next to Shin. The lookout had refused all offers for aid. The thick bandages wrapped around her head were bloodied, but she made no complaint. Her brother, Angelus, sat on the divan directly next to hers, his eyes never leaving her face, his body tense as if he was waiting to spring up and lend her his hand. Andrea had barely acknowledged the boy's presence.

Ursula stood between two men. One was skinny. His name was Charles Mild. The other was short and muscular and went by the name Gustav von Something-Or-Other. On either side of them was a woman Ursula introduced as Helena Vortrag and a rather average-looking Heiliglander named Joseph Hexenmeister. It was a small crew for an airship, even for one the size of the *Geschichte*.

There were a few representatives from the Brotherhood scattered around, too, though these seemed to be a token force, as the Cunning Lady would be speaking for all of them. Two of them flanked Kenji, who was sitting on a chair in the middle of the ring of divans. Yami stood directly behind him, his arms hidden in the depths of his sleeves, his eyes boring into the back of Kenji's skull.

Her brother wasn't present. A part of Missy hoped he would sleep through the whole thing so that she would get a chance to tell him about her decision in private. Another part of her, one she didn't like very much, wished he would arrive before they started so that she wouldn't have to look directly into his eyes and tell him she was leaving.

Her stomach felt as though it was tied in knots. Fox raised

a hand, and those gathered fell silent. Missy was almost relieved until her brother came sprinting into the hall. He saw her, sitting on the raised dais with Fox. She could tell he was puzzled, but she shook her head, refusing to meet his eyes. He took a seat between Arthur and the captain.

'Very well, ladies and gentlemen,' Fox said. 'Let us begin.'

○

Lenis gazed at Missy, who was most definitely trying *not* to look back at him. Why was she sitting with the Fox Lady? Unease ate at him, refusing to be stilled.

The captain cleared his throat, capturing everyone's attention except for Missy, who glanced at him and then turned her head to the side when Lenis tried to catch her eye. 'I would request that we keep this meeting short. Our adversary is getting ever further away from us.'

'Which one?' Fox asked, any trace of her flippancy gone. She sat with her back erect, her eyes alert. 'You seem to have many, Captain Shishi. If you wish to hurry this meeting along, I suggest you explain yourself as quickly as you can.'

The captain nodded and launched into a hasty account of the *Hiryū*'s voyages. Lenis was a little shocked by his candour – he didn't shy away from telling them the truth. He was even more surprised that the Cunning Lady didn't seem at all astonished. In fact, she didn't even blink when the captain mentioned Ishullanu and his Demon army, or the World Tree and the fate of the Totem.

Ursula was another matter. The captain of the *Geschichte* was radiating alarm throughout the captain's story, though her expression remained impassive. The captain finished his recount with a summary of their encounter with Karasu in Kolga's temple.

The Fox Lady nodded once when he was done. 'Thank you. Given the importance of your quest there seems little point in delaying your departure.'

Lenis looked to Captain Shishi, who remained focused on the Cunning Lady.

'You are letting us go?' the captain asked.

'Yes.' The woman waved a dismissive hand at them. 'You may go.'

'What of Kenji Jackson's offer?'

The woman smiled, just enough for her eyeteeth to show. 'I have had a better one.'

'What will you do with him?' the captain prompted.

Her smile widened as she turned to the *Hiryū*'s navigator. 'I have decided on a suitable punishment for his crimes.'

'Oh, good,' Kenji muttered. 'Am I to be tortured? Thrown out into the Wastelands? Perhaps boiled –'

'No, Kenji,' the woman said. 'I have decided to hand you over to the crew of the *Hiryū*. Your fate is now in their hands.'

Almost as one, each of the crew turned from the Cunning Lady to the navigator, the man who had attempted to barter everything they had been fighting for to save his own life.

'Very well, then,' Captain Shishi said, then stood. 'Let us make haste. Mister Jackson, you are needed at your post.'

'Captain!' Shin protested. 'Surely you do not mean for us to take him with us after what he did?'

The captain nodded. 'He is still our navigator, Miss Shin. Now come, we must –'

'I'm not going with you,' Missy suddenly shouted. All eyes turned to her, and Lenis saw his sister shrink down in her chair. 'I'm not going.'

'Missy?' Lenis couldn't make her words mean anything. 'What are you talking about?'

Finally, she looked right at him. 'I'm not going, Lenis. I'm leaving the *Hiryū*.'

He shook his head. It didn't make sense. 'What? Why?'

Missy glanced at the woman sitting beside her and then turned back to Lenis again. 'I have to stay here, Lenis. Lady Fox is going to teach me how to use the Quillblade properly.'

Lenis heard the words, but they didn't sink in. What was his sister saying? 'I don't understand.'

'I'm sorry, Lenis, but I have to do this. It's the only way. You can see that, right?'

Of course he didn't see that! All those years he had been so worried about being separated from his sister, about them being sold to different masters, or her being taken from him by some Demon or crazed Totem, and now *she* was the one who wanted to leave *him*? Lenis couldn't believe it. He felt something pierce his chest. His throat tightened. His eyes filled with tears. And suddenly he was running. Someone called out to him, but he didn't care. He just had to get out of there.

He burst out of the temple, pushed passed a trio of black-robed figures, and headed for the *Hiryū*. The buildings flew by him in a blur. And then he was on the gangplank, then the deck, and finally he was on the forecastle, where he collapsed on the blood-stained wood and cried. After everything, *this* couldn't be happening. Not this. *Never* this. What was the point of any of it if he lost his sister?

Lenis knew Missy had come after him long before she knelt down next to him and placed an arm around his shoulders.

'Why are you doing this?' he asked through his sobs.

Missy sighed, and the sound made her seem much older than she was. 'What wisdom forbids, right, little brother?' He glared at her. 'I really don't have a choice, Lenis. I have to learn how to use the Quillblade. Fox can teach me.'

'Tenjin can teach you!'

Missy shook her head. 'Not fully. Not like she can. You saw her fight those Demons, Lenis! Ishullanu's strong. We know that. If the Totem have fallen, and the Jinn, then what hope does Suiteki have on her own, even if she achieves her full potential? We need every warrior we can get, and if I can be a warrior, well then that's just what I'll be.'

'Then I'll stay with you,' he mumbled.

'And leave the *Hiryū, and* your Bestia, *and* Suiteki behind? No, Lenis. That isn't going to happen.'

'But I don't want to lose you.'

'I don't want to lose you either, dummy.' She poked him in the ribs, and he winced. 'But we'll see each other again.'

Lenis narrowed his eyes. 'You don't really believe that.'

She shook her head again. 'No, Lenis, I don't. Not completely. But we have to hope.'

This time it was Lenis who shook his head. 'Not good enough.' He fumbled around in his pocket and pulled out the damaged stone. 'Take this.' He pressed it into Missy's hands.

'I can't!' She tried to give it back to him, but he wouldn't take it. 'Suiteki needs it!'

'It's broken. Work out how to repair it. Then bring it back to me after your training.'

'But I can't –'

Lenis gripped his sister's hands around the orb. 'Suiteki will need it when it's fixed. You *have* to bring it back to us.'

Missy looked from their clasped hands to her brother's eyes. 'All right, little brother. When I work out how to do it, I'll come looking for you and the *Hiryū*.'

'You'd better.'

For a time the two sat together on the forecastle, holding each other in silence.

They both became aware of Kanu at the same time. The Titan boy stood at the top of the stairs leading up to the forecastle, looking graver than Lenis had ever seen him.

Lenis glanced back to his sister. It was time to put a stop to this, for Kanu's sake. He couldn't spend the rest of his life trailing along after either of the twins. He had to find his own Way.

'Kanu,' Lenis said, beckoning the boy over. When he was next to them, Lenis went on, 'Kanu, this can't go on.'

'I know,' the boy said, surprising them both.

'You do?' Missy asked.

'I cannot be in more than one place. If one of you leaves, I cannot serve Mashu.'

'We don't want you to serve us,' Lenis said, and Missy nodded. 'You aren't our slave.'

Kanu frowned. 'I'm not a slave. I am a Titan.'

Lenis and Missy exchanged a long look. How were they going to make him see?

'Your life is your own,' Missy told him. 'You can do whatever you want with it.'

'I can?'

'Yes!'

The frown vanished from the boy's face, replaced by his now familiar too-wide grin. 'That's good. Now I can decide.'

Lenis nodded, satisfied that Kanu understood he was free. 'What do you want to do?'

'I will serve you, Lenis,' Kanu said, stumbling over Lenis's name a bit. He'd only ever called either of them Mashu before.

Lenis groaned. 'No, Kanu. That's not what we meant, I –'

'That is my choice,' Kanu insisted. 'I will go with Lenis. He is weak. He does not have Adad's power or the protection of the Lady of Cunning. He will need me. I see this now. I can serve Mashu by protecting him. I will do so by his side.'

'But you don't have to do this,' Lenis pleaded.

'I am a Titan,' Kanu repeated. 'It is my duty to serve Mashu. Since I cannot be with you both, I choose to serve Lenis.'

Lenis and Missy shared another look. Lenis began, 'You don't –'

'That is my choice,' Kanu said. Then he turned and walked away from them.

Lenis groaned, but Missy laughed. 'It's not funny, Missy!'

'We gave him the choice, Lenis,' Missy said, covering her mouth with one hand.

'He wasn't supposed to choose that!'

'But he did, and you'll just have to deal with it.' She reached out to ruffle his hair. 'We chose to serve Captain Shishi when we were given our freedom.'

'Yeah, I guess,' Lenis mumbled, 'but I'm not the captain.'

'No, but I'll rest easier knowing you've got someone as strong as Kanu watching over you once I'm gone.'

They both lapsed into silence, and that was how the captain found them. He cleared his throat politely and waited for them both to notice him. 'I have discussed your decision with Lady Fox, Miss Clemens. Are you certain this is the course of action you wish to take?'

Missy was looking at Lenis when she answered. 'Yes, Captain. I will remain here and learn to use the Quillblade. When I am strong enough, I will return to my post on the *Hiryū*.'

'Very well,' the captain said. 'We will miss you while you are gone.'

Lenis saw the tears in the captain's own eyes and didn't need his empathic gifts to tell him their captain was being sincere.

'I will miss you all, too,' Missy said. She gave Lenis a quick squeeze before disentangling herself from his arms.

'Not all of us, I think,' the captain said.

Missy stood. 'What do you mean?'

'You are not the only one who will be staying behind,' Captain Shishi told her.

Lenis held out his hand so Missy could help him to his feet. 'Who else is staying?'

'I am,' Shujinko called from the deck. The cabin boy was standing just on the other side of the forecastle's railing. 'The captain has decided my injury is too severe for me to continue travelling with the *Hiryū*.'

The boy was in such turmoil Lenis couldn't sift through his emotions. Given his fear of heights, he should have been relieved to remain on solid ground for a time, but he didn't seem at all pleased with the notion.

'Miss Florona will also be staying,' the captain told them

as Missy descended to the deck, 'and the doctor has agreed to remain behind to care for them.'

Lenis didn't respond. Three more crewmates gone. Would there be anyone left to pilot the *Hiryū*?

The captain lowered his voice and leant in to whisper to Lenis, 'I would not leave your sister alone with strangers, Mister Clemens. Their injuries give me an excuse to leave them behind, but in truth Shujinko, Miss Florona and Master Long will provide much-needed support to Miss Clemens after we are gone.'

Lenis watched Missy and Shujinko over the captain's shoulder before mouthing, 'Thank you.'

The captain nodded in reply. 'As much as I am loathe to speed our separation,' he went on in a normal tone of voice, 'we must be leaving.'

'So soon, Captain?'

'We must hasten after Karasu.'

Lenis felt his tears come again. He pushed past the captain, jumped down the stairs and pulled his sister into a hard embrace. She squeezed him back. They were both crying. The captain left them alone for a moment, but all too soon he was clearing his throat and apologising, then they were pulling away from each other and Missy was heading below decks to fetch her things.

It was all happening too fast. Lenis didn't know what to do with himself, so he did the one thing he could always rely on. He went to work. If they were going to be chasing after

Karasu then they were going to need the engines warmed up and ready to go. Lenis was going to show that Shinzōn mercenary just how fast a dual-Bestia engine could outstrip his airship.

● DEPARTURE ●

Missy crammed her few belongings into the shore bag and flung it over her shoulder. This was it. It was really happening. She was leaving the *Hiryū*. She looked down at her bunk for a moment, waiting for it to sink in. Her eyes were still puffy from her cry with Lenis, and her heart was aching at the thought of leaving him, of leaving all of them. But she had made her decision, and she would stick to it.

As she passed through the airship she paused to say farewell to the Bestia. This proved harder to do than she had imagined. Trying to form a coherent image-message in her state was difficult enough, but receiving their replies was almost too much to bear. They were going to miss her. She tried to hold onto that as a solace, but it really just made her sadder. As she climbed the stairs to the deck she met her brother, who seemed to think better of entering the engine room and trailed along after her.

On the way across the deck they passed Kenji and Shin. The helmswoman's disgust for the navigator was writ large across her face, but Kenji was wearing his usual sardonic grin. Missy gave Shin a quick hug and then turned to go. A thought occurred to Missy and she paused.

'You did it on purpose,' she said, rounding on Kenji.

'What are you talking about?' he asked, sounding bored.

'You were testing me back there in Haven, weren't you?' she demanded. 'You wanted to see if I would read your mind or try to stop you. That's why you did it.'

Kenji winked at her. 'Trust moves in two directions, little girl.' Then he laughed and continued up to the bridge.

Shin looked at her, but Missy just shrugged. The navigator, she suddenly realised, was no longer her problem.

At the top of the gangplank they met the captain and Tenjin, who was leaning heavily on a crutch. Lenis was still crying a little, Missy noticed. So were the captain and the old records keeper. Her heart went out to them, but she had to do this, and do it soon. The longer she delayed the more pain she would cause them all.

Tenjin reached inside his robe. 'You will be needing this for your lessons, I believe.' He drew forth the Quillblade and held it out to her. 'I am sorry I placed this burden on your shoulders.'

As she took the *shintai* from him, she replied, 'Don't be, Lord Tenjin. Once I've learned to master the Quillblade I'll be able to help in the coming war.'

She had meant to make him feel better, but he only looked grimmer.

'Take care, Miss Clemens,' he said and patted her shoulder before hobbling off down the deck.

'Goodbye, Miss Clemens,' the captain said. He bowed low to her and then left the twins alone.

'So,' Lenis said. 'I guess this is finally it.'

'I guess so, little brother.' Missy reached up to tousle his hair. 'Look after yourself. And the Bestia. And Suiteki. And Kanu, I guess. I'll find you when I'm done here. I promise.'

'And I'll find *you* if you don't.'

Missy laughed and hugged her brother. Something squawked inside his robe and she pulled away as Suiteki poked her head out. For a moment, looking into the baby dragon's eyes, it seemed to Missy that she wasn't a baby at all, that deep inside her lurked the Totem she was one day going to become. *Take care of my brother*, she said, and was sure Suiteki bobbed her head in a nod. The little dragon gave one of her reptilian caws and disappeared back inside Lenis's robe. Without another word Missy turned and walked down the gangplank.

'I love you, sister!' Lenis called down to her.

'I love you too, little brother!' Missy waved her hand as Lenis disappeared behind the railing.

'Goodbyes can be hard,' Fox noted. The Cunning Lady was waiting for Missy at the head of the airdock. She wore one of the black coats of the Brotherhood over her flimsy gown. 'I'm sure you will see your brother again.'

Missy nodded, fighting back tears. 'I will. Definitely. In the meantime, where should I put my stuff?'

Fox smiled her wicked smile. 'Turn around.'

'Sorry?'

'Go stow your stuff aboard the *Geschichte*.'

Missy shook her head. 'But I thought you were going to teach me!'

Fox rolled her eyes. 'I am, but not for free. Remember our deal? You owe me one Peaceful Guardian, and we certainly aren't going to find him around here!'

GLOSSARY

(For a more detailed glossary, go to www.benchandler.com.au)

⬡ CAELESTIA ⬡

Apsu	(Rinjin, Njord)	God of the Sea
Ishullanu the Demon King	(Akuma, Idunn)	God of Order

⬡ TOTEM ⬡

Adad the Lord of Storms	(Raikō, Magni)	Lightning Guardian
Apsilla the Lady of Rain	(Seisui, Kolga)	Water Guardian
Silili the Lord of Healing		Peaceful Guardian

❍ BESTIA ❍

Blitzer	Bestia of Fire (the *Geschichte*)
Pog	Bestia of Earth (Haven)
Iki	Bestia of Air (Itsū)

❍ JINN ❍

Etana the Lord of Fury	Warden of Retribution
Shamutar the Lord of Destruction	Warden of Renewal
Neti the Father of the Slain	Warden of Knowledge

❍ LILIM ❍

Akandoji	Demon of the Northern Isles
Akamusaborikū	Demon of the Western Marches
Bakeneko	Cursed Yūrei no Gōshi Yami
Disma	Bonded to Anastasis Greygori
Lord Butin	Steward of Ost
Nue	Bonded to Lord Butin

○ CRITICAL DATES ○

2468 The first Kystian settlers arrive in the 'New World'

2500 Nochi is built and named the new capital city of Shinzō

2578 The Great War Starts

2585 Wastelands appear for the first time around Asheim
The Battle of Asheim – The Great War Ends
Wastelands appear along the western border of Shinzō
Emperor Kumoichi of Shinzō appoints new Warlord, Lord Shōgo Hakaru
Shinzō closes its borders

2588 The 'New World' renamed 'Pure Land'

2657 Bestia power discovered by Siegfried Huginn, an Ostian living in Heiligland

2673 First airship built in Pure Land

2835 The Divine Restoration Movement begins in Shinzō
[No date exists for the end of the Divine Restoration Movement]
Yūgure and Hajimari clans join forces against the Shōgo clan

2836 Puritan airships arrive off the coast of Shinzō and force open its borders

2865 Lenis and Misericordia Clemens are born

2878 The Ruling Council of Pure Land gifts the *Hiryū* airship to Shinzō

● PRONUNCIATION ●

When pronouncing names of Shinzōn origin, the general rule is to give each syllable equal emphasis and, even though most words end in a vowel, a word that does end in a consonant follows the same rule. For example: Shin becomes *Shi-n*, with both the 'Shi' and the 'n' carrying equal weight. Double consonants are simply twice as long.

For the pronunciation of vowels, use the following table:

a	as in 'ah'
e	as in 'eh'
i	as in 'ee'
o	as in 'oh'
u	as in 'oo'

Combinations of vowels can be tricky. Some do not affect each other (our word 'ion' would be pronounced *ee-oh-n* with three syllables). Some do affect one another:

ai	as in a hard 'i'
ei	as in a hard 'a' ('-ay')
ō or ou	as in a longer 'oh' (twice as long)
ū or uu	as in a longer 'oo' (twice as long)

● SHINZŌN NAMES ●

Shinzōn names are presented as family name followed by given name. If someone is directly related to the main branch of a clan family (for instance, a child of the head of the clan family) they take the clan name as their family name. For example, Mayonaka Shishi is the heir to the Mayonaka clan. Those not directly related to the main branch of the clan family, such as cousins, take their own family name, which is preceded by the clan name, separated by the indicator 'no'. For example, Yūrei no Gōshi Yami is a member of the Yūrei clan, but the Gōshi family is not directly related to the Yūrei family.

◦ ACKNOWLEDGEMENTS ◦

When I wrote the acknowledgements for my previous book, I wrote a bit of a story about how *Quillblade* was written. In it, I thanked the various people who helped me to see that book to completion. I'm sure it was very clever of me, but frankly it got a bit convoluted (I have a distinct penchant for convolution), so this time I'm just going to say 'thank you' to a bunch of people.

First and foremost, thanks to Zoe Walton, my editor and publisher, for believing in the series and working so hard to polish it up and get it out there. I realise the only suitable 'Thank you' at this point would be to give you a real, live Bestia to keep as your very own, so I promise I'll manage that somehow, someday. Thanks also to Cristina Briones for helping to edit *Beast Child*, and to all of the other marvellous people at Random House Australia whom I haven't met yet but who have done such great work on the series. You all both rock and roll.

Thanks to my generous readers, who read and loved *Quillblade* and will, I hope, love this sequel at least as much. To those of you who took the time to write to me so you could let me know how much you're enjoying the *Hiryū*'s voyages so far – *thank you, thank you, thank you!* Reading your messages gives me the best feeling ever.

A very big 'Thank you!' to Carclew Youth Arts for the scholarship that helped me to finish this book on time. You guys do amazing work, each and every one of you, and your organisation is both vital and generous. Thanks also to Jo and Richard Vabolis for inviting me into their home for some dedicated (cat-free) writing time, and the same to Margot McGovern and her family for the generous loan of their beachside writers' shack. (It's not really a writers' shack. It's just a shack, but I wrote a lot there.) *Beast Child* probably never would have been finished without you all, and certainly not on time.

Thanks a bunch, Nan Halliday! You are a wonderful agent, not least because you get me out of the house and listen very patiently to my whining over coffee (but mostly it's for all of the great work you do). For very similar reasons, my eternal thanks to the Keylings, who know who they are and will doubtless keep opening those doors.

Thanks to all of my friends and family, including the ones who no longer remember what I look like thanks to my increasingly frequent visits to my writing oubliette (I'm the guy with the crazy beardlike growth on his chin and cheeks, the pasty skin, the glasses . . . so, basically, the same guy you always knew). Thanks, Ash! You know why. Also, a very special sort of thanks goes to Craig and Weez, two of my oldest and dearest friends, just for being totally awesome (and not at all because you threatened dire consequences if I left you out this time). Thanks also to all of my writer friends and colleagues, who have been so supportive and welcoming of the 'new guy' and continue to be so.

If I've forgotten to thank someone in the heady craziness of getting this book ready for publication, I do sincerely apologise and will accept a swift clip around the ear as punishment (that last bit doesn't apply to you, gauntleted Jimmy). I hope a heartfelt 'Thank you to everyone in my life!' will help. So, thank you all!

○ ABOUT THE AUTHOR ○

Ben lives mostly in worlds of his own creation but occasionally misses the real world and comes home to Adelaide, where he sometimes teaches Creative Writing and English Literature at various universities. In addition to writing fantasy and things like that, he has also published academic work on popular culture, video game narrative theory, Japanese heroism, anime and manga, and creative writing pedagogy. Ben loves heroes, villains, comic books, and video games, and he believes you can learn more from watching cartoons than you can from the news. A few years ago, someone made Ben a Doctor of Fantasy, which is possibly the coolest thing ever but may have been a bit foolhardy given the number of super villains out there with PhDs. I'm not saying he's inherently evil, but don't be surprised if he gets arrested one day for trying to hijack a zeppelin. It's entirely likely Loki will have made him do it. For those of you who don't follow Ben on Twitter (@DoctorBenny), Loki is his cat. All fantasy writers have cats, even if they don't realise it.

For more information about Ben and his books, go to www.benchandler.com.au.

◉ QUILLBLADE ◉

BOOK ONE OF THE VOYAGES
OF THE FLYING DRAGON

T wins Lenis and Missy Clemens are slaves aboard the *Hiryū*. They work as Bestia Keepers, communicating telepathically with the creatures that power the mighty airship.

When the airship is stolen from under the Warlord's nose, Lenis and Missy have no choice but to obey the captain's mysterious orders. Pursued by the Warlord's airships, they must race over the perilous Wastelands, where corrupted Demons lie in wait.

It is only when Lenis tells the captain about his dreams of the Blue Dragon of the East that their quest becomes clear. The survival of Apsilla's daughter may be their only hope – but will they find the dragon's egg in time, or will their enemies find them first. The Quillblade holds the key – if Missy can use it without forfeiting her soul.

Out now!

○ EBB AND FLOW ○

BOOK THREE OF THE VOYAGES
OF THE FLYING DRAGON

Lenis and Missy have been torn apart, but will their sacrifice lead to Ishullanu's defeat, or have their attempts to thwart their fate merely brought the world closer to destruction?

Missy has left the *Hiryū* to learn the secrets of the Quillblade. Together with her enigmatic teacher, Fox, she oversees the mobilisation of Heiligland from aboard the airship *Geschichte*. When Demons attack the nation's capital, Missy and her new allies are drawn south to Tien Ti, where Missy hopes to fulfill the promise she made to her brother by restoring the cracked stone he gave into her keeping. She must also uphold her bargain with Fox and locate Silili, the one Totem who might have the power to heal the Wasteland sickness, but sinister forces are also hunting the Peaceful Guardian and are closer to discovering his sanctuary than Missy could ever imagine.

Meanwhile, Lenis and the remaining crew of the *Hiryū* seek the second stone, but in order to wrest it from Karasu they must chase the mercenary into the vast Wastelands of Garsia, a place where Bestia power alone can't guarantee their safety and Demons are the least of their troubles. Separated by empires, oceans, Wastelands, and battlefields, Missy and Lenis must face a terrible decision, but how can they hope to choose the right way when their only options either lead further into the chaos of war or on to an even more terrifying destiny?

The Demon War begins in the next instalment, *Voyages of the Flying Dragon: Ebb and Flow*!

Read on for an extract . . .

◉ THE DEMON OF THE SOUTHERN MOUNTAINS ◉

'Get Fox!' Missy launched herself forwards. She hardly knew what she was doing as she somersaulted over the heads of the guards menacing the Demon who called himself Akabasan. The power of the Quillblade was in her hand, but she didn't allow it to course freely through her as she once might have done. Drawing on her training, she channelled some of its energy through her veins and muscles, keeping the rest at bay by force of her will. As she spun down to land between the Demon and the Heiliglanders, she sliced neatly through the whirlwind that had blown in through the window. As the mini tornado parted, shards of charged air splintered around Missy, slicing into the walls and floor and, judging by the cries coming from behind her, the skin of the defenders as well.

Akabasan grinned as much as his beak-like mouth would allow, revealing an ever-widening rictus of brown teeth.

'Delightful!' he screeched and then bowed to Missy. 'You seem tasty!'

The creature leapt at her, but Missy transferred her weight to her right foot and bent backwards to duck the Demon's lunge, pulling Adad's power down into her feet to root her in place. As the creature passed over the top of her, she twisted her hips and brought the Quillblade up in a whistling arc that sent the *shintai* through Akabasan's shoulder and feathery hair, narrowly missing his scalp. A thin stream of black blood spurted from the wound as the Demon rolled head over heels between the Heiliglander guards. They hacked at him, but he moved too swiftly for their heavy broadswords to catch. As Missy straightened she decided they were in more danger of hurting one another than the Demon.

'Stand back,' she shouted, and as one they obeyed.

Akabasan reached a stretch of wall between two windows, but instead of crashing through he rolled up it and back-flipped onto his feet. He looked at his shoulder, ran a hand across the cut, then licked the inky blood from his fingers.

'Quickly, quickly, little mouse,' the Demon sang, his own blood coating his beak and teeth. 'Such a sting from a tiny thing.'

He jumped into the air and kicked off the wall behind him, flying at Missy again. She braced herself and brought the Quillblade up between them. With a thought she sent a streak of lightning crackling through the hall from the tip of her *shintai*, but the Demon rolled over in midair, dodging the attack. The bolt shattered into a tapestry, disintegrating half of the fabric and setting the rest ablaze. Thrown off course, Akabasan overshot Missy's shoulder and turned in his flight to give her a wink. Then he was behind her, entangling his arms through hers and dragging her back towards the window.

'Can your feather make you fly, little mouse?' the thing whispered in her ear. His breath stank of carrion left too long in the sun.

Missy struggled against his grip, as much to be free of his odour as his grasp. Her panic drove her training from her mind, and she lashed out, sending lightning strikes all around her, but none found their target. One blasted a nearby fire pit, exploding still-burning wood and coals around the hall. People were screaming. Many had fled, but a few were still bunched by the door, struggling against one another in their press to flee. There was no sign of Fox, and Missy knew there was no way her teacher could reach her in time through that press of Heiliglanders. She closed her eyes and tried to focus. Akabasan was a Demon, but she was the wielder of the Quillblade and had the power of a Totem at her command. She opened herself up to that energy completely, allowing its full force to surge through her. The first time she had done so, back in Erdasche, she'd injured herself badly, but this time she was better prepared.

Control, she repeated to herself. *Control. Control. Control.*

Missy gritted her teeth, her nerves seared raw by the influx of Adad's power. She couldn't fully dominate the torrential flow of spiritual energy, but she could direct and divert it. Where once it had rioted throughout her system unchecked, now she ensured it repaired as much as it damaged her. She guided the energy along its way, moving it where she willed and damming it in places so it could build up where she would need it most: within her heart, lungs, hands, and feet. The initial agony of calling on Adad's might elongated and expanded as it filled her, moving beyond pain and into an excess of sensation. Her body opened to the world around her, unprotected by the barrier of her skin, unable to defend itself from the influx of sensorial data.

At last, there came a moment when Missy knew the cadences of the elemental forces raging within her matched perfectly with the rhythms of her body. Blood and oxygen and the electric charge of Adad's soul resonated in perfect balance inside her, and in that instant Missy knew that she was in control. She threw herself backwards. Thrown off balance, Akabasan fell, still clutching Missy to him, and hit his head on the windowsill. As his skull connected with the stone, Missy thrust out with Adad's power, enveloping them both in a miniature storm of electricity. Akabasan cried out as the full force of the Lightning Guardian tore through him. His hold loosened as the voltage tortured his internal organs, his nerves, and his bones. Missy sprang free and turned to face him before even touching the ground. She swept the

Quillblade through the Demon's throat so hard she not only sliced though his neck but also opened a gaping crevasse in the stone beneath him. Akabasan's body crumpled to the floor as his head rolled out the window.

Missy felt the corners of her mouth spasm up into a grin. She'd done it. The Quillblade was hers. Its power was her power, and it moved through her body as easily and readily as blood or air. From somewhere deep inside or far away, she heard the Thunder Bird's answering cry, torn from his Demonic throat. She knew then that she could take charge of the Totem's empty vessel at will, whenever she chose to do so, and that she wouldn't need Lenis's aid to do it.

The air was heady around her. The stench of ozone filled the chamber. Little erratic charges of electricity danced across her skin, occasionally zapping and popping as they arced from her to the floor or the walls or out into the sky beyond the windows. Missy looked over her shoulder. Shujinko and Heidi were with the guards and King Asagrim, encircling the fleeing Heiliglanders. They were assessing her anew, she realised. To them she was no longer the girl pretending to be Magni, standing before them with light shows, fancy clothes, pretty speeches, and the occasional mental suggestion. Their fake Lightning-Wielder was gone, but in her place stood something more, something real. Missy might not have been the goddess the Heiliglanders thought she was, the one they worshipped in their temples and cried out for to lead them to war, but she did exercise that Totem's power, and Magni hadn't been the one to answer their prayers. Missy had.

A gust of air slammed into her and threw her backwards. She'd forgotten about Etana. The Demon Lord was still out there, lurking in the skies above Drachstadt. Missy rushed to the window and stood over Akabasan's headless body, looking out into the night. All was dark, the stars and moon hidden by the shifting cloudbanks overhead. Occasionally, a pinprick of celestial light peeked through, but Etana remained unseen. Even so, Missy knew that he was out there somewhere in the gathering storm. Her smile widened. Etana may command the winds, but Adad was the Lord of Storms. The Quillblade thrummed pleasantly in Missy's hand as she pointed it out of the window. Bolts of lightning flew from its tip into the underside of the cloud cover. The sky absorbed the electrical charge, passing it from one roiling mass to another until everything was lit by its white-blue light.

There! Missy caught sight of a talon rising up behind the cover and sent another bolt after it. She was rewarded with an outraged shriek from the Lord of Fury. Now was the time, she knew. Missy steadied herself and closed her eyes, turning her attention inwards once more, searching. Adad had drawn closer the longer she relied on the energies of the Quillblade. It would take but a simple command and the strength of her will to summon him here. Together, his strength directed by her will, they could overpower Etana.

Suddenly there was a screech, and a blast of rancid air hit Missy's face, causing her to stagger back. Adad was forgotten as slivers of air tore into her skin. The Quillblade came up before her again and, shielded by the *shintai*'s might, Missy reopened her eyes. What she saw sent a ripple of unease through her and into the Quillblade. Akabasan's severed head was floating in the window. It looked down at its body, squawked, and then turned its red eyes on Missy. She was mesmerised by its stare, by the black blood dripping from the trunk of its neck onto the wasted blue body below. The energies of the Quillblade seemed to abandon her as Akabasan's dead eyes locked her in place.

'That was nicely done, little mouse,' the Demon told her. 'You did better than I expected, though to be fair you weren't using *your* power, were you?'

Missy's mouth moved, but no words came out. She wasn't even sure she had anything to say. She was paralysed, inside and out. Her mastery of Adad's strength hadn't been enough to destroy this creature. How was she supposed to face it now? What could she do if even a Totem couldn't kill it?

'Not that I'm a sore loser, I hasten to add,' Akabasan went on, 'but you did just decapitate *and* defenestrate me, so I think I've got fair cause to be somewhat miffed about how the whole affair turned out. But never mind! To prove how generous and forgiving I am, I'll tell you something good. What you seek is far south of here. Go to Tien Ti.

Search for a place where the fire of the earth is bent to the will of humanity. Once there –'

Akabasan's head exploded. His spell broken, Missy shook herself all over and stared at Fox, who was standing on the windowsill, still hanging half outside of it, clinging to the wall there. One gauntleted fist occupied the space where the Demon's head had just been. Missy's teacher had climbed the outside of the tallest tower in Drachstadt to save her.

'Ah, thanks,' Missy mumbled, her head still foggy from whatever Akabasan had done to her.

'You didn't do too badly on your own.' Fox jumped lightly down from her perch and into the hall. 'For your first time, anyway.' Her lip quirked up in distaste as she stepped over the pool of black blood that was seeping out of the Demon's corpse. 'Though, next time, make sure the thing's dead before you throw it out the window.'

Missy nodded. Her mouth was dry, her senses still preternaturally heightened by the Quillblade's power. 'Yes, Fox. I'll do that,' she said.